JACQUI ROSE

THE WOMEN

PAN BOOKS

First published 2023 by Macmillan

This paperback edition first published 2023 by Pan Books
an imprint of Pan Macmillan
The Smithson, 6 Briset Street, London EC1M 5NR
EU representative: Macmillan Publishers Ireland Ltd, 1st Floor,
The Liffey Trust Centre, 117–126 Sheriff Street Upper,
Dublin 1, D01 YC43
Associated companies throughout the world
www.panmacmillan.com

ISBN 978-1-5290-7657-8

1 3 5 7 9 8 6 4 2

A CIP catalogue record for this book is available from the British Library.

Typeset in Plantin by Jouve (UK), Milton Keynes
Printed and bound by CPI Group (UK) Ltd, Croydon, CR0 4YY

In memory of Jackie Lee Rainbow.
May you rest in eternal peace.

BEFORE

She could hear the sound of her own running footsteps on the wet earth, but she could also hear his. He was getting closer now. Nearer. She could almost feel him. She knew if he caught her this time, he'd want to keep her. She also knew what he'd do to her, but if she could just get to the road, then maybe, maybe someone would see her. Help her . . . Save her. How many others had there been? She knew there'd been a lot – he'd told her, and she heard them screaming. What she didn't know was if any of the others had got away . . . Panting now, she glanced around. She didn't know the woods like he did: at night the whole place looked the same: creeping and twisting shadows moving in between the dark tunnel of trees. She needed to go faster but she was tired. Though she daren't stop, maybe she could hide? Yes, over there by the tree. She could hide there . . .

She hurried across, a creeping terror following her as the wind and the rain got up, muffling the sound of his footsteps. She crouched and, shaking, she tried to quieten her breathing. Quiet, she just had to be quiet . . . A noise made her turn her head. A branch breaking behind her. She tried to make herself smaller, pushing herself further against the base of the tree. She listened again . . . The silence told her he was there. Still, she had to be still . . . Her eyes darted around in the darkness, and she watched. Just waiting . . . Nothing now, only the sound of the rain hitting the leaves and the branches above her . . . Had he gone? Was it safe to move? . . . But then she screamed as she felt her shoulder being grabbed. A hand slammed over her mouth. She turned her head and stared into his eyes . . . It was over now; she knew that it was over . . .

1

PART ONE

LAST NIGHT

The burn. He always thought that was the best part of it. That first hit. That moment the coke hit the back of his nostrils. That bitter cutting taste at his throat: it was what he'd been waiting for all week . . . Oh God, yeah, this was good shit.

Sniffing deeply, he held his nose closed, making sure none of the specks of coke dropped out and went to waste.

'You want me to do it how you always like it, hun?'

Her voice ground into his thoughts, putting an irritating edge to his high. And as he sat on the edge of the bed, legs wide apart, he looked down at her, inwardly disgusted at her dirty fingernails around the shaft of his erect penis.

'What is it about you, Holly, you can never just stop talking,' he snapped.

Pouting, Holly stared up at him with doe eyes, then licked her lips suggestively. 'Just want to please you, baby.'

He bent down to her, his penis starting to droop, and grabbed hold of her thin blonde hair, his gaze darting all over her face. 'If you want to please me,' he hissed, 'then you'll shut that mouth of yours.' She was spoiling his buzz and he didn't want to start to come down already, *especially* after the week he'd had.

'Baby, I just—'

'What did I say?' Glaring at her, he gripped her hair tighter and forced her mouth over his penis, ignoring the sound of her gagging. Stupid little bitch; he wanted to relax, not have her chewing his ear off . . . Fuck. This was pointless. Now, it felt like she was chafing his foreskin with her teeth. Jesus!

Furious, he pushed her off and stood up, using his foot to barge her out of the way.

'What did you go and do that for?' Back against the wall, she rubbed her head, her naked body marked with self-harm scars. 'That frigging hurt, you bastard.'

Lowering his voice to a menacing growl, he took a step towards her. 'I've had a really hard week and the last thing I need, Holly, is you giving me backchat – any chat, for that matter. So, if you've got any sense in that empty head of yours, take that as a warning and keep it zipped.'

She snuffled loudly, tears welling in her eyes.

Ignoring her tears and needing another hit, he walked naked across the room. He leaned over the chopped lines of cocaine, snorting vigorously, chasing the high which had now been ruined.

Moving his neck from side to side to relieve some of the tension, he looked around the shabby, overheated room. A stale odour hung in the air and dirty clothes and shoes were piled up in the corner. Empty burrito wrappers and takeaway cartons, as well as a pack of nappies and a bundle of kids' clothes were stuffed in the broken cot by the window. The place was a pigsty.

His phone buzzed and he flicked a glance at it, watching it spinning around on the top of the dresser, which was propped up with a pile of magazines. He recognized the number. Fuck. He didn't want to, but he knew he needed to take this.

Swiping up the phone, he answered, trying not to let paranoia creep over him. 'Yes, what is it?' he slurred.

'It's Tony. We've got a bit of trouble.' The voice on the other end didn't sound confident. 'Sorry.'

Glancing in the mirror as he spoke, he noticed how bloodshot his green eyes were. 'I hope for your sake, Tony, it's more than a *bit* of trouble.' The cocaine made his tongue feel heavy and he rolled it around his mouth before adding, 'It's Saturday night, so like I say, this better be a whole lot of trouble for you to disturb me when I'm with my family.' He looked at Holly, rolling his eyes as she took the last of his cocaine.

'Sorry, I realize that, and I wouldn't have—'

'Just get on with it, you know it pisses me off when people don't get to the point.'

'Sorry . . . There's been an incident, and it might be best if you come—'

'Fine. I'm on my way. Oh and, Tony, just for the record, I'm not happy. I'm not fucking happy at all that my weekend is going to be messed up.' He sighed and, before the caller had a chance to respond, hung up.

He rubbed his temple, a headache beginning to form. There'd been trouble brewing for the past week and, as much as this phone call wasn't wanted, it wasn't entirely unexpected.

Grabbing the half-empty whisky bottle, he took a swig, wiping a drip off his chin with his arm. Then he took another. One for the road. After all, he had a two-and-a-half-hour drive in front of him.

Angry at that thought, he put on his watch and wedding ring, pulled on his boxers, trousers and top, checking his hair and clothes in the mirror. He looked at Holly, who now lay back on the bed, her eyes looking heavy.

Shaking his head, he threw the money at her. 'Tidy this fucking mess up, it's a shithole.'

She squawked at him. 'I'm a hooker, not a frigging cleaner . . . Same time next week, hun?'

Without bothering to answer, Governor Phil Reed marched out, slamming the door behind him.

1

TODAY

'You ain't fucking going to take my baby, you hear me! You ain't going to take him! I won't let you. He's mine. *Mine!*' Ness Davis sat on the grimy floor of the cell, hugging her large pregnant stomach, tears streaming down her cheeks.

'Listen to me, Ness, this isn't going to do you any favours. There are other ways to go about this. The official way.'

'And when's that done any fucking good in this shithole, hey?'

'Ness, open up, the sooner you do the better, then we can talk and get this all sorted out.' There was a tinge of impatience in the prison officer's tone as she spoke from the other side of the thick metal cell door, raising her voice to be heard over the banging and shouts of the other women.

How fucking long are you going to keep us in here

Tell that stupid bitch just to open up

If I lose my visit because of her, I swear, I ain't going to be responsible for my actions

I'm going to rip her a new one if I've got to be in here another hour . . . You hear me, Ness, I'm going to rip you a new one!

Ness listened to the yelling from the other women. She didn't blame them. She knew she was pissing everyone off. After all, they'd been locked up for over twenty-four hours due to the stand-off between her and the prison officers, but what else was she supposed to do? 'I ain't going to do anything unless I speak to the governor. You said he was coming, where the fuck is he, anyway?' Banging the door with her fist, she screeched back. 'You hear me, I want to see him, *now*!'

'He's on his way, but I really don't think you'll win any brownie points with him. Now stop wasting everyone's time and open up.'

Wiping her tears on the sleeve of her tracksuit top, Ness yelled so loudly she felt the words cut at the back of her throat. '*I said*, I want to see him, and I ain't going to change my mind. So just go and get him, yeah . . . I ain't going to speak to anyone else. Pointless wasting my breath on you lot. *Bunch of fucking muppets!*'

She screamed the last part, then sighed angrily. She hadn't actually met the new governor, but if he was anything like the last one, he'd sort things, listen to her, unlike the officers. The only thing they cared about was clocking off and slacking off.

'. . . Ness, look, you aren't giving us any other choice, we're going to come in. OK? So stand back.'

She heard the rattle of keys from the other side of the door and immediately shouted back again, banging on the door once more. 'If you do . . . if you do, if you even try to come in here, I'll kill her! You hear me, I'll slice her up proper!'

The jangling of keys immediately stopped, and through her tears, Ness smiled to herself. She knew the screws wouldn't risk it. No one wanted a bleeder on their hands. Not because they cared – there was just too much damn paperwork.

In fact, she had no intention of killing anyone, least of all Maureen, her cellmate. Though they suspected that was the case, none of the screws could be certain of it as she'd jammed the hatch and covered the peephole on the door.

Calming down slightly, she yawned and flicked a glance at Maureen. 'I'm sorry, Reenie. I never wanted to put you in this position, but I don't know what else to do,' she whispered, not wanting the officers to hear.

Maureen's grey eyebrows snapped together, a look of concern on her lined face. She spoke quietly: 'Sweetheart, you know me – you could do a rain dance on the roof for all I care. I'm only worried that all this shouting and screaming won't do the bairn any good.' She smiled warmly at Ness, who smiled back. Feeling her baby kick, she rubbed her stomach and closed her eyes.

Since she'd arrived in Ashcroft in mid-October, almost seven months ago now, Maureen had looked out for her: fussing and caring, making sure she ate, helping her not to fall into the group of spice guzzlers on the wing, who were so off their head most of the time they didn't even know they were banged up, which she guessed wasn't altogether a bad thing.

But Maureen had kept her well. Clean. It was the longest she'd gone without snorting or shooting anything up since she was a kid. And quite frankly, she didn't know what she'd have done without Maureen. Her head had been a mess when they'd brought her in. She was looking at ten years in this shithole and the truth was, if it hadn't been for her cellmate, she probably would've topped herself by now.

Maureen – or Reenie as she always called her – felt more like a mother to her than her own had ever been. Though that wasn't hard; Ness's mother had been nothing but a crackhead who loved the gear more than she'd ever loved any of her seven kids. And if there'd been any doubt about that, it had become evident when her mother had given her a handful of uppers and put her on the game at thirteen to pay for her habit. Fast-forward twenty years, and that was still the only career she knew.

Opening her eyes and wiping her running nose on her grey tracksuit sleeve, Ness glanced up at Maureen, who continued to knit – an illegal pastime in Ashcroft after too many women had used the needles as weapons, or worse. Tess, who was celled up on the next landing and saw herself as top dog of the wing, used them to sexually assault the women who dared cross her.

She breathed out heavily and turned her attention back to Maureen. 'Reenie, what do you reckon – should I hold out for the governor? I don't want Lynette to miss her visit, she hasn't seen her kid for a few weeks now, and I know she was supposed to come today. She couldn't wait to see her.'

'For feck's sake, will you look at that?' Maureen, cursing slightly at the dropped stitch on the yellow baby bonnet she was making, looked up. She beamed, the lines around her eyes becoming deeper as her soft Irish accent filled the air. 'You're a good girl, Nessie, so you are, and I think maybe the kindest thing to do—'

Before Maureen had managed to say anything else, the door was flung open, sending Ness sprawling across the floor as six officers in full riot gear barged in.

'*Get back! Get back! Put your weapon down!*'

'She hasn't got a weapon, you fecking eejits!' Maureen shouted in horror.

Ness screamed as the officers continued to yell their orders. They pinned her down and Maureen rushed over, her face pinched with anger. 'What the feck are you doing, you know the girl's pregnant! Get off her! For God's sake, get off her, you lumps of fuck! You're going to hurt her, *get off*! You could do her and the bairn an injury.'

Maureen started to take another step towards Ness, who was sobbing and crying out in pain, but she was immediately blocked by a tall figure strolling casually into the cell. 'Enough! This is a prison, not a zoo.' There was an authoritative tone to his voice.

'Try telling them that! What did they go and barge in here like that for?' Maureen stood to her full five-foot height.

'They were following my orders. Problem?' Governor Phil

Reed, dressed in a freshly pressed suit, threw a glance at Ness sprawled on the floor.

'Who the feck are you anyway?'

Reed smirked. 'It depends how you want to play it. I'm either your saviour or I'm your biggest nightmare. In other words, I'm your new governor.' He winked at the old woman with the mass of white hair tied up in a bun who stood defiantly in front of him. He'd read a lot of the women's notes when he'd arrived, but most of them had just merged into one big mess. To him they were all the same: druggies, whores, child abusers, husband killers, shop-lifters, wasters of society and taxpayers' money. But Maureen Flaherty, well, she was different from the others. Her notes had fascinated him: an ex-nun, who'd refused a defence barrister, had been given life, but was now a model prisoner, trusted by all the women . . . Someone who might be very useful to him.

Much to his silent amusement, Maureen looked taken aback.

'Now move it. I want a quiet word with Vanessa on my own, see if we can't sort this little problem out between us.'

At first Maureen didn't move, her gaze darting to where Ness still lay.

'Go on, get out. She'll be fine, I'll look after her,' Reed said disingenuously. 'Oh, and Maureen, I can rely on you not to stir up the other women, can't I? As far as you're concerned, this matter is closed.'

Without a word, she nodded, and he watched her shuffle out of the cell. He turned and glanced at the riot officers. 'That means you lot too . . . Now get out.'

The officers looked at each other uneasily before Officer Sharps, a small stocky woman, spoke. 'Sir, are you sure? It's not—'

'It's not what?' Reed cut in. 'You wouldn't be so stupid to start to question my authority already, would you, *Officer*?' He glared at her. 'I'm sure I can handle Vanessa on my own – let's not make this bigger than it is already. You'll learn very quickly my approach is often different to other people's, but I get results, and I also have the women's best interest at heart. And creating a bigger drama out of this isn't in the interest of anyone, especially Vanessa . . .'

Reed trailed off, wincing at the sharp bite of his headache, which he'd had since last night despite having taken several pain-killers and a tumbler of brandy. It was one of the reasons he hadn't come straight to the prison. Instead, he'd gone home, laid down on the couch and woken up this morning to several missed calls and frantic messages from Tony Earle, his deputy, who in the short time he'd known him had proved to be more of a hindrance than anything else.

He rubbed his temples. The constant noise in the prison wasn't helping. It was one of the things that a lot of women never got used to, and the biggest reason they dished out so many sleeping tablets and antidepressants. Night or day there was no real peace.

Without a word, the officers walked out, leaving Reed to gently close the cell door behind them. He looked around. The metal toilet and sink plumbed into the corner were hidden slightly by a screen made by draping towels over two plastic chairs. An attempt, he presumed, at achieving some kind of privacy. But there was no privacy here. Every sound, every stench, every bowel movement, every tampon change, was in full view.

By the side of the kettle, there was the usual array of personal items: all of them tat. He inwardly smiled at the small wooden cross hanging above the bottom bunk: what good that would do inside Ashcroft, he wasn't sure. Amused, he moved his gaze to the few photos of a life left behind. But the handful of posses-sions couldn't compete with the desperation crammed within the chipped magnolia walls of the three-by-two-metre cell.

Reed sighed and his stare fell back on Ness, who was now sitting up and rubbing her stomach. She looked a mess. Her hollow face, her scraggly thin brown hair and her skinny body with the large protruding stomach looked comical.

'I'm the new governor. I hear you've been asking for me, Vanessa.' He stretched out his hand to Ness, who took it gratefully. 'You wanted to see me.'

Ness nodded. 'Yeah, that's right.' She sounded relieved.

'It must be urgent for you to take such drastic action.'

Ness spoke quickly, her words tumbling out: 'It is . . . I was told by one of the prison workers that I ain't going to be able to keep my baby once it's born, cos there aren't any spaces in the mother and baby unit. That ain't right. It's not fair. I should be able to keep him with me until he's two – other women are keeping their babies. I can appeal, but that could take months, which is no good. So, the last governor promised me that he'd sort it, that he'd find a way for me to keep him.' She paused, fiddling with her hands, her voice breaking with emotion. 'I'm clean now, so there ain't any reason why I shouldn't have him with me.'

Reed nodded and paced slowly around the small cell as Ness continued to talk.

'So, you see, I need you to help me, like the last governor was going to do. But that's the only reason why I've done all this. I was *never* ever going to hurt Reenie; I wouldn't do that, she's like a mum to me, she's like a mum to a lot of the women. I only said that shit cos I wanted someone to listen. I wanted someone to understand that . . . that . . .' She stopped and her eyes filled with tears.

He turned to look at her. 'Go on.'

'. . . Well, after he's born is the only time I'll have a chance to have him with me. I didn't even realize I was pregnant when I came inside. I don't think I'd have gone through with it if I'd known before I was banged up. But here I am, and thing is, I'm looking at a ten stretch. I'll get out in seven, six if I'm really lucky, but by that time, it'll be too late. He won't know me from frigging Adam. But I reckon, if I can have those first two years with him in the mother and baby unit, social workers will be less likely to put him up for adoption; he'd probably just go into long-term foster care. It ain't great but at least I'd be able to see him that way, on visits and stuff.' She shrugged miserably. 'Like I say, I just want to have a chance to be his mum.'

Reed stared at her. He paused, watching as a large black fly crawled along the bars of the window. 'So let me get this straight, Vanessa, all this . . . stand-off, was because you wanted to be a good mum?'

Ness gave a small smile. She nodded enthusiastically. 'Yeah . . . yeah, exactly that.'

Without warning, Reed smashed her against the wall. Pressing his finger hard against her lip. So hard it split.

'Well, maybe you should have thought about being a good mum *before* you drove a knife into your pimp's chest.' He smirked. 'But, if it's any consolation, *Ness*, that kid you've got growing inside you . . .' He put one hand on her stomach, slowly stroking it. '. . . Well, it'll be better off without you. No kid wants a drug-addicted whore as a mother.'

Shaking, and with blood trickling down her chin, Ness went to open her mouth but immediately Reed slammed his hand over it. 'Don't scream. Understand? Otherwise, I will rip that baby out of you.'

Eyes wide and looking terrified, Ness nodded, her stare darting all over the governor's face, which was screwed up in disgust. He leaned into her, inches away, and she recoiled from his bad breath.

'Now this is how it's going to go from now on, *Vanessa*: you are never, *never* going to cause trouble in my prison again.' He grabbed her hair and banged her head hard against the wall and she let out the tiniest of squeals. 'If you ever as much as *think* about doing something like this again, your life will be such a living hell, they'll end up carrying you out of here in a body bag.' He tapped her stomach and smirked. 'And don't think about telling anyone about this little chat we've had, all right?'

He stepped back, then reached out and stroked her face, wiping the blood away from her chin with his thumb. 'So now we understand each other, how about you go and enjoy your visit, and we can put all this behind us?'

And with a wink, Governor Reed stalked out, leaving Ness shaking as she glanced miserably at the calendar: only nine years and three months to go . . .

2

VISITING TIME

'What's with the delay, darlin'? I've been frigging sardined up here for the past couple of hours. Either let us in or let us out.' Ollie Jones glared at the prison officer in the corner of the grey-painted holding room, who looked as hot and uncomfortable as he felt. He glanced around angrily. It was early May, but heat was pumping out from the vents in the ceiling like it was mid-winter, and there were at least twenty-five . . . twenty-six people jammed up close together with the only seat being the one the prison officer had her arse stuck on.

Usually, they'd be in and out of the holding room within minutes: bags checked, jackets checked, shoes checked, anywhere they felt like checking was theirs to open up and poke around in, but for some reason they'd been stuck in this room with no one telling them what was happening.

Ollie sighed and his gaze snagged on a girl. He winked at her, aware she'd been flashing her eyes at him since he'd got here. She blushed and quickly looked away, which made him smile, though it didn't surprise him. Maybe it was arrogance, but he knew he had that effect on women, always had done, ever since he was a teenager. He'd learned that his looks and turning on a bit of charm could get even the hardest-faced cow to whip off her knickers.

He saw her trying not to look and this time he chuckled out loud, causing the prison officer to glance across and frown. The girl was certainly a sort. Though she looked no older than eighteen, which always spelt trouble. They always turned out to be the clingy ones. The ones that started professing their love right after they'd given a blow job.

But in fairness, if the circumstances were different, he might have cracked on with her. Blue eyes, auburn hair, a tight, curvaceous body in proportion, what was there not to like? But he'd be a fool to go there; he didn't want to complicate his life any more than it already was. Not that he wanted to think about all the shit he had going on right now, and besides, the girl was one of the usual faces he'd seen here at Ashcroft while he was visiting Amy.

He had a feeling her name was Mina. Amy had mentioned her a few times – or rather, Amy had told him some story or other about her mother, who apparently was up the duff and on the same wing as her. Though in truth, most times his missus started bunnying on about the other women, he tuned out: there were only so many stories of prisoner cell block H he could handle. The sooner she was out of here, the better.

Undoing another button on his expensive black shirt, hoping somehow it would help with the oppressive heat, Ollie thought back. He'd had five long years of coming here. Five long years without Amy. *Shit*. Of course, in that time he'd been with more hookers than he'd bother remembering, and of course he'd fucked a few of her friends, as friends so often do. But random pussy was not the same as having her next to him in his bed. Even thinking about his wife gave him the beginnings of a hard-on, though that soon disappeared as the image of the hooker he'd been with last night came into his mind. She'd looked the part – nice ass, pert breasts – but she'd ruined the effect by spending the whole time chewing on her gum noisily and looking bored.

He sighed, bringing his thoughts back to Amy. She'd taken the rap for him, and he certainly regretted it. Not because he felt guilty – this was just another part of marriage: for better or worse, shit happens. No, he regretted it because he hadn't realized how much he needed her around. But then, that had always been the case. Since the very first time he'd met Amy, he just knew. He'd always known she was his, and his alone.

He'd picked her up when she'd been an escort, a stripper, in one of his mate's clubs. And the thought of that, even after all these years, still sent rage surging through his body. The idea that Amy was flaunting her tits, and her ass was for sale for some other geezer, made him want to kill. Within a couple of weeks of meeting her, he'd seen to it she was hardly out of his sight, or at least, if it wasn't his sight, it was one of his men's. He knew he couldn't ever be too careful, *especially* with someone as beautiful as Amy: long wavy chestnut hair, piercing green eyes, and her body always trim and tight . . . shit, he would be a fool to have her on anything but a short leash.

Ollie liked to know just what it was his woman was doing. He was old school like that. None of this women's lib crap. Seriously, he didn't get what the big need was for women to have all this freedom. What the fuck was freedom anyway? What would they do with it? It was just some daft idea they'd got into their heads. Something for them to complain about when they had nothing else to moan about. Because, in the end, if they had money in their pocket, a bit of designer gear, fuck-off wheels to drive about in, not to mention all the pedicures, manicures, all that beauty shit, as well as holidays in Marbella, what the fuck did they need *freedom* for? Christ, they wouldn't even have time for it.

He yawned noisily, thinking about the one thing that had always puzzled him, though maybe it was just a sign of Amy's strength. But she had *never* once complained about the sentence they'd thrown at her. Most women he knew, and even men for that matter, would've had a hissy meltdown: five years for money laundering, which wasn't too bad as it went, but certainly bad enough when it wasn't her rap, it was his.

However, Amy had just accepted it. Though he had thought she'd get out before now, each time she was up for parole, some ruck, some bad behaviour from her, some breaking of the rules, had caused it to be cancelled. Thankfully, there was no chance of that happening now. Unusually, she'd served the *whole* five years, which meant within the next two weeks or so she'd be home, right by his side. Where she belonged. And this time, there was no way in hell he was going to let her go anywhere again.

'OK, ladies and gentlemen and whatever else you like to call yourself these days.' The prison officer smirked, placing her radio in her wide black belt before heaving herself up and continuing: 'We've got the all-clear, so visiting can go ahead.'

What the fuck was the hold-up anyway?

An irate voice came from the back of the room, but no one bothered turning around or answering as they were led from the holding rooms back into the fresh air and across to the next block. Across to his Amy.

3

AMY

Walking into the bleak visiting room, Amy Jones automatically felt herself tensing. Each and every time she hoped it wouldn't show on her face, but the problem was, Ollie had a way of knowing what she was thinking, or at least, he had a way of getting out of her what she was thinking. The Ollie Jones way.

'Hey baby.' Seeing him at one of the small metal tables which were securely fastened to the floor – a precaution in case any of the women decided to start throwing them about – Amy plastered on a smile and purred at Ollie, the way he liked it. She'd learned very quickly that everything was about the way Ollie liked things.

The minute she sat down on the broken-backed blue plastic chair opposite him, Ollie reached across the table and grabbed her hand – a little bit too hard, as always.

'Hello, darlin', you all right? I thought I'd never get in here to see you today. I tell you what, that geezer-bird of a screw over there thought it was OK to fuck about with us.' Glaring, he spun round to look at the prison officer. 'I don't think she knows who she's playing with. I ain't one of her bitches.' He raised his voice at the end of the sentence, loud enough for the other visitors to turn and look at them.

Not wanting Ollie to wind himself up, but knowing that was exactly what he was doing, Amy put on a soothing voice. 'There was a bit of trouble of the wing. One of the women decided to have a protest or something.' She smiled as he turned back to her and stroked his face, continuing to talk. 'Anyway, you're here now, baby, that's all that matters, ain't it?'

He ran his fingers through his thick black hair and stared at her, his hazel eyes dark and brooding. 'Yeah, and you'll be home soon, *that's* all that matters.'

With the sun streaming in through the bars on the windows, Amy clasped her hands together to stop her trembling. The hum of noise in the room, like on the wing, ever present. She glanced around. She winked at the kids playing with the stained and broken toys from the box in the corner, the prison to them as normal as going to the park. The whole room was full of families snatching precious moments with their loved ones, and she watched as a tall man became frustrated with the drink and snack machine, which had never been refilled for the whole of her sentence.

She nodded at Maureen, who sat with the priest who often visited her. She had a feeling Maureen had said his name was Jack, although apparently, he was on a sabbatical. Though Reenie had told them he wore his clerical collar anyway, on account of getting better treatment wherever he went.

She smiled inwardly at the thought, and absent-mindedly continued to stare until she suddenly realized he was glancing across towards her. She quickly averted her eyes, not wanting Ollie to catch her looking at another man, even a man of the cloth. Amy knew her husband well enough to know that wouldn't make any difference; he'd kick up a fuss, especially as the priest was nothing short of astonishingly good looking.

Noticing Ness walk into the visiting room, she smiled at Mina sitting alone at a table, who smiled back shyly. Then she brought her gaze back to Ollie, who for some reason seemed distracted by Tess – D wing's self-appointed top dog – strolling in.

Amy's eyes darted over her husband's handsome face. The face that had made her think he was her prince in shining armour. Unfortunately, armour soon gets rusty.

Ashcroft was a dump. There were so many things wrong with the prison, though the one thing that prison life had given her above all else was safety. She was safely locked up, away from Ollie. Away from the life she hadn't been able to escape from. But now they were about to let her out and there was nothing she could do. And with dread in her heart she dug her nails into her palms and smiled at him as he turned his attention back to her. Hoping that her voice wouldn't crack and betray her, Amy took a deep breath and nodded. 'Yeah, that's all that matters, ain't it, darlin'? Home sweet home.'

4
NESS

'Where've you been? What's happened to your lip?' Tears pricked at Mina's eyes. 'I thought you weren't coming.'

Ness touched her mouth, which was still sore. She was feeling shaken from her encounter with Reed. She'd been in and out of prison a few times for small things – shoplifting, prostitution – and she'd come across the governor's type before. A bully who could get away with treating the women like shit because he was answerable to no one. She knew men like him deserved their comeuppance, though she wasn't about to start blowing the whistle. Even if she wanted to grass him up, she couldn't because who would listen to the likes of her? They'd laugh and see her as a troublemaker, an inmate that bore a grudge.

No, all she wanted to do was serve her time and get out early on good behaviour, which meant taking whatever Governor Reed handed out. Look on the bright side, she told herself, it could've been worse: she could've lost her visit. She supposed she was grateful for that. But none of it stopped her worrying about what was going to happen to her baby. She couldn't, she just couldn't give him up. The thought of that made her feel sick. But it felt like she'd run out of options before she'd even been given a chance.

Forcing her attention back to Mina, Ness smiled and gave a shrug. 'I didn't think I was coming either. I didn't think they'd let me, there was a bit of trouble. But it's all sorted now.' Holding her stomach and sliding herself into the hard plastic chair, she studied her eldest daughter.

Mina had just turned seventeen, and she couldn't be more beautiful: the bluest and biggest eyes, red pouting lips, long dark lashes, and high cheekbones . . . but she also couldn't look more like bait if she tried. Her daughter didn't even realize how attractive she was, but she had the sort of looks which attracted trouble, which attracted the sharks, the dogs . . . the pimps. Ness took a deep breath at the thought, knowing only too well how that ends.

They'd circle around a young kid like Mina, trying to take advantage of her. It had been bad enough before, but now Ness was banged up, there was no way she could protect her daughter like she wanted to, like she'd promised to, like she'd *hoped* to when she first held her in her arms at the hospital . . . before social services had taken Mina away within hours of being born and put her into their *care*.

Angry at the memory, angry at herself, at the mess she'd got into, Ness tried to ignore the familiar waves of anxiety. 'Do you have to walk around looking like that?' she snapped, hating herself for being harsh. All too often her words came out before her brain jumped into action, but it was hard not to react when the make-up her daughter had piled on made her look so much older, and the clothes she was wearing made her look like a mini version of Ness . . . A tart . . . A whore. She fought the tears. After all, wasn't she the one who'd told Mina to ditch her jeans and bright-coloured sweaters, the sneakers and puffer jacket, because she hadn't wanted anyone questioning Mina's age. She'd wanted her daughter to look older. She *needed* her to. She couldn't afford any busybodies phoning the social to report that her daughter was on her own in the bedsit. On her own, looking after Flo.

Flo was Mina's little sister. Their fathers were obviously not the same. Actually, she wasn't entirely sure who the father was. Her pimp or one of her clients. Though that didn't matter. All that mattered was social services didn't get their hands on Flo, which they would've done if they'd known about her. Which they still would do, if they found out.

She'd gone to a lot of trouble to hide Flo away from the authorities. Not bothering to go to any of the antenatal clinics during her pregnancy, and when she'd been seven months gone, she'd moved from Essex to Soho. Running away from her violent pimp, only to get involved with a worse one.

Still, at least she and Mina had started afresh, even if it had meant renting a shitty bedsit for cash and no questions . . . as well as the odd blow job for the landlord when she was short of the rent. And when Flo had been born, she'd used her sister's name, not that she'd seen her for the past ten years, but that was another thing that hadn't mattered either. What had mattered was that she'd been able to take Flo home the next day.

During those three years she hadn't been the perfect mum to either Flo or Mina, though she'd tried, she'd tried to get off the drugs, but the drugs always managed to find her. And she'd tried to get herself a different sort of job, a different kind of life. But no one had wanted to employ her, after all there was nothing on her CV apart from blow jobs and turning tricks.

But however dysfunctional, it had worked. The three of them had ticked over; actually, they'd done more than that. They'd been the three musketeers, and apart from her using, it was the first time in her life that she'd been anywhere near content. But then that night had happened which had started off so normally: the punters, the sex, the money, the usual Monday night. Only it had ended up with her pimp lying on the floor in a pool of blood, a six-inch blade sticking out of his chest.

She sighed and rubbed her temples, the anger, the worry churning inside her. 'You look like a cheap tart, Mina.' And once again, the minute Ness had said those words, she regretted them as she saw the hurt rush across Mina's face. This place was doing her head in, it felt like she was either being too defensive or on the attack, and her daughter often got the hard edge of that wedge.

Self-consciously Mina pulled up her low-cut red top. She knew her mum was being hard on her, but she also knew the reason: she couldn't bear that her sweet girl would end up like her. Mina had had a hard enough start in life. She'd been born addicted to crack, and between coming back to live with her mum and bouncing back to foster carers over and over again when social services swooped in to take her away because Ness was back on the drugs or had neglected to care properly for her daughter, Mina's childhood had been only a fraction better than her mother's. Yet somehow Mina had kept her loving nature.

The difference between Ness's childhood and Mina's was that she loved her daughter so much, but she just didn't know how to show it, no one had ever taught her. So, the only way she could show her love was by being hard on her, that was all she knew how to do. Ashamed of herself, Ness quickly changed the subject: 'Anyway, where's Flo?'

'With Doreen.'

'Doreen? Are you stupid, what have I said about leaving her with people? Do you want her to be taken by social services?'

Nervously, Mina chewed on her chipped painted nails. 'What was I supposed to do, Mum? You were the one who told me not to bring her here.'

Ness leaned over the table, lowering her voice. 'That don't mean you can leave Flo with anyone. You should know better.'

'Doreen's not anyone. She helps me out. Anyway, she's your mate, so I don't know why you don't want her to look after Flo.'

Ness sighed and instinctively rubbed the side of her stomach as the baby began to kick. 'Just pay for the babysitter like you were supposed to do.'

Mina's face flushed. 'With what?'

'What the fuck do you mean, with what? You had that big bag of dough. Oh, please, please don't fucking tell me you've rinsed through it already?' She glared at her daughter. The money had belonged to Steve, her pimp, and when he'd been lying there bleeding to death, instead of calling an ambulance, she'd taken the opportunity to take his money, or rather *take back* what he'd earned from the likes of her. 'Ten grand, Mina. Ten frigging grand. Tell me you're joking. That was your security. Yours and Flo's.'

'It ain't all gone . . . well, not entirely. There's a bit left . . . Not much.'

Ness covered her face with her hands for a moment then, dropping them, she shook her head. 'Go on then, where's it gone? And it better not be on frigging drugs and partying, I'm warn—'

'On the rent, Mum,' Mina interrupted. 'You were behind by eight, nine months.'

'It was fine, I had a deal with him. You didn't need to cough up all that.'

'No, Mum, it *wasn't* fine. He threatened to kick us out. And your deal was something that I *wasn't* going to do.'

Ness felt her cheeks burn. A wave of anger rushed through her. She also felt humiliated, which was crazy; she'd always been open with her daughter about being on the game, but she didn't need to be reminded, not like this. The stark reality of how she earned her living and what she had to do to get by felt like a curveball had hit her.

Although it was true, the deal she had with her landlord before she'd been banged up was something she wouldn't want her daughter to do; in fact, she'd kill her if she did. Giving blow jobs, being pawed over and having sex with a man who was old enough to be her grandfather, all to keep the rent down, certainly wasn't her finest hour.

'How much are we talking about, Mina? How much have you got left?'

Mina shrugged uncomfortably. 'I don't know. There was the rent, Flo's clothes – she needed them – and . . . and food . . . and the babysitter is expensive and there's only so much time I can take off school to look after her. I needed stuff for my exams, Mum, books and . . . Look, I'm trying my best. It's not easy.' Tears began to run down Mina's cheeks.

Guilt washed over Ness, but as so often happened, it turned to fury. 'What do you think it's like for me in here, hey? Do you think I've just booked myself into a frigging Airbnb for the next ten years? What are you going to do now, Mina?'

Trembling, Mina shrugged miserably. 'I don't know. We'll manage, I've still got a bit left.'

'A bit ain't going to last. Jesus, Mina. It's not like I can get any more money for you, stuck in here, is it?'

'Well, you wouldn't be in here if you hadn't brought Steve into our lives,' Mina muttered under her breath.

Ness leaned over the table and grabbed Mina's hand. 'What the fuck did you just say to me? What the fuck did you say? How dare you. How fucking dare you.' Incensed, Ness raised her voice, causing the other visitors to look across.

'Everything all right, babe?' Lynette, one of the women who had a cell two doors along from her, smiled, her black skin shining with the coco cream she always used. There was a tinge of sadness to her, though, and Ness had a feeling she was trying not to cry. By the looks of things, her daughter, Evie, yet again hadn't bothered to show up, something Ness knew Lynette found painful.

30

Feeling her baby kicking, Ness took a deep breath, and nodded. 'Yeah, you know what kids are like, Lynn.' She gave a quick, cold glance at Mina, who was silently crying. 'Drive you mad, don't they?'

'Well at least your kid turns up. I thought Evie would be here today, but my sister just told me that she still doesn't want to come. I ain't seen her in nearly a month now. I don't know what I've done to her; she won't even pick up the phone to me . . . but then again, I guess I don't blame her . . .' Lynette trailed off and shrugged, before glancing at Mina. 'You all right though, hun? How's school?'

Mina wiped her tears on her jacket. 'It's OK. We've got exams next week.'

'Make sure you work hard for them, yeah? I was always shit at exams, never bothered with school. Maybe that's why I ended up in here.' She grinned and, getting up to walk back to the wing, she rubbed Mina's back as she passed. 'Promise me you'll work hard, girl, get out there, see the world. You don't want to end up like me . . . or your mother – especially not your mother.' Lynette winked at Ness.

Mina giggled. 'Thanks, Lynn . . . see you later.'

'*Time please, everyone.*' The prison officer suddenly came to life, shouting unnecessarily loud.

As Mina went to get up, Ness kept hold of her hand, her voice icy. 'You owe me, Mina. You owe me that you'll look after Flo, you hear me . . . Cos I might have brought Steve into our lives – and God do I fucking regret that – but let's face it, so much of this mess, this shit, is because of you.'

5

MINA

'You want a lift, babe? I'm driving past your manor.'

Standing miserably in the prison car park as it started to rain, Mina gazed at Iris sitting behind the wheel of her new ice-blue Range Rover. Still upset by the way her mum had treated her, she wiped away her tears. She hated arguing with her, especially as she knew she wouldn't see her mum for another week. She missed her and everything seemed such a struggle.

They were always at loggerheads now, and it upset her because they hadn't argued when Ness had been on the outside. Yeah, they'd had their disagreements, but not like this, it was like everything was falling apart. And she wasn't sure how to stop it. The truth was, she was terrified. She couldn't see a way out, and the problem was, her mum's sentence was really only just beginning.

'Come on then, unless you're trying out for the wet T-shirt competition. You hoping to impress someone?' Iris winked and giggled.

'Hey baby, how are you, darlin'? Long time no see!' Roz Watson, Iris's friend, waved from the passenger seat at her before elegantly clambering out.

'Yeah, I'm good thanks,' Mina said quietly, feeling even more self-conscious about the way she was dressed. Roz and Iris were everything she wasn't.

'I'm in a rush sweetheart, got a little bird to catch.' Roz winked, laughing, as if somehow Mina was supposed to be in on the joke.

Hurrying to her side, Roz – smelling of expensive perfume, and as loud and dramatic as always – gave her a kiss on the cheek. Her eyes sparkled as she said, 'We must get together soon, go for a drink or something, yeah? All three of us. Don't be a stranger, hun.'

Before Mina had a chance to reply, Roz tottered off in a towering pair of heels, across the car park towards the main road.

'Mina, move your beautiful arse and get in,' Iris hollered again, and this time Mina moved towards the car.

She shivered slightly, trying not to feel envious of Iris's life, or Roz's for that matter. She liked both of them, but especially Iris. From the very first time she'd visited her mum, Iris had reached out to her and shown her nothing but kindness, which she had to admit, had surprised her. She never thought that someone like Iris would bother with the likes of her. After all, she had nothing, owned nothing – apart from cheap clothes and an even cheaper fake Louis Vuitton bag – and she lived in a dive which she called home. Whereas Iris seemed to have everything.

She was graceful, tall, a model figure, beautifully kept long flowing corkscrew blonde hair with golden highlights running through it. A pretty face. And she wore all the latest designer gear along with the obligatory diamond Rolex watch. But even though Iris had a life which Mina could only dream of, their differences hadn't stopped them becoming friends, because in spite of everything, there was one similarity that had thrown them together. One similarity which couldn't be denied: they were both COPs: children of prisoners.

Mina had initially found the whole of prison life, of having a parent inside, totally alien and overwhelming. Frightening even. She'd never felt so alone – which was saying something, given that she'd been in and out of care throughout her life. And she hadn't been able to confide in any of her friends. What was the point? They wouldn't understand. They wouldn't know how it felt to wait in line in the cold week after week to undergo a body search, a bag search, personal belongings search, just to be able to sit opposite their mum for a couple of hours. To Mina it felt like she was as much a prisoner as the women in Ashcroft.

But Iris, well, she'd understood. Her mum, Steph, had been inside for the past six years for murder, though she was looking at a life stretch. Iris had told her that her mum had sliced up some guy she'd been doing business with, and ever since, Iris had to come and visit her mum here at Ashcroft most weekends.

Roz, on the other hand, had been banged up herself, along with her sister, who still had six months of her sentence to go, for buying and selling stolen designer goods. Though neither of them had been locked up in Ashcroft. They'd served their sentence at a prison outside Nottingham, where Iris's mum, Steph, had originally been sent while on remand.

Iris had struck up a friendship with Roz, starting first in the visiting room, and it had continued after she'd been released. She wasn't entirely sure what Roz had been banged up for, but she did know that Iris's mum didn't like her hanging out with Roz for some reason. But she also knew that it just made Iris more determined to be mates with her.

As much as she liked Roz, Mina always felt slightly intimidated by her. It was the confidence she walked around with. The opposite to how she always felt.

'Mina, you're well soaked.' Iris, her blue eyes lighting up, giggled again.

'You sure you want me getting in your car like this?'

'Of course I am. I ain't going to leave you to walk, am I? Hurry up, you look like a drowned rat.'

They both laughed as Mina climbed in, but as she did, she glanced behind her.

Iris saw her looking. 'Were you hoping for a better offer?'

Mina tilted her head and grinned as she put on her seatbelt. 'What are you talking about?'

'You know what I'm talking about.' Iris gestured with her hand. 'I saw you looking at him.'

Immediately, Mina blushed. She could feel her cheeks burning. 'Who?'

Putting the car into drive, Iris headed for the exit. 'That Ollie geezer.' Iris glanced at Mina. 'And don't try to deny it, you're always looking at him . . . Well smitten, ain't you?'

'No,' Mina shrugged, then squealed with embarrassment and pushed herself down into her seat as Iris beeped her horn as they drove past Ollie, who was stepping into his large, blacked-out four-by-four.

'Oh my God! I can't believe you just did that! Do you think he saw? Did he see us?'

'Er, yes! Duh!' Iris hooted with laughter, turning towards the motorway that would take them back to London. To Soho. 'I don't know what you see in him, Meen.'

'What, you wouldn't if you had a chance?' Mina looked at Iris, smelling the brand-new leather of the cream seats.

'No, I frigging wouldn't. He's a creep. Well muggy. He reckons he's God's gift. Yuk! He once tried to chat up Roz, but she was having none of it. Evie, though, God, she was well into him.'

Irrationally, Mina felt a streak of jealousy rush through her. She didn't really like Evie, who was around the same age as them, though Iris was slightly older; she'd just turned eighteen. The flashy new Range Rover a present from her mum, Steph. Roz was older still, twenty-five, twenty-six. Mina didn't know much about her background, but she hadn't ever seen her without a Louis Vuitton bag hooked on her arm and a pair of Louboutins.

'Evie's got no chance,' Mina replied sullenly. 'As if he's going to look at her, have you seen the way she dresses? It's like she's got shares in an old woman's shop.'

Iris spluttered, showing off her perfect white teeth. 'Meow . . . You have got it bad, ain't you? Anyway, I haven't seen Evie for ages, so you don't have to worry about the competition, he's all yours.'

'I wasn't worried . . . What's happened to her, anyway? I saw Lynette in the visiting room.'

'I dunno, maybe she just doesn't fancy coming anymore. I swear down, I wish I could swerve this place. If I miss a week, my mum's right on my case, she's such a fucking bitch. And she's giving me proper grief about Roz coming down to see me. I swear that cow doesn't like me to have any mates, apart from you, that is.' Overtaking a lorry too quickly as she hit the motorway, then sticking her middle finger up at the driver, Iris continued in a snarl: 'Even though she's inside, she really thinks she can still run my life. Like she's got this mobile phone she keeps stashed away, and she always calls, checking where I am, checking what I'm doing, who I'm seeing. She's on it all the time.'

'Then don't answer,' Mina suggested.

Iris raised her eyebrows. 'I wish. If I don't, she sends one of her goons around to the house, to check on me.'

'What about your stepdad though, is he still away?'

'I told you already that he can't say nothing, and besides, he's well under her thumb. And anyway, this past year he ain't really been around. He spends most of his time sunning it up in Marbella on her money, but she doesn't really bother with him anyway.'

Mina remembered that Iris had told her that her real dad had been stabbed to death when she was only little, and her stepdad was one of life's ponces.

'But I'm telling you, Mina, I ain't going to put up with it much longer. I'm sick of her trying to control me. She's a part-time mum, so she ain't entitled to get a full-time say. I'm eighteen now, and I'm going to find a way to earn my own money, then I'm going to leave everything behind and just fuck off out of here.'

'Really?'

'Yeah, really, I'm going to walk away from it all, every single thing . . . well maybe not this car, maybe I'll take this baby with me.' Laughing and relaxing, Iris quickly glanced at Mina before concentrating again on the road. 'You can come with me, if you like. Maybe we could go to the States or . . . or Australia or Germany even. Apparently, German men are well fit. Let's fuck them all off and leave them to it – what do you say?'

Mina turned and looked out of the window, watching the rain slink down the outside of the car. The idea of being able to leave it all behind, leave behind all the responsibility, never having to answer to her mum, or to her conscience, was something she could only dream of. But then what about Flo? What would she do with her? She hadn't actually told Iris about Flo, and although she trusted her, Mina knew she couldn't have anyone finding out about her little sister. She'd been in care herself and it had been tough; the memories of the abuse she'd suffered never went away. And there was no way she was ever going to let her sister go through what she had. But that didn't stop her wishing that life was different.

Speaking in almost a whisper, and knowing her reply was just a pipe dream, Mina smiled wistfully. 'Yeah, I'd like that. I'd be well up for it.'

For the next half hour, they drove in silence, swerving through the heavy traffic of central London, both in their own thoughts. Eventually they drove down Shaftesbury Avenue and Iris indicated right, turning into Greek Street before pulling up outside the French Tavernier.

Swivelling round in her seat to look at Mina, Iris frowned. 'I'm being serious. I ain't doing this no more. I have to work a few things out first, but then I'm gone. If you're serious, then we can go together. What's stopping us? It's not like we've got kids, is it? Your mum is looking at ten years, and mine, thank fuck, is in there for life. So why not? It's not our crime, so why should we have to serve a prison sentence too? I'm breaking out, Mina, and if you've got any sense, you'll come too . . .'

6

'*Just untie me, OK. Please.*' *In the small basement, she pulled on the ropes which cut into her wrists and ankles. Her arms aching from being above her head as her long hair became wet from tears and sweat.*

'*And why the fuck would I want to do that? Why would I let such a pretty thing as you go?*' *He leaned down and whispered in her ear, his erection pushing against the zip of his trousers.* '*Besides, we've tried that and look how it went. You opened your mouth, didn't you? You could get me in trouble.*'

'*I wouldn't tell anyone, I swear.*'

'*Swear as much as you like, sweetheart, it won't make any difference. I'd be a mug to trust you. I mean, how do I know that the minute you leave this place you won't go running and tell the first person that you meet? And then where would we be?*'

He laughed and she turned her head, staring into his eyes. All she could see was a cold darkness. Vacant eyes staring right back at her. '*You have my word. I wouldn't do that to you . . . I love you.*'

He sneered. '*Of course you do, like I love you.*' *The sarcasm dripped off his tongue cruelly.*

'*I wouldn't get you into trouble. I wouldn't do that.*' *Her voice trembled.* '*I just want to go home.*'

Stroking her head, he smiled at her, his eyes turning even colder. '*Oh, we both know that's exactly what you'd do, don't we? Besides, this is your new home now . . . You see, all of this could have been avoided if you'd just listened to me. I would've let you go, but how can*

I, after what happened? Don't forget, you were the one who wanted this in the first place, sweetheart. You were the one who thought this would be fun. What's changed?' He laughed nastily again, then paused and looked down intently at her on the bed before adding, 'Look, let me give you some advice. The best thing you can do is just accept it. Accept this is home now. Who knows, you might even enjoy it more than you think you will.'

She let out a scream, her words muffled by her tears. 'You fucking bastard, you fucking bastard! Just let me go.'

'Temper, temper.' Pushing back her hair, he kissed her gently on her forehead. 'You need to calm down – you're all tense, and that ain't good for either of us.'

He reached across to the pot of cream on the small, chipped round table next to the pile of condoms and tubes of lubrication. He undid the top, his fingers slipping from the excess cream which had been left on the outside of the lid.

'How about a massage? Here you are, keep still, sweetheart.'

The cold cream between his fingers contrasted with the warmth of her body. Her shoulders were tense; he could feel it. Then he slipped his hand underneath the arch of her back, rubbing the cream in firmly.

Slowly he let his hands move around, caressing the cream into her stomach. 'Sshhhh, stop crying, just stop, OK? It's all going to be fine . . . as long as you listen . . .' He bent down and kissed her naked breasts, feeling his penis throbbing. But as much as he wanted to, he held back.

To stop himself going any further, he stood up from the small metal framed bed and spoke soothingly. 'Try to get some sleep, baby.' Heading for the door, he stopped. 'I almost forgot.'

Turning back, he picked up the gag, walked over and put it on her. As he pulled the bedsheet over to keep her warm, he smiled again, though something told him she was big trouble.

7
LYNETTE

Lynette lay on her bed staring up at the grey ceiling as she tried not to cry. This place wasn't going to break her, she wouldn't let it. But everything seemed so hard. Each day seemed to become more difficult. She wasn't cut out for it like some of the other women were. She hadn't been in and out of care or had neglectful, drug-addled or alcoholic parents, which was such a familiar story here at Ashcroft. She'd never been in trouble in her life. OK, she'd left school with no qualifications, but she'd always worked. She'd been in the same job for the past fifteen years: a dispatch coordinator for a chocolate company. And whether people thought it was boring or not, she'd loved her job, loved the girls she'd worked with but in just one moment she'd thrown it all away, and now, now she was looking at an eight stretch.

Cradling her arms around her knees, she rocked back and forth, listening to the endless banging and shouting coming from the wing. Then she closed her eyes, feeling her tears rolling down the side of her face. And once again she thought back to that moment, the moment it had all gone wrong, and she groaned audibly. Why, why, why, had she been such a stupid cow and reacted the way she had done? If she hadn't, none of this would be happening. She'd be at home with Evie watching crap on the TV, arguing about who had the remote, ordering Chinese, but no, instead in that moment, in that second, she hadn't thought about anything else apart from herself. So, she knew she only had herself to blame.

'You all right, Lynn?'

Opening her eyes, Lynette saw Maureen, dressed in a grey prison tracksuit identical to her own, standing at the door of her cell, a look of concern etched into her face. She tried to smile. 'Yeah, you know how it is. Some days are better than others.'

Maureen frowned and stared at Lynette's arm. 'Lynn. Oh, Lynn,' was all she said before hurrying over to her. 'Let's see, darling.'

Lynette shook her head as the blood seeped through onto the arm of her tracksuit top.

'Oh sweetheart.' Maureen's eyes filled with tears. 'Please, let me see. I'm not judging, sweetheart.'

This time Lynette didn't object; instead she let Maureen roll up the sleeve of her top, exposing the deep self-harm marks. 'That's a fair brutal cut you've made this time. I think we best take you down to the medic, get them take a look at it.'

'No.' Lynette furiously shook her head again, wiping away the tears with the palm of her hand. 'They'll just throw me in the psych ward like last time, and I know if I go in there it'll make it worse. At least here I've got you lot.'

'I don't know, it looks nasty.'

'No.' Lynette sounded adamant. 'I'm not going.'

'In that case, will you let me clean it up?'

'OK . . . OK.' Lynette nodded and sniffed loudly. She hated the way she felt about herself. As a teenager, there'd been a period when she'd self-harmed, and that was because she'd been relentlessly bullied at school. She'd thought all that was way behind her – until she'd been locked up in Ashcroft. Within a week of being banged up on the wing, she'd found herself once more picking up a blade to cut into her own flesh. 'Thank you, Reenie. I'm sorry, I really am.'

'Now that's an eejit thing to say, Lynn. There's no need to be sorry. I just wish, each time you got the urge to do it, you'd come and find me. Talk to me. What brought it on this time, anyway? What happened?'

Lynette glanced up at the window, the rusty bars a constant reminder of where she was. As she began to talk, Steph appeared at the door and smiled, giving a sympathetic shrug as she caught sight of Lynette's arm.

'Mind if I come in?' Steph asked warmly.

Lynette smiled at Steph, though the sadness felt like it was overwhelming her.

'Of course not. I was just saying to Maureen, I know it sounds stupid, but when my sister came to tell me that Evie was going to be a no-show again, it hurt. You know it's like, if I see her, if I talk to her, I can get through this . . . just. But with her not coming to see me anymore, I can't deal with this place or the way I feel. It's like there's a build-up inside me, like I'm a frigging pressure cooker, you know?'

Steph nodded, listening intently to her.

'And . . . and it just gets to a point where my head can't take it no more. It feels like the only way to release the pressure, that bubble in my head, is to cut myself.' She covered her face, feeling shame, the tears running out between her fingers as she began to sob. And it took a minute or so for her to be able to compose herself enough to add, 'And the weird thing is, for a second, it works. The pain of the razorblade cutting into my flesh, overrides the fucked-up feeling in my head.'

Steph walked over to her, pulling her hands gently away from her face, then she gave her a hug which Lynette gratefully accepted. 'You shouldn't even be in here, darlin'. It's wrong. What you did, anyone would do. I tell you, if I found out my sister was fucking my old man and had a kid with him, he'd be ten feet under. And now she's shacked up with him in your house looking after Evie, playing happy families.'

Maureen nodded. 'Steph's right, you shouldn't be in here. I know they made out your sister and your old man were the innocent parties, but they were the ones who pushed you to it. They should've let you off with a slap on the wrist and probation. I mean, in France, what you did, they'd call it a crime of passion: a *crime passionnel*.'

Steph flashed a grin. 'Yeah, but here they just call it, you ramming your car through the wall of your sister's front room when she's watching *Homes Under the Hammer*. Though in fairness, that's a fucking crime right there.'

Grateful for Steph trying to lighten the moment, Lynette laughed. As Maureen dabbed her arm, wiping away the blood, she winced and looked at her. 'Thank you, you're what I needed. It's too easy to start feeling sorry for yourself in this place, ain't it?' She swung her legs onto the floor, holding the wet rag which Maureen had just given her to stem the bleeding from her latest wound.

Steph popped gum into her mouth. 'Seriously though, why do you think Evie hasn't come to see you? You reckon your sister is saying shit, trying to poison Evie against you?'

Lynette nodded thoughtfully. 'Yeah, maybe. Cos every time I call the house, she always says Evie doesn't want to talk to me.'

'Have you tried her mobile?'

Lynette shrugged. 'It's always turned off.'

'Well, it's a fucking shame,' Steph continued. 'Cos you always seemed to get on. Not like me and my ungrateful madam of a daughter. I tell you, Iris is becoming a full-on bitch.'

'Look, why don't you call Evie now?' Maureen suggested.

'Here, you can use my phone.' Not waiting for an answer, Steph dipped her hand into her joggers, fumbling around for a moment as she pulled a face, grinning. 'It's up here somewhere. That's what happens when you have kids, it's like one of them big black holes. Stephen Hawking could've done worse than use my pussy as research for one of his theorems.'

Maureen squealed, her face breaking out into a flushed grin. 'Oh, saints preserve us, please tell me you're not really expecting Lynn to use that after it's been hidden up your noonie.'

Retrieving the small mobile phone and wiping it on her top, Steph shrugged. 'I don't see Lynn complaining.' She passed it to her.

'Trust me, I couldn't care less where it's been as long as I can speak to Evie.' She punched in the number, but within moments it clicked into her daughter's voicemail.

'Hey, this is Evie, make it worth my while . . .'

'Evie, it's Mum. I'm just calling to speak to you, darlin' . . . I haven't heard from you, and I haven't seen you either, and I get you might not want to come to this shithole. I mean, who wants to spend their Saturdays here? I understand that but, I feel like you've just cut me out of your life, and I miss you . . . But I'm sorry, I'm sorry for this mess I got myself into, and I know me being inside has hurt you, probably more than it hurts me, but please talk to me, Evie, write to me, just . . . just let's sort this out somehow, yeah? I love you, Evie. To the moon and back.' She ended the call and sat staring at the phone before passing it back to Steph. 'Thanks, babe, I appreciate that.'

'Yeah, anytime. If you want to try again later, let me know,' Steph said quietly.

'Why do I get the feeling that something's wrong, Steph?'

'It's just this place, it makes you paranoid, that's all.' But even as she said it, she didn't sound very convincing.

8
TESS

'Nothing in here is free, darlin' and you fucking owe me. I don't know why you thought it was OK to ask me for gear, knowing that neither you nor your poxy family could pay. You must be some dumb bitch, cos, let's face it, pet, it's not like you can hide from me, is it? You've got nowhere to run. And you must have a short memory, because what did I frigging tell you the last time this happened?'

'I . . . I . . . I . . .'

Tess Witham stood in the small shower room of the gym with one foot on the toilet bowl, and the other foot on the back of a woman who was kneeling on the dirty tiles and sobbing silently.

She laughed nastily at the frightened woman. 'You'll need to do better than that, love.' And she held on to the woman's hair, twisting it in her hand to pull brutally on her scalp. 'So, come on then, why didn't you listen to me when I warned you before? Cos I told you loud and clear what would happen . . . Or perhaps you didn't hear me? Could that be it? Maybe what you need is your ears cleaning out, pet . . . I tell you what, this might help . . .' And with that, Tess plunged the woman's head into the unflushed toilet, holding it below the soiled, toilet-tissue-filled water.

She cackled as the woman struggled and flayed her arms, prompting Tess to press her foot harder onto the woman's back and plunge her head deeper into the toilet bowl.

'You reckon she'll learn her lesson, this time?' She glanced over her shoulder, winking at the three women standing next to her: her bitches. Her prey. They were the women who did her dirty work a lot of the time, who were prepared to do what she wanted, as well as giving her sexual favours whenever she felt the urge. She had their undivided loyalty. And in return? Well, they had her full protection, along of course with the perks: the first in the meal lines, the first in the showers, a pick of any of the other women's possessions: it was theirs to take, especially as not many of the women were prepared to go up against her. The only women who stood up to her, who were prepared to question her authority, were Ness, Steph, Amy and Maureen. They weren't afraid to speak up and, although it wasn't always paradise between the four of them, they stuck together. Power in numbers. Though soon there was going to be one less. And without Amy, Tess was certain the cracks would begin to show.

And then yes, there were the cell warriors in Ashcroft: spouting shit, talking crap, but when it came to face to face, they were meek and mild, hiding their brewing resentment towards her.

Though, in her opinion, she'd earned her position. She deserved to be top dog. The war scars from the batterings she had taken, too numerous to count, were dotted all over her body – and she wore them with pride.

Everything had been thrown at her when she'd started to challenge for the number one spot. From being jumped on in the showers to being attacked in her cell to being raped in the gymnasium by the last dog and her crew. It had all been thrown at her. But none of it broke her. If anything, it had made Tess stronger. Because that's what it took. That's what it took to become untouchable, and it had all been worth it to get to where she was now. Inside, fights and favours were currency – and Tess had certainly paid out handsomely.

It hadn't come easily though. It had taken her a few years to really settle into Ashcroft, establish herself, and it had been one hell of a feat: the last top dog had been in power long before Tess had arrived, and not everyone had liked the idea of change. But neither had she liked to take orders from another inmate.

So over time, she'd pushed back: bribing and promising favours to the other women, and when that didn't work, she'd resorted to coercive means: the violence, the intimidation, the fear. And eventually she'd had enough women on the wing behind her to overthrow the competitor. Steph, who'd tried to challenge for top dog at the same time, hadn't got enough backing to pull it off. She hadn't even managed to get Amy onside, which, much to Tess's amusement, caused a hell of a lot of friction between them, even to this day.

In the end, it had only taken Tess two days of bloodshed to claim the crown.

And the fate of the last top dog? She'd been found in the showers – a ligature round her neck – no one had seen a thing.

Tess smirked at the memory but brought her attention back to the matter at hand. 'Hopefully now, Sandra, you'll hear me when I tell you not to take the piss.'

She lifted Sandra's head up out of the water, curling her lip in disgust. Then without giving her a chance to speak, Tess slammed Sandra's face on the edge of the ceramic toilet bowl, smashing her nose wide open. As blood spurted out all over the cubicle, Sandra screamed in agony.

'Howay, man, stop all that crying, you'll give me a headache.' And with that, Tess brought Sandra's arm behind her back, pulling it around until she heard a loud snap. Then, smiling, she left Sandra writhing on the floor in agony, in a pool of her own urine.

Walking out of the cubicle whistling, Tess nodded to the screw, pushing a fifty-pound note – along with Sandra's 18-carat gold wedding ring – into her hands. She'd learned long ago that everything in prison had its price, and everything was up for sale.

Five minutes later, having marched from the gym back into D wing, Tess – already in a fighting mood from the altercation with Sandra or, as she liked to call her, *the bag head*, one of Ashcroft's heroin addicts – stood in the doorway of Lynette's cell, her tracksuit straining at the seams, the ankles of it lightly sprayed with Sandra's blood. 'As cosy as this is, get the fuck out, I want a word with Lynn. All of you, move . . . *Now!*' She stared hard at Ness, Steph and Maureen, who were huddled in the tiny cell with Lynette.

Her body took up a lot of the doorway. She was almost as wide as she was tall. Something else she was proud of. She'd never understood the obsession for thin. A cream cake and a slice of sticky chocolate pudding was what she measured life on, not a number on the scales. Her face, marked with acne scars, screwed up into a snarl. Behind her as usual stood two of her cronies: a tall black girl no older than twenty, who celled up at the end, and a short, older woman who never seemed to be far from Tess's side. 'Am I talking to my fucking self?' She grinned at them nastily.

'Seems like you are, Tess.' Ness stared back defiantly. 'Seems like no one here is interested in what you've got to say. So if I were you, I'd piss off.'

Tess sniffed loudly, stepped closer into Ness. She placed her hand on Ness's pregnant stomach. 'Don't think this little bastard is going to protect you. I'll fuck you up and take you out as quickly as I take anyone else out.'

Incensed, Ness grabbed hold of Tess's throat, but immediately Tess used her weight, pushing Ness forcibly across the cell. 'Come on then, Ness, show us what you've got!' Tess spat out her words.

'Don't you fucking touch her!' Steph screamed, diving in and grabbing hold of Tess's hair.

Maureen ran forward, trying to separate the women. 'Enough! For feck's sake!' Her face flushed, she turned to Ness, who was staggering to her feet. 'Are you all right? Ness, go on, go. Get out of here.'

'The fuck I will.' Enraged, Ness pushed Maureen out of the way, glaring at Tess as her two cronies waded in: grabbing Steph and flinging her onto the floor, then laying in with hard, brutal kicks, while Ness, still furious, leapt at Tess. 'You don't get away with calling my kid a bastard, you hear me?'

'What, you're going to stop me, are you? How about I kick that bairn out of you right here, right now?'

'The hell you will, Theresa! Because you'll have to kill me first.' Maureen's cries rose above the screeches of the women as Ness lunged again at Tess. And tears welled in Maureen's eyes, the worry in her voice apparent. 'Ness, enough! Ness! Think of the bairn! Ness! Holy mother of God, just stop, will ye!'

'Animals. Nothing but filthy, filthy animals.' Above the women's yelling, Governor Reed's voice came from behind them, his words spat out viciously, startling them into frozen submission.

Rigid with fury, he stood next to two of his deputies: June Walters, a hard Caribbean woman who'd been in the service since leaving school thirty years ago, and Tony Earle, his deputy, who did as little as he could while trying to look busy.

Crammed into the cell, Reed gazed around, his eyes stopping at Ness in a look of disgust. 'You again? Even after our little chat, you still want to cause problems in my prison.' It was a statement and not a question. 'There are some people in life who never learn, but let me tell you, you *will*, Vanessa. You will learn no matter how long it takes or what it takes.'

'She's been nothing but trouble since she arrived, sir,' Deputy Walters smirked nastily.

'That's bullshit and you know it!' Ness retorted.

'Less of your mouth, Vanessa,' Tony Earle snapped. 'Unless of course you want to lose your next month's visiting rights.'

'These are hardly the actions of someone who's keen to keep their baby. From what I've seen of you so far, I think it was a whole lot of fresh air you were spouting about wanting to keep your child. The only person you're interested in is yourself.' The scorn was written all over Reed's face.

'That's not fair, sir! That ain't fair!' Panic rocked through Ness's words. 'Nothing's changed.'

'Oh, I think it has. I think that before, you had next to no chance of me recommending you to the mother and baby unit, and now, after this performance, there's zero chance.'

Ness burst into tears and was immediately comforted by Maureen as Steph, getting up, dusted herself down, but not before she threw an angry glare at Tess.

'It ain't right to blame Ness. She wasn't the problem here. We were just minding our own business. It's not how it looks. It wasn't what you think. It wasn't like that, sir.'

Looking at all the women, Reed sneered. Sounding bemused, he said, 'Then would someone care to tell me what it *was* like?'

At first none of the women said anything, then Tess, her Newcastle accent bouncing off her words, spoke. 'We were just practising.'

Reed's green eyes narrowed. 'Practising?'

'Yeah, practising for . . . for . . . for . . .' Tess trailed off, looking blank. She shrugged at the others, folding her arms under her large breasts.

'Jesus Christ, how hard was it to think of something. Dumb fucking bitch,' Steph muttered under her breath.

'And you're a dead fucking bitch.' Tess threw a punch at Steph, catching her under her chin. Reed stood in between them before it went further. 'That's enough!' he bellowed. 'Take them to solitary, *now*. I think a night or two down there will do them good.'

'My pleasure.' Deputy Walters sounded and looked delighted as she started to push Steph roughly out the door, but as Deputy Earle went to grab Ness, Maureen shuffled towards the governor.

'She's pregnant, she can't! Ness can't go down there! It's not right.'

He stared at her, a look of irritation rippling across his face. 'I think anyone that's up for a few rounds with Tess can take a couple of nights down in the hole, don't you? They can keep each other company. Tess and Ness, how quaint.' Vitriol coated his words.

'It's wrong, you can't!' Maureen put her hand on the governor to stop him walking out of the cell.

He gripped her arm and paused dramatically before speaking. 'Seems you'll be joining them too.'

Maureen's eyes were wide open. 'I don't care about meself, but if anything happens to Ness, if the baby starts to come early, what then? You must be able to see that? She'll be on her own in a cell. You know how long it takes for anyone to come if you press the bell down in solitary – if they even bother, that is.'

'Then you need to pray the baby doesn't arrive, don't you . . . Maybe you can have that job.' He winked and hauled Maureen off with him. 'Now move it.'

As they marched out, without Deputy Tony Earle or the other officer noticing, Tess quickly threw something out of her pocket and onto the floor.

★

Scrambling up from the bed, Lynette, making certain everybody had gone, hurried to pick it up. She turned it around in her hand and realized it was a home-made shank: the sharpened end of a plastic toothbrush – as vicious and as deadly as any razorblade. Then, making sure no one was coming, Lynette closed the cell door, climbed up on the locker and hid the shank under the edge of the fluorescent light.

9
STEPH

Lying back in solitary, Steph sighed. She wasn't sure why she'd got involved. Though she guessed when it came to Tess, it was hard to ignore her constant jibes. She, like a lot of the women, hated Tess with a passion. Her constant peddling drugs to the most vulnerable, bullying the weak, and simply not caring about the other girls, made her a pariah, though paradoxically, the crimes she committed made her somewhat of a hero within Ashcroft's walls.

Tess had killed her brother, who'd been a prolific sex offender, having abused several young girls all under the age of twelve. She'd also, in her killing spree, beaten her father and uncle to death with a metal baseball bat. Rumour had it the whole family had been in a paedophile gang and Tess had been on the receiving end of their abuse since she'd been a little kid. Although her heart went out to Tess on that level, it didn't stop her hating her for the way she tried to rule Ashcroft with sheer brutality. And if it wasn't for Amy, she would've been top dog by now and not Tess.

When Amy had first arrived in prison, she'd taken her under her wing, looking out for her, showing her the ropes. Introducing her to the other girls. Pointing out who to avoid and who to befriend. Because who you knew was more important inside than outside. It could even be the difference between getting through the sentence, and not.

The other girls had taken to Amy. Her easy personality had

made her one of the most popular women on the block. There'd been no jealousy from Steph; she'd been pleased for Amy, and she'd felt their friendship was solid, unbreakable. But when it had come to the crunch, Amy hadn't backed her for pole position, instead she'd given her vote to the last top dog.

It had felt like a personal betrayal; she'd been genuinely hurt by Amy's decision not to support her. And aside from Tess becoming number one, for her personally, the fallout had been even greater. Their friendship was done. The trust was gone, and now all she did was tolerate her. What Amy did was unforgivable. The sooner the bitch left Ashcroft, the better.

Steph closed her eyes and shifted her thoughts to Iris. A lot of the women inside were tough on their children, and she was no different. For all the hard life she'd lived, marrying a gangster to become a gangster's wife, then taking over the business when he'd been stabbed to death, parenting from inside the walls of Ashcroft was her toughest challenge.

There was no rule book to tell you how to go about being a good mum while banged up. There was no guide to show how to be loving yet strong. Because the fear always was, if she was too soft, too lenient, how would she stop Iris from falling into the same traps as she had done? She'd had so many conversations with Ness on this very subject. How to be a mother when you're not even there. Especially how to be a mother to someone like Iris, who was so similar to herself: headstrong and sassy. A disaster waiting to happen.

'You all right, Steph?' Ness's voice floated through from next door.

'Yeah, why wouldn't I be? This shit is a piece of cake!' She laughed, knowing it wasn't true, knowing that Ness knew it wasn't true either. Solitary was never easy, and sometimes it was a question of bullshitting your way through. That was the key to success in this place. Pretend all was fine during the day, and cry into your pillow at night. 'What about you, doll?' she shouted back to Ness.

'I'm fine. Like you say, a piece of fucking cake, mate!'

Biting back the tears, Steph put her hand down her joggers, pulling out her phone. Sometimes she needed Iris more than Iris needed her, and with that thought she dialled her daughter's number . . .

10

JACK

Soho was buzzing. The Sunday evening tourists were out in force and the restaurants and bars were full to bursting. The noise of traffic and music filled the streets and the harsh winter chill had been replaced by a balmy spring temperature as Jack Walsh strolled down Wardour Street.

Smoking a cigarette and avoiding banging into a group of rowdy teenagers who were busy taking selfies, his mind flitted to Maureen, and he tried to recall exactly how long he'd known her. Twenty years? Twenty-five? It was certainly something close to that. It was crazy, he certainly never imagined he'd still be visiting her after all this time, but life seemed to have a strange way of turning out: the nun and the priest, or rather, the fallen nun and the fallen priest.

Not that priesthood had ever really been his calling. Not once had he thought about it – quite the opposite. The things he'd endured during his years at a Catholic boarding school as a kid back in Ireland had made him doubt there even was a God.

The priests had promised their pupils would benefit from retreat, pilgrimage, care, culture, but instead all they'd received was abuse. Physical, verbal, and for some – though he was one of the lucky ones – sexual, and there was certainly no God to call upon for help. They'd been at the mercy of those bastards . . . they'd been at the end of their beatings.

He breathed deeply at the thought of those dark days, taking the smoke right down into his lungs. That school at one time had been his whole life, having been placed there as a baby after his parents – no doubt young and unmarried – had put him in the care of the priests. And it was when he'd been sixteen, maybe seventeen, he'd met Maureen.

Mixed in with maths and English lessons, there had been lessons on humility, on service, on duty, all in the name of Christ. Every Friday, he and the other sixth formers from Our Virgin had been sent out into the community, each pupil being allocated the lonely, the needy, the wrongdoers of society. Their mission: to encourage them to relinquish their sins and rediscover God. And Maureen had certainly been a star sinner: a nun, a double killer. Jack had been given the task of visiting her in the prison just outside Waterford in the province of Munster, where she'd already served sixteen years of her life sentence.

On their first meeting, he'd sat opposite her with his Bible, ready to read a passage from the book of Isaiah: *let the wicked forsake his way, and the unrighteous man his thoughts*, but she'd leaned across the table and taken his hands in hers, and asked him to tell her about the outside world, about the smells and scents of summer, about the trains, about how a roast dinner tasted on a Sunday. It had thrown him. Not so much her questions but her warmth. Her tenderness. Not the behaviour he'd imagined for a double killer, though since then, life had certainly taught him that the devil came in many disguises.

And so, he'd never actually got to read that passage to her, they'd never actually got around to talking about God. Instead they'd laughed and talked football and life, and he'd visited her ever since. Even when his lifestyle had been something other than it was now, he'd made the trip to see her. She was as close to a family as he had.

Then when he'd moved across to London, Maureen had somehow been able to persuade the Church to put pressure on the prison system to help her transfer to Ashcroft prison – highly unusual, given that the Republic of Ireland and England were different authorities, but, he guessed, either the church had a long and powerful reach when they wanted to, or it was because one of her victims had been English, which had given good grounds for extradition. But however it had happened, Jack was certain the church was behind ensuring she ended up in Ashcroft. And now – after her friend, a nun who'd worked in the boarding school he'd been at as a kid, had died – he was her only visitor.

Sighing, Jack threw his cigarette down and continued to walk through the streets of Soho, passing Desires nightclub before turning right and heading towards Richmond Mews. It was strange to be back here. Everything looked the same: the deli on the corner, the Greek restaurant at the end of the street. The walk-ups. Even the graffiti on the side of the small wall leading to the garden of St Anne's church was still there. It felt like Soho had stopped in time. Why had he even come? He didn't know, not really. For so long he'd stayed away, though the pull had always been there. The smells and sounds of his old stomping ground calling to him.

Walking into the Mews, a girl he thought he recognized hurried past but she offered him no acknowledgement, so he continued to stroll along until at the end of the narrow street he came to a small set of stairs which led down to a basement.

Stopping in front of them, he stared down, thoughts and images rushing through his mind. Then, taking another long, deep breath, Jack headed down the stairs to the private member's bar. At the entrance he paused, ripping off his clerical collar, shoving it down into his pocket. Then he unbuttoned his top shirt button, put his hand on the large, black door and pushed it open . . .

The heat and the smell of sweat was overpowering. The music

was cranked up loud: old school R & B, Mary J. Blige. And he smiled to himself, memories of all the good times he'd had here, but it quickly faded away as recollections of the dark times hit him harder. Once again, he questioned why he'd come. What the hell was he looking for? This wasn't his haunt. His life. Not anymore, anyway. He was stupid to even think this was going to be anything but a bad idea.

He quickly turned to go.

'Hello, stranger.' The voice purred behind him.

He jolted, and for a moment, Jack didn't move. Then slowly, he turned with a smile – slightly forced – as he held the stare of a tall, olive-skinned woman dressed in a tight black skirt and gold top. Her green eyes shone with delight, enhanced, Jack suspected, by the effects of alcohol or being high. But perhaps that was him just being harsh.

'Hello, Rebel, how are you doing? It's good to see you.'

Rebel licked her lips. She looked stunned. 'Not as good as it is to see you, Jack. You're looking well, as handsome as ever . . . We weren't sure if we would ever see you again, not after you found your god.'

She laughed warmly but Jack detected a hint of bitterness. He could see her trembling slightly and he shrugged. 'Well, I couldn't stay away forever, could I?'

They fell silent and Jack felt the awkwardness clutching him. Eventually, Rebel stepped forward, wrapping her arms around him and Jack smelt her musky perfume, the one she always wore when she was working. For the punters.

'I missed you, Jack,' she whispered in his ear, but like he'd just had an electric shock, he drew quickly away from her, holding her at arm's length. A flash of hurt crossed her face.

'Do I offend you now, Jack? Ain't I pure enough for you?

Well sorry, darlin', my Virgin Mary badge disappeared a long time ago.'

He shook his head and both sadness and bemusement ran through his words. 'No, no, fucking hell, it's not that, it's . . .' He searched to find the words, 'I guess some things are best left in the past.'

They held each other's stare again and finally Jack said, 'Let me get you a drink, you can catch me up on all things Soho.' He took hold of her hand, his tall, strong figure standing head and shoulders above most of the crowd as he led her across to the bar.

Under the flashing coloured lights, he turned to her, raising his voice above the music. 'Are you still drinking the same poison?'

She nodded and immediately he waved to the barman, who sauntered across.

Not paying any real attention, Jack spoke as he looked in his jacket pocket for his wallet: 'A twin vodka with cranberry. Hold the ice. And I'll take a whisky. Make it neat.'

The barman nodded, but then he did a double take at the same time as Jack looked up. 'Jack? Oh my God, *Jack*!' His grin was wide. 'Rebel didn't tell us you were coming. How are you, mate? Fucking hell, it's good to see you.'

Recognition rushed through Jack. 'Hello Harry. Likewise.' The warmth exuded from him. 'Actually, Rebel didn't know – *I* didn't even know I was coming myself until I got here. Spur-of-the-moment shit.' He grinned, though he wasn't sure how long he'd be able to hold it. The truth was he felt lost. He didn't know where he belonged anymore. Who he was.

Drinks. Hello, can we have some drinks down here.

Pouring the shots then refusing to take Jack's money, Harry gestured to the group of men at the other end of the bar who were calling him. 'I'll be there in a second, mate.' He glanced at Jack again. 'Look, my shift doesn't finish till four a.m., but I hope you're going to hang around a bit – it'll be good to catch up. Nine years is a hell of a long time.'

Jack watched him go off to serve the other customers, then he turned his attention to Rebel. 'Wow, Harry hasn't aged one bit, has he?'

Before Rebel had time to answer, a tall well-built man grabbed her shoulder, spinning her round. 'Hello, Reb.'

'I'm not working.' It was a curt reply to an unasked question.

The man snorted in disgust, looking in disdain at her. 'Bitches like you are always working.'

Jack smiled slowly, then picked up the glass of whisky. He knocked it back, rolling the alcohol in his mouth before slamming the glass on the bar. He turned his head, glancing over his shoulder. 'She told you, she's not working.'

The man, swaying slightly, stared at Jack, stepping in closer. 'And who are you, her fucking keeper?'

'Something like that.' Jack cricked his neck, the old familiar feeling of adrenaline rushing around his body.

'Is that right?' Slurring, the man prodded Jack's chest.

Momentarily, Jack said nothing, then, stepping in front of Rebel, he smiled. 'A piece of advice, mate . . . Get out of here . . . *now*.' He clenched and unclenched his fists, adding, 'And whatever it is you're thinking of doing, make sure you really *want* to head down that road. Because if you know what's good for you, you'll turn around and walk out that door . . . Now, if you don't mind, I'm having a drink with the lady.' Jack winked at Rebel.

The man's face was rigid with anger as Jack turned his back on him.

'Who the fuck do you think you're talking to?' the man bellowed, incensed. The next instant, Jack heard the sound of smashing glass. He whipped around in time to see the man break his bottle of beer on the side of the bar, drink and glass spilling and shattering everywhere.

He lunged at Jack, slashing at him with the jagged bottle, which caught and nicked the corner of his mouth.

Spitting out blood and without hesitation, Jack snarled, charging, wrapping his arms around the waist of the man, sending them both sprawling backwards. They slammed down onto the floor.

'Jack! Jack! *Jack!*' Rebel yelled. The urgency in her voice rose above the music.

Quick to move, Jack sprang, twisting the broken bottle out of the man's hand, then he threw his full weight on top of him as they lay on the ground, their faces inches away from each other.

Jack pushed the jagged bottle against the man's neck, drawing a drop of blood. He spoke through gritted teeth. 'Tell me one good reason why I shouldn't kill you now?'

'Jack, baby, leave it. Leave it. He's not worth it.'

Ignoring Rebel, Jack continued to press the glass deeper into the man's neck, feeling him shaking underneath him. '*One reason.*'

'Jack, *please*, baby, just give me the bottle.' He felt Rebel crouch next to him and touch his hand.

'Look at me, baby. Jack, look at me.'

He lifted his head and stared at her, only slightly aware of the other people in the bar standing watching him.

'Jack, you've got to give it me.' She reached out and tried to unprise his fingers from around the bottle. 'That's it, that's it, baby. He ain't worth it.'

Jack blinked, looking around, a sudden blast of realization rushed through him. He let go, dropping the bottle into her hand as if it was a burning piece of coal. He scrambled up to his feet, quickly heading for the exit.

'Jack! Jack! Jack, wait!'

Hurrying outside, the cold air hit him. Fuck. Fuck. Fuck. He knew it was crazy to come back, but he'd thought he was ready. He really thought things would be different this time, but within minutes, he'd gone back to the person he'd been before, the person he'd been trying to escape from.

And they'd told him, hadn't they? They told him that would happen. They'd all said he wasn't ready to leave the priesthood. They'd looked at him with pity, telling him to take his time, not to rush into it, pray, take a sabbatical, which was exactly what he was doing right now.

He'd wanted to prove them wrong so badly, he'd wanted to prove that he was more than just a sinner, a troubled man who'd needed the crutch of a God he didn't even believe in. He was determined to show them he was his own man. Changed. Better. Stronger . . . Wiser. But they'd known he'd fail the first test he came upon, even if he hadn't known that himself. And maybe that's ultimately why he'd come here, to see if he still fitted in. Turning up like the prodigal son. To see if he felt more comfortable with sinners than with saints.

'*Jack!*' Rebel caught him up. 'Jack, listen . . . That wasn't your fault. You were looking out for me.'

'Yeah, but I never had to take it that far, did I? How long have I been back?' He looked at his watch. 'Less than an hour and I'm already playing the tough guy.'

She regarded him kindly. 'The guy was a wanker anyway, he deserved it.'

He shook his head, looking down at the ground as the rain began to fall. 'Maybe, but nothing's changed, has it? After nine long years, I'm still the same. And you know something, Reb, you know the worst thing about it, is that I enjoyed it. I enjoyed how it made me feel. I felt alive for the first time in a long time . . .

Fuck.' He headed for the stairs. He needed to get the hell out of the area. It was like a drug.

'Jack, wait, don't go. *Please* don't just walk away from me again.' She moved up towards him, glints of tears in her eyes. 'Not yet, Jack. You can at least give me that after all this time.'

He looked at her, holding her gaze. Then she carefully dabbed his bleeding lip with her fingers, before leaning in and kissing him. A beat. Then he kissed her back and she slid her hand down his chest, slowly, to the buckle of his trousers, pushing herself close, closer to his body, as he felt every inch of her against him. He pulled away. 'Rebel, I can't, I can't give you what you want.'

'I'm not asking you to, I'm just asking you for one night, for old times' sake . . . I missed you, Jack.'

'I don't know, it . . . it . . .' He trailed off before adding, 'and what happens tomorrow? What then? How will you feel when I get up and go? I don't want to hurt you.'

'You mean *again*? You don't want to hurt me *again*?'

He shook his head. 'Let's not go there, Reb.' He started to head up the stairs, but she pulled him back.

'Jack, I'm a big girl, I can look after my own heart, you don't need to look out for it, not anymore.' Stroking his face, her eyes locked into his. 'Don't you want to spend the night with me . . . or aren't you allowed now?'

He gave her a wry smile, feeling the sting of his mouth. Everything told him to turn and walk away and just keep on walking, but the thought of her warm body next to his, the idea of waking up to something other than a cold room and an empty bed, was seductive. He tilted his head and smiled. 'I'm a priest, not an angel.' He wanted to be with someone tonight. He needed that. Pushing away the thought he was using Rebel, and holding back the feeling he was taking advantage of how he knew she felt about him, Jack let her lead him to the flat above the club.

11

MINA

It was getting late, and Mina hurried along Greek Street. She didn't like to leave her little sister alone in the bedsit, but what other choice did she have? She was desperate. She'd told her mum that she'd got a bit of money left. The truth was, she was down to her last twenty pounds. And now, if either of them was going to eat this week, she needed to find Doreen, who owed her a hundred quid. She'd lent it to her and now trying to get it back was proving to be much more of a problem than she first thought it'd be. Knowing Doreen, she was either with a punter or getting high somewhere. But she guessed it was her own fault. Even though she liked Doreen, who often worked the street with her mum, she should've known not to lend it to her. Doreen had a worse drug habit than her mum used to, and that was saying something. When she'd come knocking, needing some money, she'd felt sorry for her. But now she and Flo were out of pocket.

She sighed, shivering as she tried to hold back the tears. Then for some reason, Iris suddenly came into her mind. God, how she'd love to leave everything behind. Just go, not look back. Start a life somewhere else . . . Anywhere else.

She was only seventeen, but she constantly felt tired. She couldn't remember a time when she hadn't. And she couldn't remember a time when she hadn't woken up with anxiety in her stomach. Even when she was growing up, she'd had the same feeling of worry. When she'd been in foster care or at home, it was always the same. But now her mum was banged up, it'd got worse. Most mornings it got so bad, she'd throw up. So, the idea of getting away from her life was something that certainly appealed to her.

But could she do that to her mum? She wasn't sure. Because as much as she was a pain, always putting pressure on her to be the sensible one, the grown-up one, Mina loved her so much. And then there was Flo. What would she do with her little sister? Maybe she could take her? Her, Iris and Flo could leave Soho behind. Though as soon as Mina had that thought, she shut it down. She was being stupid. It was like when she was a kid and she used to wish upon a star that her mum would stop messing with the gear. And that never came true. She'd learned a long while ago that there was no point in wishing, no point in day-dreaming. She just had to get used to it because, whether she liked it or not, this was her reality: running around Soho in the middle of the night looking for cash.

Stepping over a homeless man who was asleep and sprawled across the corner of Bateman Street in his own vomit, Mina shut down all thoughts and shivered again as it began to rain harder. Annoyed with herself that she hadn't put on her thicker jacket, she quickly looked behind her, not wanting anyone to see her out at this time of night.

She'd spotted the priest who visited Maureen over in Rich-mond Mews. She actually hadn't realized he hung around Soho, but then, why would she? She only hoped he hadn't recognized her. Because if he told Maureen that he'd seen her, there was a high possibility she'd tell her mum. Then Mina would be in *big* trouble.

Her mum would ask a thousand questions: where was Flo, why was she out, were there boys involved, were there drugs involved? And no matter what she said, she knew her mum would see right through her stories; she always seemed to know when she was lying.

Yawning, Mina decided to try one of the walk-ups Doreen sometimes sold sex out of and she headed towards Dean Street, but turning into it by the Red Lion pub, she jumped and let out a tiny squeal.

'Hello darlin', what are you doing around these parts?'

She immediately recognized the voice. The laughter loud and familiar.

'Not touting for business, are you?'

Ollie Jones stepped out of the shadows, a large grin on his face. Handsome as always.

Mina blushed for several reasons, though her first thought was that she looked a mess. She quickly pushed her hair behind her ears, hoping that she didn't embarrass herself. *Hoping* that she didn't look self-conscious. 'No, no, no, it's nothing like that. I . . . I live here, well not here, but over in Berwick Street, above the Indian takeaway. I'm . . . I'm . . .'

Ollie laughed harder. '. . . Calm down, darlin'. I'm only winding you up, girl.'

She suddenly felt stupid.

He drew on his cigarette and stared intently at her, the smoke making him squint. 'So, what are you doing here – sneaking out to see your boyfriend?' He winked, causing her to blush even more, she could feel her cheeks burning.

She spoke quickly: 'God no, I haven't got one . . . I mean, not that I want one, no, I mean I do want one, not that I'm looking, I . . .' Then she trailed off her rambling, wishing the ground would just open up and swallow her.

Ollie's handsome face lit up. 'It's OK, sweetheart, there's no judgement here. And don't worry, I ain't a grass, I won't be telling your mum, your secret's safe with me. I was young once.'

Mina bristled at his words, hoping that he didn't think of her as a silly kid. She tried to sound older. 'Like I say, it ain't nothing like that, I was just looking for a taxi, but I forgot my purse at my mate's house, and I needed to get home.'

'I thought you said you lived here.'

'I do, it's just that . . .' She was hopeless at lying and she quickly looked at the ground, feeling even more self-conscious than ever before.

She felt his hand underneath her chin as Ollie gently lifted her head up and inexplicably, tears welled in her eyes.

'It's Mina, ain't it?'

She was both surprised and pleased that he knew her name. 'Yeah, yeah it is.'

'Well, Mina, I don't know what's going on, babe, and I'm not prying, but I just want to make sure you're OK. Are you in any kind of trouble? Is there anything I can do, mate?'

She stared into his hazel eyes. 'No, I'm OK, I swear down. I just forgot my purse and it's a right pain cos I've got college tomorrow.' God, why did she have to say that? She could kick herself; he'd know how old she was now.

Dropping his hand away from her chin, he nodded, then went into his pocket. 'That won't do, will it? I tell you what . . .' He pulled out his wallet, flipped it open, taking two fifty-pound notes out. 'Take this, doll.'

Mina shook her head. 'No . . . no, it's fine. I can't, and I wasn't saying about my purse so you'd give me some money.'

Ollie grinned again, making Mina's stomach flutter.

'I know you weren't, darlin'. I'm just trying to help you out, that's all. Ain't that what neighbours do, help each other out? Go on, take it.'

She shook her head again. 'It's really kind of you, but I wouldn't be able to pay you back.'

He pulled her into him slightly and slid the fifty-pound notes into the back pockets of her jeans. She caught her breath.

'I'm not asking for it back, Mina. Call it a present.'

He stepped away and winked. 'I can afford it.' Though it didn't sound arrogant.

For a second, Mina contemplated not taking it, but then Flo came into her mind. She could buy some food for the week. Treat her to the strawberry yogurts she liked, and maybe she could even buy the textbook she needed for college.

She looked at him and smiled, her mind racing over the fact that he'd stood so close to her. If she didn't die of embarrassment, the first thing she was going to do when she got home was call Iris and tell her. 'Thank you. Thank you, Ollie . . . I really appreciate it.'

'Anytime, sweetheart.' He leaned in towards her ear, whispering, 'And don't worry, it can be our little secret.'

12

OLLIE

Walking into his townhouse in Dean Street, Ollie yawned. He threw his car keys down on the green leather couch in the hallway as well as his jacket, and he thought about Mina. The way she was dressed and the way she'd done her make-up, she could've easily been mistaken for a cheap little tart. But then, he guessed the apple didn't fall far from the tree: brass for a mother, whore for a daughter.

He chuckled to himself, but as he'd thought many times before, if circumstances were different, he would've cracked on with her. But the problem always came down to one fact: he wouldn't mind his dick in her mouth, but he certainly wouldn't want his name there. Girls like that liked to talk – he'd certainly learned the hard way – which always caused agg. Ultimately it was a shame though, because the way Mina had been looking at him just now when he'd handed her the money, he would've bet his life that he only needed to give her the nod and she would've been whipping her knickers off like she was Harry Houdini.

He laughed again at the thought and yawned.

'Where the frig have you been, Ollie? I've been standing around like a cunt waiting for you.'

Ollie jumped, rubbing his chest.

'Fucking hell, do you want to give me a heart attack?' He glared at his ex-wife, who was standing stony-faced in the hall-way. A dark anger washed over him. 'Do you get off on sneaking around like that?'

'Oh, grow up, Ol. I didn't have you down as a pussy.'

'No, but I've certainly got you down as something. Oh, and may I remind you, *yet again*, Martha, as I always seem to say to you these days, you ain't my wife anymore.'

'And as I've said before, *thank fuck for that*.'

He clicked his fingers, pointing at her. 'Feeling's mutual . . . Which means, your days of coming and going like it's frigging Paddington station are long gone. Well and truly over.'

Martha Jones glared back just as hard. 'Like I say, grow up, or do we have to go through the same thing as we go through each time: you complaining and boring me into a fucking stupor.' Humming, she walked through to the newly decorated white kitchen and threw her brown leather Valentino satchel down on the table. 'Where've you been anyway?'

Having to bite on his lip, Ollie followed her, going over to the fridge to grab a cold beer. He broke it open, the froth dribbling down the side of it. 'That's another thing I don't have to do any more: answer to you.' Angrily, he slurped the beer. Martha had always had a way of getting under his skin. They'd been divorced for over ten years, but the way she spoke to him and the way she grated on his nerves made it feel like only yesterday they were hitched.

She probably knew him better than anyone else, which he suspected was the cause of his constant irritation when it came to her. He couldn't get away with bullshitting; she could see right through his gab, and unlike so many women, including Amy, he'd never been able to put Martha in her place. She'd always given as good as she got.

Taking another swig of beer, he glared at her. Martha was the opposite of anything he'd ever found attractive. She walked like she'd just got out of the army, like she'd got something stuck up her arse. A straight up and down figure, short, cropped pixie hair, no tits to speak of, no hips, no curves. And fucking her had been like fucking a piece of cardboard.

The only reason he'd married her in the first place was because of his dear departed ma. She'd thought Martha, whose mother had been a family friend, was the perfect match for him. And never wanting to disappoint his ma – especially by that time, when the cancer had spread throughout her frail body – he'd walked down the aisle with Martha, ten minutes after shagging her bridesmaid, with his ma sitting with an oxygen tank and looking on proudly from the front row of the aisle.

Ollie sighed, watching Martha as she opened one of the cupboards to take out a packet of crisps. She tore the bag open, shoving a handful into her mouth, her shrew-like features hard and angular. 'Let's get one thing straight, Ollie.' She spat out crumbs as she spoke. 'I ain't interested in who you've been boning, all I care about is that you were supposed to meet me here at ten, and now it's gone midnight. I don't appreciate having to wait around.'

Throwing the beer can in the black marble sink, Ollie shook his head. 'You know full well I had business to attend to, it just took longer than I thought it would.'

Martha didn't bother answering, instead she unzipped the satchel and emptied two half kilogram packets on the table. 'According to Sammy, it's perfect. Not like the shit you got a couple of months ago.'

Lighting another cigarette, Ollie sneered. 'Fuck me, Marth, you can't resist a dig, can you? Any opportunity and you're on it like a ferret.'

'I ain't wrong though, am I? The cack you got, not even a fucking caterpillar could've got high on. But this stuff is supposed to be the dog's bollocks. And there's plenty more where this came from. He's just taken delivery of another shipment. What makes it sweeter is we've got this lot at cost. He owed me and he knows only too well not to fuck me about.'

Ollie couldn't help but laugh. Martha might be many things but, when it came to business, she knew her shit. They'd been in business together since they'd been married, and although he couldn't wait to sever their marital ties, it had never once crossed his mind, or hers, to sever their business connections.

The roof he had over his head, the money he had in the bank, his lifestyle, was all predominantly down to her. She was the brains – sometimes even the brawn – behind every penny he'd earned. Ruthless and cruel were certainly two of Martha Jones's top traits.

'I have to hand it to you, darlin', you're one dark bitch.'

She smiled, looking genuinely delighted at his words. 'That's the nicest thing you've said to me in a while.'

They both roared, but a loud knock on the door interrupted them. Immediately, Martha glanced down at her watch. 'At least someone's on time.'

Before Ollie had a chance to reply, Martha walked out of the kitchen.

A moment later she came back in, followed by Deputy Tony Earle.

'All right, Tone. How's tricks? And how's my gorgeous missus? Is she all right? Behaving herself, I hope?' Ollie gave Tony a nasty smile. He'd always thought the guy was a greedy sleazeball, and he couldn't stand the bugger. To him, a screw would always be a screw. But then, liking someone wasn't the point. It never had been. Martha being a good example. The only thing that mattered was how useful a person was to him.

Looking uncomfortable, and not holding Ollie's stare, Tony nodded. He shuffled on the spot, looking down at his tan lace-up shoes. 'Yes, Amy's good. I'm sure she's keen to get home as soon as she can. Not long now.' He glanced up and smiled cloyingly.

Not replying, Ollie sauntered over to the drawer and pulled out a large envelope. He threw it across to Tony, who fumbled the catch.

'Same rates, it's all there,' Ollie said. 'You don't need to count it, unless of course you don't trust us.'

Tony hurriedly slipped the stuffed envelope into the pocket of his blue anorak. 'I trust you. Both of you. I don't think it's in either of our interests to turn the other one over, do you?'

Not bothering to answer the question directly, Ollie instead asked, 'When are you thinking of taking it in?'

'The day after tomorrow. Walters should be on the gate with her girlfriend, so it won't be any problem. As long as I carry on bunging her a couple of hundred quid here and there, she's happy.'

Martha stood leaning against the kitchen cabinets, peeling an apple. She nodded. 'Make sure she stays sweet, any fuck-ups and it's on your head.'

Seemingly irritated, Tony snapped, though he held his syrupy smile: 'I've been doing this for long enough, Martha, and so far there haven't been any problems. I've never given you any reason to worry, have I?'

Martha stared at him, her small brown eyes cold. 'Wind your neck in, Tone. I don't like your attitude. No one likes a cocky cunt, least of all me.'

Tony flushed scarlet.

'I just hope that you ain't getting complacent. You know what they say: pride comes before a fall. And if you fall, we'll be there waiting – and believe me, we won't be picking you up. You understand me?'

The threat hung in the air as Tony strapped the bags of heroin under his shirt in the home-made body belt he'd made, exposing his large hairy belly which hung over his trouser belt. 'I understand loud and clear.'

Martha's face darkened and she sauntered up to him, patting Tony on his stomach and placing the point of the sharp apple knife she had in her hand against his skin. She pushed it slightly, drawing a nick of blood. 'I'm glad we've got that sorted, *Tone*. You really wouldn't want to get on the wrong side of me. And don't think for one moment that because I'm a woman, I won't come after you. Believe me, darlin', I can slice your neck open and put you in the ground as good as any man.'

13

THE GOVERNOR

The clock changed to midnight as Governor Reed undressed in the darkness, the outside streetlights of the small close in Hounslow he lived on outlining his slim, toned naked body: impressive for a man his age who didn't bother going to the gym, even if he thought it himself. Being a lardy arse like Tony Earle wasn't and would never be on his agenda. The man was a dead weight, both literally and metaphorically. He didn't know one person in the prison who had respect for him, not the staff or the inmates. They all saw him for what he was.

Not wanting to think about Tony or about work too long, Reed shut down the thought. It had been a long day and he was tired; he hadn't been able to sleep from the coke he'd taken earlier and instead he'd sat aimlessly staring at the television as he'd flicked from channel to channel. He'd contemplated watching a bit of porn, but by the time he'd found his laptop – moved by the cleaner to the top shelf of his bookcase instead of it being where it was supposed to be – he'd lost interest in the idea.

Yawning, and light-headed from the whisky he'd drunk, Reed got into bed next to his wife. He could tell she was awake, just pretending not to be, and he shivered, feeling the coldness exuding from her. She was a frigid bitch. He couldn't remember the last time they'd had sex. Not that he'd wish that on his worst enemy.

His wife, Shirley, was hardly what anyone would call desirable. She couldn't be further from that description if she tried. God knows, he couldn't imagine any man lusting over her, though right now, that was beside the point.

Moving closer to her, Reed pulled on her shoulder. 'Shirley, Shirley, are you awake?'

There was silence, but he could feel her stiffen up as he pushed his erection into her back. There'd always been an iciness to her when it came to sex. Even on their wedding day she'd made him come to bed in his pyjamas, preferring a quick fumble in the dark, a roll-on, roll-off job. Afterwards, she'd always get in the shower and scrub herself as if he'd given her scabies. To his wife, sex was dirty, and she'd openly welcomed, almost encouraged his regular visits to hookers. In her words, it gave her *a bit of peace*.

'Not now, Philip, I'm tired.'

Angrily, he hissed through his teeth, pushing himself up on his elbow. 'You're always tired. It's hardly much to ask, is it. A man has needs.'

She tutted loudly. 'Yes, and you should've left them at the door. I'm not one of your whores.'

He pulled her round to face him. Her hair, as usual, was done up in large sponge rollers, sitting under a night net. 'And more's the pity, Shirley.'

As the streetlight shone into the bedroom, he could see her expression: a scrunched-up look of disapproval.

'Can't you just go to the bathroom, Philip, and do what you have to do? But don't get it on the towels.'

The disgust in her voice made him laugh, loud and bitterly.

Grabbing her violently, he slapped her hard across her face, watching the inevitable tears come as she squealed in pain. The noise was high-pitched and aggravated him, and without thinking, he found himself slapping her harder, over and over again.

She tried to push him off, but she was no match for him.

'Philip! Philip! *Stop!*'

His anger continued to rush through his body, the way she was acting was like he was a stranger attacking her.

'Just shut up! For God's sake, Shirley, shut the fuck up.' He grabbed at her nylon nightie, the static electricity from the material causing sparks in the darkness, like fireflies. He pulled her close to him. He was sick of her saying no. After all, she was his wife and he had his needs . . .

14
IRIS

On the other side of London, Iris listened to the home phone ringing as she sat on her king-size bed in the large, plush house in Mill Hill. Everything around her was expensive and pristine. Even now, her mother arranged for the place to be cleaned, making sure it was always showhouse ready. Everything was about the front with her mum, how it looked from the outside, even if the inside was vacant and rotting.

She'd never been entirely sure how her mother had earned *all* her money; she'd had various businesses over the years that were no doubt a smokescreen for all the criminal activity that went on. Her grandad had left her mum a portfolio of properties as well as a huge scrapyard in his will. On the day of his funeral, the police had raided the yard, found six sawn-off shotguns as well as hundreds of thousands of pounds' worth of stolen jewellery.

Rubbing her head, Iris continued to let the phone ring. She felt groggy from the half a bottle of vodka she'd drunk. It was her way of managing life and it made her feel better, warm, and sleepy.

At first when she'd started to drink alone, it had been just a small measure, the odd alcopop here and there to help her sleep, but when that had stopped working, she'd tried the harder stuff. A vodka, a gin, a whisky, it didn't matter, although she hated the taste of most of the drinks, but rather than giving it up, she'd stuck to vodka, which was easier to stomach. And now, if she needed the odd drink during the day, which she found she did more and more, at least with vodka, she knew no one could smell it. The last thing she wanted was her mum finding out; she'd only give her more grief than she already did.

Hearing the phone stop, Iris sighed with relief, but it was short-lived as, almost immediately, it started up again. She knew exactly who it was: her mother. She also knew eventually she'd have to speak to her, otherwise she'd send round one of the men, her paid knuckleheads – who kept her mum's business ticking over and were still on the payroll.

She shivered at the thought. They were creeps, and since her stepdad had thankfully taken himself off to Marbella, being around them was even worse than before. Taking a deep breath, she swiped up the phone from her grey bedside cabinet.

'Yes,' she growled.

'Is that any way to talk to me? A "hello" would be nice. I've been trying to get through to you for ages,' her mum whispered.

'So.'

There was a long pause followed by a sigh.

'You know, I'd watch your attitude if I were you, madam. Has it ever occurred to you that I might want to talk to my daughter? That I miss you?'

Even though her mum was whispering, her voice was still hard and shrill, and Iris sighed loud enough to make sure her mum heard. 'Look, it's late, what do you want, Mum?' She threw herself back on the bed, hoping she didn't sound too slurred.

'In case you've forgotten, I'm your mother. Most daughters would be pleased to get a call from their mum.'

'It depends on who their mum is, don't it?'

'Why are you being like this? I'm here, stuck down in solitary, and if I get caught using this phone, I'll be stuck down longer than just a couple of nights.'

Iris stared up at the bespoke chandelier above her bed,

watching the crystals glittering as they caught in the light of her bedside lamp. 'I didn't ask you to call, did I?'

'No, you didn't, but here I am making an effort, more than you ever do. Even when you come and see me, you've got a face like a wet weekend. How do you think that makes me feel, when I look forward to seeing you all week, and rather than a bleedin' ray of sunshine walking into the visiting room, I get a fucking storm cloud? Iris, what is going on? Look, I don't know how many times I've told you, but I'm sorry that it's like this. I know it ain't ideal.'

Iris laughed bitterly. 'That must be the understatement of the century, Mum. Has it ever crossed your mind that I might not want to get up every Saturday morning and travel twenty miles to see you.'

'Do you know how hurtful that is to hear?'

Tears rolled down the sides of Iris's cheeks. 'It's always about you, Mum. It always has been, ever since I can remember. You've never asked me how I feel, or what I want. And you know, I ain't a kid anymore.'

'Then try not acting like one.' Her mum raised her voice and Iris hoped that one of the screws would hear her; at least then they'd confiscate her phone, and her mum would struggle to call her for the next few days until she managed to get a replacement burner. 'I mean, let's have it right, Iris: you've got everything, you've got it all. I try to get you everything I can. It's not like you have to bus it on a Saturday, like that poor cow Mina. Count yourself lucky you ain't in her boat.'

'Is that what you really think, Mum? You think I've got it all?'

'Yeah, I do. How many eighteen-year-olds get a pukka Range Rover for their birthday? Or a tasty Rolex in their Christmas box? You're one lucky girl, Iris, you need to see that.'

There was so much Iris wanted to say. She wanted her mum

to see that not everything could be bought. The most important thing. The thing that had always been missing in her life was free . . . Love was free.

'I haven't got you, Mum.'

'Yeah, but there's not a lot we can do about that, is there . . . And . . . and anyway,' her mum continued, changing the subject as she always did when the conversation got difficult. 'You weren't where you were supposed to be earlier. I called the house and you never answered. I told you to go straight home after the visit. Where the hell were you?'

Iris closed her eyes. The truth wasn't very exciting: after she'd dropped off Mina, she'd decided to get herself a manicure, then she'd pottered around the shops until they'd closed, and after, well she'd sat in her car having a drink feeling miserable, lonely, listening to music, and wishing she had a different life.

She'd lost touch with all her friends; they'd been bitches anyway, so there were no tears shed, because when they'd found out her mum was inside, most of her friends from the private school she'd attended had backed right off. Though as much as they'd been cows, it didn't stop her being lonely.

The only real friends she had now were Roz, who her mum hated, and Mina. She'd surprised herself how much she liked her, especially as Mina wasn't exactly what she'd look for in a friend. The girl had no style, no designer gear, she'd never been on a holiday, and she wasn't into partying either. In fact, even though Mina's mum was banged up, Mina was actually a total goody two shoes.

But despite all those things, Mina was kind, she was funny, she listened when nobody else did, and although she didn't know it, Mina was probably one of the most beautiful girls she'd ever seen . . . both on the outside but especially on the inside.

'I'm waiting. I've just asked you a question, lady. Where were you?'

Her mum's voice jolted Iris out of her thoughts. She chewed on her lip. She'd known she was supposed to be back at the house. Her mum always called the home phone to check she was really there. But she was sick of it. 'I was just out, OK?' she snapped.

'No, it's not OK, Iris. Don't you get it, I'm trying to keep you safe . . . You know the rules.'

'And they're fucking shit,' Iris shouted down the phone, surprising even herself.

'Who the hell are you speaking to like that?'

The tears continued to run down the sides of her face as she screamed in hurt and anger. 'You, Mum, you! You can't be inside; you can't be absent and still expect to tell me what to do. You stopped being my mum a long time ago.'

'No, that ain't true. I may be inside but I still love you, and I'm still your mother.'

'Yeah, and a fucking shit one too.'

Her mum hissed down the phone, the anger swirling in her words: 'You're lucky I ain't there, otherwise you'd see the hard edge of my hand. So, here's what's going to happen: tomorrow, I'll be sending one of the men around to sort you out, to have a little word in your ear.'

'A little word, Mum, or a fuck?'

The call fell silent but not before Iris heard her mum gasp. She was too upset and too unhappy to care. She hadn't wanted to tell her mum like this, and in truth, she probably would've never told her mum at all, she hadn't seen the point. What could she do from inside?

'What did you say?'

Iris sat up. And it felt like something inside of her had snapped.

This time there was no backing down. 'I said, are they coming around to fuck me? Yeah, that's right, Mum, they always come around now you're not here, you know, to tend to me. Give me a good seeing to. But hey, I should be used to it by now. After all, they ain't doing anything different to what my stepdad did.'

And with that, Iris, crying hysterically, put the phone down on her mum. She reached for the bottle of vodka by the side of her bed, gulping it down and more determined than ever to leave her life behind sooner rather than later. And now she knew exactly how she was going to do it.

15

Through the keyhole she watched him kneel next to the naked woman. She had to keep quiet, otherwise they'd tie her up again, and gag her. And she hated that, so as silently as she could she stared at the other man who was there, the one with the blood on his hands. He stood shaking. 'She just passed out.'

'She didn't just pass out, you fucking strangled her.' He glimpsed at the filming equipment and flicked off the camera: the red light immediately stopped flashing. Then she watched some more as he roughly picked the woman up off the floor by her shoulders, shaking her roughly while her head lolled back and forth.

Trying to steady her breathing, she saw the man with the bloodied hands, his voice on the verge of hysteria, turn pale.

'No one can find out, my wife can't find out . . . Oh my God, what are we going to do?'

He looked at the other man, his eyes cold, his voice steady. 'We're going to calm the fuck down.'

'But I swear I thought she'd be fine, I was just having fun, I thought she—'

'. . . Shut the fuck up and let me think . . . Fucking hell, this is a mess.' She watched his eyes travel along the woman lying lifeless on the floor. Her stare did the same: the cuts, the bruises, the lacerations. 'What is wrong with you? This is not what I wanted to get out of bed for and come and see at 4 a.m. in the morning. When my guy called me, I couldn't believe what I was hearing. I didn't think anyone could

be so fucking stupid, cos doing what you like, does not mean frigging killing her.'

'But I—'

'I said keep fucking quiet.'

And she saw him raise his hand and strike the man, sending him reeling across the room.

'Now help me get her up.'

With his right eye swelling, the man hesitated, but then he staggered to his feet, and she noticed the blood wasn't just on his hands, it was over his naked body.

Trembling, she moved away from the keyhole. She shivered. And she felt cold, so cold, even though the night air was warm. And she felt sick and wondered, not for the first time, whether she'd be the next.

16

D WING

'All right, ladies. Party's *here!*' It was Tuesday morning and Ness walked with her hands in the air, a large grin on her face as she strolled up from solitary to a loud cry of cheers from the other women on the wing who were waiting for breakfast.

'Hey, how was it? You look like shit.' Amy Jones grinned as she sauntered up to Ness, who was still dressed in the same grey tracksuit she'd been wearing when she'd been taken down. 'Lynette told me what happened.' Amy looked over Ness's shoulder at Steph. 'Hey, you all right?'

Steph, who'd arrived back from solitary a moment after Ness, shrugged. She stared vacantly, her eyes red and puffy. 'What's it to you?' Then she turned away, walking along the landing to her cell, closing the door behind her.

'She still hates me, doesn't she?' Amy asked Ness with a frown.

Ness – who was still suffering from pregnancy sickness and at this point trying not to vomit from the smell coming from the kitchens – shrugged. 'I dunno if it's you this time. She ain't said anything much to me either. I tried to talk to her on the way up, but she as good as ignored me . . . Hey, Maureen! *Reenie!*' Delighted, Ness called over to Maureen, who ambled slowly into the wing. 'You all right, darlin'? How was it? I was worried about you.'

'Ach, what's a couple of nights down there?' Her Irish accent was stronger when she was tired. 'If Christ himself could do forty days and forty nights in the wilderness, what's two frigging nights down in Ashcroft's shithole?'

Ness roared, shouting cheerfully as she looked around the wing. 'So, it's official then, ladies, solitary *is* a piece of piss!'

The other women laughed along as Ness winked at one of the screws, who glowered, causing her to laugh even harder.

'Keep it down, otherwise I'll be taking you back, and you'll be spending the rest of the week there, Vanessa.'

'*Fuck off,*' Ness mumbled under her breath at the screw, who wandered off to break up an argument further down the wing.

She felt tired from lack of sleep, and in fact, solitary hadn't been a piece of piss at all, it'd been hard. Really hard. It had messed with her head. Every minute seemed like an hour down there, and there was too much time to think: about the baby, about Mina, about the fact she had another nine years plus of her stretch to go. Solitary had a way of dissolving the survival walls she'd had to build up to cope with life on the inside, and now, not that she'd admit it to any of the other women, she felt scared: she didn't know how she'd get through such a long road ahead.

Putting on a fake smile, she looked around to see if Lynette was about, then she leaned against the wall, feeling the kick of her baby. 'Hey, Reenie, come and feel this. He's kicking proper hard.'

'He's probably got a whiff of the breakfast and he's like the rest of us: he can't face any more of their fucking crap food,' Amy said loudly.

'Just think, you'll be able to eat proper food in a couple of weeks. What are you going to munch on for your first meal as a free woman? What about the Ivy? Get Ollie to take you, make him spend some of his dough.'

Amy gave a tight smile but said, 'Nah, you know me, I'm fur coat and no knickers, darlin', not one for that fancy grub. I'll be heading for the kebab shop in Camden High Street . . . I can taste it now.'

Ness grinned and opened her mouth to say something, but she was distracted by Maureen trudging up towards her. 'I think you should have a lie-down, Reenie.'

'Oh, don't mind me, nothing that another night in Ashcroft won't fix.' Maureen placed her hand gently on Ness's stomach as she spoke.

Ness grinned at her, noticing how tired she looked, but then, the hole always had a way of making everyone feel tired. The mattresses were harder than the ones in the cells, which said a lot, and the noise from the boiler room kept everyone who went down there awake. 'Oh shit, he's proper kicking now. Can you feel it?'

'Yes, it's beautiful.' Maureen's face lit up, but within moments it clouded, and Ness noticed tears well up in her eyes.

'Reenie, are you all right?'

Before Maureen had a chance to answer, Tess strolled up to them, barging past Amy and Maureen. She pushed Ness hard in the chest. 'You owe me. Two nights down in those fucking cells.'

'What's that got to do with me?' Ness stood defiantly. 'If I remember rightly, sweetheart, it was you who thought it was OK to come into Lynette's cell and give it the big I am.'

Tess leaned into her, her bulky frame towering over her. 'I'm not talking about that. I'm talking about the fact that I lost business, time down in the hole was money lost, and secondly' – Tess looked at both Ness and Maureen accusingly – 'I couldn't sleep because of your mate.'

'What are you rabbiting about? You love to chat shit.'

Tess glanced around, seemingly making sure none of the screws were watching, then grabbed hold of Ness's neck. 'Remember who you're speaking to.'

Knocking her hand away, Ness glared. 'Oh, I remember all right. But the thing is, I don't know what the fuck you're on about. Who kept you awake?'

'Your mate, Stephanie, hollering like a fucking lunatic. Didn't you hear her crying last night?'

'I was dead to the world,' Ness said, watching as Steph came out of her cell, moving towards the breakfast line. She didn't look herself and, as much as Steph could be a hard bitch, a hard mother, underneath she was both a caring friend and a loving mum, and Ness had a lot of time for her. They had a lot in common, and it also helped that Mina and Iris were friends.

Noticing Steph, Tess yelled across to her angrily. 'Do you get off on keeping people awake? Two fucking nights solid, man. It was like I was celled up next to a frigging hyena, all the fucking wailing you did. Next time, save all that crying crap for the muppet ward.'

Steph flushed and for a moment she looked taken aback, but she soon composed herself with a snarl. 'Oh, do me a favour, Tess, and fuck right off. Of course it wasn't me, it was probably your fat fucking stomach rumbling.'

Tess pointed at Steph. 'I warned you before that you were a dead bitch! I'm coming for you.'

'No one's coming for anyone!' From over by the server, Tony Earle hollered to Tess. 'Just calm down, if there's any more fighting on the wing, you'll have the governor coming down – and you wouldn't want that, would you?' He gave Tess a strange look which didn't go unnoticed by Ness, though before she could think any more about it, a woman she'd seen a few times on the wing but didn't know the name of scuttled up to Tess, carrying a tray of underdone scrambled eggs.

'You got anything, mate?'

The urgency in the woman's voice was profound and, looking

agitated, she moved on the spot from one foot to another. Even from where Ness was standing, she could smell the woman's rancid breath, she also saw the large gap where her front teeth were missing. The other thing Ness noticed was her stomach: she was clearly further on than her own pregnancy, looking like she could pop at any time.

'What are you after?' Tess sniffed, wiping her nose on the back of her hand.

'Spice, brown. Anything.' The woman, who was trembling slightly, shrugged.

Over the din of the chatter on the wing and the sound of cutlery scraping and clattering, Tess glanced around again then gave a small nod. 'Come to my cell in ten.'

'For God's sake, Tess, she's pregnant!' Maureen admonished her. 'Stop flooding the wing with that rubbish. We don't need drugs in here. You're hurting the women. Have you got no shame?'

'Shame?' Tess laughed nastily. 'Howay, man, piss off from me, you're a joke. Aren't you the same nun who murdered two men then lobbed them under the floorboards? I reckon they'll be getting a restraining order for you if you try to walk through them Pearly Gates. So don't talk to us about shame, love.'

Maureen turned red, she stepped back and supported herself on Ness's arm, looking like she'd been slapped.

'You stupid cow, just take your shit and go.' Ness drew her attention away from Maureen and, clearly enraged, she turned to the woman: 'You've got a kid inside you; doesn't that mean anything to you?'

'It's none of your fucking business. I ain't keeping the kid, so what difference does it make? It's my body, I can put whatever I want in it. It's a free fucking world, you know.'

Ness shook her head in disgust. 'You best find someone else, cos she ain't going to give you any . . .'

'There is no one else, otherwise I wouldn't have had to wait two fucking days while she's in the hole, would I?'

'Do I look like I care? *No* . . . Now go on, go. You heard me.' Ness gestured with her head to leave. 'Go and find your gear elsewhere.'

The woman didn't move.

With a smirk on her face, Tess cracked her tattooed knuckles and spoke directly to the woman, who was now visibly shaking, a thin layer of sweat on her face. 'Like I say, love, my cell, ten minutes.'

The woman nodded and shuffled off, leaving Ness, Amy and Maureen facing Tess, who absent-mindedly picked at one of the large acne scars on her face. She yawned widely and grinned again at Maureen. 'Anyway, I'm only the monkey, you need to speak to the organ grinder. The mastermind of the operation.' She pointed at Amy. 'If you want all the drugs in here to stop, ask her.'

Amy stared at Tess as the other women stared at her. 'What crap are you talking now? What have I got to do with it?'

'Oh, come on, Amy, don't pretend, you're not fooling anyone.'

'Piss off, Tess, you're off your head if you think I've got *anything* to do with bringing gear in here. The only woman who does that is you. Everyone knows – not only are you the scum of the earth for supplying in here, but you've made it known that anyone else selling on the wing will have you and your frigging yes-girls to answer to.'

Laughing, Tess flashed a smile at Amy as various other women came to join the group, listening with interest to the conversation. 'Come on, love, don't try to turn it on me. Every woman here knows you've been fucking up your chances of getting out each time your parole comes around.' Animated, Tess turned to the other women. 'And now you know the reason! She wanted to make sure she could keep an eye on her business. After all, what better way than being on the inside to do it. A canny lass is our Amy.'

The women were now all staring at Amy hard, and she flushed, grabbing hold of Tess's arm. 'Take that fucking back, and stop trying to wind everyone up. What I do with my parole is down to me, but I can promise you this, it certainly ain't anything to do with drugs.'

Steph, still red-eyed and looking uncharacteristically subdued, strolled over. She spoke to the small group but kept eye contact with Ness. 'I think I'd rather eat my own vomit than eat that shit they call breakfast. If getting decent grub means having to give one of the screws a blow job to bring it in, then I'm down for that, though I draw the line at Tony Earle. No one wants to gobble down his dick.'

She laughed but it sounded forced.

'Am I missing something here?' Steph pulled a face, at the same time cutting a hard stare at Tess. 'What's going on?'

'I was just telling them: if you want to discuss anything to do with the wing having gear on it, maybe you should be speaking to Amy. Like I told these bitches, I'm only the monkey.'

Steph looked puzzled. She glanced at Amy for a moment but just as she opened her mouth to say something, a loud scream echoed through the wing, and Ness saw Lynette come rushing towards them. Shaking and with tears streaming down her face, Lynette struggled to get her words out. 'I knew it . . . I knew it . . . I knew it, cos it wasn't like her.'

Ness held on to Lynette's hand. Most of Lynette's arms were bandaged, but she could still see some of the weeping sores of her self-harm wounds. 'Slow down babe, you're not making sense. What did you know?'

Lynette gulped for air. 'Evie. It was all crap, what my sister told me. She hasn't seen her for over a month.'

All the women's faces drained of colour.

'Oh my God. Oh fuck . . . How do you know?' Steph asked, concerned. 'Who told you? Your sister? You sure she ain't winding you up?'

Trembling uncontrollably, Lynette shook her head. 'No, I wish she was. The governor asked to see me earlier. He was the one who told me. He got a call from the Old Bill; apparently my sister reported her missing, but only after a month . . . After a whole fucking month. I'm going to kill her.' She raised her voice, an edge of hysteria in it.

Ness raised her eyebrows at Maureen but continued to speak to Lynette. 'Maybe Evie has just run away? Maybe she didn't want to hang around with your sister now she's shacking up with that bastard old man of yours.'

'No, Evie wouldn't run away. She ain't like that. She'd always tell me if there was something wrong. I mean, yeah, of course I knew she wasn't happy that I was banged up, and I know she hated my sister and hated her stepdad cos of what they'd done to me, but that wouldn't make her run away without saying nothing . . .' Lynette's voice faded off, but then, sounding like she was speaking more to herself, she added, 'I should've followed my gut. I knew there was no way Evie would ignore my calls if there wasn't something wrong.'

'But why didn't your sister tell you?' Maureen looked at her in confusion. 'And why wait a whole month to inform the police? It makes no sense.'

Lynette pulled her hand away from Ness's and covered her face.

It was a few seconds before she managed to speak. She dropped her hands. 'My sister thought Evie was going through a bit of a phase. She was being secretive, apparently, and so she thought Evie was just being a typical seventeen-year-old. When she didn't turn up one night, she reckoned Evie had gone to stay with her boyfriend or something.' Lynette's face twisted angrily. 'But I guess it suited my sister that Evie wasn't there.'

'Wow, what a stupid cunt,' Amy said quietly. 'Anything could have happened to her.'

Ness dug Amy hard in her ribs and scowled. That was the last thing any mother needed to hear, *especially* when they were banged up. Ness knew it was hard enough being inside, but trying to be a parent as well seemed impossible.

She'd spoken to enough of the women to know that most of the mums inside felt the same. The guilt that their kids were being punished too, never went away. The worry about them on the outside sat in all their stomachs like a lead weight. They were the first thing and the last thing on everyone's minds: hoping they'd be safe, hoping the kids didn't fall into the wrong crowd and make the same mistakes as they had, as well as hoping that somehow life would treat them kindly, even though on the day the judge had passed his sentence, their kids had been given their own sentence too.

And Ness also knew that one of the biggest misconceptions everyone had of them was that they didn't care about their kids. The fact they'd made some lousy choices or mistakes that had landed them in here didn't mean they loved their kids any less than other mums. The only difference was that their love was shut behind bars, inaccessible, and the worry was crippling, the powerlessness to protect their children was absolute.

Lynette's eyes widened. 'So, you think something's happened to her? You think she's in trouble?'

'No, no, Amy didn't mean that, did you, Amy?' Ness prodded her again.

Amy smiled warmly. 'No, of course not. I . . . I only meant; she was bang out of order not telling you before. Your sister is probably right, Lynn: she's shacked up with some fella, loved up. I know what I was like at that age.'

'Evie doesn't even have a boyfriend, though.'

'Are you sure she doesn't?' Steph asked. 'Kids hide a lot of stuff that we don't know about.' She closed her eyes for a moment then, taking a deep breath, opened them. The women gave her a strange look but once again didn't say anything.

Lynette wiped her eyes and nose on the bandage, struggling to get the words out through her tears. 'Yeah, I'm sure. She would've told me if she had. What am I going to do? How am I going to find her, how am I . . .'

She trailed off, sobbing loudly.

Ness spoke gently. 'Lynn, listen to me, darlin': it's going to be OK. Now the police know, they'll do something, I'm sure of it. And I'll call Mina, see if she's heard anything. Steph, maybe you can call Iris?'

Steph shrugged, looking non-committal. Ness gave her a cold glare.

'Babe, you know they won't give a fuck about Evie. No one does. Even when I spoke to my sister this morning in the governor's office, you could tell she didn't give a fuck. And we all know the police ain't going to do anything for a kid like Evie: a black kid, the kid of a prisoner. Fucking hell, they would've made up their minds already about her from the get-go. Plus, she's turning eighteen next week, so all she'll be is another adult in their missing persons file.' Her face crumpled. 'But she's my baby, she's my baby.'

'Oh Lynn, come here, love.' Maureen opened her arms and Lynette collapsed onto her shoulder. She stroked her hair. 'We'll find her, Lynn; I promise we'll find your Evie.'

17

AMY

An hour had passed since Lynette had told them the news of Evie, and Amy hurried along the corridor having left Maureen and Ness trying to comfort her. She didn't have children, so she could only imagine the fear and worry Lynette was going through. Though out of all the women of the wing, Lynette was the worst person this could happen to. She was already on the edge; like a lot of the women, her mental health was suffering from being inside. Some women coped so much better than others, but Lynette wasn't one of them. And right now she certainly wasn't her usual self.

For Amy, life with Ollie on the outside was so much worse than being banged up. For Lynn, being torn away from her daughter for eight years because of one stupid moment of madness, was torture.

Sighing to herself, she pushed past a group of women she didn't know well but who gave her a dirty look anyway. It was so easy to get in a fight around here, but she had more on her mind than confronting a group of spiceheads.

She made her way towards the prison showers, following Tess, who she'd seen a few minutes ago carrying her towel. She wanted to get to the bottom of this. To find out why Tess was intent on stirring trouble for her. There was already enough bad feeling towards her from Steph, something she'd never wanted. And looking back, perhaps it was all of her own making. She'd backed Yvette, the old top dog, because at the time, she really thought

Yvette would make the better top dog. Everything ran smoothly under her, so why fix it when it ain't broke?

She hadn't realized how much it would hurt Steph. That decision to back Yvette had cost her Steph's friendship. But the other thing she hadn't realized was how much she'd miss being friends with her.

It was true, she had less than a week to go inside – a prospect which made her sick to her stomach – but that didn't mean there wasn't time for the other women to jump her if they thought she was taking the piss. Then again, perhaps even a stint in hospital would be preferable to going home.

Looking around, making sure there weren't any screws about, Amy quietly slipped into the shower room.

For once the shower rooms were empty, which Amy was pleased about. Usually, they were filled with women, though mostly that was nothing to do with taking showers. It was one of the few places that didn't have CCTV, so it was a perfect place to buy and sell contraband, to settle arguments – or to start them, to deal, to smoke gear. As a result, the shower rooms were often livelier than a Soho club.

Turning the corner to where the cubicles were, Amy came to a stop by the end one where Tess was washing her hair and singing loudly. She was about to confront her when she heard the door open.

'Tess?'

Recognizing the voice, Amy quickly jumped into the adjacent cubicle where she crouched, listening in surprise as Deputy Tony Earle called out to Tess again.

Male officers were only supposed to come into the shower rooms in an emergency, like a fight or a code red – when a woman had cut her wrists – or a swinger – when a woman had hung herself. So what was Earle playing at, coming in here now?

'Tess?' Earle's voice got louder, and Amy thought she picked up a tone of frustration.

A pause, then the shower was turned off, and eventually she heard Tess's voice . . .

'Howay, Tony, have you come to get an eyeful? Want to see what a real woman looks like? Go on then, take a picture – you can use it to wank off later,' she cackled.

'Don't be so disgusting – and put some clothes on.'

'Why? You uncomfortable seeing a full-bushed ginger minge?' She laughed again. 'Don't tell me you're only used to bare down there? Not keen on that look meself, man; nothing to rub your face in.'

'I won't tell you again. Put your clothes on.'

'So I can't tempt you to a bit of a roll-about?'

'Clothes, *now*!' Earle raised his voice, making Amy jump.

'Has anyone told you that you're no fun? Well, if you change your mind, you know where my cell is, pet. So, go then, if it's not my pussy you want, what can I do for you, Mr Earle?'

'The shipment came through. I've put it in your cell. Usual place. Though, just a heads-up, we're going to do a surprise search of the prison tomorrow; the area inspector wants to have a crackdown on drugs, so we all have to go through the motions. Anyway, I'll be in charge of the search on D wing, and either myself or Walters will do your cell, so you don't have to worry.'

'You mean, *you* don't have to worry. I'm already doing life, but where would a drug bust leave you?' Tess mocked nastily. 'I reckon you've got a lot more to lose than us, hey, Tone?'

There was a long silence and Amy suspected that the deputy was seething. She knew only too well how good Tess was at getting right under your skin.

'Still, make it discreet,' Earle continued. 'No being blatant, Tess. Because if for some reason one of the other officers decides to join me when I'm turning your cell over tomorrow, and they find the package and confiscate it, it'll be you who's owing Ollie Jones a lot of money, not me.'

Amy's blood ran cold. Ollie. How? When? She knew that he was into all sorts, she only had to look at her own sentence: five years for money laundering. *His* money laundering, not hers, though she'd been more than happy to take the rap when it meant getting away from him. But she'd had no idea that Ollie was into selling gear. Not like this anyway. Yes, she'd known him to deal in kilos of coke, but only to give to the faces of Soho, to the rich, to the famous, to the infamous, not to women who were desperate. And in here, right under her own nose.

A lot of the girls on D wing were her mates. Ness, a prime example. She was also a classic case of coming inside and, for the first time in probably forever, having a chance of getting clean. But with the amount of drugs in prison on top of the stress and the boredom, it was only a matter of time before Ness and others like her gave in to temptation. And Ness had already confided in her that she wanted better for this baby than she'd been able to give Mina.

Anger coursed through her. The idea that somehow Ollie had gone behind her back and hooked up with Deputy Earle blew her mind. She knew only too well how low Ollie could go. But this? It was typical of Ollie to take advantage of any opportunity he could.

When did it even happen, though? This year? Last year? Was it right at the beginning of her sentence? Was that why he was always so keen to visit her? Though it was no good confronting Ollie. She knew what his reaction would be. She was his wife to walk down the street with, to have sex with any which way he wanted, she was his wife to do what he said, to take the fall if he wanted, but what she wasn't there for was to question him. So, if she wanted answers, Tess was her only option.

Amy heard Tess yawn loudly. 'Is that all, Tony? Only I've got some paint I want to watch dry.'

'Tess, I'm not joking, if you don't—'

'What?' Tess cut in. 'If I don't what, *officer*?'

'Nothing.' Earle sounded sheepish. 'Nothing, it's fine.'

'Howay, that's what I thought.' And with that, Tess roared with laughter as she and Earle walked out of the shower room.

18
TESS

'Have you ever heard of knocking?' Tess, her cheeks flushed, raised herself off the pillow as she stared at Amy who stood at the door of her prison cell.

Then she winked at Amy. 'Come to join us?' Tess glanced down at the skinny naked woman with scars all over her back and her head between Tess's large, thunderous thighs. 'I'm sure she won't mind . . . but leave your clothes on the side.'

'I want a word,' Amy snarled at her.

Cackling, Tess grinned as the other woman continued to pleasure her, clearly unbothered by the fact that Amy was standing there. 'You know, pet, you can get into trouble for being a peeping Tom. You could get sent to prison for that.'

'Shut up, you stupid cow.' Amy stepped into the cell, she glanced at the other woman, tapping her leg. 'Move it, darlin'. If you want to go deep sea diving, you can come back later. Now get out, I want a word with Tess.'

The woman sat up and angrily wiped her mouth. 'Fuck off, who the fuck do you think you are, telling me what to do?'

Before Amy could speak, Tess kicked the woman off the bed. 'Oi, where's your manners? She's a guest. Now, you heard the lady, *get out.*'

As was the case with most of the prisoners, the woman didn't challenge Tess. Instead, she grabbed her clothes and slipped them on quickly before walking out of the cell, but not before she'd barged her elbow into Amy's side on the way out.

Tess moved her gaze to Amy. 'So, you've got me alone now, what do you want?'

'I want to know what the fuck that was all about.'

Sitting on the bed, Tess pulled on her tracksuit, giving Amy her full attention. She looked bemused. 'What, no one told you about the birds and the bees? Or in our case, just the bees.' She winked, licking her lips suggestively.

'I'm not here to play games, Tess.'

Tess shrugged. 'Then what are you on about?'

Amy looked over her shoulder. She waited for a woman who was hovering outside the cell to walk by, then she brought down her voice. 'I heard you . . . I heard you with Deputy Earle.'

It was a few seconds before Tess said anything. She pulled a face, sniffed loudly, shrugged. 'In that case, what are you doing here talking to me? It's not like it was news to you, is it. Come on, Amy, don't pretend your old man didn't tell you.'

Amy could feel the anger rushing through her again. 'You know full well I had no idea what was going on. You only said that to the women to wind them up, and it succeeded.'

'How could you accuse me of something like that?' Tess mocked her. 'A girl's feelings could be hurt.'

'Enough of the shit, Tess! I'm fucking warning you. Why are you out to get me?'

Tess smirked. She liked the fact that she'd rattled Amy. There was only a week to go before she was released, so she had to make the most of the time she had left. Though Amy was stupid enough to think this was about her. Far from it. This was about Steph.

Only last week, she'd heard rumours that Steph was interested in being top dog again. Challenging her for the crown of D wing. Well, the hell that was going to happen. This was her territory, and hers alone.

The problem was that Steph had started to become more popular. The women respected her. Worse still, they liked her. So, she needed to get Steph out of the way.

When she'd first taken over from Yvette, her and Steph had come to a tense agreement that Steph wouldn't cause trouble. She would respect the law of the prison. Tess had rightfully won the title of number one lag. And up until now, those unwritten rules had worked.

But she wasn't going to leave anything to chance. This was her prison, so she needed to get Steph out of the way. But to do that, she had to be smart, she had to get rid of her. She also needed to divide the group of women, split their loyalties. Cause problems.

She knew Steph was a fireball and that she had a sticky history with Amy. And there was no doubt Steph would be only too happy to believe some shit about Amy, given the chance. So, if she could stir trouble between them, make out that Amy was behind the gear coming in, then hopefully that would cause enough agg for Steph to bite.

Aside from the agg between Steph and Amy, it would also lead to divisions among the women, some believing Amy, some not. And she knew Steph, once charged up, wasn't a woman to back down. Before she could say top dog, Steph would've pissed so many of the girls off, she wouldn't be able to get the votes to challenge Tess. And if she was really lucky, if Steph caused enough beef, they might even ship her off to another prison. Most probably Ollie wouldn't be too happy with her talking his shit, but if it meant she continued to wear the crown, it would be worth it.

Moving her attention fully to Amy, Tess pointed to herself. 'You're warning *me*? That's very brave of you, Amy.'

'Whatever, I'm not scared of you,' Amy snapped. 'And you can quit the bullshit, we both know the truth . . . But what I want to hear though, is about Ollie. How did you even get involved with my husband? How long's it been going on for? Did he visit you, or was it all through Earle?'

Rubbing her wet hair with a balding grey towel, Tess as usual, laughed viciously. 'You sound like a spurned wife . . . Are you jealous, man? Oh, don't worry, Amy, it's all platonic. You know I'm into my birds, though thinking about it, I've never said no to the odd fat cock here or there.'

'Oh, I ain't worried about that darlin', Ollie might have his faults, but he has got taste, and he wouldn't touch you with a bargepole.'

'No, you're right. But maybe he'd touch Martha.'

Amy was visibly taken aback. 'Martha. Ollie's ex-wife. How . . . how do you know Martha?'

Tess laughed hard. She knew that mentioning Martha would rock the stupid cow. It was probably the only good thing about Tony Earle: he couldn't keep his mouth shut, which only played into her having the upper hand. 'It'd surprise you, the things I know, Amy. It's amazing how much people talk, telling me stuff they shouldn't . . . I mean, take last night: Martha was in your bed, sucking him off.'

Amy lunged at Tess, grabbing her hair and dragging her off the bed. 'You ignorant bitch! You're just a wind-up!'

Tess's elbow slammed violently into Amy's nose and immediately, the blood spurted out. For a moment she felt dizzy and staggered backwards, giving Tess the opportunity to pounce on her.

Amy ducked in time to avoid Tess's clenched fist. A second later, Tess's teeth sank into the top of her ear. Amy yelled out, kicking and flaying her arms, trying to push Tess off her. Outside, the corridor filled with the excited yells and screams of the other women. Hearing the ruckus, they'd come running to watch the fight and were now bellowing in delight:

Go on Amy, kill her

Slap that bitch

Fucking have her

Batter the cunt

Get her, Tess

'Get off me, Tess, fucking get off me, you stupid bitch!'

To the banging, stamping and screaming of the other inmates, Amy managed to twist herself out of Tess's clutches. Then Tess's nails scratched down her face, digging into her flesh. Amy yelped as she grabbed Tess into a tight neck lock, pulling her down, turning her round and then banging her head hard on the floor. But Amy's weight wasn't a match for Tess, and immediately the bigger woman let out a roar and used all her strength to pick Amy up and slam her against the cell wall.

Amy slid down the wall, but Tess, incensed and enjoying herself, picked Amy up and threw her against the wall again. Once, twice, like a ragdoll. Amy screamed out as Tess, laughing, lifted her up again, ramming her against the wall, pushing the full force of her weight against her.

The noise in the wing was deafening but then it unexpectedly went quiet.

The sudden hush caused Tess and Amy to stop fighting. Amy wiped her nose, a small trickle of blood running from it. All eyes went towards the wall where Tess had slammed her. Concealed behind an array of photographs, part of the wall had given way. A moment later, a brown-wrapped package which had been hidden in the cavity of the wall tumbled slowly out onto the floor.

Tess picked it up, throwing it over to Amy, and in front of the women, she shrugged. 'Yours, I believe, pet.' She nodded towards the hole in the wall. 'Looks like you'll have to stash it yourself.'

She winked at Amy just as Steph appeared in front of the group of women watching her.

Amy looked awkward. 'It . . . it's not what you think, Steph.'

'Oh, it's exactly what you think, Steph,' Tess said, grinning. 'See, I told you she was part of it. We took it in turns to stash the gear.'

'Stop lying!' Amy's voice was desperate. 'You can't believe this cow!'

Tess glared at Amy, delighting in the fact that fate was on her side, and it was going much better than expected. This was going to be easy pickings. 'We've been working together for a while. She just didn't want you to know. Suited me, the deal was, she'd give me a bigger cut, if I kept my mouth shut.' She chewed on the wick of her nails. 'But howay, keeping someone else's secret, gets a bit boring.'

'Fuck off, Tess . . . Just fuck off . . .' Still holding the package in her hands, Amy quickly turned back to Steph. 'Listen it's really not—'

'Don't bother.' Steph cut her off, shaking her head in disgust. 'But don't think this is over, Amy. Not by a long way.' And with that, Steph walked off.

Amy yelled after her. 'Steph, wait up! Steph.'

'Whoops, someone's not best pleased,' Tess giggled.

'This is all your fault.' Angrily, Amy threw the package of heroin to Tess, who caught it at the exact moment Governor Reed appeared at the door . . .

19

THE GOVERNOR

An hour later Reed sat back in the leather chair in his large office, looking out over the gardens that the prisoners kept pristine. Ashcroft was over twenty miles from London but he could see the city skyline on the horizon. He could also see the prison yard, giving him the perfect opportunity to view the women, watch their dynamics, the hierarchy, the nuances, because he knew it was often in the smallest moments that he learned the biggest things.

He yawned widely, eyeing the bottle of whisky which sat on the metal filing cabinet in the corner. He could almost taste it, and he was looking forward to a large glass once he'd sorted out what he needed to do.

Feeling the heat from the sun burn through the window, Reed pulled down the blind slightly and spun around on his chair, staring at the package of drugs on the desk which he'd confiscated from Tess.

Drugs in prison was a real problem. Only last week he'd had a memo about an area-wide crackdown. Though each and every one of the staff knew that the memo wasn't worth the piece of paper it'd been written on. Drugs and prison went hand in hand.

A massive percentage of the women who came through the gates of Ashcroft were addicts, and the reason they'd been sent down in the first place was to feed their habit. The system just wasn't large enough to accommodate proper rehab and detox, so the only option open to the women was to keep on using, which meant drugs needed to be smuggled in.

In truth, it suited a lot of the officers for the women to carry on with their habit. It made their job easier. Life was quieter. And he had to agree with them: women who were doped up to the eyeballs were certainly preferable to stone-cold sober women. If there was any doubt in his mind, he only had to look to his wife. But then he doubted even a rock of crack would mellow that miserable bitch.

He sighed at the thought of her and absent-mindedly chewed on the top of his blue biro. One of the things he knew he had to do was report the find to one of the idiots from the HM Inspectorate of Prisons. But then, knowing what he had to do wasn't the same as doing it, was it.

He glanced up and nodded at Tess. 'So this conversation we've just had goes nowhere else. Understand? Now get out of here. Officer Sharps will take you back to the wing.'

She nodded and sauntered out without a word.

He watched the officer – who'd been waiting outside – lead her away. Then he reached for the long-awaited whisky and poured himself a large glass, knocking it back as if he were drinking a large glass of squash.

He immediately poured himself another and thought about Tess. She clearly hadn't given up all the names involved, which didn't surprise him. The prisoners had some warped sense of allegiance. It was ridiculous really, because paradoxically, they didn't think twice about plunging a knife into someone's back, though figuratively speaking, it wouldn't ever be up for consideration.

But the one name Tess had given him, had been interesting. *Very* interesting. But rather than pick up the phone to the police or to the authorities like he should, he was going to sit on it and wait. After all, he'd been in this game long enough to know, having something over someone was always very useful. It gave him power. Because in the end, Phil Reed realized that was all that mattered in life: power and revenge.

20

JACK

It was mid-afternoon the same day, and Jack leaned against the bar, knocking back another glass of whisky. He knew he should be hitting the road but being here in Soho was so familiar to him. Comfortable. But then he also knew being comfortable wasn't always the right thing.

Since he'd hooked up with Rebel, he hadn't been home. Not that there was anything at home to miss. Now he was on a sabbatical, he no longer stayed in one of the residences the Church provided for parish priests. Instead, he stayed in the sprawling gated mansion in Henley-on-Thames. He'd bought the riverside property a few years ago. For cash. When his life had been very different to the one he lived now.

Like everywhere he went, his house was filled with memories of his past. A past he no longer belonged in, but then, he wasn't sure where he *did* belong. Locking himself away as a priest had been the perfect antidote to what he'd thought he was running from. But over time, he realized the only thing he'd been running from was himself. So, for now, he'd accept comfortable because comfortable was better than being lost.

'Jack! Well, well, well, I never thought I'd see you again.'

Jack froze at the voice behind him. Then he felt a hard pat on his back, the pat he knew was meant to get right under his skin – and it did.

He played with his glass, swirling the ice around it. Then, composing himself, he slowly turned. 'Hello, Raymond.'

'I thought it was you. I see priesthood ain't taken away those handsome looks of yours.'

Jack stared right into the eyes of his past. He could feel the tension rush into his body, his breathing becoming staggered as a pulse on his jaw began to throb. Eventually, he gave the smallest of nods. 'And I see your bullshit ain't been taken away from you either . . . Shame really.' He gestured to Harry for another drink. 'How are you doing, anyway?'

Raymond laughed, the row of gold front teeth giving his grin a macabre appearance. And his sharp features were emphasized by the scar across his cheek, while his shaved head accentuated his thick frame. He winked at the two henchmen next to him. Then he wagged his finger at Jack, speaking with a part Turkish and part cockney accent: 'You know, when I first heard you were back, I thought they must have got it wrong, cos I said to myself, he wouldn't be that stupid. But then someone else told me you were here, and I thought, well two people can't be wrong, can they . . . So, I came to see for myself, and look, they were right, here you are.'

'I'm glad to see you do a lot of thinking, Ray. Makes a change.'

'Don't try to be a funny cunt.'

In the dim light of the members-only club, Jack stayed silent and watched Raymond take out a tin from his leather coat. He opened it, tapped out the contents before pulling a flick knife out of his pocket. Then, pressing the metallic stud button with his thumb, Raymond released the sharp blade. And in plain sight of the other punters in the exclusive club, he proceeded to chop up the cocaine on the bartop.

When he'd finished cutting the powder, from the back of his trouser pocket Raymond produced a gold engraved toot.

'Care to join me?'

He offered it to Jack.

Cricking his neck to try to relieve the tension, Jack shook his head. 'I'm not into that anymore. It's a mug's game.'

Raymond grinned nastily. He licked his lips, eyeballing Jack hard. 'Is that right? So, what, you calling me a mug now, are you? That ain't very nice.'

Jack laughed loudly, causing one of the punters to look over. 'You're just chomping at the bit for a fight, aren't you, Ray?' His scorn oozed out. 'Why don't you cut to the chase? Have it out with me. Whatever your beef is, why don't you just say it?'

Raymond feigned innocence. 'I just think it's rude not to partake, especially after all this time. I mean, you and I go way back, don't we?'

'That's in the past,' Jack said coldly.

'Oh, come off it, don't you miss all those good times? I know you, Jack, and all this – this religious shit, this facade you've got going – well, it don't fool me. You ain't changed, after all. Look around you. Look where you are. This club is hardly St Peter's, is it? The only thing you'll find here are sinners.' He laughed. 'I know you must miss it. Remember all that partying, all those women, the business, the money—'

'—the killing,' Jack cut in drily. 'Don't forget the killing.'

Raymond opened his arms in an exaggerated manner. 'Oh, come on, Jack, what's with you bringing down the vibe? You used to be much more fun than this. We'd be peeling you off the wall by the end of the night . . . Don't tell me all that Bible shit has given you a conscience?' He grinned again. 'But you know, I reckon you're wasting your time, Jack, cos I'm not sure that even Jesus Christ himself could wash off all that blood you've got on your hands.'

Determined not to rise to the bait, Jack shook his head. 'I'll ask you once more, what do you want, Raymond?' he said after a

long pause, though he could still feel the tension rising up in him
like flames.

Raymond held out the toot again. 'The question isn't what I
want, it's what *you* want. Why are you back? And don't give me
any bullshit . . . You looking to reclaim your crown?'

Jack took another swig of brandy. 'I don't know what part
you're missing, Raymond, but all this, this here, is all in the past
for me. I'm not interested.'

Raymond nodded slowly then, exuding sarcasm, said, 'And
that's why you're here, is it, because it's all in the past?' He
stepped nearer and smiled at Jack. His face inches away from his.
He pushed the toot into his hand. 'You know, it's rude not to join
in . . . Take it. *Now.*'

Feeling the knife in his side, Jack leaned over the lines of
cocaine. He hovered over them. He could almost taste it. And he
knew, after all this time, that hit of the coke rushing into his
system would be a high like no other.

'Go on, Jack, what are you waiting for? Worried it's going to
take a hold of you again?'

Jack stared at the coke again, but he suddenly shook his head
and slammed the toot back into Raymond's free hand. 'Do what
you want to me, but I ain't taking it.'

The laughter filled the club. Raymond winked again. 'It nearly
had you though, didn't it? Still your poison, I can see.'

'No. No, it ain't.'

'Are you sure about that? Your eyes say different.'

'Like I say, it's a mug's game.'

Raymond glared at Jack, hostility coming off him in waves, but
then he smiled, though it didn't hit his eyes. 'How's Rebel, by the
way? I take it you two have hooked up again. She said as much
when I called her the other day. Pity really, she and I had a good
little thing going. But then, second-hand goods never really was

my thing. You can take it or leave it, can't you?' he smirked. 'Oh sorry, didn't she tell you about me and her? It must have slipped her mind when she jumped out of your bed into mine . . . *again.*'

Jack shrugged. 'No, she didn't tell me, but she's free to do what she likes.'

'You weren't saying that a few years ago, I remember.'

'All water under the bridge.' Jack turned to go but, as he walked away, Raymond grabbed his arm, the grip hard enough to leave a bruise. 'Be careful, Jack. Things have changed a lot since you've been away, you ain't number one around here anymore, and all you've got behind you now is Christ's army, and I ain't sure that will do much good when you go up against me.'

'Like I said, it ain't my thing, not now.'

'Well, make sure it stays that way. Make sure, while you're here, you're only on a tourist visa. Do you get my drift?'

Jack glanced around the club, then he brought his stare back to Raymond. He scoffed. 'Oh, I understand, Ray, but I'm not sure how many times I need to tell you, I ain't interested in the business anymore. I've got my new life now, so if you'll excuse me.' He pulled his arm out of Raymond's clutch and walked away, listening to Raymond shout after him.

You sure you don't want a line, Jack? I'll give you a wrap – you can keep it for later if you like.

Walking through to the back stairs of the club, Jack took a deep breath. He could still see the lines of cocaine in his mind's eye, and although he was pleased that he'd abstained, the urge was obviously still there.

Climbing the stairs slowly, Jack could smell sex and stale alcohol in the air. The girls who worked in the club often brought punters back here, taking them into one of the numerous rooms on the floor below Rebel's tiny flat. She'd been living here for more than fifteen years, just a year short of the time he'd known her.

At the door on the top landing of the converted Georgian building, Jack sauntered in without knocking, making his way into the bedroom opposite the entrance. He called out:

'Rebel? Rebel?'

There was no answer.

Glancing around, he popped his head around the kitchen door, then went into the lounge before making his way down the small hallway. But then he quickly threw down his jacket and stood motionless, taking in the scene that greeted him. Rebel was slumped on the floor of the en suite bathroom, her head lolling forward on her chest.

'Oh Jesus, Reb! Reb!' He ran forward, crouching by her side. Immediately, he lifted up her arm, checking her wrist for a pulse.

'Reb, talk to me, baby.' Placing her hand down gently on her lap, he put his fingers under her chin, lifting her face up towards his.

Blearily, Rebel began to open her eyes. She gave a half smile before her eyelids closed again.

'What have you taken? Reb, tell me, baby, what did you take, sweetheart?' He looked at her arm to see if there were any track marks. Not finding any, he glanced around and by the base of the toilet bowl he saw her freebasing equipment.

Continuing to kneel, he brought her in for a hug, kissing her gently on the forehead. 'Reb, I thought we said this wasn't going to happen anymore. Remember? How long have you been back on it? Tell me it's just a blip, and you're not down that hole again.'

It was a moment before Rebel stirred and she opened her eyes, pushing him gently away. She managed to speak but it sounded slurred. 'How are the kids, Jack? How are the babies?'

Jack stared at her, memories rushing through him. He took

a deep breath and stroked her hair, which was wet from sweat, one of the side effects of smoking heroin. 'We haven't got any, remember?'

'Haven't we, Jack? I thought we did.' She looked at him, her stare hazy as she frowned.

He rubbed his face and a wave of emotion hit him. He knew some memories were best left in the past. 'No, honey, we haven't.'

She giggled. 'Stay with me until I fall to sleep tonight, Jack.' Then she touched his face, keeping her hand there for a moment before leaning across to kiss him.

He hated seeing her like this. For so long Rebel had fought her demons, and he knew what that was like. They'd all partied, all stayed out longer than the night was, and as Raymond had put it, they'd *needed to be peeled off the walls*. But Rebel, well, she'd always taken it further, almost to the point of no return. And maybe he wasn't around as much as he should've been. He knew that.

It had always been different with her; she'd never wanted to let it go. She'd loved the drugs to the point where she'd watched it destroy everything. Nothing had been sacred to Rebel . . . *nothing* at all.

And her being high like this, well, it just brought back unwanted memories which Jack thought he'd laid to rest nine years ago.

Sucking in air, Jack watched her head roll to the side and rest against his shoulder. He spoke gently to her. 'I told you this morning, Reb, that I needed to go. I'm getting too comfortable, I'll end up staying.'

She peeked at him through one eye. 'And would that be so bad?'

He smiled sadly at her. 'Yeah, for us, I think it would, Reb. I can feel myself getting drawn back into it all, and that isn't good.'

He chuckled but there was a hollowness to it. 'I was only supposed to pop in for a drink.'

Drowsily, she smiled back. 'I'm sorry, babe. What can I do?'

Jack kissed her again on her head. 'Maybe try not fucking my best mate.' He corrected himself. 'Former best mate.'

Tears filled Rebel's eyes. 'Jack, he was here, and you weren't. You left me, Jack. What was I supposed to do?'

'Anything but that, baby. Anything but that.' He rubbed his head. 'You know Ray was one of the reasons I left. Maybe not the main reason' – he took a deep breath as the tension rose inside him – 'but one of the reasons. So, it's kind of a bitter pill when I find out you and him, even after everything, had something going on.' He rubbed his temples again, and after a moment said, 'You know what, ignore me, Reb. What you do is your business, if you're happy, I'm happy. I'm not your judge or jailer.'

'Do you hate me, Jack?'

'I could never hate you, though that's not to say I haven't tried. Jesus Christ, back in the day, Reb, and even after I left, I tried so hard to hate you. I thought I did for a long time, but I couldn't, not really . . . But I do need to go home, you know that?'

Panic rose in her voice. She grabbed him, holding on as if she were drowning. 'Jack, no . . . No, don't leave me. Not again.'

He wiped her tears and, unable to look into her stare, which was full of pain, he glanced around the grey-tiled bathroom. 'Reb, this is what I didn't want to happen.'

'Then why did you come back? Look at me, Jack.' Her voice was slurred and her gaze hazy. 'Why did you come back if you were going to disappear again?'

'Reb, you said you'd be OK.'

'*Please*, Jack, just give me a couple more days.'

'I've done that already, and the longer I stay the harder it'll get for both of us.'

'Please . . .'

He didn't answer immediately. Would it be so bad if he stayed? Did he really want to go back to his empty house, lost, having no direction to speak of? Maybe her asking was actually doing him a favour.

He glanced at Rebel again and slowly nodded, knowing that him staying was probably less about her and more about him. 'OK, I'll stay. But I do have to get out of here eventually. It's not going to do either of us any good . . . But, Reb, while I'm here I'd appreciate it if you stayed away from the punters, and Ray. Not sure if I could stomach it.'

In her haze, Rebel smiled. The expression on her face looked something like relief. 'I love you, Jack.'

He kissed her gently on her lips, saying what he knew she wanted to hear, though only a part of it was true. 'I love you too. Always did.'

Her eyes began to roll back and he picked her up and carried her out of the tiny bathroom into the whitewashed bedroom, and carefully laid her on the bed. Almost immediately, she closed her eyes and began to snore gently.

Sitting on the bed next to her, Jack watched her sleep for a while. About to get up, he felt his phone vibrating in his pocket and pulling it out he saw the number was withheld, though he answered it anyway.

'Yes?'

'Jack – it's Reenie, lovey. One of the women has got a bit of a problem, and we need your help.'

21

EXERCISE YARD

The next day, with lunchtime having come and gone, the women mooched about outside in the yard. There was a light spattering of rain and Steph, Maureen and Ness stood in the corner huddled up, watching Tess and her cronies on the far side of the concrete yard, sitting on the bench.

'Stupid cow's blatantly selling her gear. She's proper taking the piss, even after what we said to her,' Ness grumbled angrily.

'You know what Tess is like – she doesn't care, it's all a fecking game to her. The more women she can hurt, the better,' Maureen agreed. 'And it's not as if there's anyone to stop her either.'

'Yeah, cos no one's going to grass her up. The worst thing that happened in this place was her becoming top dog. If it wasn't for Amy, that wouldn't be the case. The bitch has a lot to answer for,' Steph said this as she glared at Tess, who was in the middle of dealing with one of the known spiceheads on the wing.

'It's not all her fault,' Ness said calmly. 'And I think she regrets it now.'

'Too little, too late.' Steph rubbed her head, closing her eyes for a moment.

Ness frowned at her. 'You OK, hun? You seem tired.'

'I'm OK, just got shit on my mind.' Steph shrugged and both the women noticed her bottom lip trembling, but they knew better than to push Steph with questions. When she was ready, she'd tell them herself.

'It's terrible,' Maureen mused, going back to the subject of

Tess. 'We're just supposed to do nothing and watch her? She's always enjoyed causing trouble, and all that stuff with Amy—'

'Which could well be true,' Steph cut in and Maureen gave her a sad look.

'I wasn't going to say that, Steph. I know that there's bad blood between you and Amy, but Ness is right. Amy told me herself she regrets not backing you but, at the time, she thought it was the best thing to do.'

'Best for who?' Steph snarled. 'I'd been backing her all the way since she'd arrived, and when I needed her to back me, she screwed me over. Gave her vote to Yvette. She betrayed me, Reenie, and you know it. So, finding out that she's been serving up with Tess behind our backs don't surprise me. She's not to be trusted, and I found that out the hard way.'

'You're not thinking straight,' Maureen tutted.

'Oh, I am. And believe me, Reenie, I'll be getting to the bottom of it. I just haven't had time to have a word with Tess about it yet.'

'Ignore her. Even if what Tess says is true, Amy will be out of here soon.'

'That's not good enough. She doesn't get to just walk away from this,' Steph growled.

Maureen looked flustered. 'Stop all this. Amy's a good girl.'

Steph gave a tight smile. 'And that's why she's in here, right? Because she's a good girl?'

When Maureen gave no answer, continuing to glare at Tess, Steph added quietly, 'Anyway, what Tess needs is to be stopped in a way she understands.'

Ness, keeping most of her attention on Tess, asked, 'Who's going to do it? I would be up for it, but . . .' She pointed at her ever-growing pregnant stomach.

Steph shook her head. 'No, we need to be cleverer than that. A pasting won't do much good and, anyway, knowing Tess, she'll

'I want a word with you.' He spoke angrily, his face pinched with red.

'Can't you see I'm busy getting my daily exercise in. Now, if you don't mind, you're disturbing my karma. Come back later, will you?'

'*Now!*'

Earle's anger was apparent, and she looked around at the others and grinned, mocking him. 'Howay, man, whatever happened to *please* and *thank you*? Did your mam never teach you?'

Clearly incensed, he grabbed her arm, squeezing it tightly and dragging her out of the yard and into the outside walkway. He clenched his teeth as he pulled her along, hissing under his breath. 'What the hell did you tell Reed? You better not have dropped me in it.'

Tess, delighted as always by someone else's distress, laughed loudly. 'You sweating, Mr Earle? Worried the old boys in blue will be coming around?'

He shook her, tension brimming over in him. 'Just fucking tell me, for God's sake: am I going to get a knock from the police any minute? And don't play games with me.' Earle was breathless.

She shook him off. 'If you don't calm down, you'll be blue-lighted away. By the looks of you, you're going to have a heart attack any minute, man,' she giggled.

Earle licked his lips; he was visibly shaking. 'Tess, *please.*'

She stared at him for a moment and grinned widely. 'You of all people should know the saying by now: if you can't do the time, don't do the crime,' she trilled chirpily and turned to go. 'Maybe you should be wishing the pigs get to you before Ollie does, though I wouldn't fancy your chances with Martha either. I may only have met them once like, but what I saw of them, and what I've heard of them from my own sources, I reckon you might be in a lot of trouble, man . . .'

She drew her finger across her throat and winked, then looked up to the sky, 'Mmmmm, Ollie, the governor, or the Old Bill – now which one of them will it be?' She returned her gaze to him and winked again. 'Or maybe it won't be any of them.' She shrugged. 'I've always liked surprises, Mr Earle. It's like all your birthdays are coming at once.'

'You better hope nothing happens.'

'And how do you make that out?' Tess said with a grin.

'Because without me, you're nothing. Who's going to bring the stuff in for you?'

She leaned forward. 'Oh, Tone, you stupid, stupid little man. Rule number one: never think you're indispensable. There's always twats like you, they're ten a penny.' She roared with laughter, walking away. But then she spun around and blew him a kiss, just as Steph came into view.

'Oi, Tess, I want a word.'

Tess smirked. 'I'd love to oblige, but I've got an aversion to talking to people that talk shit.'

She barged past Steph, leaving her standing opposite Deputy Earle, who looked positively ill. She gave him a strange look but didn't say anything, though as she was moving away, Earle called her back. 'Stephanie, a moment.'

Steph sighed. She pulled the neck of her tracksuit jumper up as the rain started to trickle down her neck. 'Are you about to tell me that I was supposed to wipe the gym machines down? Cos that wasn't my job this week – you need to speak to that silly cow Alison. I'm rota-ed in to do the book trolley, ask Miss—'

'Shut up, Steph.'

Visibly taken aback, Steph frowned. 'I thought you wanted to know about the gym, I already—'

'Be quiet!' Earle stepped forward and grabbed Steph. His voice was low, and his eyes darted around. 'If you just listen, maybe you'll learn something.' His face was drawn.

'What's happened, is this to do with Lynette? Have they found Evie?'

He shook her and Steph tried to pull away, but his grip on her arm tightened. 'Just *listen*. I know that Tess has been causing problems for a long time, and this place has eyes and ears. I know that all the women on D wing want rid of her. I also know that you've been planning on taking her crown . . .' He paused and looked around again. 'I'd be more than happy to help you. Whatever it takes. And I'm saying this because I think you want to get rid of Tess as much as I do, and if we work together, I have a feeling we can be free of her once and for all.'

22

MINA

It had just turned four o'clock and Mina relaxed back on Iris's bed. It was actually the first time she'd been to her house, and she had to admit that if she had a house even half as nice, she wouldn't be thinking of leaving it behind. Iris's place was everything she'd dreamt of, even her front garden, let alone the sprawling back one, was so much larger than the squalid bedsit that her and Flo lived in. And it was hard not to envy all that Iris had, and the creeping thought that other people's lives always seemed so much better than her own sat with her.

But despite that, it did feel lovely to sit and chill in Iris's house, and for once, she'd been able to pay the babysitter from the money Ollie had given her, which meant she wasn't panicking to get back, thinking that Doreen might leave Flo on her own. It was the first time she'd been able to unwind in longer than she could remember: she could certainly get used to it.

'So, what do you think? Will you come with me?' Iris sat on the sofa opposite the king-size bed and grinned at Mina as she drank a large glass of vodka, her legs curled up underneath her.

'You wanna know what I think? I think you're fucking crazy.' She squealed with laughter and shook her head. 'I couldn't, Iris. I can't.'

'Why not? What's the big deal? Come on, Roz will be there, and she thinks you're so cool. It'll be . . . it'll be a laugh.'

'A laugh! I think there's a lot of words for it, and a *laugh* ain't one of them. Going to some brothel is hardly my idea of a good time.'

'It's not crazy. I've been talking to Roz about it for a long time. She works at this place and she earns so much money. She was always trying to get me to go.'

Mina raised her eyebrows and wondered if that was why Steph hated Roz so much. She knew her mum would feel exactly the same if she knew she'd been hanging out with Roz.

'I've always said no, until now. But it's perfect. I need money, Mina. You told me yourself that you did. This is the solution to all our problems . . . Oh, please, Mina, I won't be able to do it without you.' Iris stared at her, her long blonde hair falling over her shoulders.

'I'm sorry, no.'

Iris looked disappointed and she took another large sip of vodka from the crystal glass. 'But why? At least tell me why.'

Mina quickly looked away.

Iris started to giggle. 'Oh my God . . . oh my God, are you telling me that you're still a virgin? You are, aren't you?'

Mina could feel herself flushing red, but she didn't hold Iris's intense stare. 'No, no, I'm not.'

Iris jumped off the couch, glass in hand, and skipped across to the bed where Mina was sitting. Her voice was high-pitched and slightly slurred. 'It's true, isn't it?' Her face was lit up. 'I ain't judging, I'm just surprised, that's all.'

Mina looked up at her. 'Why? Because of my mum?' She suddenly sounded defensive. 'You think cos my mum sells herself that I'm the same as her?'

Iris raised her eyebrows. 'No! I didn't mean that.' She sounded upset.

'Yes, you did. And you know what, it's not like it's the first time

I've heard that, but I thought you'd be different.' She could feel the tears cutting at the back of her throat.

Iris placed her glass on the small black Swarovski bedside cabinet and took Mina's hands in hers. 'Fucking hell, Mina, how can you think that? I'm your mate – and I told you, I ain't judging, cos what your mum does is *her* business. Jesus, I'd rather have her for a mum than mine, any day. I just thought it was cute.'

Mina frowned. 'Don't take the piss.'

'I ain't taking the piss. I was just surprised cos, let's face it, you could have any guy. They'd be lining up in the street for you—'

'Shut up!' Mina cut in.

Iris shook her head, staring right into Mina's eyes. 'You really don't get how beautiful you are, do you?'

Mina leapt up from the bed. 'I knew you were taking the mick out of me. I want to go home; will you just take me home?'

Iris grabbed her gently. 'I'm sorry, I'm sorry, yeah . . . Don't go, *please*. I really didn't mean what you thought I did.' She leaned in and kissed Mina on her lips, then stepped back and grinned. 'See, even I fancy you.' She laughed, which made Mina laugh as well. Then her face grew serious again, and she stepped forward once more and kissed her again. Though this time it was Mina who stepped away.

'Iris, look, I'm flattered but—'

'But you're not into girls.'

Mina nodded and shrugged.

'Neither was I, until now.' Iris laughed, unabashed, and they sat down again on the bed, hugging each other in a warm, friendly embrace as they giggled hysterically.

Eventually, Mina pulled away gently. She wasn't offended by the kiss, far from it, she was as she said, genuinely flattered. One of the good things about being brought up by her mum was that she'd seen enough to accept everyone for who they were, and if Iris was into both girls and boys, it didn't matter to her one bit.

Iris's eyes twinkled. 'You're amazing, Mina. And look, we'll be able to leave everything behind for good. I thought you wanted to escape this shitty life as much as I do. If we do this, we can get away.'

'I can't.'

'Don't you want to leave here?'

Mina glanced around again, taking a sip from the can of Coke Iris had given her earlier. 'Yeah, of course. I mean, getting away from everything sounds great when you say it, but . . .' She trailed off, not wanting to get into how complicated her life was.

'OK, don't think about that now. I get it, it's a big decision. But at least come with me on Saturday. We'll be back by Sunday lunchtime. It'll be easy, well, it'll be easy for me. You don't have to do anything, just keep me company.' She shrugged. 'Even if you don't come with me, I'm going to go.'

'You can't go on your own.'

'I won't be on my own. Like I say, Roz will be there. And it's no big deal, not for me. I've done this sort of thing once before, a couple of years ago, though it only lasted a month or so as the brothel owner got busted and ended up in Cookham Wood on a twelve stretch.' Iris rolled her eyes. 'And even back then, I didn't regret it. Tell you the truth, I felt disappointed that it had come to an end. Sleeping with some geezer for money, especially when it doesn't involve working for any scummy pimp, is no different from picking up a one-night stand at a club.' She shrugged. 'It beats giving it for free, or someone taking it for free.'

Mina frowned, hearing the hardness in Iris's voice. 'What do you mean?'

Iris looked away, fidgeting with her hands. 'Nothing. I'm just saying.' She paused before continuing, 'But the days of being told what to do, where to go, being threatened with getting cut off financially by Mum if I don't do what she says, are going to stop. This way, Mina, I'll have my own money and there's nothing Mum can do about it.' She sighed. 'I ain't staying around longer than I have to, and doing this on Saturday will be the start of my ticket out of here . . . If I don't do this, I'll never be able to leave – and I can't stand it anymore.'

'I need to see my mum on Saturday,' Mina said lamely.

'Just fuck her off, tell her you're ill or something,' Iris urged. 'You can say that you caught a cold from me. Then that covers both of us, and it also means my mum will believe me when I tell her that I'm feeling rough. Look, there's some things that you don't know, shit that's been happening to me for a long time, and I can't say what it is, but trust me when I tell you I can't stay here anymore.'

Mina stared at Iris and was surprised to see tears running down her face. Iris always seemed the strong one, the teen ice-queen with everything going for her.

She leaned over and wiped her tears with the palm of her hand as memories flashed through. So many times, when she was growing up, when she wasn't in care, her days had been spent waiting for her mum in various walk-ups, while she serviced some punter or other. And how many times had her mum got herself into trouble, being roughed up, slapped around by them? It was a dangerous game, and sex and violence seemed to go hand in hand.

She didn't want Iris going through what her mum did. She didn't want her to get hurt. When she'd been a kid, she hadn't been able to do anything to help her mum, all she'd been able to do was cover her ears and hide in a cupboard. But now was different.

Though the main problem, if she did go, was Flo. How the hell was she going to get around being able to afford to have someone look after her for over twenty-four hours? It's not like she could tell Iris the truth. Flo had to be kept a secret. But then, she couldn't let Iris go off on her own. That wasn't even an option.

'Don't cry, Iris. Look at me . . . if you need me to come with you, I will. But I'm not saying that I'm going to get involved or anything, you understand?'

'Of course.'

'Then I'll come along to make sure that you're OK. But I have to be back for Sunday lunch, yeah?'

Once more, Iris's face lit up. She threw her arms around Mina. 'I love you, you're totally the best mate ever . . . Nottingham here we come.' Then she looked at Mina and kissed her on her lips again, and this time Mina didn't pull away.

23
STEPH

It was Tuesday morning and Steph picked at her scrambled egg, though it wasn't so much scrambled as sloppy and under-cooked. Irritated, she pushed her plate away, sending it skidding down the breakfast table. It crashed to the floor, but she made no attempt to pick it up. Leaning back in her chair, she let out a long sigh.

'What the fuck's got into you?' Ness, sitting opposite, stared at her as she slurped on a milky cup of tea. 'I've told you already, that's why I never eat breakfast in this place, scared I'll get frigging salmonella.'

'And it's got bloody worse since that stupid cow Allie got a job in the kitchen. Have you seen the state of her frigging nails? It's like she's scraped out the toilet bowl with them.' Amy pulled a face.

Maureen spluttered out her orange juice. She grinned. 'Don't say that, I've just had a bacon sarnie from her: she told me she'd made it personally. Jesus, Mary and Joseph, I feel like soaping me mouth out now.'

'Why don't you have some toast, Steph?' Ness suggested helpfully. 'It's so fucking burnt that I reckon any bleedin' germs will have been incinerated.'

All the women laughed, apart from Steph.

Steph stood up and banged her chair hard into the table. 'Fucking hell, Ness, not everything revolves around food you know, we're not all eating for bloody two and stuffing our face.'

'I only meant—'

'I don't care what you meant. Why don't you just try for once, just for once shutting that mouth of yours and giving it a rest. And as for her sitting with us.' She pointed at Amy. 'It feels like a complete mug-off. Didn't you hear what Tess said? You're not even going to consider it, are you? She could be responsible for flooding this wing with shit, yet here you all are, playing happy fucking families. Well, you can drop me out. And you need to choose which side you're on. Hers or mine.'

Not giving Ness or the others a chance to answer, Steph stormed away, barging past a small group of women who were busy arguing. She stalked towards her cell, rubbing her temples. The noise in the wing seemed so much louder than usual, the constant clattering, along with the incessant raised voices and the shrieks of laughter echoed around the cell block, filling every corner.

She couldn't think straight, and she longed for some silence. Even in the chapel, which was situated between D and C wing, there was noise. There was no escape from it, but right now, peace was exactly what she needed.

And it wasn't helping that she'd hardly slept last night, partly because Lynette, who was bunked up in the cell next door, had been crying her eyes out. And although she had a lot of time for her, she hadn't reached out; the truth was she couldn't. She'd found it triggering. It had made her think of what Iris had said and the sickness in her stomach it had caused sat there.

Since she'd had the row with Iris, and Iris had told her, she hadn't actually spoken to her daughter. She didn't know what she was going to say. The idea Iris had been abused by her stepdad and the people that had worked for her . . . *were* working for her, well, she couldn't get her head around it. She'd failed Iris. And now she was stuck in here, not being able to do anything about it, not being able to put her arms around her girl and face it together.

Why hadn't she seen the signs? Why hadn't Iris told her before? Had it started when she'd been banged up, or had it happened right under her nose, when she'd been at home? And why now? Why had Iris decided to blurt it out now?

There were so many questions, and she wasn't even sure if she'd be able to get answers to them . . .

She came to a halt right in front of her cell door as the tears began to pour down her face. She pictured Iris. Her beautiful, crazy, hot-headed daughter who she loved with every fibre of her body had been hurt in a way no one ever should be. And she hadn't been there to protect her.

She felt a physical pain and wrapped her arms around herself to stop the scream which was building up inside her. Walking quickly into her cell, she sat on her bed and gazed around. The walls of Ashcroft felt like they were closing in on her. And all she could hear in her head was the pain in her daughter's voice when she'd told her about what had been happening.

She curled up in a ball and buried her face in her pillow. She was here in Ashcroft for life and her days of being able to protect Iris in the way she should and be her mother in the way she wanted, were long gone. She doubted she'd see the outside world again, so her daughter was having to face this alone. She felt sick at the thought, so helpless, so angry, but there was one thought she kept hold of. Somehow, she was going to make sure she got revenge. No one was going to hurt her baby and get away with it. Not now, not ever. And with that thought, Steph screamed into her pillow.

24

LYNETTE

In the next cell, Lynette paced around, clutching her hands as anxiety swelled in her. It felt like there was something stuck in her chest, pushing down and making it hard for her to breathe. Starting to cry again, she breathed in deeply, wiping her running nose on the back of her sleeve, her whole body shaking with terror.

It had been days since her conversation with the police and the governor, and nobody had heard anything more about Evie, or come to speak to her about it. Not the prison social workers or the well-being officers, no one. It felt like they'd left her to drown. Worse still, it felt like they'd forgotten Evie.

Even her sister and her ex hadn't called. She'd left a voicemail, but they hadn't bothered getting in touch. Steph had even let her give the number of her burner phone to them, but there'd been nothing. No texts, no missed calls. They simply didn't care. But then, did that really surprise her? It had taken over a month for her cow of a sister to contact the police about Evie, and now they were probably all cosied up in the same house where she'd once tucked her daughter up in bed.

Holding her head, Lynette squeezed her eyes shut. She couldn't stop trembling and she felt like she was going out of her mind, but there was nothing, *nothing* at all she could do about it. Her Evie was out there somewhere, alone, frightened, and she was stuck in Ashcroft, unable to help, unable to do anything useful.

If she could only speak to Evie's friends or go to the places she used to hang out, or if she was able to ask in the coffee shop her daughter worked in . . . well, even that would be better than being stuck inside these four walls, worse than useless. And the reality of doing nothing when Evie needed her the most . . . frankly, it was killing her.

She glanced down at her arms, which were still bandaged from where she'd cut them. She could feel the sting of the deep wounds rubbing against the material of the dressing, and although it hurt, she was grateful for the pain, anything to help distract her from the waking nightmare she seemed to be living in.

She'd wanted to speak to Steph. She was always good at listening and giving advice, but when she'd approached her yesterday, she'd had her head bitten off. Of course, Steph had apologized, but she'd backed off from speaking about it to her.

The problem was, there were a lot of women in here whose kids at one time or another had run away from home, or from foster care. Sadly, it was nothing unusual. But she knew, she knew in her gut, her Evie wouldn't run away. No matter how much she hated her old man and her aunt, there was no way Evie would just get up and go without a word. No, something had happened to Evie. Call it a mother's intuition, but whether other people believed it or not, she was in no doubt.

'Being a Billy No-Mates, that's a bit unsocial of you, isn't it? What happened to all those cows you usually hang around with? Abandoned you, have they?' Tess stood at the door of Lynette's cell before walking in and closing the thick metal door behind her. 'Oh, you don't mind if I come in, do you? No, that's what I thought.' She laughed.

Lynette stared at Tess, but she didn't have the energy to object.

Tess plonked herself on Lynette's bed, tapping it. She grinned. 'Come on, pet, come and sit down next to us.'

'What do you want, Tess? I'm not in the mood for talking.'

'Well, it's a good job I am then . . . Come on, I don't bite . . . well, I do, but who's splitting hairs.' She roared with laughter and Lynette begrudgingly sat down. It was easier to comply. She knew that Tess enjoyed games, so her refusing wouldn't put her off, it would just encourage her to stay longer. And all she wanted was to be left alone so she could think about Evie and what she was going to do. The powerlessness of being in here at times like this was unbearable.

'I heard what happened to Evie. It's terrible.'

Lynette jumped up off the bed, stumbling back. Tears burned her face as she pointed at Tess, her voice raised in hysteria. 'Don't you go near that, don't you dare start talking about my Evie. She's off limits, you hear me? Completely off fucking limits.'

Tess stood up; her stare hardened. She stepped towards Lynette. 'Howay, what do you take us for, a monster?' She winked. 'And if you must know, I actually came here to make sure you're all right.' She moved away and walked about the cell. Then she stopped at a photo on the wall. 'She's a pretty thing, isn't she?' Tess stared at the picture of Evie.

'I don't know what sick game you're playing, but I'd rather you went.'

Tess glanced at her. 'That's not very nice, especially as I've been thinking about you. I thought you might need a bit of friendship.'

Lynette shook her head. 'Just stop it! Stop it! I need you to go!' She began to cry again, hating that she was breaking down in front of Tess.

'That's it, man, let it all out, don't bottle it up.' Tess grinned as she towered over Lynette, then she opened her clenched fist. 'See, I told you I was thinking of you.'

Lynette stared at the wrap of heroin in Tess's hand. She shook her head. 'I don't take that crap.'

'I know, pet, but sometimes there are circumstances where we need to rethink things, be kind to ourselves. No one would blame you; we all have to have an outlet from time to time, love.' Tess gently lifted Lynette's arm and stared at the bandages. 'That looks nasty. I hear you've done yourself some real damage this time around . . . You've got to be careful to keep it clean, you don't want to get that sepsis shit. I knew someone once who cut herself on a paperclip; next thing you know, she was in hospital getting both her arms and legs removed. After I heard that, I stuck to fucking Pritt stick . . . Point is, there are easier ways to lessen the pain, Lynn. You don't have to gouge out your arm, love.' She shook the wrap of heroin in front of Lynette's face. 'Go on, pet, take it. My treat. No one deserves to go through what you're going through.'

Lynette stared at it. 'I . . . I . . .'

'I get it. You've never taken it before. It's not your thing, I understand.' Tess smiled widely, and Lynette could smell her breath: a mix of egg and unbrushed teeth. 'But then you've never had a missing daughter before, have you?'

The tears continued to pour down Lynette's cheeks and she shook her head, trembling more than ever.

'I don't know how you do it, Lynn,' Tess continued. 'How do you even get through another day knowing that you're stuck in here when your precious Evie is out there somewhere? It's not right . . . Go on, love, give yourself a break, you look like you need a bit of kip. It'll help you forget about things for a bit.'

Lynette held Tess's stare, then slowly she reached out and took it from her hand. 'Just this once though, Tess, cos you're right, I'm so tired, and I don't want to think anymore. I want to forget, just for a little bit.'

Tess chuckled, then she reached into her other pocket and pulled out a syringe. 'Then I'm happy to oblige . . . You need some help with it? Though I'm sure you've seen it done enough times in this place.'

'I'm fine.'

Tess nodded and turned to go but at the cell door, she hesitated. 'And if you like it, there's plenty more where that came from, Lynn. If you want some more, just let me know. But that one's free, on the house. I like to look after my customers, especially when they're first-timers.' She winked. 'Enjoy, love. And let me tell you, in times like these, I swear, that little wrap you've got in your hands really will be the best friendship you've ever had.'

25

EVIE

'Hello! You've got to let me out! Let me out! You've got no right! *Hello!*' Evie screamed through the locked door, banging on it with her fists. 'Hello? Is anyone there? Hello? Please, please just let me out . . . I want to go home. *Please.*' She screamed again but, feeling her throat becoming sore after shouting for the past hour or so, she rested her head against the door, breathing hard as she closed her eyes.

But she didn't cry; it felt like she was all out of tears. And the fear she'd originally felt when she'd first been locked up seemed to have faded and been replaced with a cold numbness, like she was disjointed from her body, trapped inside her own head and all she could hear was the sound of her own screaming.

The only thing she wanted to do was call her mum, speak to her, get a hug, tell her how much she loved her. She *needed* to hear her mum's voice, and the idea of never being able to again caused an icy terror to sit in the pit of her stomach.

Rubbing her hands and seeing the redness on them from where she'd been banging on the door, Evie thought back. How could she have been so stupid? How could she have thought that she was anything special to him? She'd acted like a lovesick schoolgirl. *No*, she *had* been a lovesick schoolgirl, and before she knew it, everything had spiralled out of control.

Thinking about it now, there'd been so many red flags that she'd just ignored. She'd been looking down a tunnel and hadn't been able to see anything other than what she'd wanted to see.

She'd shut out everybody and become secretive, thinking that she was protecting something precious, something romantic, something only she had. And right now, that was probably one of the biggest mistakes she'd made, because no one knew about *him*, so no one would know where to look for her.

She was the biggest joke, not just to him but to herself. A cliché. Falling for someone who had no intention of falling for her. She'd read about stuff like this in magazines, watched stuff like this on TV, girls getting caught up in things, just like this, and she'd always thought them stupid. She could even remember when she'd sat eating snacks and shouting at the television, shouting at the documentary, wondering how any girl could be so stupid as to fall for the charms of a man who would ultimately take her prisoner . . . or do something worse still. And now she was *that* girl.

At the sound of the door being unlocked, Evie forced herself to focus. She heard the key and the bolts being slid back . . . And then, there he was, smiling at her as if he'd come to pick her up for a first date: Ollie Jones, looking as cool and as handsome as ever. 'Hello, sweetheart, everything all right?'

'I want to go home,' she screamed. 'I want to fucking go home, this is sick, you can't just leave me locked up in here forever.'

'At least that's something we agree on, but the problem is, what do we do with you? Though I know what I'd like to do.' He winked suggestively.

She flew at him, her long nails scratching at his face as she flayed her arms about.

'Fucking hell, you stupid bitch!' Ollie held his hand over his cheek, the blood trickling through his fingers. He glared at her. 'Now that was a stupid fucking thing to do, wasn't it?' He slapped her hard and she went flying, crashing down backwards onto the floor.

The sound from the open-palmed slap rang in her ears and the sting on her cheek burnt. 'I hate you! I *hate you*!' she screamed at him, tasting her own tears.

'I can't say, right now, that the feeling ain't mutual. Jesus Christ, you're like an alley cat.' He touched his face again.

Evie stared at him as she sat on the floor weeping. How could she ever have thought that Ollie had liked her? He'd been charming at the prison gates, flirting with her while she'd flirted back. He'd even given her a few lifts to Streatham, even though South London was completely out of his way, and she had genuinely thought that he had liked her. She had stuck up her nose when Iris and Mina, and that bitch Roz, had seen her giggling with him, because she'd thought she'd bagged herself something special, something they didn't have. God, how stupid was she? And on her birthday, a couple of months ago, he'd bought her a present, a cute dusty pink Gucci purse.

Then things had got complicated . . . After she'd given him a blow job, and after she'd slept with him, things had taken a messy turn. Ollie had been all she could think of, and stupidly, she thought of him as her boyfriend. God, she knew now how crazy that seemed, but he had made her think that she was something special. And now, although it was too late for hindsight, she could understand part of the reason why she'd fallen for him so hard: she'd been missing her mum, who'd always been her best friend.

Her mum being sent down had come as a knock for her, and she'd sunk into a bit of depression, getting low marks at school and shutting herself away in her room, though that was partly down to her auntie moving in and shacking up with her stepdad. But she guessed none of that mattered now.

'Why are you doing this to me?' She stared at him, her eyes full of tears.

'I'm not doing anything to you, darlin'. You've done this all yourself.'

Evie could hear her voice becoming hysterical. 'How can you say that? You knew how I felt about you. And you used me.'

'Used you?' Ollie roared with laughter at the same time as he dabbed his cheek with a tissue. 'You make it sound like you and me had something special. You were nothing to me, sweetheart. I mean, let's face it, if it wasn't for all this shit that's gone on, I wouldn't remember you from Adam. Your pussy was no different to any other cheap little whore's. What made you think you were any different? You couldn't have whipped your knickers off faster if you'd tried. All you were to me was a bit of a distraction, a bunk-up, so don't flatter yourself. But then you had to go and threaten me . . . And that wasn't very nice, was it?'

Evie began to cry harder. Iris had warned her about Ollie, but she hadn't listened, in fact, she'd been an outright bitch to her when she'd tried to warn her off him. She'd thought Iris was jealous of the attention he was giving her, but clearly that couldn't have been further from the truth. What a joke. And then they'd had an argument, and after that, her and Iris hadn't bothered talking. They'd just blanked each other.

'I don't know what I saw in you.'

He winked at her again. 'We both know that ain't true. You were gagging for it . . .' He trailed off and tilted his head. 'Maybe you're still gagging for it? What do you say, Evie, for old times' sake?' He walked towards her, and she scrambled up onto her feet.

'Keep away from me, you understand? Just stay away from me.'

He shrugged. 'That's not what you were saying before. You couldn't get enough of me.'

'I'm warning you.' She banged into the wall behind her as he moved nearer, his body inches away from hers.

'Stop trying to resist, Evie.' He reached out and grabbed her, bringing her close into him. She struggled but his strength overwhelmed her.

Laughing, Ollie kissed her, but she snapped at his lip, bringing her teeth down on his mouth. 'Fuck!' He let her go, licking his lip and pushing her back hard, causing Evie to slide down the wall in tears. 'You ain't worth it, darlin'.' He sniffed indignantly. 'But suit yourself, I don't need to fight for pussy, especially one I've already rinsed out.'

Evie could feel herself trembling. She had no idea what was going to happen to her, or how far Ollie would go to keep her quiet. Though maybe these past few weeks were just a way of frightening her so she'd keep her mouth closed. But then, she'd seen what had happened to Pippa, hadn't she?

Pippa had tried to run away on two occasions that she knew of. She heard the conversations, the shouting. The first time, she'd watched through the keyhole as they'd dragged her back, kicking and screaming. She'd also seen the damage they did, knocking the girl about. Terrified, Pippa had broken down, begging them to stop. Then, yesterday, she'd made a second attempt to escape. And Evie had watched through the keyhole as they dragged Pippa's lifeless body from the filming room.

Breathing deeply, trying not to let panic get the better of her, Evie fought to shut the image out of her mind. Maybe . . . maybe Pippa was all right, maybe they'd only knocked her unconscious, and she'd blacked out, and that was as bad as it had got for her. And right now, Pippa was back home and was absolutely fine. Yeah, yeah, that was what she was going to think, because she didn't have any actual proof that Pippa was dead, did she? So why was she trying to frighten herself by thinking that?

Rubbing the middle of her chest, focused on calming her breathing, Evie pushed away any other thoughts about Pippa. 'Just let me go home. It'll be the last time you hear from me, I promise. I won't make any agg for you, I won't even tell my mum.

I'll say I ran off cos I was upset about her being banged up . . . Please, *Ollie.*'

He smirked and she watched the trickle of blood dry on his cheek. She didn't know how long she'd been locked up in the basement. All she knew was the house she was in was a large sprawling property in the middle of the woods, miles from anywhere.

Ollie went to open his mouth but, as he did, Evie heard footsteps coming from the main filming room. The next thing she knew, she heard a voice which sent shivers down her. 'What the fuck is happening here? Why is she in that state, and what the hell have you done to your face?' Martha stood at the door dressed head to toe in black, firing questions at Ollie. Then she glared at Evie, her features tight and fierce, the effect exaggerated by the way she wore her hair scraped back into a tight bun. 'I hope you ain't been messing around with her again – it's your dick that got us into this trouble in the first place.'

'I'm not a fucking kid,' Ollie snapped at Martha as Evie looked on. Although she'd only spoken to Martha the one time, the time that Ollie had brought her here, Evie knew that out of the two of them, Martha was by far the worst, the most brutal. She had been the main perpetrator when she'd watched them give Pippa a kicking, and she was the one who made all the decisions. 'So, I'd appreciate it if you didn't talk to me like a cunt.'

Martha spun around and stared at Ollie. 'Maybe if you didn't act like one, I wouldn't have to.' She reached up and touched Ollie's scratched face, shaking her head. 'You're a fucking idiot,' was all she said before turning back to Evie. 'This is a mess.' The comment was to Ollie, but her stare continued to be locked on Evie.

'I want to go home, you've no right to keep me here!' Evie, against her better judgement, shouted at Martha.

'You're a feisty cow, ain't you.' It was a statement, not a question, as Martha walked across to where Evie was sitting on the floor.

Taking Evie's face in her hands, Martha squeezed it hard, and Evie could feel the pressure on her jaw. 'You're a little scrubber and you've caused us a lot of trouble. You never thought about how it was going to end, did you? You were way too quick to jump into bed with him, weren't you?' It was another statement and Evie could see the hatred burning from Martha's eyes.

'It wasn't like that.' Evie's voice was distorted as Martha continued to squeeze her face. 'I liked him. I thought he liked me.' Her tears dripped onto Martha's hand.

'Then not only are you a little scrubber, you're a stupid one as well, ain't you? I could just about stomach that, but why go and threaten him? Why be a stupid bitch and start talking about calling the police?' Martha dropped the grip on Evie's face, then, without warning, she slapped her hard across the face. Harder, more brutal than Ollie's slap. Then she stood and glanced over her shoulder at Ollie. 'You've made a right fuck-up. You're right, I can't see any other way: she'll have to stay here.'

Hearing those words, Evie leapt up. 'I'm not! I'm not staying.' She looked at Ollie and, weeping hysterically, she directed her words to him. 'Tell her, Ollie, tell her I won't be any trouble, please! You know I won't say nothing.'

Martha's voice was icy cold. 'Calm the fuck down . . . I *said*, calm down.' There was an underlying threat to her words.

'No, no, you ain't doing this to me.' She ran to Ollie and grabbed hold of him, begging and pleading. 'Help me, please help me.'

Martha spun her around and slammed her fist into the side of Evie's head.

Despite the pain and the room seeming to spin around her, she managed to keep her balance and jumped back to Ollie. 'Leave me alone – Ollie, tell her to leave me alone!'

'Do you see what you've done, now?' Martha spat her words at Ollie. 'Shut her up.'

'No, you ain't shutting me up, I saw what happened to Pippa, I saw what that guy did . . . And I saw what you did to that other girl right at the beginning when I was waiting for Ollie in the car.'

Martha stared at her. She laughed nastily. 'See, right there, darlin', was your chance to say nothing, pretend that you never saw a thing, pretend you'd forgotten about that night which got you into trouble in the first place . . . So the thing is, if I was ever going to let you go, how could I now? How could I even think about it, knowing you clocked on about Pippa? Don't look at me like that, don't try playing the victim. This whole thing is down to you. The only person you've got to blame, Evie, is yourself . . . You stupid, stupid, cow. There's absolutely no going back now.'

Ollie and Martha began to walk out of the room, locking the door behind them.

Panicked, Evie banged on it. 'No, don't leave me here, please, don't . . . My mum will be worried, she'll be going crazy not hearing from me. Please, please, come back.' Her words rushed out in a jumble of tears as she collapsed on the floor screaming . . .

26

STEPH

Still lying on her bed staring up at the ceiling, Steph sighed to herself. The noise of Ashcroft kept penetrating her thoughts. She'd wanted to get away from everything on the wing, and shutting herself in her cell on her own had been the nearest thing to that. Her head was swimming with thoughts of Iris, imagining all the horrific things she'd been through. But it was also filled with thoughts of Amy and Tess, which fed the anger she was already feeling towards Iris's abusers. And the other pain she felt in her heart was for Lynette, Lynette and Evie, and how guilty she felt for leaving her friend to get on with it.

She'd listened to the wailing on the other side of her cell wall last night and ignored it, and she'd noted this morning that Lynette hadn't bothered coming to breakfast. Even if the women didn't eat anything from the total crap they liked to serve up here in Ashcroft, they came for the morning chat, the morning banter to escape themselves. A night in the cell, especially if you were bunked up alone, like Lynette, was hard, so the morning chatter over a cup of tea helped them reset.

Her awareness of Lynette on the other side of the wall made it impossible to think. And as much as she tried to ignore the wails, like she had done last night, she couldn't. She'd already failed her daughter, failed as a mother, she certainly wasn't going to fail as a friend.

Sighing again, Steph sat up, swung her legs off the bed and stood. She yawned and rolled her neck to try to alleviate some of the tension built up, before walking across to the small kettle to make herself a coffee. Not because she wanted a drink, but because it put off having to go and do the thing she'd been dreading. Apart from it being triggering for her, Steph knew it was going to be terrible, worse than terrible.

At the best of times, a child going missing was excruciating, desperate, frightening for the mother. Being banged up behind Ashcroft's walls only added to the hell Lynette was already living in. For a start, what was there to say? What could anyone say to Lynette to ease her pain? It wasn't as if she could say, *It'll be fine, don't worry, they'll find her, we'll find her, why don't you go and check her friends, check the places she hangs out* . . . None of those were an option, so instead all she could do was go in there, hold Lynette's hand and sit and cry with her. Because, apart from the women in here, no one gave a damn. Not the prison officers, not the police – no one cared about Evie.

She watched the steam beginning to rise from the kettle, but then she shook her head. What the hell was she doing? Lynette needed her, not in ten minutes, not in an hour, not when she'd had a fucking cup of Nescafé, but right now. Because that's what got the women through the long days and months and years behind bars: the friendships, the togetherness, the bonds that acted like a life raft. Driven by that thought, Steph walked out of her cell to go and be with her friend.

'Lynn, Lynn, mind if I come in, darlin'?' Steph popped her head around Lynette's cell door. She glanced around, noticing how gloomy it was. Lynette had put a towel over the small, barred window, blocking out the sun.

'Lynn, you sleeping, babe? I can come back later if you want?' There was no reply and Steph smiled as she looked at Lynette crashed out on the bed. It was probably exactly what she needed; she doubted that Lynette had caught any sleep last night.

She'd speak to her later and make sure that she was properly there for her this time. Turning to go, Steph was about to walk away, but then something made her stop. She frowned and peered into the cell again before she found herself walking in completely.

She pulled off the towel over the window, then turned to Lynette.

'Lynn? Lynn? Lynn?' Moving over towards her, Steph leaned over her. 'Come on, Sleeping Beauty, what's going on?' Once more she frowned, then she let out a piercing scream, 'Oh my God, no! Lynn! No! Shit! Fuck, you stupid cow, what have you done, no, baby, *please*, Lynn!'

She pulled the needle which was sticking out of Lynette's arm and slammed the red emergency button, before picking Lynette up in her arms, cradling her, watching as green vomit trickled out the side of her mouth. 'Can somebody come and help, please!' she screamed as loud as she could, but then brought her voice down to a murmur: 'Lynn, you can't do this. Lynn, you've got to wake up, darlin'. Baby, why didn't you come to me, you didn't need that shit, Lynn. Please. Just open your eyes.'

At that moment Amy and Maureen and Ness appeared at the door, along with some of the other women in D wing. 'Oh fuck! Oh Jesus Christ!' Ness whispered, but it was loud enough for the others to hear.

'Help! We need help in here!' Maureen shrieked behind her as she came rushing over to Lynette.

'She's smacked up, she's fucking OD'd, Reenie!' Steph spoke to Maureen as she gently shook Lynette, her heading lolling back and forth. 'Wake up, Lynn! Wake the fuck up! Come on, come on, don't do this to us. Lynn, Evie needs you, come on, babe. Fight, sweetheart, fight it!'

'Out of the way!' Three prison officers entered the room. 'Out! Get out! We'll sort it from here.'

As Steph shook her head, the tallest prison officer began radioing for help. 'No, we ain't going anywhere.' Steph stared at them, panic rushing through her. There was no way she was going to leave Lynette. 'We've got to stay with her. She needs us.'

'Stephanie, I'm not going to tell you again: move out, all of you. This won't help her.'

'I said, fucking no!' Steph, having gently laid Lynette back down on the bed, screamed at the top of her voice and stepped towards the officer aggressively, causing him to flick out his baton.

'Stay where you are, Steph . . . I said, stay where you are. I won't tell you again.'

Maureen and Ness pulled on Steph's arm. 'Give them space, Steph, give them space.' Maureen's voice cracked and Steph glanced at them both, but eventually she nodded and, without saying another word, she moved out of the cell as another two prison officers came running in with the resuscitation equipment.

As the women walked out, the officers closed the cell door, but not before Steph had seen them take out the Naloxone, the emergency antidote for an opiate overdose.

She stood in the corridor shaking. 'I let her down, Reenie. I should've made sure she was all right. I just couldn't fucking deal with it last night – I know I was being selfish, but I had my own shit in my head. I should've gone to her before lock-up, instead I put a fucking pillow over my head to drown out her crying. Same thing this morning . . . *Fuck*.'

Steph put her hands on her head, fighting back the tears. She had known Lynn needed someone, they had all seen her struggling, cutting herself and sinking into a depression. So as much as she wished Lynette banging up gear had come as a total surprise, it hadn't. The only thing she was pleased about was the fact that Lynn hadn't put a noose around her neck instead.

'It wasn't your fault, babe.' Ness swiped away her own tears. 'I didn't even know she took gear. She was a cutter, not a bag head.'

'Yeah, she was, until a certain person went and gave her it, and there's no prizes for guessing who that is. It can only be one person.' Steph turned to stare at Tess, who was over the other side chatting to some of the women who always hung around her.

'You reckon she's going to die?' Ness asked.

'How the fuck do I know?' Steph snapped, though she knew it was only because she was scared for Lynette. In her time, she'd seen a lot of people overdosing; she'd also seen a lot of people dying. She only hoped that if they did manage to bring her through, she didn't have brain damage, because who knew how long ago she'd fallen into unconsciousness.

'How long do you think she was out of it for?' Maureen asked. 'I never saw her at breakfast, I only hope to God that it wasn't last night that she took it.'

Steph shrugged. 'I was just thinking the same thing. Say a prayer for her, Reenie, cos she'll need all the help she can get.'

Maureen nodded and gently squeezed Steph's hand.

'She looked so bad though, I thought she wasn't breathing,' Ness continued. 'Maybe she wasn't.' Her eyes widened.

'Can you just shut the fuck up – how is this helping?' Steph glared at Ness, then, catching a group of D wingers staring over at them, she hollered angrily, 'Can I help you? What, have you suddenly got some business over here? No, I thought not, so piss off and stick your noses somewhere else.'

Breathing heavily, Steph turned her back on them. It was only natural when something happened for the women to stand about watching, because even though not all the women talked to each other, the atmosphere, the vibe, any fights, any trouble . . . any deaths, affected everyone in their own way.

'It's terrible. God, poor cow.' Amy looked just as upset as Ness. 'I feel so bad, it's the worst thing that could've happened.'

Steph pushed Amy hard in her chest, causing her to take a step back. 'Is it? Really? Are you sure about that?'

'What the fuck are you talking about?' Amy sounded shocked. 'Of course, this is terrible. It's fucking awful.'

Steph licked her lips in irritation, she could feel her temper rising. 'If this is to do with you and the crap that you've been bringing in—'

'Don't fucking put this on me, don't use this as an excuse to have a go at me. This has nothing to do with me.'

Steph shook her head. 'And why don't I believe that? You're a shady bitch, everyone in here knows that.'

'Back off, OK, Steph.' Amy's eyes flashed in anger. She pushed her hair from her eyes and glared. 'Lynn's just as much a friend to me as she is to you. I can't even bear to think of her in such pain and in such a state, and I'll be gutted, *properly* gutted if anything happens to her.'

'*If* something's happened? Something's *already* happened to her, you stupid bitch! She's hanging on to life by a fucking thread! How much more of a *something* do you want?' Steph screamed in Amy's face.

But before Amy had time to say anything, Tess shouted over, a grin on her face.

'Problem with your mate, love?' Tess laughed.

'I'm going to kill you!' Steph screamed at her and began to run over as Maureen tried to grab her, but she darted past and flew at Tess, taking out the home blade that she always carried on her.

She slashed the blade at Tess's face, nicking her slightly on her cheek before Tess managed to grab Steph in a headlock, twisting her into a neck hold as Maureen tried to pull her off. The hold was too strong, and Steph could feel the air being cut off and she struggled to breathe as her windpipe began to crush. But then a flash of Iris came into her head, and she felt the anger rise up in her. And with the anger came a renewed strength. A renewed determination.

She turned her head slightly and sank her teeth into Tess's fleshy arm.

Tess yelped and instinctively released her hold, allowing Steph to twist out of the grip. 'You stupid bitch!'

'Go to fuck, Tess,' Steph snarled back.

The atmosphere was tense now, and as the other women stood looking on, for once not goading or calling out anyone, Earle came hurrying down from the far end of the wing. 'What the hell's going on?'

'She just leapt on me,' Tess smirked.

'That's not what happened, sir.' Steph glanced at Earle. 'Ask anyone, I was just here minding my own business,' she panted, shaking her head. She knew that what she'd done so publicly was a challenge for top dog. There was no backing out now.

Earle looked at Steph and then at Tess. 'I think you both need to go down to seg. Now move it.'

'I already told you, it wasn't me,' Tess said calmly. 'I'm the victim here.'

Earle's face screwed up. 'I won't tell you again, Tess. Start walking.'

Tess grinned at him maniacally, crossing her arms. 'No. You don't tell me what to do, *Tone*. Haven't we had these little talks before?'

Steph stared on, curiosity building in her.

Earle flushed. 'Be quiet, Tess, and start walking.'

'Aren't you going to do anything about her? You should be locking her up, not going after me.' Tess's eyes flashed with anger. 'Everyone around here knows she's always up for a fight, man. So how come all of a sudden I'm getting the blame?'

'Tess, I haven't got time for this nonsense. So, I won't tell you again: *move it.*'

Tess stepped towards Earle, and it was clear to Steph who had the upper hand.

'Are you sure you want to annoy me? Do you really want me to start opening my mouth? After all, I know a lot about you, don't I?' She roared with laughter.

Earle was looking distinctly uncomfortable. 'Stop talking crap, Tess.'

'Oh, crap, is it? Are you sure about that, Mr Earle? Why don't we test that theory – let's see what the women have to say, shall we? Though, of course, Amy knows all about it already. Don't you, pet!' She winked across at Amy and, as Steph and the other women glared at her, Amy turned as red as Earle.

'Just get back in your cells then. *Now,*' Earle mumbled, humiliated.

And as Steph made her way back to her cell, watching as they stretchered Lynette away, she didn't need any more proof to know that Amy was up to her neck in it with Tess. She hadn't seen it, even though it was clearly happening right under her nose, and she hadn't seen what was happening to Iris either. But now she did know. And just like Iris's abusers were going to pay for what they did, so was Amy.

27

OLLIE

It was late Friday night and Ollie sat with Martha in Fat Eddie's office above his members-only club which looked out over Hyde Park. The air was thick with smoke and Eddie's desk was covered in takeaway cartons, an empty bottle of JD and several lines of coke which, for once, he'd declined to take part in: his thoughts were already a mess. The situation he'd got himself in was, to put it bluntly, pretty shit.

His mind kept wandering from the crap that Eddie was chatting about to Evie. How the fuck had he got himself in such a mess? He knew he should have left well alone, but she'd been giving him the eye from the first time he'd seen her at the prison gates, clearly gagging for it.

What was he supposed to do? He was a full-blooded male and she, Little Miss Come On, was putting it on a plate for him. No man he knew would say no, but he'd thought he could just fuck her and dump. Sadly, it hadn't turned out like that, to put it mildly. Because now it was a frigging nightmare.

He should never have taken her to the place in the country, but Jesus, it was only because he knew he had a busy week in front of him that he'd gone there at all. Rather than make another trip to the country the next day, which would've taken him a good couple of hours there and back, he'd decided to take a detour.

It was innocent enough at the time; they'd been passing on the way back from the outing he'd taken her on. He'd bought her a few bits to keep her sweet – it was amazing how a couple of designer tops would make a woman work harder when they were on their knees, more eager to please. So, at the time it made sense. Stop off at the house, save time. Five minutes, that's all he'd needed. And he'd truly thought Evie was asleep in the car. How the fuck was he supposed to know that she'd wake up and panic, wondering where she was, where he was, and come looking for him. Even then, it might have been all right if it wasn't for one of the stupid whores that worked for him. She'd been bang on the gear, and had started to cluck, so of course he'd had to calm her down, show her who was boss, slap her about a bit. Normal stuff.

But then Evie had found them. And by that time, the stupid whore was covered in blood, *and* naked. She'd seen Evie, and had started screaming for help, for Evie to help her. Then the shit had hit the fan. Evie had panicked, tried to run off, he'd grabbed her and then she'd started to threaten him with the police.

He'd tried to calm her down, sitting her in the kitchen, giving her the old charm offensive, but she'd tried to run away again, and then one thing had led to another, she'd started screaming again. He'd only slapped her a little, trying to bring her back to her senses. And OK, maybe looking back he'd gone in a little too hard, cos she'd blacked out. So he'd done what he'd thought was best: put her in one of the rooms the girls who worked for him stayed in, but every time he went to try to talk to her when she'd come around, she'd either been hysterical or threatening to tell the Old Bill.

And then Martha had got involved. Soon as she'd found out about Evie, the shit really hit the fan. He knew then there was no going back for Evie. It was fucked up.

'Am I boring you? Oi, Ollie! I said, *am I boring you*, cos each time I've looked at you, you're staring out the window, mouth open, looking like a gormless fucking cunt watching a peep show,' Fat Eddie snarled at Ollie.

Ollie blinked, and stared at Eddie, wanting to say yes, yes, there wasn't anyone more of a boring cunt that he knew than Fat Eddie. He reckoned even if Eddie were covered head to toe in diamonds, somehow he'd still manage to take the shine off and make them look fucking dull. But he didn't say that. Instead he winked and chuckled, 'You, boring? Come off it, Eddie. You're the fucking life and soul of the party, everyone knows that . . . I'm sorry, mate, I've just got my head on a few other matters. What were you saying?'

Martha gave him a cold stare which he returned just as coldly. The last thing he needed was her on his back. Ever since the mess with Evie, she'd been chewing his ear off more than normal, which made it harder to think of a way out of this mess. He knew what Martha's take was on it: shut her up permanently. He didn't want that, but if he didn't come up with anything better, and fast, it was looking more likely than not that Evie was on a one-way ticket out of here.

A naked girl, no older than seventeen, eighteen, draped herself on Eddie's lap. His face was round and sweaty: Fat Eddie was no picture of health: there was a waxy pallor about his skin and, looking at him now, Ollie reckoned he was a heart attack waiting to happen.

'I was saying, I ain't happy with what happened to Pippa . . .' Eddie sniffed, then he glanced at the girl sitting on his knee, and with a look of disinterest, he shoved her off and onto the floor, not missing a beat as he spoke. 'OK, I wouldn't be crying at her funeral, and I ain't saying that I would've wanted the little whore back working here again, but this ain't good for business. And I don't want any comeback. I don't want a trail back to me if the Old Bill started sniffing around.'

'Ain't no one going to miss her,' Ollie said, at the same time thinking about Evie. The problem there was, she had people who *would* miss her, had already started to. Another reason why the situation needed to be sorted as soon as possible.

'What happened is too risky: you've got to be able to see that.'

'It was a mistake, these things happen,' Ollie snapped.

Eddie shook his head and his finger at the same time. 'Do me a favour, Ollie. A mistake is putting too many sugars in me fucking coffee, or forgetting to buy the frigging bog roll, a mistake ain't breaking a bird's neck and mauling her all over like a fucking dog . . . I saw the tape of it – why did you let him film it?'

'We didn't.' Martha's voice cut through the air. Her tone harsh.

Ollie touched the scratch on his face from Evie's nails as he watched Eddie lean forward, narrowing his gaze as he stared at Martha. 'What do you mean, you didn't? I saw the footage.'

'That's not the same as us *letting* him film it. We didn't know what he was going to do. I'm not sure he knew himself. Got carried away, I guess. These things happen.' She laughed coldly. 'My point is, *Eddie*, the reason we can charge the punters so much is because they can have fun with the girls, do what they like, no boundaries, and then they get to take away a home movie of them doing it. Relive the experience anytime they want . . . And it makes them want to come back for more.' She smiled and even Ollie thought how dark and sinister she looked, her shrewish, sharp-angled features emphasized by the dim light. 'We can't pick and choose who can film stuff. The filming is what makes our package so attractive.'

Eddie lit a cigar, sucking on it vigorously to get it burning. He blew out the smoke. 'The girl's dead, she's pushing up daisies, or being nibbled by the fishes at the bottom of the Thames or wherever it was old Ollie here put her, and you, Martha, sound like you're talking about an advertising campaign for fucking sausage rolls.'

'And you sound like a pussy.'

Eddie pushed himself up out of the chair, and instinctively Ollie jumped up as well, and it was only Martha who sat back casually smiling.

'Who do you think you are . . . I'd watch it if I were you, Martha.'

Martha tilted her head to one side and smiled again. 'Or what, Eddie? What are you going to do to me?'

He sneered. 'You're a hard fucking bitch.'

Martha nodded. 'Like I said to Ollie recently, I take that as a compliment. Now, what's your point, sweetheart?'

Eddie glanced at Ollie, who stood ready in case anything kicked off. Then he glanced at Martha and, looking defeated, he sat back down. 'Listen, I ain't asked you here to argue. All I'm saying is, it ain't good for business if the girls I sell and send to you, end up brown bread. Talk gets around, and some of the girls ain't keen to come to you guys in the first place. Most of the time, a bit of persuasion is needed – if you get my drift. Pippa being the prime example. She was a pain in the arse when she was here.'

Ollie agreed. 'Yeah, well she wasn't that much better with us. She tried to leg it a couple of times, ended up having to do a bit of the old Houdini with her, to keep her in place.'

'That's my point: we've got a good thing going on here. I provide you with my leftovers, the ones that have been rinsed through a bit too much, which is perfect for your little enterprise, cos you need girls that you can do what you want with. You pay me and we're all happy. So you see, it's in everyone's interest to have girls that *want* to come to you. They know it'll be a bit rough at times but, moneywise, it'll be worth it for them. The ones that ain't got no choice in coming to you, you don't want them to be difficult, fuck knows. And what happened to Pippa isn't great publicity. We ain't doing snuff movies, you know.'

Martha yawned widely, not bothering to cover her mouth. She stood and gestured with her head to Ollie that it was time to go. 'More's the pity – that's where the real money is. Still, beggars can't be choosers . . . So, is that all?' Her tone was full of disdain, and she turned to go but stopped as Eddie called to her.

'Did you know, Jack's back?'

'Jack?' She sounded puzzled.

Eddie nodded, looking solemn. 'Jack Walsh, I heard it through the Soho grapevine. He's hanging around with Rebel again. You know, the whore he used to be with, the one who killed his kid and fucked off with his best mate.'

'What does he want?' Martha pulled a face. 'Why's he back?'

'No one knows. Apparently, when Raymond spoke to him, he said he was only back for a bit of pleasure, he ain't interested in business anymore. Taken up the priesthood, would you believe! I suppose he'd done everything else. Even the devil needs a rest.' He laughed. 'I'm going to keep my head down for a while. Old wounds and all that. I've got enough shit going on without dealing with him.'

Martha looked scathing. 'Yeah, that's because you owe him money.'

Eddie shrugged. 'Well, I was hardly going to track him down to a monastery to give him his drug money, was I?'

They laughed again.

'Was he with anyone else?'

'Why, are you worried? Worried he's come back to claim Soho as his?' Eddie let out a loud belch.

'Don't be stupid. You were the one who shat himself whenever Jack was about. And it ain't me that owes him. I'm curious, that's all.'

Ollie looked at Martha, shrugged. 'Who's this Jack?'

'He was around before you moved to Soho, though I'm

surprised you ain't heard of him. He was a face, number one face, and he was ruthless in his time.'

Ollie smirked. 'I'm not sure he'll make me quake in me boots. What's he going to do, set the three wise men on me?'

'That's what a lot of people said. But he was one of the untouchables. He'd kill you before you had a chance to open your mouth . . . Believe me, whether or not he's wearing a cross around his neck, Jack Walsh is no angel.'

28

EXERCISE YARD

It had been four days and four nights of twenty-three-hour lock-up on the wing, a punishment for the incident with Lynette, but finally the women were able to see each other.

'Can you believe that they've cancelled our fucking visits?' Ness stalked over to where Maureen and Steph were standing. 'I've just heard Earle tell some of the others. It's a fucking disgrace, that means I won't be able to see Mina today.' She nibbled on her nails. 'I left a message; I just hope she gets it. I don't want her turning up at the gates and then being told she needs to go home.'

Steph nodded. 'I was hoping to see Iris today. I needed to talk to her, I wanted to . . .' But she trailed off, chewing on her lips, feeling the tears beginning to fall again. Then, taking a deep breath, she attempted a smile. 'Anyway, has anyone heard anything about Lynette, and Evie for that matter?'

Maureen shook her head and without asking what was wrong, she took Steph's hand in hers. 'The police are hopeless. I think they've probably stopped looking for Evie before they even started.'

Ness rubbed her stomach as she sat on the bench, the morning sun beating down on her back. 'I asked Mina if she'd heard from her, or knew where she hung out, but they weren't really close. Not like with Iris.' She smiled at Steph.

'Yeah, at least they've got each other. That's something, ain't it?' Steph said, sounding listless.

'It's so hard being a mum inside. All you do is worry,' Ness said quietly.

A small, older woman walked across to them.

'Thought you'd like to know: I've just heard that Lynette's still unconscious. It's not looking good.'

'Jesus, if anything happened to her . . .' Maureen shook her head but didn't say anything else, instead she closed her eyes, strain showing on her face.

'Thanks, Babs, really appreciate you letting us know.'

'Sorry it wasn't better news.'

Ness nodded to the woman, who walked away looking downcast. Leaning back on the bench, Ness sniffed, her tone suddenly darker. 'That Tess needs to get what's coming to her. Most of the women had a lot of time for Lynette, so they won't be happy.' She glanced at Steph. 'The sooner you bring her down, the better. Apart from the junkies, everyone will be behind you, I'm sure of it. I can speak to people if you want me to, and I'm sure you'll be able to rally some of the women, won't you, Reenie?'

'Just give me the word. I want her to fall off her perch as much as everyone else does,' Maureen agreed.

As they were talking, Steph nodded to Earle and got a discreet nod in return as he walked into the exercise yard. 'Thank you, Reenie. And who knows what other help we may get with knocking her off her perch once and for all.'

Maureen and Ness gave her a strange look, but they didn't say anything as Steph continued to talk. 'But before that, we need to make sure a certain other person gets their comeuppance.'

'What are you on about?' Ness asked, swiping away a fly.

'Oh, not this again.' Maureen sounded worried. 'Tell me you're not talking about Amy.'

Steph's face darkened. 'Yeah, I am. She's leaving tomorrow,

and there's no way she's going to walk out of here without getting what's coming to her.'

Ness pulled a face, but she said nothing.

'She's part of what happened to Lynn, and I've already had a quick chat with some of the women this morning at breakfast. Let me tell you, they are *so* up for it. I'm done with letting people take advantage of women who can't stand up for themselves. And now she's got me to answer to. I'm going to give her a lesson she won't forget. She's had this coming for a long time.'

'What's going on with you, Steph?' Maureen asked. 'This isn't right.'

Steph shook her head, hating the fact that she could feel the tears beginning to sting. In that moment it was all she could do to bite back her anger at Maureen for defending the bitch. She couldn't help it. Her emotions were all over the place: she'd never felt so helpless and scared in her entire life. 'You and me have never had a problem, Reenie, so let's not start now, yeah? Best keep your opinions to yourself.'

Ness stood up. 'Back off, Steph. Reenie's off limits, understand? You and I are friends, our girls are friends, but you start on Reenie and you start on me – and I ain't afraid of you. I'll take you on in my sleep, if I have to.' She glared at Steph, who stared back.

'Ness, it's fine, you don't have to defend me,' protested Reenie.

Not looking at her, still fixing Steph with a glare, Ness said, 'You're right, I don't have to, Reenie, but I want to. You're the nearest I've ever had to a proper mum, and I won't let her throw her weight about and disrespect you like that.'

Maureen gave Ness an appreciative smile.

'Well?' Ness said. 'I'm waiting . . . Apologize to her, or you and me are going to fall out badly. And I don't want that.'

It took a moment, but after a long sigh, Steph conceded. 'Look,

I shouldn't have said that. I'm sorry, Reenie . . . But Amy and I have history, you know that. She's sly. She's not to be trusted. She did what she did to me, then there's all that shit with her parole. I mean, you tell me what woman here wouldn't jump at the chance to get parole, especially when they've got a set-up like Amy. She ain't like old Mo or Betty who have nowhere to live after they leave here. For them, Ashcroft's a better bet than being on the streets, but for Amy, it's different. Yet each time she has an opportunity to get out, she fucks it up. And now, with what's happened to Lynette, she's due payback.'

'We're all supposed to be friends,' Maureen insisted.

Steph snorted. 'Friends? You may be, but I'm not. Not with her. Our friendship finished the day she backed Yvette. How can you call her your friend, anyway? She's not an open book like us. Friends aren't supposed to keep secrets from each other . . . well, not really.' Steph began fidgeting with her hands as she looked down at the ground uneasily while Maureen and Ness exchanged tight smiles.

There was silence and the only noise was the buzz of the exercise yard. The awkwardness sat in the air until Steph, changing the subject, said, 'Anyway, what did your solicitor say about trying to keep the baby here? Did he say you could appeal?'

Ness blew out her cheeks, tears welled in her eyes. 'It does my head in to even think about it. It's so fucked up. Time's running out and all they said was the same old shit: they're looking into it. I swear, half the women wouldn't be banged up if it wasn't for the crap solicitors we're all given. Sometimes I think they're dragging it out on purpose so there'll be no chance of me keeping him and he can be put up for adoption by some *nice* family.'

'Is there no one else you can ask? Like a relative or a family friend or something? That way, if they don't let you keep him here or move you to another prison, at least he can go and stay with them. It'll stop the adoption, won't it?'

'There's no one.' She wiped away her tears and Maureen held her hand.

As they continued to talk, a woman whose cell was on the landing above them walked up to Steph. After glancing around furtively, she slid something into her hand. 'Are we still on?'

Steph nodded and the woman hurried off without saying another word.

'What did she give you?' Ness stared at Steph. 'Steph, *what did she give you*?' she pushed some more.

Looking across to Deputy Earle, who was deep in conversation with the governor and a couple of the women from the wing, Steph slowly opened her hand.

'Oh my God, Steph, what's that for?' Maureen stared at the blade lying on the palm of her hand.

'I already told you.' Closing her fingers around it, she stared back at Maureen. 'Today, Amy gets what's coming to her.'

And from the far side of the yard, Tess looked on, delighted. She'd been watching the whole conversation, and she could see there was trouble in paradise. Her plan was working. There was no way she was going to give up her crown, and the threat from Steph was real. There were a lot of women who'd back her, unless of course the women were divided, and already she could see them parting like the Red Sea.

29

NESS

Walking into Amy's cell, Ness smiled. Her mind was full of all sorts of things. Lynette and Evie, for a start. She couldn't even imagine it if something happened to Mina. In all honesty, she probably would've done what Lynette did. It was horrible. And it was obvious that most people had put it down to a teenager running away. No one was going to look for her, apart from Reenie's friend, Jack. That was something, but she doubted it would be enough.

The whole of the wing had been affected. Even though the women were trying to put on a brave face, have a banter, keep each other's spirits up, it was hard to do. Every one of them knew that what had happened to Evie and Lynette could so easily happen to them, and that fear sat in the air like a bad smell.

She tried not to think about what Steph was planning either because, apart from anything else, she really liked Amy. But since she'd arrived in Ashcroft, she hadn't known a time when one of the women wasn't arranging the downfall of another. It seemed to be the favourite pastime. In prison, friendships were built and friendships were destroyed in the blink of an eye. And somehow, along the way, Steph had decided that Amy deserved *the treatment*, using Tess's accusation as an excuse.

She knew better than to try to persuade Steph not to go through with it. Chances were it'd only make her more determined, and as so many of the other women were involved, she knew she couldn't stop it. Nevertheless she had spoken to

Maureen about what they should do, though they both knew ratting out a fellow inmate wasn't really an option. And although it didn't sit well with her, the only thing she could do was hope. Hope that Steph would come to her senses before this evening.

'Hey, Amy, I ain't disturbing you, am I?' Ness spoke warmly as Amy – who was sitting on the bed – smiled back at her, her piercing green eyes lighting up.

'Hardly. You know one thing I won't miss about this place is the frigging boredom, you know? And the other thing I won't miss, is the way the same thought can go around and around in your head like it's on a loop. Too much time to think is not a good thing . . . You OK, darlin'?' Amy said, frowning. 'Is everything all right with Mina? I'm sorry you won't be able to see her today, I heard everyone's visits are cancelled: Earle told me before he pissed off home for the weekend . . . That guy is such a wanker, it's untrue.'

Ness sat on the bed. She grimaced as her baby kicked hard against her sides. 'I tell you what; this kid keeps me on the rails.' She breathed deeply, trying to get comfortable.

'How long have you got now?'

'About eight weeks, but I was a couple of weeks late with the other two, so—'

'. . . I thought you only had Mina?' Amy regarded her strangely.

Ness could feel herself blushing. She could kick herself. 'Yeah . . . yeah, I have . . . sorry, baby brain. My mind's mush! I don't even know how many kids I've got!' She laughed but it sounded hollow as it echoed around the cell.

Amy said nothing and the women fell silent for a moment before Ness asked, 'Didn't you ever want kids?'

And for a moment, Ness thought that Amy looked uneasy as she sighed. 'I guess I would've liked kids.'

Ness shrugged. 'It's not too late. How old are you? Thirty?'

'Thirty-three.'

'Same age as me . . . So, if you want kids, why not?'

Amy stood and went to grab the KitKat on the locker. 'It's different if you're on your own, but if you're with someone, that someone has to be right, don't they?' was all she said before shrugging.

'So, you're not planning on having kids anytime soon?'

Amy broke the KitKat in two, offering Ness the other half, which she took with a smile. 'No, I can't imagine that. Why all the questions?'

Ness's eyes filled with tears. 'I need your help.'

'Hun, what is it?' Amy, looking concerned, came and sat next to Ness again. 'Sure, whatever I can do, what's up? *Ness*?' Amy reached out and wiped the tears from Ness's eyes. 'What's going on, sweetheart? Why are you crying? Is it Tess? Steph?'

Ness shook her head.

'Hun, you've got to tell me if you want me to help you,' Amy urged.

Ness played with her hands on her lap, listening to the spring rain falling outside the cell.

'*Ness*?'

She looked at Amy, staring into her eyes again. Then she blurted out the words: 'I want you to take my baby. I want you to have him.'

Amy could only stare, aghast. 'I . . . Ness, I . . . I don't know what to say.'

'Just say yes. *Please*. Tell me that you'll have him.' She spoke faster as her emotions rushed out. 'I mean, not forever, but while I'm in here. It'd be perfect. You could have him until I'm out and . . . and then I could have him back. You could come and visit me with him . . . and when my sentence is up, I could earn money to pay you back. I mean, what's a few more blow jobs between friends?' She laughed again but then she grabbed Amy's hands tightly, squeezing her eyes shut as she pleaded, 'Please, please don't say no, please say anything but that.'

It was a few seconds before she dared open her eyes and, when she did, she could see the pity on Amy's face. 'Don't look at me like that. Don't look at me as if you're about to say something that's going to break my heart. Amy, Amy, just think about it. You're my last hope, cos it looks like the solicitor and that cunt of a governor won't pull their finger out to help me, and I ain't got anyone else I can ask.'

Amy began to shake her head. 'Ness, I—'

Ness let go of Amy's hands and she slammed her hand – not hard but quickly – over Amy's mouth. 'Don't say it! Don't say it, I can't hear you say it. Just think about it before you decide. I know it's a lot for me to ask, and I know that it's a lot of responsibility, but it won't be forever, and I don't want to sound like I'm taking the piss, but I know you've got money and a pukka place in Soho, so it's not like you'll be struggling.'

Amy blew out her cheeks, looking around the cell before returning her gaze to Ness. 'This is so out of the blue, Ness. It's like . . . I dunno, I—'

Ness interrupted. 'I know, I know, but like I say, he ain't due for another eight weeks, so we'll have time to sort it.'

Amy looked down. 'I'm sorry, Ness, I'd love to help you, but I can't.'

'Why not?' Ness could feel herself panicking. 'Why can't you? It's not like you're in here for a violent crime, is it? So, they'll let you. There's no reason why social services won't agree to it.'

'It's not that . . . It's my lifestyle. I, just can't.'

Ness bristled. 'Your *lifestyle*? I'm asking you to help me and stop my kid going into care, cos we both know what that's like, don't we? And you're talking about him getting in the way of you wining and frigging dining and having your nails done.'

Amy shook her head. 'That's not what I'm talking about. There are things that go on, that . . . Look, me and Ollie are . . .' She trailed off.

Even though she didn't want to, Ness could feel herself getting angry. 'You and Ollie, what?'

Amy stood up. 'Nothing, it doesn't matter . . . Look, I don't want to argue with you, Ness. But don't you see what you're asking me?'

'I know exactly what I'm asking, and what I'm asking is a big ask, but it ain't as big as me having to let him go forever. That's what you're really going to make me do?'

'Don't put this on me.' Amy turned away and began to walk out but Ness grabbed hold of her arm.

'Amy, I'm begging you.'

Amy shook her off and walked out into the communal area with Ness following her.

'Amy! Amy! Don't fucking walk away from me!' Ness was shaking and crying hard, at which point Tess called over from the communal chair she was slumped in as she stuffed her face with biscuits.

'Trouble in paradise again? This place is like a scene from *The Bold and the Beautiful.* Best front-row drama there is.'

'Shut the fuck up!' Ness snarled at her, which caused Tess to laugh out loud.

'Or what, Preggers? You going to sort me out?'

Glaring at her, Ness hissed, 'Yeah, if I have to, I will.'

Tess feigned biting her nails. 'Ooooh, I'm scared. Please, Vanessa, don't hurt me . . . *Muppet!*' Tess shouted the last word and Ness was torn between whether or not to continue the argument with Tess or go after Amy.

'We'll sort this out later!' Ness shouted, pointing a finger at Tess as she hurried after Amy.

'Well, you know where I am, pet!' Tess bellowed in raucous laughter.

'Amy! Amy!' Ignoring Tess now, Ness ran to where Amy was, running in front of her to block her way. 'Just wait.'

'Ness, you ain't going to change my mind. This is crazy, I'm sorry.'

The noise of the wing began to rise as the women made their way to the dining room for afternoon tea, something that only happened on a Saturday.

'You're not,' Ness growled. 'Cos if you were sorry, you'd say, yes. What's the big deal, it's not going to be forever, is it? I'm looking at a ten stretch, but if I behave myself, I could be out in, four, five years at the most.'

Amy looked bemused, but then her expression softened. 'Ness, I love you, but I can't, I can't for so many reasons, most of them you don't understand. I wish it was as simple as you're making out, but it's not.'

Unable to stop herself, Ness pushed Amy in the chest. 'No, cos you're not making it. But I suppose now you're leaving, I don't matter.'

'That's not true. Can't you hear yourself, Ness?'

'Yeah, I can, and what I hear is someone desperate – but not for myself. This ain't about me. It's about him.' She pointed at her stomach as she continued to cry. 'I fucked up, I have fucked up so many times in my life it's unbelievable, but I know it can be better this time around. I just know it. All I need is a chance . . . I need you to give *him* a chance.'

Amy moved her glance away. 'You're asking me for something I can't—'

Ness moved around to where Amy was staring. 'I've been looking out for you, sticking up for you, making sure you didn't get a good hiding from the other women when they thought you were too big for your fucking boots. Steph's always gunning for you, but it was me that calmed them down. Me, and all I'm asking is you return the favour.'

'It's hardly equal, is it?'

'What are you doing here?' Officer Barrett, a tall Asian officer in his late forties, walked towards them, interrupting the conversation. He stood in front of Amy. 'I've just asked you, what are you doing here?' His tone was sharp.

Amy frowned. Worked up after the conversation with Ness, she snapped back, 'Have you had a bang on your head? I ain't leaving until tomorrow.'

'Barrett was born with a bang on his frigging head,' Tess hollered, a large grin on her face.

Barrett scowled and whipped around. 'Enough of your lip, Tess, otherwise it'll be early lock-up for you.'

'Howay, man, haven't you heard of free speech?'

The officer didn't bother to respond, instead turning his attention back to Amy. 'Maureen said that you'd got a one to one with her in the chapel.'

'Me?' Amy looked surprised.

'Well, that's what she's just told me. She's in the chapel now.' Barrett frowned and suddenly regarded her suspiciously. 'She said she'd forgotten to write it in the wing book.'

With Ness glaring at her, Amy nodded, not sounding very convincing. 'Oh yeah . . . yeah, sorry, I forgot.'

'Go on then, hurry up. But make sure you sign out first.' He gestured with his head, and she began to move towards the small guard room to sign the book.

'I ain't going to forget this!' Ness called angrily after her. 'You're nothing but a selfish bitch! You know that! You stupid cow, I hope you get what's coming to you!'

30

MAUREEN

Maureen hurried down the long corridor and through the double doors at the end of the wing. At the bottom of the stairs, she caught her breath: she wasn't as young as she used to be, and slower than she wanted to, she made her way up the stairs. It was one of the good things that being the wing's support advocate brought her. She was trusted to leave the wing during the day to speak to the prison social and mental health workers on behalf of the women, as well as speak to the governor, as long as she had an appointment with him of course.

The other thing she was able to do was visit the small prison chapel whenever she wanted, unlike the other women, who had to get permission from the wing officer whether they wanted to see the priest who came once a week, or they wanted to speak to her in private. The chapel was one of the few places that felt like a sanctuary. It was *also* one of the few places in Ashcroft that there wasn't the sense of constant chaos and desperation which filled every inch of the prison.

Walking into the chapel, Maureen was immediately struck by a sense of calm, although she had to admit it was noisy, something that Steph often complained about. And it was true, from where she stood, she could hear the screams from C wing, which was where they kept the women with mental health issues and women who were detoxing. Though it never spoilt her time here; the chapel was where things made sense for her.

There were ten rows of wooden pews and hymn books piled

up against the grey breeze-block walls. At the end of the aisle by the altar, she knelt on a red velvet cushion which had a gold embroidered cross on it. She crossed herself, looking up to the small stained-glass window which was actually made of plastic due to the fact that there'd been a couple of occasions where the glass had been broken by the women in order to use the shards as a weapon.

She closed her eyes, clasping her hands together, 'I know it's been a long time, but sometimes I can't bring myself to talk to you, so I can't, but I'm struggling now, and I ask you to bring me strength. I think seeing Ness pregnant and glowing, stirs things up inside of me, things that I thought I'd locked away. But I suppose none of us can run away from our sins . . . and our regrets. I don't know how long I can—'

'Reenie?'

Maureen stopped and opened her eyes. 'I . . . I . . .'

'Sorry, Reenie, I didn't mean to disturb you . . . Oh, don't worry, I didn't hear anything . . . Carry on if you like.'

Maureen smiled in relief, but she was also pleased to see Amy. She shook her head, then with a slight struggle, stood, and walked towards her. 'No, I can talk to Him later. It's you I want to speak to. That's why I told Barratt that you were scheduled to see me but I'd forgotten to write it down in the wing diary . . . I hope you don't mind?'

'No, of course not. I didn't know what he was on about, but it's OK, I covered.'

Not saying anything, Maureen nodded, watching as Amy glanced up at the large wooden cross which the prison had screwed to the wall. After a moment Amy shrugged. 'I've never seen the appeal of all this myself. I can't imagine how it helps.'

'Then you should try it one day.' Maureen spoke warmly.

Amy's eyes twinkled. 'I think I'll stick to a large gin and tonic, thanks.'

Laughing, Maureen nodded. 'I can't say I don't feel the same sometimes, but my tipple was always a good whisky.'

Sitting down in the front pew, Amy stared at Maureen. 'Don't you mind being in here? You know, stuck in Ashcroft, cos you never seem to complain.'

Maureen raised her eyebrows. 'Same could be said about you. I've never once heard you say anything about hating being in here . . . I often wonder why that is.'

Amy continued to stare but she said nothing.

'As for me,' Maureen went on, 'I do more good in here than I would stuck in a convent, away from life. It's my path, and I accept what is thrown at me, Amy. I did wrong and I have to pay for that.'

'Yeah, but there must have been a reason why you did it. You're not the type to just kill two people and stick them under the floorboards without a reason.'

Maureen bristled. She'd never spoken about what had happened and didn't plan to. What had gone on was between her and God, and that was enough. Even when the court case was happening, she had refused a defence barrister and had simply pleaded guilty. The judge had given her a double life sentence, and instead of feeling upset about it, all she'd felt was relief. 'Yes, there were reasons,' was all Maureen said.

'I take it from that you ain't going to tell me.' Amy smiled. 'So, why am I here? Not that I mind, it's good to have a chat, especially as I'll be leaving tomorrow . . .' She took a deep breath which didn't go unnoticed by Maureen. 'You've been a proper friend, Reenie, I won't ever forget that. But it still doesn't explain all this cloak-and-dagger stuff.'

'It felt a safe place to talk. I want you to look me in the eye,

Amy, and tell me you really didn't have anything to do with what happened to Lynn.'

Amy shot up out of the pew. 'Are you for real? Fucking hell—'

'I'd rather you didn't swear in here, please,' Maureen cut in.

Looking exasperated, Amy nodded. 'OK, whatever . . . But it's ridiculous. It's stupid. This place creates its own dramas. Tess started this crazy rumour out of nowhere. That must be a flag for you. And of course Steph is going to believe it. She doesn't trust me, not anymore, not after Yvette. And I don't blame her. I was wrong to back her, but Steph ain't one to listen to an apology. She's never going to forgive me, is she?'

Maureen watched her pace up and down the aisle. 'So, you don't know anything about it then?'

There was a pause before Amy answered, 'That's right, I don't.'

Getting up from the pew, Maureen walked over to Amy. 'Now everything else you've said to me I believe, but why have I got the feeling that you're not telling the truth on this one?'

'How should I know?' Amy snapped, turning her head away as Maureen held her hands.

'Look at me, Amy, *please*. If I'm going to help you, I need to know the truth, whatever that is.'

'Help me? What are you talking about?' Amy frowned.

Before answering, Maureen walked down the aisle and stuck her head out of the chapel door. Certain no one else was about, she shuffled back to Amy, dropping her voice to a whisper. 'I don't want to break the other women's confidence – I know the rules in this place, we don't tell tales. But I can't sit back and do nothing . . . They're gunning for you, my darling. The women are going to jump you tonight.'

'What?'

'They want to do it before you leave. Teach you a lesson. They all think Lynn lying in a coma is down to you.'

'Oh my God, that's stupid, crazy . . . That's what Ness must have meant.'

'What do you mean? She told you?' Maureen was surprised, because although she and Ness had spoken earlier about what to do, they both knew that ratting on Steph and the other women was dangerous.

'No, no, she didn't tell me. She was upset, she'd asked me to do something I couldn't.' Amy fell silent and chewed on her lip, and when she spoke again, she sounded worried although it quickly turned to anger. 'No prizes for guessing that Steph is behind all this.'

Maureen didn't say anything, but she knew it was obvious. Steph was always there on Amy's shoulder, checking, pushing, holding her to account. It was a tragedy really, because their friendship had been good and Amy's decision to back Yvette as top dog had been naive rather than spiteful.

The betrayal Steph had felt had cut her deeply. Friendships inside were important, though first and foremost was trust – and that had been lost. To make matters worse, Amy and Steph shared the same group of friends, so it was impossible for them to avoid each other, even though the tension between them was always simmering under the surface.

'You still haven't answered my question fully. What do you know? *Amy*? I can see you're hurting; I just want to help you. I want you to trust me. Whatever it is, you can talk to me. I promise, I'll make no judgement.'

Amy sat and stared at the tiny altar at the front of the chapel. For several minutes she stayed motionless as the sun came through the window. Then without warning her eyes filled with tears. She began to talk, almost as though she was talking to someone other than Maureen.

'My husband, Ollie – no one knows what he's really like. When people see him, they see a confident, good-looking guy. Charming, helpful, protective – and that's what I saw, at first. When I was working in the clubs, he came along and swept me off my feet.' She glanced at Maureen, her beautiful face drawn in sadness. 'I sound like a cliché, don't I, Reenie? But sometimes desperation can make you take the wrong choices.'

Maureen nodded and she felt her chest beginning to get tight as she battled not to let her own memories overwhelm her.

'But I was desperate, Reenie. It was the usual story, the same for so many of the women in here: I was just trying to survive. Then, like I say, Ollie came along, and I thought he was everything that I was wanting.'

'Which was?' Maureen asked.

'I was wanting someone to love me.' Her voice cracked. 'It's stupid, I know, but I'd never had that before. I was in care, you see, and after I was kicked out at sixteen, I ended up working in the clubs: dancing, escorting . . .' She shrugged. 'You know, where anything goes . . . So, between the clients, and the clubs of Soho, love's a little short on the ground.' She gave a wry smile. 'And Ollie came along, and I saw what I wanted to see. But seeing someone isn't the same as them being that someone . . . The truth is, Reenie, he's violent, controlling, and I'm terrified of him.' She wiped away her tears. 'That's why I messed up my parole each time: better Ashcroft than being at home. The truth is, I'm dreading tomorrow . . .' She looked down, sitting with her hands clasped together on her lap.

'And the drugs?'

Amy nodded. 'I know about them.' She put her head in her hands for a moment. 'I feel so ashamed. But it's not what you think. I only found out recently, but Ollie is involved. Somehow, he got involved with Earle.'

Maureen gasped.

She dropped her hands and glanced at Maureen. 'I don't know how, but Earle is bringing it in for Tess to sell. It's been going on for a while. I don't know if it started before or after I arrived. Knowing Ollie, it was probably the latter. He probably saw an opportunity he could take advantage of . . . So you see, Reenie, part of what Tess said is true. I don't know who I hate more, Tess or Ollie . . . I'm so sorry.' Tears spilled from her eyes.

From where she stood, Maureen could see Amy trembling.

Amy took a deep breath. 'And as Ollie's my husband . . . well, if it wasn't for him, Lynette would be OK. That shit she took was obviously too pure. I feel responsible for it. I might as well have given her the injection.'

Crossing herself, Maureen went to sit close to Amy. She stared into her piercing green eyes, and her voice was warm but firm. 'It's not your fault, but you know Lynn might die – you do know that, don't you?'

To the sound of someone from C wing wailing, Amy gave the tiniest of nods.

'You have to understand, I'm not blaming you, Amy, but just because it isn't your fault, that doesn't mean that it isn't your responsibility to do something.'

'Like what?' Amy squinted from the bright sunlight which continued to flood in.

'I think you owe it to Lynn to help find her daughter. We both know that the police won't do anything about Evie. They'll have her filed as a missing person, and that's it. Lynn has no one else to help her, but you're leaving here tomorrow, which is perfect . . . Just think how Lynn will feel when she pulls out of her coma and we're able to tell her Evie's safe . . .' She paused a moment. 'But if the worst does happen to Lynn, we can't just leave Evie out there. She can't be forgotten . . . That's if Evie's still alive.'

Amy blinked rapidly. She rubbed her head, her chestnut hair falling over her eyes. 'How? I mean, I'll do what I can, but . . .' She stopped and stared at Maureen.

'You know a lot about Evie. Lynn's told us so much about her, which might help. You know the things she likes to do, where she likes to hang out—'

'Jesus, Reenie, I'm hardly Hercule Poirot. It's not like I can go out and start asking questions. I wouldn't even know where to begin, not really.'

'No, but Jack does.'

'Jack? Who's Jack?' Amy looked at her blankly.

Taking a deep breath, Maureen gave her a tight smile. 'The priest. You know, the one who comes to visit me. I've already spoken to him about Evie, and he's happy to do what he can, but I'm sure your help will make all the difference.'

'Are you kidding? I'm not being funny, Reenie, but I think we need more than a few prayers to help find Evie.'

'Jack wasn't always a priest. Trust me, he knows a thing or two about life.'

'I don't know, it sounds . . .' Amy looked like she was searching for words, '. . . well desperate.'

Maureen leaned in, holding her gaze. 'We haven't got many options open to us. At least try. Do it for Lynn.'

'I don't know if I'll be able to, Reenie, even if I want to – which I do. Obviously, I want to help Evie . . . But you don't know what you're asking . . . I've told you what Ollie's like. He'll never just let me go out and about, especially with Jack. I'd have to do it all in secret, and Ollie will kill me if he finds out. He's always got one of his men following me wherever I go.' She looked scared.

'I'm sorry, Amy, I really am, but you'll have to find a way . . . *Please*, Amy, you getting out means you're the only one who can help. You must see that. The police aren't going to do anything.

Evie needs you. She's a young girl and she's out there some-where . . . And Lynn needs you to find her.'

'But—'

'But nothing,' Maureen cut in firmly.

Once again, the women fell silent. Then Amy said, 'Is this why you wanted to see me?' Sighing, she leaned back on the wooden pew, looking up to the ceiling.

'Partly.'

Hearing a noise, Maureen glanced towards the chapel doors. She waited until the footsteps passed before continuing: 'In the laundry room later, that's where they're planning to jump you. Obviously, I can't rat the women out, so I've had a word with Jenkins, and she's going to try to sort something out.'

Amy sounded surprised. 'Officer Jenkins never does anything for free. She's a total money grabber. What did she make you give her?' Amy stared at Maureen but then she suddenly became ani-mated. 'Your cross. Reenie, where's your cross that you always wear? Please don't tell me you gave it to her?'

'Look, it's fine, it's just a necklace . . . And here, you'll need this.' Maureen pulled up her tracksuit top and took out a kitchen knife. 'For protection.'

For a moment, Amy just stared at the knife, then carefully she took it and, standing up, she slipped it in the waistband of her joggers. 'I . . . I don't know what to say. You did all this for me . . . Thank you. Thank you, Reenie, I owe you.'

Maureen stood up as well. 'In that case, you'll try to help Jack find Evie. It's Lynn you owe, not me . . . So, this is what's going to happen. In a few days, Jack will get in contact with you – he'll do it discreetly, I promise . . . Trust me, he knows what he's doing.'

Amy's eyes darted around until eventually she nodded slowly. Her face was showing the strain. 'OK . . . I'll do what I can.'

Maureen smiled. 'You're doing the right thing, Amy . . . Oh, and please, *please* be careful with Steph and the others.'

'I will. And don't worry: I won't let on that you told me.' She hugged Maureen, who hugged her back. 'I'd better go.'

Maureen watched Amy walk towards the doors of the chapel.

'They raped me.'

Amy turned around and stared at her.

'Those two men I killed, they were paedophiles in a position of power . . . And I did it because they raped me.'

31

MINA

It was late Saturday afternoon and Mina and Iris stood outside an inconspicuous house on a pretty street on the outskirts of Nottingham.

'You sure this is it?' Mina glanced around. 'It's not what I was expecting.'

Iris blew a large bubble from the gum which she'd been chewing on for the past half an hour. It popped and she twisted it around her tongue as she spoke. 'What were you expecting?' She grinned.

Feeling nervous, Mina shrugged, and not for the first time that day she wondered if she was doing the right thing. Especially as Flo seemed so far away. Though thankfully, she'd persuaded Doreen to look after her for the night in exchange for writing off the money that Doreen owed her. It wasn't ideal, but it was the only option available to her, and as Doreen had been bang on it recently, the only thing Doreen wanted to do was rest, so the likelihood of her leaving Flo on her own was slim.

'I don't know what I was expecting, but not this.'

Iris giggled, her blue eyes lighting up. She gave Mina a quick kiss on her lips and squeezed her hand. 'It'll be fine . . . We can have a few drinks and—'

'No.' Mina interrupted quickly. 'I said I was coming with you, that's all.'

'OK, OK. I hear you . . . Come on.' And with that, Iris knocked on the door . . .

The inside of the house was just as nondescript as the outside. Spotless whitewashed walls and doors, wooden floors, and a staircase leading up to the next landing of the three-storey house. The only oddity was how strong the smell of Dettol was, almost overpowering.

'Yay! You actually came. I totally didn't think you would.' Roz grinned at Iris. Her long, poker-straight, blue-black hair was tied up in a high ponytail and she wore a crisp white dress which skimmed the top of her knees, reminding Mina of the beauticians who worked in the nail bars along Shaftesbury Avenue. 'Hiya, babe, so good to see you. You look lovely.' Roz winked at Mina.

Iris grinned. 'Yeah, I thought Mina was going to blow me out.'

'You can talk. I dunno how many times you said you'd come and never did.' Roz gave her a hug and Mina could smell the floral perfume she was wearing.

'You fancy a drink? Come on.' Without waiting for an answer Roz led them through into a front room which had two new-looking red leather sofas in it and a glass drinks cabinet. Roz continued to direct her conversation at Mina as she made the drinks. 'I hear you're a bit unsure about all this.'

Knocking back the tumbler of vodka Roz had just poured her, Iris winked at Mina. 'She's a good girl, that's why.'

'Well at least someone is.' Roz flashed another grin.

Sitting down with the glass of vodka which she didn't really want, but drank quickly anyway, Mina felt the burn of the alcohol as she replied, 'I came to keep Iris company, that's all. Make sure she's OK.'

Roz seemed bemused. 'That's a bit stupid.'

Mina felt herself blushing again.

'Oh, shit, I didn't mean to be rude,' Roz said, apologizing. 'I just think it's a great opportunity for you.'

'That's what I said.' Iris, who'd poured herself another large drink, nodded and pointed. 'Listen to her, Mina, she knows what she's talking about.'

Smiling, Roz came and sat next to Mina and started playing with Mina's hair, pushing it back behind her ears. 'You're so beautiful, they'd love you. They really would.'

Mina pulled away slightly. She shot a glare at Iris. This wasn't why she was here, and Iris knew it. And she certainly didn't like the pressure she was feeling. 'No offence, but it just ain't my thing.'

Roz's big eyes shone warmly. 'No offence taken. Like I say, I think it's a shame, but if you don't want to . . .' she shrugged, 'you don't want to.'

Skipping over to join them, glass in hand, Iris threw herself down at the other end of the couch, the leather squeaking under her. 'Oh, come on, Mina. Have another drink, get wasted and then go for it – you won't even think about it then.'

'True. That's what a lot of us do,' Roz agreed. 'Seriously, I don't want to push you into anything, but I swear it's no big deal. I mean, if you want some coke, I've got a couple of grams left – you can have that, if you think it will help?'

Mina shook her head. 'I'm fine . . . but thanks.'

Roz gave Iris a side glance. 'You're better than me, girl, I could never turn down a monkey. You must be rolling in it!'

Mina blinked. She stared hard at Roz and then at Iris. 'A monkey? As in five hundred quid.'

Roz giggled. 'Yeah, as in five hundred big ones. Why, what did you think it would be?'

'I . . . I didn't know.' Mina shrugged but said nothing else at the same time as trying to push away the fact that the sort of money Roz was talking about would change her and Flo's life. When Iris had told her, she had no idea it was that amount of money. Her mum had never earned anywhere near that, partly because the pimps took most of it, in return for giving her mum 'protection'. Which was the biggest joke going. Mina couldn't recall how many times she'd seen her mum being smacked around by one pimp or another. Split lips, broken ribs, bruises all over her body, a broken nose. And those were just a few of the injuries.

But not wanting to think about that anymore, Mina brought herself back to what Roz was saying.

'More tempting to you now, is it?' Roz giggled. 'Most of the time it doesn't last longer than twenty minutes. Five hundred pounds for twenty minutes, for fucking some geezer. I looked it up, that's more than heart surgeons get. And it's not like we're picking them up from some street corner – no dis to your mum like . . . Oh sorry, Iris told me.'

Mina threw Iris – who already looked slightly drunk – another hard glare.

'But you'll be safe. You don't have to worry about getting attacked or anything.'

Mina bristled.

'Oh, go on, Mina, what do you say?' Roz pushed again. 'Well? We'll all have a laugh.'

Mina glanced from Iris to Roz again. 'And the whole five hundred is ours to keep?'

Roz nodded. 'Yeah, but what a lot of girls do is give a little tip to the person who's working the house: greeting the punters and all that crap. We take it in turns to work that shift, and cos you're not in with the clients, you ain't getting the money. And as it's my turn on the door tonight, feel free to tip large.' She smiled and Mina could see why Iris liked Roz so much, but she could also see how manipulating she was. Making selling sex sound like going for a trip to Disneyland. 'So, we do that to make it fair,' Roz continued, 'and working house, you can still go away with more than a grand or so, if it's been a good night for the other girls.'

Mina could feel her eyes widening. 'A grand?'

Roz laughed again. 'Yeah, cos each client we charge a straight five hundred for fucking, a couple of hundred for blow jobs.'

'Wow, my mum only got about twenty quid,' Mina said at the same time as realizing she'd never been so open about her mum's work before.

'Well, when she's out, get her to come and work for us,' Roz said jokingly.

'I think I'll take a rain check on that one.' Mina took another large sip of vodka, feeling better as the warmth inside her stomach grew. 'She'd kill me if she knew I was here.'

'Then don't tell her.' Roz glanced at the slim Rolex watch on her wrist. 'I'll have to start getting the rest of the rooms ready soon. It's been quiet today, but our next few clients will be here in less than an hour. So, come on, girl, it's decision time. If you're worried about having some strange, weirdo geezer, don't be. I mean, yeah, what geezer isn't strange, but all of them are our regulars, some of them are all right looking as well. I had a well-fit guy last week; I would've been happy to pay him.'

Iris snorted with laughter as she continued to knock back the vodka.

'And the ones that are coming later,' Roz added, 'they don't want any kinky sex, you won't have to start spanking them or be dressing them up in a baby-grow or any shit like that. Trust me, those lot come during the week when they're here on *business*. It'll be straight sex. That's all. But I get it, if you want to build up to the full works before you start straddling cock.' Roz roared loudly, making Mina cringe as she vividly pictured the scenario in her mind. 'Look, Iris told me you ain't popped your cherry yet.'

'What haven't you told her?' Mina said, glancing at Iris, who shrugged non-committally.

Roz took hold of Mina's hand. 'The only thing about that is, we ain't got any oral only today. So, you won't be able to earn anything. But if you *do* want to earn, and you don't mind the full works, I can put you in one of the rooms, and you'll be guaranteed at least five hundred big ones. Your call.'

Mina finished off her drink and Roz went over to make her another one. How bad could it actually be? Especially if she got drunk, or at least semi-drunk. That kind of money would change everything. She wouldn't have to worry, and if she ever did it again, at least then she'd have some money to pay for a proper babysitter, so she wouldn't have to rely on Doreen.

And maybe then, if she decided to continue, if she did it only when she needed to, she could keep Flo safe, she could keep them both clothed and fed and pay the rent. She could go to college and get her qualifications without worrying about her sister. And if all went well, really well, perhaps she could even keep it going until her mum came out of prison . . .

As Roz handed her another drink, the thought of what her mum would say rippled into her mind. The reality of how disappointed her mum would be if she even knew she was thinking about it, hit her like a slap. And as much as the money would be the solution to all her problems, it was ridiculous to even go there in her head.

Taking a large gulp of vodka, she smiled at Roz. 'I'm sorry, I just can't do it.'

32

EARLE

Stirring his cup of tea, Tony sat at the table. He was exhausted from his shift and was grateful that for once he'd been rostered to have the weekend off. Sighing, he looked around the poky kitchen with its tired, yellow laminate cupboards and the ailing cream stove which had to be at least twenty years old. The whole place needed decorating – no, the whole place needed bulldozing. There weren't any redeeming features about the property at all, though somehow, Tony had lived his whole life here. Fifty-six years in a high-rise on the wrong side of Hounslow.

It had been his mother's flat, and begrudgingly she'd left it in her will for him, having no one else to leave it to. Though while she'd been alive, she'd often toyed and threatened to leave it to one of the various animal charities she'd supported, if he ever moved out. So, he'd stayed, hoping that her ill health would put an end to her miserable, bitter life sooner rather than later. Instead, she'd lasted the better part of ninety-two years. Ninety-two years of moaning and complaining before dropping dead of a heart attack. That day certainly hadn't come soon enough for Tony.

Now though, it seemed his life had ebbed away in the blink of an eye. No wife. No girlfriend. No prospect. Nothing. But he was determined for that to change. It was one of the reasons, when the landlord of his local pub – someone he'd known since school – suggested if he wanted to make a quick bit of money, he should have a word with a woman he knew called Martha, he'd agreed to it almost straight away. He'd learned the hard way that life wasn't kind to those that sat back.

Martha had been looking for someone to help take gear into a few of the prisons around the London area, and it so happened that her goon of an ex-husband, Ollie, who had his wife banged up in Ashcroft, was wanting to take advantage of that fact as well.

Everything had fallen into place, including getting Tess on board, which had been easy. A case of scratching each other's backs. Though, thinking about it, Tony realized having Tess as part of the equation had been a mistake. The money he'd earned was far from a mistake. He wanted to start a new life abroad. Spain maybe. Brazil. The Philippines. Anywhere but here. He hated the prison, his life, and his bitch of a mother, because although she had left the flat to him, she had put in a clause that he couldn't sell it or rent it. Even from the grave she knew how to punish him. Well, he was going to get the last laugh, because this time next year, he'd have enough money to get the hell out.

Loud banging broke Tony's thoughts, and he jumped up from the brown plastic chair he was sitting on. For a moment, he didn't move as he stared at the front door, but then he heard a louder crash as it was booted open . . .

Standing in the doorway were Ollie and Martha.

'Hello, Tony. I've been calling you, and you ain't been answering me. I think that's rather rude, don't you?' Martha walked in with Ollie only a few feet behind her.

As Tony watched them, he could feel himself beginning to shake, his heart pounding hard against his chest. For a moment, he thought about running, but that idea quickly faded as the pair walked towards him and into the kitchen. There was no way he could get past them, and perhaps they were here only to talk, though the flicker of the knife in Martha's hand told him different.

His mouth felt dry, and he struggled to swallow. 'I . . . I've been busy,' was all that Tony managed to say.

'Too busy to call your pals.' Ollie walked up to him and put his arm around Tony's shoulder. Ollie winked, and Tony could feel the tight embrace getting tighter.

'I'm sorry, we've been busy at the prison. I was meaning to get back to you.'

Martha laughed scornfully. 'Oh, I bet you were. Well, we've saved you the bother, ain't we?' She pulled out a chair and sat down on it, staring at Tony so intently that he had to avert his gaze.

'Two guesses why we're here.' Ollie continued to drape his muscular arm around Tony's shoulder.

'I'm sure you're here to talk about why there hasn't been any money put through the account.'

'Bingo. He ain't so stupid after all, hey, Martha?' Laughing, Ollie let him go and began to open and close the kitchen cupboards, while all the time the sick feeling in Tony's stomach was growing.

'Look, I can explain. I can explain what happened.'

Martha tilted her head to one side. 'Can you? Can you really explain to me how, usually by this time each month, there's money coming in from the gear Tess has sold, but for some reason I'm seeing nil pound signs in there. And then, Tone, once you've explained that, can you tell me why, if there was a problem, you didn't come to us right away. Saving us the bother of coming to pay you a little visit.'

He nodded, slightly too exuberantly. 'Yes . . . yes, I can.' Even to him, his assurance sounded hollow, pitiful. And just looking at them both, he knew he was going to have a hard time convincing them that he was on top of the situation, especially as Martha was correct when she said that usually money was filtering through by now.

Tess sold the gear mainly to the women who had families on the outside, who were basically the guarantors. They were the ones who were paying for it, either through money they already had or would earn, or having to sell things to pay for the gear. And if for some reason a woman's family didn't cough up, a couple of Ollie and Martha's men would go and pay them a visit.

Unfortunately for him, Martha and Ollie were making a personal appearance this time.

Martha leaned forward, resting her elbows on the table, her sharp features crueller than ever as they twisted into a smirk. 'Well, this is going to be good.'

Tony cleared his throat, jumping each time Ollie slammed a cupboard door closed. 'I . . . Well, I can see how it looks, but . . . the thing is, the gear's been confiscated.'

Martha sat up. 'You what?'

'Don't worry, it's all in hand.'

Ollie stared at Tony, his immaculately ironed black shirt straining at the seams. '*Don't worry* – are you having a laugh? Confiscated, *how*?'

The thought of making a run for it passed through Tony's mind again, but as if he could read his thoughts, Ollie walked to the kitchen door and closed it. 'You need to start opening your mouth, Tone. *Now!*'

Ollie bellowed the last word and immediately Tony began to stutter. 'The governor, he came along, wrong time, wrong place. Took the gear, but . . . but it's OK, Tess hasn't said anything, well I don't think she has . . . I don't think the governor knows anything. I haven't said. I . . . I wouldn't do that. Not to either of you.' His eyes darted between Ollie and Martha, who were staring at him.

'So let me get this straight,' Martha snarled. 'You *think* it's OK? You *think*, Tess ain't said anything, but you don't actually know.'

It was a moment before Tony said, 'Yes . . . cos if she had, the police would have been round, I know that—'

'The police would have been round *where*, Tone?' Ollie strode over to him and pushed Tony hard in his chest. 'Cos, I know you ain't saying the police would even sniff towards my postcode. You see, I reckon you'll be singing like a canary if anyone starts to ask questions, and that makes me feel really uncomfortable.'

'I wouldn't do that. We've been working together long enough. Come on, Ollie, you know I wouldn't.'

Ollie turned to Martha and nodded. She threw the large, jagged knife across to Ollie, who caught it, then smiled, his green eyes narrowing as he dragged the tip of the blade down Tony's cheek.

'No, please.' Tony stared at Ollie, fear eclipsing his jumbled thoughts.

Ollie roared with laughter. 'You don't even know what I'm going to do to you yet, mate.' He winked again, then quickly put Tony in a headlock, twisting his body around and slamming him down onto one of the kitchen chairs.

The next moment, Tony felt his hands being pulled and tied to the chair. Desperately, he pleaded: 'Look, I'm not going to say anything. I wouldn't, I swear, I won't say a word.'

'I know you won't. But I just want to make sure you don't—'

And with that, Ollie pulled open Tony's mouth. The next moment, he felt the most excruciating pain.

33

STEPH

Steph paced around in her cell, and pressed dial again on her phone, but each time it went straight to voicemail. She didn't know why Iris wouldn't pick up. Did her daughter hate her that much? She wouldn't blame her if she did. She'd let her down, allowed this to happen to her. She hadn't been there to protect her. She hadn't even spoken to Iris since she'd told her the news. Not that she hadn't tried, but it was as if Iris had just cut her off.

But she wanted to be there for her daughter, comfort her, if that was even possible in a situation like this. She wouldn't mind if Iris was angry. If she told her she was the worst mother, told her that she hated her. She'd understand that. She'd even agree with her. Whatever Iris did or said would be all right, but not this closing off, shutting down. Anything but that. But it looked as if that's what she was doing.

She'd thought about calling Mina, given that her and Iris were great mates, but she didn't want to put Iris in an awkward position. She actually didn't know what to do for the best. She'd thought about speaking to Reenie, but since what happened to Lynette, and with Evie still missing, a lot of the women were on edge. It had brought home the enormity of life on the inside, the helplessness. Reenie had been swamped by women wanting to talk to her, and Steph didn't want to add to that, to be a burden to her.

Truth was, she was a tad relieved that Reenie was busy with the other girls, because she felt so much guilt and shame for being such a terrible mother. She hadn't even noticed what was going on with her precious daughter. She'd been too busy laying down the law, reading the riot act to her, to see what was really happening.

Dialling her daughter's number again, she began to leave a message.

'Hey Iris, it's mum . . .' Shame hit her again when she said that word; she didn't deserve to call herself that, but she continued with the message. 'So, I'd love to talk to you, hon. I'd love to talk some more about . . . well, you know what you told me. Can you call me, please. It would be great maybe if we could arrange a visit. If you'd come and see me. There's so much I want to ask you . . . but of course, if you're not ready to talk, I get it. I . . . I just want to see you. Make sure you're all right, or as all right as you can be. Call me, yeah. And Iris, I'm sorry. I'm so sorry . . . I love—'

'Everything all right?'

'Fucking hell, Ness! Have you ever heard of knocking?' Steph quickly clicked off the phone, anger surging through her. 'There is such a thing as privacy, you know.'

'I'm sorry, I—'

'How long were you standing there for?'

Ness looked puzzled. 'I wasn't, I just came along to see if you wanted to get a cup of tea, they've started serving—'

'Yeah, well I think I've been here long enough to know what time they serve tea, don't you?' Steph snapped. She knew she was being unreasonable, but she couldn't help herself.

'I don't know what's going on with you, but if you're not careful, you'll start pushing people away.'

Steph shook her head. 'There's more to life than this fucking place, you know. Why would I care?'

Ness looked over her shoulder, bringing her voice down. 'You will if you want to be top dog. The women are looking for a strong leader, not a bitch. We've already got that with Tess.'

'Go to hell.'

Looking hurt, Ness turned to walk away, but Steph grabbed her arm. 'Let the women know, whether they like it or not, I'm going to be top dog. If they've got a problem with that, tell them to come and see me . . . Now get out. *Get out!*' Steph screamed. Looking like she was about to cry, Ness hurried off.

Slamming the door on Ness, Steph closed her eyes for a moment, then collapsed on the floor, weeping into her hands.

34

AMY

Amy carried her tray through the noisy eatery, placing it in the dishwash pile. She hadn't eaten anything; apart from it being yet another bland, greasy meal, she didn't have an appetite. The thought of going home tomorrow played on her mind and made her feel sick. And even if Ollie wasn't in the picture, she would still be nervous. For a moment her thoughts turned to Evie and Lynette, but that was so painful to think about, she didn't want to dwell on it.

Everything about prison life had been a routine: waking, eating, sleeping, exercising, all timetabled. Even though she'd only served five years, the idea of leaving, knowing that she was free to make her own decisions, her own mistakes, deciding on even the smallest of things, made her feel nervous . . . Or maybe she was just being stupid, she didn't know. Her emotions were all over the place. Leaving behind some of the women she'd made friends with, cried with, fought with – well, it seemed like the end of an era. Most of them, she knew she'd never see again, though the special bond, the situation they'd found themselves in was truly unique.

There was no doubt, prison institutionalized everyone, and even though the thoughts of tomorrow were filling her mind, she guessed the more immediate problem was Steph. If she didn't have her wits about her, worrying about going home to Ollie was futile, because she doubted that she'd see the inside of her house again for a very long time.

During her stay at Ashcroft, she'd seen many women get the *treatment*: punishment for whatever wrongs the women thought had been committed. Ironically, the prisoners of D wing became judge, jury, and executioner to whatever level and on whatever scale the women saw fit. And Amy had a very bad feeling that her retribution would be one of the severest.

At supper, Steph had actually spoken to her. And if it hadn't been for the heads up from Maureen, she wouldn't have known that Steph was planning anything. She had a good poker face. She guessed that was exactly what Steph wanted: for her to be completely unsuspecting. The only clues were the sideward glances she'd caught Steph giving to some of the other women. But she'd noticed something else about Steph. Her eyes. If she didn't know better, she'd lay a bet that Steph had been crying, which was crazy. Steph was the ice queen, through and through.

'You all right, Amy? I bet you're gagging for your old man to give you a good seeing to, you won't be able to walk for weeks. Lucky bitch!' Stopping Amy's thoughts, Ness called across to her from the other side of the dining room. Though Amy noticed she didn't look too happy either.

'Yeah, something like that.' She smiled but it was an effort to force it and she glanced at Steph, who glared at her but said nothing.

'Five whole fucking years. You won't recognize Soho. What do you think it'll feel like to get out of here?' Tiny Webber – a woman she'd shared a cell with when she'd first arrived in Ashcroft, who was far from tiny – shouted to her.

'I'll let you know.' She walked away but stopped as she heard Steph talking to her.

'Well, I wish you the best, Amy . . . It's been a long time coming.'

Slowly, she turned around and, seeing Steph smiling, it took everything Amy had not to blurt out what Maureen had told her. She certainly wanted to wipe the smirk off her face, but she couldn't – she wouldn't do that to Reenie. All the same, she was sick of the way Steph was treating her. She'd apologized more times than she could remember for backing Yvette, but Steph was having none of it. She'd held the grudge for years. Reenie had told her it was because she'd been hurt by her choice, but she doubted it was that. It was obvious that Steph was just a hard cow.

Anyway, Reenie had trusted her not to break her confidence, and no matter what happened, she would never rat on her. Inside, rats, paedophiles and child killers were all on the same level. If any of the prisoners did fall into one of those categories, they'd have to watch their backs every moment of every day.

Rolling her tongue around in her mouth, it was a second or so before Amy answered. 'What's been a long time coming, *Steph*?' she said in a low tone, and from the corner of her eye, she could see Reenie shake her head.

Steph stared at her, biting on her thumbnail. 'You, getting out. Why, what did you think I meant, Amy?'

Amy shrugged. She could feel the tension in the air. All the women were on edge, mainly because of Lynette and Evie. Whenever there was a real problem, it was like a ripple effect. Everyone felt it. 'I don't know, Steph, that's why I frigging asked you.' She moved to go again, but once more, Steph stopped her with her words.

'It's been nice knowing you.'

Amy heard the snickering behind her, but this time she didn't bother turning around.

Come on, ladies, the clothes won't wash themselves. Those on laundry duty, start making your way down, those on cleaning, make yourself useful and get along to the gym, likewise with the book monitors – Officer Riley wants you to meet her in the library. Every-one else, back in your cells . . . Now!

There was an audible groan from the women as Officer Bailey, playing with her keys, stood beside Amy rounding up the prisoners.

'Why do we have to go into our cells? It's too early. Fucking hell, there are laws, you know.'

Bailey glared at Ness. 'Yeah, and you, my love, broke them.'

Ness's face flushed. 'That ain't an answer. And you know what, I ain't in the mood for any more frigging crap from this place.' She threw Amy a hard glare.

Bailey pointed. 'I'd watch your mouth if I was you, Vanessa, otherwise you'll be paying another visit to solitary.'

Ness shook her head. 'Anytime anyone says anything to you lot, that's the first frigging thing you threaten.'

Bailey smiled. 'Then at least we're consistent. Right, move it. Cell, *now.*'

Ness crossed her arms, resting them on top of her large stomach. 'I ain't going anywhere until I know why we're all being locked up straight after supper.' She glanced around at the other women. 'Ain't that right, girls? What do you reckon? How about we stay here until we get a proper answer. You can't put us all down into solitary.'

A murmur went around, and Amy looked at Bailey as she began to talk to Ness. Most of the prison officers knew which battles to fight, and it was clear that Bailey thought this one wasn't worth it.

'Fine. If you must know, we're short of staff,' Bailey said. 'A couple of officers haven't been able to make it in.'

Ness shrugged. 'Why?'

Bailey sighed and sniffed loudly. 'I don't actually know, and if

I did, I wouldn't tell you. So, are you happy now? Have I answered all your questions?'

Ness nodded and slowly got up from the chair she was sitting on, her pregnant belly stretching the prison tracksuit top she was wearing. She glared at Bailey again. 'That wasn't too hard, was it? You know, a little bit of respect goes a long way.'

Bailey smirked. 'If you've got any complaints, take it up with the governor. Until then, move it.' She winked. 'And I won't be asking you again.' She swung around to look at Amy. 'As for you . . .' she stopped to look down at the clipboard she was holding, '. . . according to the list, you're supposed to be on laundry duties and until that clock strikes 3 p.m. tomorrow afternoon, you still belong to Her Majesty's prison service. Understand? So don't think about slacking off.'

Again, Amy didn't say anything; instead she slowly began to walk along the corridor to the laundry room, the noise as usual filling Ashcroft's air. One thing she wouldn't miss.

At the end of the hallway she headed down the stairs, feeling the heat as she descended: both the boiler and the laundry rooms were located down in the basement and, even in the winter, the heat was oppressive.

'Amy. Amy!' At the bottom of the stairs, Officer Jenkins beckoned to her from the shadows, her pasty white face appearing to glow in the dark.

Amy threw a glance up the stairs, feeling the knife she was still carrying under her jumper.

'Amy! Pssst!' Jenkins beckoned her over.

Making sure none of the women were going in or out of the laundry room, which was in clear view from where she was standing, Amy moved across to Jenkins, who was probably one of the most manipulative screws in the whole of Ashcroft.

Anything was on sale if the price was right. With Jenkins, a pound of flesh probably wasn't out of the question.

'What?' Amy whispered, staring into Jenkins' dark brown eyes.

'Here, take this, it's the key for the cleaning room. I've already unlocked the door via the code pad, so you don't need to worry about that. All you need is the key.' She paused, and they both looked up to the top of the stairs as they heard a group of women pass by. 'When it kicks off – if it does – make your way in there. Lock yourself in, then head along the corridors through to the back stairs. You know how to get there?'

Amy nodded.

'Good. I'll make sure the cage door is left open for you – I'll leave it ajar. You'll be able to get through that way, and back up onto the wing. But again, close it behind you.'

'What about a key for that?' Amy asked, her heart beginning to race.

Jenkins shook her head. 'You don't need one, it'll click shut on its own.' She glanced at her watch. 'I've got to go, I'm on C wing lock-up with Officer Doyle . . . Oh, and make sure you ditch the key for the cleaning room. Slip it behind the bottles of bleach and I'll collect it tomorrow, OK?'

Taking the key from her, Amy nodded, then hissed through her teeth. 'I'd thank you – if you weren't such a devious, greedy cow. What sort of scum trades a bit of help for Reenie's cross?'

Jenkins gave another smirk and Amy noticed the crumbs of biscuit at the corner of her mouth. 'I don't know, you tell me. After all, you're the one who's taking advantage of my help, and let's face it, if it wasn't for you, she'd be wearing that baby round her neck now. So, if I were you, Amy, I'd get off that high horse, since this all begins and ends with you.' And with those words, Officer Jenkins spun round and marched up the stairs, leaving Amy to head to the laundry room . . .

35

MINA

Mina stood against the door of the small, whitewashed bedroom. She couldn't see straight, she wasn't sure what was happening, and she was beginning to panic, though the strange thing was, she couldn't get her bearings. She tried to focus on the room she was in, but it was spinning around, and it felt like she was struggling to keep her balance.

Holding onto the wall to steady herself, she could see a bed in front of her. But there was someone there. Lying on it. Even in her confused state, her heart began to race and she tried to head for the door, but she was beginning to see double and struggling to walk.

'Where are you going, little lady?'

A man's voice came from somewhere in the room, but she couldn't see where. The next thing she knew she could feel his hands on her, pulling her towards the bed. She tried to shout out, but her tongue felt heavy, and it was almost as if she couldn't get her legs to move.

'Aren't you going to introduce yourself? I'm Matt. Roz told me you're new to this game. Don't worry, I'll be gentle with you.'

His face suddenly appeared in front of her, and she smiled but it looked manic. And somewhere in the back of her head, she knew that he was naked, fully aroused, grinning at her as he began to play with himself.

'How about you and me have a little party?'

She tried to shake her head at him, but for some reason her body wasn't connecting with her thoughts.

'Come on, daddy needs a little help.'

Desperately trying to shake him off, she felt herself being pushed onto the bed. It was as if she was trapped inside her own body, unable to scream.

The next thing Mina knew, she felt her jeans being tugged off. Then everything went black.

36

AMY

The heat and the tension in the laundry room sat in the air in equal measures. Amy stood on one side by the industrial-size washing machines making small talk with Reenie and a few of the other women about what she was or wasn't going to do in the first week of freedom. Though in truth, she was only half listening, her attention was mainly on Steph, who she could see over in the far corner by the folding and steam press.

Standing with Steph, huddled and whispering away, were Ness, as well as Mo and Betty and Tiny, and some of the women from the landing above her.

The laundry room was one of the places where there was usually banter, loud music from the radio, and singing, but right now, there was a strained silence, save for the hum of the machines.

Catching Ness's eye, Amy called over, her voice cutting through the quiet. 'I didn't think you were on laundry duty today. Special occasion?'

'Yeah, she just can't get enough of your kegs!' Tiny grinned, but it fell flat with the other women.

Ness screwed up her face. 'I know you can't be talking to me, cos as far as I'm concerned, you and I are nothing now, so do me a favour and fuck off!'

A loud *ooooh* went around the laundry room and Amy quickly looked away from the hostile stares. She didn't want it to be like this with Ness, but what she had asked her was impossible . . . Yes, they'd been close, but she hadn't known her for long. Six months? Seven at most. Of course, being in prison it was possible to build tight bonds in a short space of time, but to ask her to bring up her baby? That was crazy, wasn't it? She couldn't . . . even if she wanted to. There was no way Ollie would let her have him, and there was no way that she would want a baby, not with Ollie around. The little mite would be better off going into care – nothing could be worse than living with her psycho husband.

'I think she told Bailey that she wasn't feeling great,' Maureen leaned towards her, whispering in her ear. 'You know, a bit claustrophobic. And the last thing she wants is a sick pregnant woman on her hands during her shift, so she let her come down here.' She continued folding the towels as she added, 'What's going on between you two? When I asked her, she wouldn't tell me.'

Amy gave Maureen a small smile. 'It's not my place to say, Reenie. She's just having a hard time of it. Do me a favour, will you – when I'm gone, make sure she's OK.'

'You know I will. For some reason, that girl sits right in my heart, she always has done.'

'I know she does, and I know she feels the same way about you. I reckon the next few weeks will be really tough for her, trying to get her head around giving up her kid, I think—'

Seeing Steph and Tiny making their way towards her, Amy broke off and indicated with her eyes for Maureen to move away.

'Oi!' Steph's voice was loud and aggressive. 'Me and the girls thought we'd give you a proper send-off, what with you leaving and all, Amy. After all this time, we couldn't see you go without a bit of a fanfare, could we?'

Amy continued to separate the laundry into baskets. 'You don't need to bother. I wouldn't.'

Steph leaned against the side of the long towel table, giving Amy a sickly-sweet smile as two of the women she'd been whispering with walked over to the laundry door, poking their heads out to see if any screws were about, before closing the door and barricading it with some of the metal tables. 'Well, that's the difference between you and me, ain't it?' Grabbing the sheet that Amy had in her hands, Steph hissed at some of the other women to move away. Knowing exactly what was about to begin, others began to move towards them, circling Amy.

Looking Steph in the eye, Amy hissed, 'You don't need to do this, you know that?'

Steph looked around, grinning at the other women. With a scornful laugh she threw the clean sheet on the floor then stepped in closer, standing on it. Amy could smell the slight whiff of coffee coming off her breath. 'I'm sure you'd like that. But you don't get to prance out of here and play happy families while Lynn is lying in hospital because of you.'

Amy's glance wandered down to Steph's right hand, which was clenched into a fist. There was no doubt in her mind that Steph was carrying a blade. She'd seen it all before, she'd also seen the injuries a home-made shank could inflict.

On her guard, Amy continued to meet Steph's eye. 'You don't know what you're talking about.'

'Is that right?' Steph tilted her head and winked at Tiny, who stood next to her.

'Yeah, it is. And to tell you the truth, it's really sad. Now back off.'

Steph sneered. 'You wouldn't know the truth if it stepped on you, sweetheart.'

Amy shook her head. 'Five years I've known you, and it comes to this. Us, arguing in the laundry room. Come on, Steph, we're better than this.'

'I might be, darlin', but you ain't.' Steph opened her hand and slashed through the air with the blade, screaming, 'This is for Lynn, you stupid cow!'

Amy ducked and tried to step back, but the women behind her pushed her towards Steph. Quickly she pulled the knife from the waist of her joggers, and for a fleeting moment she saw Steph's expression change from anger to surprise.

She pointed the sharp kitchen knife at Steph. 'We end it here, OK? There'll be no winners.'

Steph bared her teeth. 'We'll see about that, shall we? Cos I ain't planning to lose!' She lunged at Amy again, and this time Amy felt the blade cut through her top and graze her stomach, then she felt a trickle of blood. Rather than stopping her, it acted like a trigger. With her left hand, Amy grabbed the pile of folded sheets from the table next to her, throwing them hard in Steph's face, then seizing the opportunity to dive at Steph with the knife.

The blow caught Steph on her shoulder; she yelled and staggered back as the noise of the women began to rise, and Amy could see blood pouring from the wound. Then she saw the determination on Steph's face as she came charging towards her again.

'You're going down for that, bitch!' she screeched, ripping through the air with the home-made weapon. Instinctively, Amy jumped back but a searing pain tore through her as the blade sliced her earlobe. Feeling sick, Amy stumbled to the side, trying to keep her balance but as she did, Tiny stuck out her foot, tripping her up and sending her sprawling across the floor.

A cheer went up and the next moment Amy felt someone jump on her back and grab her hair, then they slammed the side of her face into the ground. She screamed, but she fought hard at the same time, twisting and kicking, all the while keeping a firm grip on the knife.

Steph's anger squawked around the laundry room. 'You're going to pay today!'

'Go to hell!' Amy yelled back, blood from her ear trickling

down her face. Then she kicked out hard, flipping her foot into Steph's spine. The impact knocked her aside, allowing Amy to roll over, but Steph immediately recovered her balance and straddled Amy. In the scuffle that followed, the knife was knocked from her hand and she found herself looking up at Steph, the home-made blade hovering above her neck.

She was about to bring it down into Amy's throat when Amy reached up and grabbed her wrists. The muscles in her arms quivered as Steph tried to push down harder on the blade, edging nearer to her jugular.

'Bye bye, baby.' Steph's eyes were full of hatred.

'Steph . . . Steph . . . Don't . . . Steph, think about what you're doing . . .' Amy's voice came out in a hoarse whisper as the yelling around her became louder. The next moment, Amy felt a tug on her joggers as a group of women began to pull them down, loud screams and screeches of laughter mixed with the tension in the air.

Fuck her up, Steph

Give that cunt what's coming

Shut that bitch up once and for all

Teach her a lesson for Lynn

A couple of the women moved in to grab Amy's head, holding her down and covering her mouth. A fist smashed into her face. She tried to scream as the pain whirled round her head, but her mouth was covered by one of the prisoners, and in the next instant, Amy felt her knickers being pulled off as the blade Steph was holding started to press down into her throat.

'*Open this door! Open the door! Now! Open up!*' There was banging at the door as the prison officers, obviously having heard the yelling from the women, tried to enter the laundry room. Steph, clearly not caring, continued to push the blade towards Amy's throat. 'I don't know how you sleep at night, knowing Lynn is messed up because of that shit she took.'

Amy stared defiantly into Steph's face. 'Don't pretend this is because of Lynn . . . just fucking admit it, you've been wanting to do this for a long time.'

Steph grinned nastily, pressing the blade into her neck, causing a spot of blood to appear. 'Maybe I have, but that doesn't mean this isn't about Lynn, you stupid cow.'

'That's enough, Steph! You've proved your frigging point, now let her go! I said, *let her fucking go*, or I swear to God!' Ness stood above Steph and the other women, holding the knife Amy had dropped. She pointed it directly towards Steph's temple, the tip touching her skin. 'One move, that's all it'll take, Steph. And don't think I won't. I ain't in this place for nothing,' Ness yelled, and the women fell silent as she pushed the knife against Steph's face, nicking her skin.

Steph held perfectly still, the only part of her body that moved were her eyes. 'You're backing the wrong dog, you know that, Ness. And don't think I'm going to forget this in a hurry. What's going to happen tomorrow, have you thought about that? Oh, and I'm happy to wait, darlin', I'll wait till that baby pops, and then I'll come after you, understand?' Steph hissed through her teeth, her face going red. 'And what do you think your Mina will say when she finds out that you've put a blade to her best mate's mum's throat? I don't think she'll appreciate it, do you? You are so making the wrong choice.'

'No, I ain't. This has gone too far. I don't know what's got into you, but you need to stop this. Lynn wouldn't want it.'

'Hun, walk away before it's too late.' Amy looked up at Ness. 'You don't have to do this, darlin', not for me.' It crossed her mind to fess up, tell Steph that although she wasn't part of it, Ollie was. But then, maybe that would only make things worse.

There was no way Steph would believe she didn't know. And what if Ollie found out she'd been blabbing? Her life would be more than a living hell with him. A beating, even a knifing from Steph, would be preferable.

'I know I don't, but this ain't right. Look at you . . .' Ness turned her attention to Steph again. 'Get off her . . . *slowly* . . . That's it, now stand up . . . And don't make any clever moves. Understand?'

'Oh, I understand, all right,' Steph sniped as she moved off Amy, allowing her to get to her feet.

'*Open up now!*' The officers continued to bang as the emergency alarm went off, but it didn't deter any of the women.

Steph stood staring at Amy and Ness, a smirk on her face as she addressed Ness. 'Ain't you seen the movies?'

'What are you talking about now, Steph? What shit are you going to come out with next?' Ness answered contemptuously.

'You should have told me to drop it.' She flashed the blade, which was still in her hands, then she leapt at Amy, slashing and catching the top of her forehead with the weapon.

Blood spurted out, Amy let out a yell and the other women, seeing it as some sort of signal, piled in.

In pain – but realizing that, if she didn't do something before the officers forced their way in, the women would take matters into their own hands and finish off what Steph had started – Amy grabbed the knife from Ness, not wanting her to be in the line of fire. She stood in front of her, pointing the blade at Steph as the blood from the slash across her face continued to stream down into her eyes, blurring her vision.

'Back off, Steph, and back off from Ness. I'm happy to do more time, believe me – home is overrated anyway,' Amy hissed. She could see how much discomfort Steph was in from the injury to her shoulder, but she was surprised to see tears in her eyes. That wasn't like her at all, and the thought that maybe Steph was going through something else crossed her mind.

Some of the women stood behind Steph, their faces twisted in anger, hellbent on continuing the fight.

The situation wasn't looking good, but knowing that she had to front it out, Amy glanced towards the cleaning room to the side of her and discreetly dropped the key which Jenkins had given her. She knew with the level of noise in the room, the sound of the key hitting the floor would go unnoticed, unheard, but she moved her foot over it. Then, still standing with the knife pointing at Steph, she darted a glance at Maureen, giving her a silent message with her eyes.

'Make the next move, go on, I dare you, cos I'm ready for you, darlin'.' She spoke loudly to Steph, hoping it would divert attention from Maureen, who was moving to stand behind her. Aware that this might be her only opportunity, she flipped the key from under her shoe to where she thought Maureen was, though she didn't turn around, and she held Steph's stare: poker face.

The emergency bell droned on, and the officers continued yelling as the hammering got louder. Amy shouted over the din, hoping that Maureen had noticed the key by now, though she still didn't want to look behind her and draw attention to it.

Steph grinned and laughed nastily, but as she spun around to wink at the other women, Maureen's voice suddenly broke through the noise: 'Run. *Run!* Amy! Ness!' Maureen gestured, standing at the open door of the cleaning room, beckoning the women in. Immediately, Amy sprinted over, dragging Ness, before Steph and the others realized what was happening.

They tried to slam the metal door closed behind them, but throwing her whole weight against it, Amy could feel the force of the women on the other side, attempting to push it open. 'Help me! Help me close it!' Amy screamed and Maureen jumped forward to lend her weight.

Ness also went to help, but Amy shook her head. 'No, no, you can't! The baby! Forget it! Forget it!'

'I'll be fine!'

But as Ness answered, the arm of one of the women edged around the door.

'Ness! Look out! *Ness!*' Maureen yelled, pointing.

To Amy's surprise, Ness leapt forward and sank her teeth into whichever woman's arm it was. There was a loud shriek and the arm retreated, allowing Amy to slam the door shut.

Scrabbling to lock it with the key, Maureen shook as she glanced at Amy, but she also sounded breathless. 'Holy Mother of God, I thought you were done for . . . Jesus, look at ye, look what Steph's done to your head . . . you're bleeding everywhere.' She reached up to Amy's forehead, gently wiping the blood away with her hands, which were trembling.

'It's OK. I'll live.' Amy smiled weakly as she took the key from her and placed it – as Jenkins had asked her to do – behind the bottles of bleach lined up on the shelves. 'At least that lot can't get to us now . . . Thank you, for everything, Reenie.' Then she turned to Ness as they listened to some of the women shouting threats from the other side of the door.

You'll fucking pay for this, Ness, you stupid bitch, just wait!

At least we know where your loyalties lie

Call yourself a friend of Lynn's, you backstabbing cunt!

'As for you, Ness . . . well, what you did, you didn't have to, you know, especially after our chat earlier. The way Steph was looking at me, I really thought she was going to kill me, it was crazy.'

Ness sighed, rubbing her stomach.

'You'll need stitches in that, Amy,' Maureen continued as she took a deep breath.

'You OK, Reenie? You look well messed up.' Ness peered at her, worried.

Amy, noticing the same thing, agreed. 'Yeah, you're white as a sheet . . . the sooner we get you back into the wing, the better. Jenkins said she'd leave the gate open to the stairs, so we could get back up on to the wing. We'll just say it all kicked off and someone had left the doors open. Come on.' She looped arms with Maureen as Ness trailed behind them. She was slightly dizzy, and now the adrenaline was beginning to wear off, the pain was making itself felt.

They moved along the various corridors in silence: she knew the way from when she'd had to help one of the officers carry items from the delivery gate down to the laundry.

'Reenie, are you sure everything's all right? I'm worried about you.' Ness, breaking the silence, paused to take a closer look at her cellmate. 'You sound like you're struggling to breathe. You want to take a break?'

Maureen attempted to laugh, 'Jesus, no! I think I'll be able to get down the corridor in one piece, it's hardly Everest, is it? Now come on, stop mithering, and let's get back.'

Ness looked unsure but they continued anyway. A moment later, Amy let out a groan. 'Oh for fuck's sake. That bitch!' she hissed through her teeth.

'What?' Ness glanced at her.

'Look at the gate – Jenkins hasn't left it open. *Fuck*.'

'I'm not getting why Jenkins is involved in all this.' Ness frowned.

Amy sighed and, frustration getting the better of her, snapped, 'Time for that later, Ness. Point is, how are we going to get out of here?' The heat in the corridor was beginning to feel oppressive.

'Why don't we just go back the way we came? The screws will have got in by now, it'll be fine,' Ness suggested, frowning as she watched Maureen struggling for breath beside her.

'Firstly, we don't know that. More importantly, we can't. Jenkins had overridden the code pad for us to get in, so all we needed was the key. But to get back through, we'll need the code, and we ain't got that . . . Fuck!' She kicked the gate and it clanged noisily. 'Hello? Hello?' She rattled it hard.

'What if someone other than Jenkins hears us?' Ness asked.

'I don't care. We can't stay stuck down here, can we? Anyway, the bitch has turned us over. I've got a good mind to tell . . .' But Amy stopped talking as she stared at Maureen. 'Reenie? Reenie? What's going on? Reenie, what's the matter?' She bent down to look into the woman's face.

'Reenie! Talk to me!' Ness's voice took on an edge of hysteria. '*Reenie!*'

Amy could see that Maureen was clutching at her chest, her face going from white to a purplish blue as she struggled to breathe. Before they could get to her, she dropped to the floor.

Ness let out a scream: 'Reenie! Oh God, no! Amy, Amy, you got to do something! Help her, Amy, you got to help her!'

'Oh God, no . . .' she whispered, then leapt into action. 'Get out of my way, Ness, move out of the way. Come on!' Amy knelt by Maureen's side, then glanced up at Ness. 'Keep calling for help—'

'But—'

'Just fucking do it!' Amy yelled.

Ness nodded and began to call through the gate, her voice ragged with panic, while Amy leaned over Maureen, checking the pulse in her throat before quickly starting to pump her chest, performing CPR. 'Come on, Reenie, breathe.'

Ness glanced over her shoulder, tears streaming down her face. 'No one's coming!'

'Then keep calling until they do! We need help, *now*.'

'What's wrong with her?' Ness trembled.

Still pumping Maureen's chest, Amy looked up at Ness. 'I think she's had a heart attack . . . and if there's any time we need her God, it's now . . .'

37

IRIS

'You OK, Mina? Baby, you OK?' Iris looked at Mina, who was fast asleep on the bed. 'Mina, hey, sleepy head, how are you? You're lucky you decided to duck out. You didn't miss anything. I tell you, my guy was such a wanker, but then ain't all men . . . Mina?' She shook her gently, stroking her hair. 'Come on, Sleeping Beauty . . .'

Still with her eyes closed, Mina murmured, 'Go away!'

'Mina, what's wrong?' She leaned down to kiss Mina on her lips.

Mina's eyes shot open and she sat up. 'Get the fuck away from me.'

Iris stared at Mina. 'What's going on?'

Mina's eyes filled with tears. 'I thought you were my friend, I thought, well . . . I thought I meant something to you.'

'You do. You know you do.'

'Then why?' Mina wiped her tears away and Iris could see she was trembling. 'You think what you did last night was funny? You think because I said no, then it was OK for you and Roz to set me up? How could you do this to me?' Mina covered her face and wept into her hands. 'All my life, I've had to fend off fucking creeps because of what my mum does and who she hung about with, and then you . . . you go and do that to me. I'll never forgive you. *Never.* I hate you!'

Hurt and puzzlement rushed through Iris. 'Mina. Mina, I don't know what you're talking about.'

Mina dropped her hands. 'Liar!' She clambered out of bed, pulling her clothes on as tears rolled down her cheeks.

Tears pricked in Iris's eyes as well. 'I swear down, I don't know what you're talking about.'

Mina's gaze darted all over Iris's face and she could see the pain in her eyes. 'My drink was spiked.'

Iris fell silent, watching Mina begin to shake.

'What, what do you mean?' Iris grabbed Mina's shoulders. 'Tell me what you mean.'

'The drinks. They were laced with something. And . . . and there was this guy.' Mina took a noisy deep breath in between crying. 'I can't even remember most of what happened last night. How it happened. But I was talking to you and Roz . . . Then . . .'

'. . . I went to get ready,' Iris prompted. She shook her head in dismay, anger and hurt for Mina rushing through her, as well as guilt. 'I left you with Roz, I was half-cut by then. I did a few lines in the room, then the client came in. I thought you'd be all right. I thought you were all right, I . . .'

Before Iris had finished speaking, Roz came in, holding an envelope in her hand, waving it around. A large smile on her face. 'How does it feel to be a big earner, babe?' She directed her conversation to Mina. 'Five hundred big ones, doll. All yours.'

Without warning, Iris flew at her, screaming, grabbing hold of her hair. 'You fucking bitch, I'm going to kill you! How could you do that! She said no. She said, fucking, no, she didn't want to do it!'

'Leave it! Iris, just leave it!' Mina yelled, but Iris, ignoring her, continued to slap Roz about, pushing her into the wall.

'Iris, no! Don't!' Mina grabbed her, pulling her off Roz, who had a nasty scratch down her face.

'You spiked her drink!'

Panting and looking shocked, Roz stared at Iris. 'I was trying to do her a favour. I was trying to relax her.' Roz pointed at Mina but continued talking to Iris. 'You were the one who told me she needed the money. I felt sorry for her, OK! I like Mina, you know that, and I could see she wanted to earn, but she couldn't quite bring herself to do it.'

'So, you thought you'd put shit in her drink and let some guy bang her?'

Roz shook her head. 'Oh, excuse me for trying to be a mate, and anyway, it wasn't like that. It wasn't about the guy, it was about wanting to help her.'

Iris rubbed her head. 'Can you hear yourself?'

'I don't get what the problem is. She ain't hurt. And besides, once you've done it once, then it ain't a big deal. And see . . .' Roz picked up the envelope she'd dropped, throwing it over to Mina, who caught it. 'She's got a monkey for it. It wasn't like I was trying to rip her off. Quite the opposite. Oh, come on, guys, where's the fucking harm? She had to pop her cherry at some point, so she might as well get paid for it.'

'You sick bitch.' Iris glared at her.

Roz, looking genuinely puzzled, shrugged. 'Suit yourself. Next time, I won't bother. See yourself out.' She glared at them both before slamming out of the room.

Nothing was said for a moment. Iris looked at Mina. She didn't know what to say, especially as it was clear Roz didn't think it was any big deal. But then, why would she? Roz and her sister had been selling sex and making a good living from it since they were in their teens. To them, it was just a commodity like anything else. But the guilt she felt for bringing Mina along was beginning to grow. If it wasn't for her, none of this would be happening.

'Mina, I'm so sorr—'

'I don't want to talk about it,' Mina cut in.

'You can't pretend it didn't happen.'

Mina wiped away her tears. 'That's exactly what I plan on doing.'

'But . . .'

'But nothing, Iris. What's the point in talking about it? It's not like I can report it to the police, is it? It happened. End of.'

They fell silent again, and Iris had no doubt that Mina was putting on a tough face, something she'd probably had to do so many times in her life before.

'Shit, what time is it?' Mina's voice suddenly sounded panicked.

Iris glanced at her watch. 'It's already after eleven.'

'Oh my God!' Mina jumped up out of bed and hurried to get her day clothes out of her bag. 'Eleven! For fuck's sake! We have to go, come on, quick!' Mina visibly began to shake. 'Oh God, I needed to be back by midday.'

Iris glanced at her watch again. 'We won't be able to make it. It'll take us at least three hours from here. I'm sorry.'

Tears ran down Mina's face and Iris could see how agitated she was. 'I told you I had to be back . . . I knew I shouldn't have come.' She pulled out her phone from her jacket. 'Look at all the messages I've got!'

'From your mum?'

'No . . . no, from Doreen, she ain't going to wait past midday. Oh my God, this is a nightmare.' There was a tinge of hysteria to her voice.

'Who's Doreen?'

Tears were streaming down Mina's face, but she didn't answer.

'We can set off now,' Iris suggested. 'It'll be all right, Mina.'

'Just shut up! Just shut up, OK. It's not going to be all right. None of it's all right.' She pushed the envelope of money into her jeans pocket. 'I'm going to get the train back.'

'Let me drive you.'

Before Iris had time to say anything else, Mina rushed out the door and set off running down the stairs.

'Mina! Mina! Just wait, please . . . Mina, don't go. *Please*.' Iris raced after her and pushed herself in front of the door, blocking Mina's exit.

'Get out of my way!'

'Not until you tell me what's going on. *Please*.'

Mina went to open the front door, but she was on the verge of hysteria and Iris found that she could easily slam it shut again. 'Mina, I ain't letting you leave here like this. You need to calm down. You don't even know where the station is. I'm so sorry, I'm so sorry what happened. Let me look after you.'

'I can't, I haven't got time.'

Iris grabbed hold of Mina's arms. 'Why do you need to get back so urgently? What's going on? Tell me.'

Mina's shoulders slumped, the fight leaving her. 'I can't. I can't.'

Iris wrapped her arms around her. 'Mina, Jesus, you're scaring me. You know you can trust me. You can tell me anything.'

Mina shook her head. 'Not everything.'

Iris drew Mina away from her and she looked directly into Mina's eyes. 'I have *never* felt about anyone the way I feel about you, Mina. And I don't even know what this is, and you know what, that doesn't matter . . . Look, I ain't saying this very well, but what I'm trying to tell you is that you can trust me. Whatever it is, you can trust me. I swear . . .' She paused, then sounding nervous, she asked, 'Has this got something to do with that woman who texted you? Have you and her got something going on? If you have, that's OK, we can still be friends, yeah . . . I might not like it, but I still want you in my life – you're the best thing that has happened to me.'

Mina gave Iris a warm smile through her tears, and she wiped her running nose with the back of her sleeve. 'It's not that. I wish it was.'

'Then what is it?' Iris felt and sounded relieved. 'It can't be that bad, can it?'

'It is though.'

'Mina, please, let me help you. Tell me.'

Mina nodded, sobbing as she spoke. 'So, Doreen, she's . . . she's my mum's mate, they used to work together . . . and . . .' The unease oozed out with Mina's words. 'But now she's the babysitter, well kind of. Like I say, she used to work for the same pimp as my mum, but she helps out now and then.'

'Babysitter? Mina, what are you talking about?' Iris spoke gently, struggling to make sense of it all.

'Flo. She looks after Flo sometimes.' Shaking, Mina began to cry again. 'Flo's my little sister. No one knows about her – not the social, not the hospital, not the prison. No one. Mum's told none of the other women at Ashcroft either. Not even Reenie, and Mum loves and trusts her with her life.'

Iris was shocked. 'I had no idea, babe. But why ain't she told anyone?'

'Because she doesn't want Flo to end up in care, like I did. My mum's never been clean in her life. She always tries, but then ends up scoring again. Prison is the first time she's been off the gear, so if they'd known about Flo when my mum was pregnant with her, they would have had a care order for her before she was even born. Even now, social workers would just take her away if they knew; there'd be no chance of keeping her. I don't want that for her. I love Flo so much, but it's so hard to look after her. To keep her safe. To clothe her, to feed her, and it's not like I can even get money off the social for her. I had some money, but it's all gone. And somehow I'm still supposed to look after her and get myself to college and give her what she needs. I can't afford the proper babysitter, that's why I've got Doreen, but she likes the gear as well, so leaving Flo with her ain't great.'

Iris didn't say anything straight away. 'I'm so sorry you've had to deal with all this. I can't even imagine how you've been coping. I wish you'd told me earlier; I could've helped. You could've brought her round. Stayed with me.' She stared at Mina, and they locked eyes, and she gently kissed her on her lips before pulling away, and saying, 'I'm so sorry, Mina, but I can help you now. Now you've told me. I can get some money for you. If . . . if I can sweet-talk Roz, she'll let me work here again.'

Mina shook her head. 'No, no way. I don't want to have anything to do with her. Not after what she did.'

'But you won't have to, it'll be me. I want to help, Mina . . . I know it's not ideal, none of it's ideal. But I owe you. What Roz did to you was wrong, and I can't change that, but I can try to make things better for you.'

'No . . . no, you can't. I won't let you do that, not for me . . . This is such a mess. This is all just a frigging mess.'

Iris, who was crying nearly as hard as Mina, nodded. 'I know, that's why we need to get away. So our mums can't ruin our lives anymore. No disrespect, but it's not fair of your mum to give you that kind of responsibility. My mum's the same – she expects me to trail behind the mess, the shit she's made out of life. And she don't care she's making a mess of my life as well.'

Iris could see Mina bristle.

'It's fine.'

But she didn't look fine.

'It's not fine though, Mina, you've just told me how much you're struggling. And I know you love your sister, but it could be another eight, nine years before your mum gets out. It's not fair on you, and it's not fair on Flo.' She felt so upset for Mina.

She knew what it was like to be trapped in a situation of someone else's making.

Mina's stare darkened as she looked at Iris. 'I already told you, I'm fine, and I've made my decision. And it ain't got anything to do with you. This is my choice.'

Tears flooded from Iris, mirroring Mina's tears. 'But it isn't, none of this is our choice, don't you see that?'

Mina, upset and overwhelmed, shrieked, 'Just stop, just stop, OK! You have no idea what you're talking about.'

'But I do . . . I do. Don't you get it: I'm in the same position as you.'

'You're not though! You're not! It's you that doesn't get it. I owe her. I owe Mum.'

'What? That's crazy. How do you make that out?'

'Cos it wasn't her. It wasn't her! I was the one who killed her pimp. She took the blame, but it was me, Iris. I was the one who stuck the knife in his chest and killed him.'

38

THE GOVERNOR

Phil Reed stood by Gate C, watching the Sunday visitors walking through the car park. He nodded to them and most, if not all, nodded back, regarding him as if he was a headmaster, as they filed into assembly. It amused him, how a little bit of power went a long way. He smiled to himself, though that quickly faded as he saw Ollie Jones sauntering across. He gestured to him, calling him over. 'Mr Jones.' Reed stepped forward, putting out his hand, which Ollie duly shook. 'Mr Jones.'

'Call me Ollie.' His voice was gruff, and he ran his fingers through his thick black hair, his hazel eyes full of hostility.

'*Ollie* . . . I don't think we've had the pleasure of meeting, I'm the governor. I bet you're looking forward to taking your wife home today. No doubt it's been a long five years.'

Ollie nodded. 'Tell me about it. I can't wait to see the back of this place.'

'Well, you won't have to wait long . . . Though I do need to tell you, yesterday evening, there was an incident . . . It's fine, your wife's OK, but for some reason she was attacked by some of the other prisoners. She managed to make her escape along a corridor with another couple of prisoners. Luckily, one of the officers was alerted to their whereabouts, but it was certainly an unfortunate incident. Another of the women had to be taken to hospital. It's still touch and go. These things are a waiting game, aren't they?' He held his smile as Ollie's eyes darkened.

'What the fuck are you talking about?' Ollie snarled.

'Some of the other women jumped on your wife. She's been seen by Medical, and she's had to have a few stitches.'

'You're joking, right?' Ollie raised his voice. 'She's banged up in this shithole and you can't even keep her safe. I've got a mind to sue you lot.'

Reed bristled. 'I'm sure that's not what Amy would want.'

'How the fuck do you know what my wife would want?'

'Mr Jones . . . *Ollie*, I'd appreciate it if you'd lower your voice. I realize you're upset, but this behaviour, trust me, won't help anything.'

Ollie rubbed his chin, agitation showing on his face. 'Upset? Listen, you don't know the half of it.'

Reed nodded. 'Oh, I think I do.' His tone was sickly-sweet, and he smiled, feeling a headache begin at the back of his head. 'Any minute now, Amy will be getting her things handed back to her, but it'll still take a good hour for all the paperwork to be done – the administration takes a little while.'

'So where do I go? Where am I supposed to meet her?'

'She'll exit at a different gate, but if you come with me, I'll show you where you can wait.'

Ollie nodded but didn't say anything and Reed led him through the car park and around to the side gate, walking along the corridor in silence towards the door where Amy would eventually be released. He could feel Ollie's seething anger oozing out behind him, though he didn't bother trying to appease him.

After a few minutes they reached the reception desk, where two officers were busy sifting through a pile of letters. Reed stopped, turned to Ollie. 'I've got an office down here. You're more than welcome to sit and wait in it. Come on, I'll show you.'

'Getting the royal treatment ain't going to stop me taking this place to the cleaners.'

'Well, that's down to you, isn't it?' Reed's voice was oily

smooth. He opened the door of the plain, drab office he used to speak to visitors. 'Take a seat.'

Ollie stalked past him and Reed gently closed the door, moving across to the large black desk by the window. He sat behind it: the imbalance of power needed to be sustained. 'I bet you've got a lot of things planned with Amy. Obviously, I don't know her very well as I haven't been at Ashcroft long, but from what I know, and what my staff tell me, she's certainly one of the more *pleasant* guests we have staying here.' Again, his voice was super smooth, but Ollie just stared at him contemptuously.

Going into his desk drawer for something, he continued to talk. 'At least the weather's lovely, you'll be able to go to the parks, have a picnic . . . You may even want this.' Without warning, Reed threw something to Ollie, who instinctively caught it. Then, seeing what it was, he dropped it and blanched.

Reed stood, coming around the desk to pick up the package. 'I take it you recognize it, *Ollie?*'

Ollie shook his head. He stood up to go, hurrying towards the door. 'I don't know what the fuck you're talking about. I don't even know what that is.'

'Really?' He smirked. 'Is that why you're looking ill suddenly? Maybe I could get you a drink of water?'

'This is a set-up!'

Holding the package in his hand, Reed turned it over, chuckling. 'What's a set-up? I thought you didn't know what this is. For all you know, it could be your Amazon package gone astray: couriers, they can never be trusted.' He laughed heartily, nastily.

'Fuck you, I don't have to listen to this.'

Reed sat back on the edge of his desk, watching as Ollie reached for the door handle. 'Oh, but you do, Mr Jones. For one thing, this is a prison, you can't just wander about. And secondly, I only have to press this button on my radio, and those officers out there will come running in. And even if this package didn't have your fingerprints on it originally, it does now.' Reed turned the package around in his hand, feeling the weight of it. 'What would you say? Half a kilo? A kilo of heroin? Whatever it is, you're looking at a long stretch, Ollie.'

Ollie pointed at the governor. 'You won't get this to stick.'

'You and I both know that's not true. After all, I already know who your accomplice is, and they'll sing like a bird. Plus, I suspect this stuff is part of the reason one of our women overdosed.'

Ollie visibly gritted his teeth. He began to pace, and Reed could see the film of perspiration forming on his forehead. 'This is bang out of order.'

'My sentiments exactly.'

Ollie lurched towards him, but Reed put up his hand, 'I wouldn't, if I were you. You're only going to make your situation ten times worse. Game's up, Mr Jones . . . Shame. But there you have it; you should never have brought that shit into my prison.'

For a moment, Ollie closed his eyes, breathing loudly, heavily. 'So, go on. Go on then, whatever. Do what you have to do . . . Well, what are you waiting for? Let's get this over and done with, shall we?'

Placing the package on the desk, Reed walked up to Ollie and stood close to him, staring into his eyes. Then he hovered his thumb over the red call button on the radio.

And the seconds passed by.

'Just fucking get on with it,' Ollie snarled again. His whole body was visibly tense.

'OK.' Reed lowered his thumb, skimming it on the button. 'How about a countdown?'

'You're enjoying this, aren't you?'

'I am, very much so . . . OK then, here goes. Ready?'

'Fuck you.'

Reed tilted his head and laughed, but then said, 'Or maybe there's another way. Maybe you and I could sort this out together.' He grinned, then walked round the desk and sat in his chair. Ollie's face turned to shocked bemusement. 'Take a seat, Mr Jones.'

'What?'

'I said, take a seat.'

Ollie shook his head. 'What is your game? What do you want from me?'

Reed gestured to the chair again. 'If you sit down, I'll tell you.'

Ollie didn't move for a moment, then, after a beat, he stalked to the chair and sat down, his shoulders slumping. 'Earle always said you were a cunt.'

'Earle?' Reed raised his eyebrows, though he didn't want to sound or look surprised. Although chatter around the prison had made him suspicious, he had no actual proof that the spineless Tony Earle had been involved. If anything, the news that Earle had been bringing in quantities of gear made him go up in Reed's estimation. Not much, but it took a fair bit of guts to bring heroin into a prison.

Ollie frowned, clearly picking up on the surprise that Reed was trying to hide. 'We weren't talking about the same *accomplice*, were we?' he snorted.

Reed opened his arms. 'No, I was talking about Tess, but thank you for that. It's always good to know who you're dealing with. Knowledge is power.'

Ollie licked his lips, and Reed could see the anger and hatred in his eyes.

His work phone beeped and he looked at the message, reading it off the screen. 'All the paperwork has been done for your wife . . . She's now a free woman. Congratulations. If you go back through the door, you'll see her in the holding reception . . . Go on, off you go. Enjoy.'

Ollie looked confused. 'You can't just leave it like this. What the fuck? What do you want from me?'

Reed locked the package of drugs in his desk drawer. This little meeting had gone even better than anticipated. Not only did he have Ollie's fingerprints on the gear, he also had another name. He smiled. 'I'll let you know . . . Oh, Mr Jones, before you go, do you want to talk about that little matter of suing the prison?'

Ollie's face was a picture of fury, and he pulled the door wide open.

Reed laughed. 'No, I thought not . . . Oh, and Ollie . . . You do realize that this is *far* from over. You owe me, and when I come calling, even if it's next week, next month, next year, I expect you to jump . . . And Mr Jones, believe me when I say, I always, *always* pull in a favour.'

39

EVIE

'Hello! Hello! Hello, is anyone there?' She banged on the door, her whole body shaking. 'Hello! You can't just keep me in here. You have to let me go! Hello! Please, *please*, just let me go home!'

The door opened and immediately Evie began to back away.

'What is it about you that doesn't learn?' Martha smiled nastily, walking towards her. 'I think my idiot of an ex-husband was a little too soft on you. But that's Ollie all over – too full of sentiment for his own good.'

Evie could feel her heart racing. 'You've got to let me out of here. You can't keep me in here any longer.'

Martha was inches away from her, and she didn't say anything for a moment. Then she nodded. 'You're absolutely right, Evie, we can't . . .'

PART TWO

FOUR WEEKS LATER

40
AMY

'In four weeks, we haven't got a single lead. No proper ones anyway. I know you've spoken to lots of people, but speaking and getting answers are two different things.' Amy sat in the front pew of the church in Soho Square. Since her release, she didn't know how many times she'd been to church, she'd lost count. Apart from when she'd been in the chapel in Ashcroft, never in her life had she seen the inside of a church, but now it seemed to be a regular pastime.

Standing in front of her, Jack fixed his dark green eyes on her. He smiled, his handsome face lighting up. 'I know, I think Reenie thought there was going to be a miracle somehow. I keep telling her we'll find her, but . . .' His face dropped and he stopped talking for a moment, then, looking like he was trying to compose himself, he smiled again. 'Someone must know where she is, hey.'

'Maybe,' Amy said solemnly because, much as she hated to admit it, her instincts were telling her that something was very wrong. 'We've checked with all her friends and all the places I remember Lynette told me Evie hung out in, and each time we drew a blank. I think we have to face it: Evie's not coming home.' She didn't want to say out loud what she was thinking for fear that, if she did, fate might do the rest.

Jack came and sat down next to her. Instinctively, she touched the almost-healed scar on her forehead, a reminder of Ashcroft. It was funny because some days she really missed the place, the girls, the banter, even the noise, but other days she woke up with nightmares, thinking that she was back inside.

The past four weeks had been a struggle, what with trying to adjust to life on the outside in between meeting up with Jack whenever she could. Jack had been following leads and trying his best, not just for Lynette and Evie, but for Reenie and the women back in Ashcroft. It was almost like they needed it as much as Lynette did. Having something like that hanging over the women's heads made serving time so much harder.

She glanced at her phone. 'I have to go. Ollie will be back soon – he went somewhere with Martha, God knows where.' She shrugged. 'Not that I'm interested; he just can't know that I'm out and about.'

'I thought you said he bought your story about finding God while you were in Ashcroft.' He gave her a wry smile.

She stared at him, feeling uncomfortable that she'd had to open up about her life to him. Reenie said he could be trusted, but at the end of the day, he was still a virtual stranger to her, and the fear that Ollie would somehow find out was never too far away. 'He has, kind of, but what he still ain't keen on is me going to church all the time – and I can't say I disagree with him, though his reasons are different to mine. He was worried about the priests. I reckon he's been reading too much of the *Thorn Birds*.' She smiled, but as always Jack made her feel self-conscious, though she wasn't quite sure why.

'So, what's your reason, if it isn't to do with wanting to rip Father Doherty's robe off?'

She roared with laughter, and so did he. The tension broken, their merriment echoed around the high-domed ceiling of St Patrick's Catholic church. Father Doherty must have been eighty at least.

'That hour every Sunday morning, and Thursday evening,

feels like a month. I don't know how you ever did it. Even the guy Ollie sent to watch me has given up coming. He's probably told Ollie no one in their right mind would put themselves through Doherty's sermons if they didn't need to.'

Jack winked at her. His messy dark brown hair fell over his forehead, and not for the first time, she wondered why he'd ever become a priest. He was so . . . so . . . un-priestlike. Here he was, dressed casually in jeans and a black shirt, looking strong and handsome, the twinkle in his eyes making her feel something she hadn't felt for a very long time. She told herself to get a grip and stop being stupid.

Maureen hadn't mentioned anything about his past life, and he'd only said in passing how different his life had been before. Though that much was obvious. She'd seen his on-off girlfriend, Rebel, and although she didn't know the woman personally, she'd made a few enquiries with some of the girls she knew from her days working in the clubs. The high-class escort world was a small one, and people knew each other.

The information that had come back didn't surprise her in the least: Rebel had once been a top-class hooker, before she got bang on the drugs, that was. After that, she'd ended up in the tiny Soho members-only club, still on the game, but certainly not earning the thousands she used to.

Amy didn't know the timeline between Jack getting together with Rebel and her past as a high-class hooker and drug addict. She sensed it was a sensitive subject, and that they went back a long time. But she also knew that the only time she'd spoken to Rebel was when she'd been with Jack, and the look, the hatred in Rebel's eyes towards her, had told her all that she needed to know. And she had to admit, the feeling wasn't far from mutual.

'So you see, it did the trick,' Jack said. 'You coming to church like a good Catholic girl took the heat off you.'

'I guess.' She shrugged again. Ollie had always been suspicious, jealous, but for some reason he seemed distracted of late. Even on the day she'd been released from Ashcroft, it had been obvious his mind was elsewhere. He'd hardly commented on her injuries, which had looked especially shocking that first day.

But the thing she'd found strangest was that he'd stayed away that first night. Not that she was complaining. The days of her wanting him to touch her were long gone. Fleetingly, it had made her curious, though not curious enough to care. All she wanted was to get answers about Evie, even if they weren't the answers anyone wanted. It was the not knowing that was toughest for everyone.

'That still looks nasty.' Jack's words broke her train of thought, and she glanced up to see him reaching to gently touch her head.

'It's fine, I've had worse.'

He looked at her. 'Have you?'

For a moment, she held his stare but then quickly moved her gaze away, looking at anything but him. There was something about Jack that made her feel . . . vulnerable. Soft. Free. Something about him that allowed her to take down the walls that she'd put up over the years since she'd been with Ollie. She didn't even know him. She was being stupid. And she guessed that's how sad her life had become: all someone had to do was be nice to her and she started getting all girly. Because that's all it was. Instead of putting her down all the time like Ollie did, he was always positive and encouraging.

When she'd first met him, a month ago – though it felt longer – Jack had been abrupt, abrasive with her. She'd even go as far as to say he'd been bloody rude. She hadn't liked him, and she'd taken exception to that; after all, she'd been risking a lot to meet him at the church, to help Lynn, and all he could do was be impolite. But maybe that was a trust thing. She didn't trust him, and he didn't trust her.

But his abruptness had begun to dissolve when word came back that Maureen was getting better. It had been touch and go for the first couple of weeks, the heart attack she'd suffered very nearly proving fatal, but now Maureen was making a good recovery. And once Amy had realized Jack's moodiness was purely down to him worrying about Reenie, she'd warmed to him. Though warming to someone certainly wasn't the same as trusting them. She'd learned that the hard way.

Finding herself catching her breath, she moved away from Jack, trying not to show how flustered she'd suddenly begun to feel. 'So, when are you going to visit Reenie again?'

'Tomorrow. You want to come? I think you should, you haven't seen her since you saved her life. I owe you.'

Amy blushed. 'You don't owe me. I love Reenie. Anyone would've done the same.'

He stared into her eyes. 'But it wasn't anyone, it was you . . . Come with me, she'd love to see you.'

'And I'd love to see her. I miss her, but I can't. It's one thing sneaking to church and convincing Ollie that I've found religion, but it would be another thing entirely, me getting in a car with you.'

Jack pulled a face. 'He doesn't have to know, we can get round it.'

Amy glanced at her watch again and she stood up, accidentally knocking a hymn book which had been left on the pew to the floor. 'No, I ain't risking it. I could just about explain if he saw me talking to you in here with that clergy collar on. I could say that Maureen put me in touch with you, especially if he recognized you from the prison. But it's another thing altogether, me hanging around with you . . .' She paused, watching him pick up the book from the floor, and decided not to explain to him that the fact he was so good looking, probably one of the most good-looking men she'd known, would serve only to enrage Ollie. So instead she said, 'Even if I went there on my own, he'd find out. Like I told you, he's in with one of the officers there, as well as that cow Tess . . . You don't know what he'd do if he ever found out.'

Jack's eyes darkened. 'Believe me, I've come across enough guys like him to know how he operates.'

Amy gave him a small smile and went to turn away, but he grabbed hold of her hand, his handsome looks brooding. 'You will tell me if there's anything I can do. Just say the word.'

'Sorry, am I interrupting something? This looks very cosy.' A loud, sarcastic voice came from the back of the church, followed by the sound of heels tapping on the marble floor down the aisle.

'Rebel, hey, it's good to see you. How are you doing?' Amy trilled, but it sounded disingenuous, and it was only made worse by the fact that it echoed around the church.

'Oh yeah, I'm doing great, but clearly not as good as you two.' Rebel's speech was slurred. Dressed in a tight black skirt and top, she looked pointedly at Jack's hand holding Amy's.

Quickly Amy pulled away, knowing exactly what Rebel was thinking, though she didn't take the bait. She could see Rebel swaying on her feet, and she wondered if it was only alcohol or something harder she'd taken.

'Yeah, I was just telling Jack about a few issues I'm having, wasn't I?'

Jack didn't say anything, only nodded. So she added, 'It's hard to adjust to life outside Ashcroft.'

Rebel, her face caked with make-up that made her look hard, sneered, 'Well, you can always go back, darlin', if you miss it that badly. That can always be arranged.' They held each other's stares, but still Amy didn't jump to the bait. It wasn't wise to annoy Rebel any more than she had already.

Rebel lived and worked in Soho, and even though Jack had assured her that Rebel would keep her mouth shut, she wasn't so sure. She knew what a woman scorned was capable of. Even though there was nothing between her and Jack, Rebel didn't see it like that. From the first time she'd met her, Rebel had clearly taken an instant dislike to her.

And she knew that Rebel wasn't a shrinking violet. You couldn't be an escort, high class or otherwise, if you weren't tough. She remembered how she'd seen Ollie as her knight in shining armour, riding in to save her from that life. Maybe that was how Rebel saw Jack. Unlike Ollie, Jack seemed to be the real deal. Though, thinking about it, all the men she'd ever known had let her down, and maybe Jack was no different. Maybe being a priest wouldn't stop him turning out to be a prick eventually.

But if Rebel did open her mouth, she had no doubt word would filter through to Ollie. Soho was a community, a small one, and the Soho grapevine ensured news travelled. And that was something she couldn't afford to happen.

'Reb, I think maybe you should go and lie down.'

Jack's words were like a red rag to a bull. Rebel's eyes flashed and she turned on him. 'You're a condescending cunt, you know that? Or maybe it's you who wants to lie down, with her.'

Amy's heart went out to Jack. She knew only too well what it was like to be humiliated in front of someone. That was Ollie's party piece.

Jack's voice was calm though. 'Why do you do this every time, Reb? When will you realize there's no need for it?'

He reached out to her, but she stepped back and snapped, 'When you stop talking to whores like her.'

Jack gave her a hard stare. 'You're out of order, so back off.'

She pushed him hard in the chest, her expression full of anger. 'Don't tell me what to do, understand? Don't ever fucking tell me.'

Amy watched him roll his tongue in his mouth, cricking the tension out of his neck. 'And that works both ways. Who I speak to is nothing to do with you. *Nothing*. Reb, we've gone through this before.' He turned to Amy. 'I'm sorry, Amy.'

Rebel was swaying on her feet, her skirt hitched up to her thighs. 'Why are you apologizing to her? It's me you should be saying sorry to.' She pushed him again, then slapped him hard across the face, though he didn't react. He just stared at her, as if he'd been through this a thousand times with her already.

'You're a mess.'

'And who's fault is that, hey, Jack? *Yours*. Me being like this is your fault.'

Tense, he shook his head. 'Keep telling yourself that, Reb, but I've been gone for nine years.'

Feeling all kinds of awkward as well as anger towards Rebel for the way she was acting, Amy said, 'I better go.'

Without waiting for a reply, she hurried down the long marble aisle, feeling Rebel's stare. And once again the same thought came into her head: Rebel was trouble waiting to happen.

41

VISITING TIME

'Sweetheart, please talk to me.' Steph held on to Iris's hands from across the table. 'You've hardly said anything. I don't know how to help you if you won't talk to me.'

'I already told you, Mum, I don't want to talk about it. That's why I haven't been calling you or coming to see you, because you only want to talk about that.'

Steph's eyes brimmed with tears; she leaned across the table. 'You can't just tell me this and expect me to forget about it, sweep it under the table. You know I hate the Old Bill, but maybe we should talk to them. I don't want those fuckers getting away with it.'

Iris snatched her hands away. 'Stop. This isn't about you, it's about me, and there's no way I'm going to start talking to the Old Bill. If I hadn't been so angry, I wouldn't have told you either. It was only because I was upset.'

Steph took a deep breath. 'Well, I'm glad you did. You shouldn't have to go through any of this on your own.'

Iris shook her head, looking around the visiting room. 'Is that supposed to be a joke?'

'No.' The hurt was etched on Steph's face.

'Mum, since you've been banged up, I've been alone. Apart from the ponces who work for you and your sorry excuse for a husband – who, apart from getting his leg over, was never there – I've been on my jack jones.'

Steph closed her eyes. She visibly swayed in her seat. Then she opened them, staring at her daughter. 'I swear to you, if it's the last thing I do, he will not get away with it. Do you understand? I will make sure he pays. I just need to know the names of the others.'

Iris frowned. 'I can't do this now. I'm going to get a drink from the machine.'

As Iris got up, across the other side of the visiting room, Mina sat listening to her mum, who looked far from having a rosy pregnant glow. Her hair was scraped back, and she looked pale, the grey prison tracksuit jumper making her look even worse.

'You OK? You don't look so well,' Mina said.

'What do you expect? I'm banged up in here, and I'm ready to drop.'

Fiddling with her fingers, Mina tried to smile. 'I'm just worried that . . . that you might go back on the gear . . . I'm scared, I'm scared you're going to throw it all away again. You've got that look, you know, really agitated.'

Her mum chewed on her lip. 'It's hard. I'm not saying I ain't tempted. Truth is, my head's done in. This place, it gets to me.'

Mina shrugged.

Ness looked hurt. 'Is that it? A shrug – that's all you've got for me.'

'I . . . I just don't know what to say.'

'Really?' Her mum's voice dripped with sarcasm. 'I can think of something.'

'Like what?' Mina mumbled.

'Like, I'm sorry.' Ness's eyes filled with tears. 'Like, "I'm sorry for stabbing Steve to death and putting you in this shithole for the next ten years."'

Mina burst into tears, covering her face. 'You told me that was what you wanted to do.'

'Oh yeah, cos giving my baby up and sitting in Ashcroft is what I wanted to do.'

Trembling, Mina dropped her hands. 'You didn't even know you were pregnant. You never knew until you came inside. I told you not to. I told you not to say it was you, Mum. I begged you. I said I'd fess up.'

'I had no choice! What was I supposed to do, sit back and do nothing?'

'That wouldn't be anything new.' Mina whispered the words before she could stop herself.

'What did you say?' Hurt poured out of Ness.

'I didn't mean it, I didn't mean it. But . . . but you talk like this is what *I* wanted, you make out that it's easy for me on the outside, looking after Flo, trying to make ends meet.'

'Then maybe you shouldn't have done what you did.'

Mina sat back and started furiously shaking her head, but she made sure she spoke in a whisper. 'No, no, no, I ain't taking that. Yeah, I stabbed him, Mum, but you were the one who brought him into our house, you were the one who was always bang off your head. And let's face it, you were the one who got pregnant by one of your punters or by Steve. But you're right, *Mum*, I was the one who killed him, because he was hurting Flo while you were out . . . Should I have left him to hurt Flo like he hurt you? Is that what you wanted me to do? Did you want me to leave him to batter her about because she was crying for you while you were out earning money for him and to feed your habit?'

Ness was weeping now and shook her head. 'I'm so sorry. I shouldn't have said that. I'm just scared, and I take it out on you when I shouldn't.'

Mina reached across and touched her mum's hands, but she stopped short of saying it was fine, because it wasn't. She was so tired of having to deal with her mum's ups and downs, and tired of trying to make everything all right for her. For once she wanted her mum to make everything all right for her.

'Oh my God, he's the last thing I need right now.' Ness wiped her eyes and her nose on her sleeve. 'He's a right wanker. He swans around this place like he's fucking king of the castle. I hate him, I'm telling you, that cunt needs to get what for.' She stared over Mina's shoulder. 'I'm ready to pop, and he's done nothing. I'm telling you, Mina, if I have to wait ten years to get him, I will. He knows that I'm desperate to keep the baby, but he's done nothing to help. They told us that he was away on conferences, but does that suntan look like he's been in a bleeding conference in Telford? I'm telling you, that smarmy bastard's been larging it up on the coast while I've been going off me nut worrying.'

Mina sighed as her mum went off on yet another rant. 'Who are you talking about?'

'The governor. Mr Phil Reed. Fucking arsehole.' Ness spat out her words.

Mina turned to see who her mum was looking at, then she quickly stared across to Iris, who looked as unhappy as she felt as she walked back to Steph, holding a can of lemonade.

'Mina . . . Mina . . . Don't you think that's terrible?' Her mum's voice broke through her thoughts.

'Sorry . . . sorry . . . what did you say?' She turned back to her.

Ness smiled at her daughter and let out a big sigh. 'I'm saying, one of the officers told me that Lynn still doesn't know that Evie hasn't been found. She's awake but it sounds like the doctor doesn't think she's strong enough to hear it. Poor cow. But then, when is any mum ready to hear that their daughter's gone missing?'

Mina smiled back, but she could feel it was forced; her thoughts were spinning.

'Yeah, it's terrible what happened.'

'I'm just hoping she's run off with some geezer. Anything else don't bear thinking about . . . Look, I'm going to get a coffee from the trolley, you want one? And I'm sorry again for saying what I did. You wouldn't think that I get excited to see you, would you? But I do, only then I go and fuck it up. Then that's me all over, ain't it.'

Mina watched her mum walk across the visiting room and quickly she called across to Iris, who was sitting looking upset opposite an equally grim-faced and red-eyed Steph.

'Iris . . . Iris. I need to speak to you.' She gave a quick smile to Steph, who gestured to her daughter that it was fine for her to go and speak to Mina.

Looking relieved, Iris sauntered across to the chair Ness had been sitting in, opposite Mina. She grinned at her. 'Thank you for saving me. Oh my God, my mum was doing my head in. I know she means well, and she's being all caring, but I can't deal with her, not right now. I told her some stuff, stuff I ain't even told you even – but I will, one day – and I know she's gutted, but she wants to fix it. Like she wants to fix everything. Only she can't. I just don't want to talk about it – well, you know what that feels like, when you don't want to talk about stuff . . .' Iris trailed off and stared at Mina and frowned. 'Is everything all right, Mina? You look terrible.' She glanced across to Ness, who was busy chatting with the prison volunteers serving her coffee. 'Is she doing your head in too? Who needs parents.'

Mina could feel herself shaking. 'No, no, it's not that.' She took a deep breath.

'Then what's going on? You want me to go and get your mum? You feeling ill? Do you think you've picked up the cold Flo had? She was all snuffles this week, wasn't she?'

'No, it's not that. I just . . .' She took another deep breath.

'I'm going to get your mum. Maybe it's cos you didn't have

breakfast this morning.' Iris went to stand up, but Mina grabbed hold of her hand.

'Just sit down, yeah. Sit down.'

Looking surprised, Iris gave a small nod. 'What's happened?'

Over the noise of the visiting room, Mina said, 'Look over to your right. But don't make it obvious.'

Iris did as Mina had asked. She turned back and shrugged.

'Yeah, what? What am I supposed to be looking at?'

'Remember Matt – the man . . . well, the man that I slept with in Nottingham.'

'You mean the man Roz tricked you into sleeping with,' Iris said angrily.

Mina brought her voice down even lower. 'Well, he's here.'

'Here! Oh my God!' Iris looked shocked.

'But that's not his name.'

Iris shrugged, looking puzzled. 'How do you know?'

'Because he's over there . . . Phil Reed. The governor of Ashcroft.'

42

MAUREEN

'How are you feeling, Reenie?' Jack sat opposite Maureen in the visiting room. 'You're looking better than the last time I came.'

'I think the good Lord was kind to me, don't you think? He obviously has plans for me, he clearly wants me to spend a little more time here in Ashcroft before he takes me.' She laughed but the tightness of her chest made her pull on her breath, though she didn't want to worry Jack. There was no point. There was nothing he could do for her apart from pray, and even she wasn't sure that would do any good.

She glanced around and saw Mina and Iris huddled together. 'Look at those two, they're thick as thieves, but it's nice to see that they're such good friends. It's a shame Ness and Steph can't be the same. I hoped that with all the worry about Lynette and Evie, it would bring everyone closer together, but it hasn't. Though Tess is the one to blame for that, and Steph for some reason hasn't been herself lately, so she gunned for Amy and caused such a divide between the women. The whole wing has been on edge for the past month. Though if you ask me, I think that was Tess's plan all along. I may be wrong, but that's my guess.'

Jack let his eyes wander across to Mina and Iris. 'I'd say those two were more than that, Reenie.'

Maureen frowned. 'More than what?'

Jack smiled. 'Haven't you seen the way they look at each other? Iris more than Mina, I think, but maybe that's because Mina seems more reserved. I've noticed it over the past couple of months. I'd lay a bet on the fact they were an item.'

Maureen glanced at them again. 'Oh Jesus, that's all we need.' As always, her Irish brogue became more accentuated as she grew agitated. 'Can you imagine the fuss if Ness or Steph found out? They'd go mad. The last thing either of them want now is to be forced together any more than they already are. Not now when they're sworn enemies.' Her laughter was warm. 'I think for now, I won't mention it. Iris and Mina will just have to play star-crossed lovers for the time being . . . Anyhow, how's it going with Evie? Any word?'

Jack's dark green eyes saddened. 'No.'

'Please don't give up looking, Jack. Lynn needs it, we all need it. We all need her to be found.'

'I'm not giving up, but so many of my leads have dried up.' Then he smiled. 'Amy sends her love, by the way.'

'Oh, how is she?' Maureen's face shone.

'She's good. Really good. But her husband Ollie continues to be a bastard. I think she's terrified of him. She would've come to see you if it wasn't for him. Such a fucking idiot – excuse the language, but she deserves better. Much better.'

Maureen stared at him. She didn't say anything for a moment, but she did take another deep breath, and took his hands in hers, holding them across the small table that stood between them. 'Well, she's a beautiful woman with a good heart but, as they say, her life is complicated.'

Jack nodded and tried to pull his hands away, but Maureen held on to them.

'I don't know much about this Ollie. But I do know he's not a man to be messed with.'

This time Jack did pull his hands away. 'Reenie, I'm not a kid.

I can look after myself. How long have we known each other? Twenty-five years? More?'

'To me it feels a lifetime.'

Jack raised his eyebrows. 'Well in all those years, you've never stopped worrying about me. You've never thought that anyone was good enough for me or right for me.'

Maureen leaned forward. 'You're a priest, maybe on sabbatical, but a priest nevertheless, so of course I don't think anyone's right.' She sniffed haughtily.

Jack shook his head, there was a slight tone of irritation to his voice. 'Oh, come off it, I haven't always been a priest, and even then, you had a strong opinion, Reenie. And besides, we both know why I became a priest: I was running away. Hiding. Ashamed.'

Maureen shook her head. 'We all come to God on different paths. Our journeys are all unique to get to him.'

'Stop! Stop!' he whispered, hissing through his teeth. 'Reenie, why do you always do this? I love you, but why try to make out I'm some fallen angel, some harmless sinner who's been reborn? You and I both know what I was . . . what I am.'

'You're not that anymore.' Her voice was firm and once again she felt her chest tighten and she struggled to catch her breath. 'We all make mistakes.'

There was warmth in Jack's eyes, but he laughed sadly. 'Reenie, I have blood on my hands. *Blood*. I lost count how many men I killed. I lost count how many lives were ruined by the things I did and the way I lived my life. That never goes away.'

'Oh, Jack.' Maureen covered her face for a moment. She could hear the pain in his voice. She wished he wouldn't speak about himself like that, she wished he would see that he was a changed man. 'Why won't you forgive yourself? Why torture yourself with the past. Haven't you paid enough?'

Then she felt him move her hands away from her face, his smile, his warm eyes looking at her. 'Reenie, it's OK. I'm OK. Please, don't get upset.'

'But I do . . . Those men, those people you talk about, they knew the risks of the life they led. Faces, and gangsters, drugs and guns and violence, that all comes with a price. Do you think they'd have given you the time of day, Jack, if something had happened to you? I'm only thankful you got out when you did, because it could've been you that was being buried in Epping Forest . . . And anyway, you didn't have the easiest of starts. To know what they did to you, the way they treated you in that children's orphanage, well, it haunts me, Jack.'

He laughed kindly. 'I think if I ate the moon, Reenie, you'd give me an excuse as to why I did it. What did I do to deserve to have you in my life, to meet such a good, kind, protective woman like you?'

Despite herself, Maureen laughed too. She swallowed down her tears. 'Now who's making excuses? Look around you, Jack. Look where we are. I'm hardly a saint, am I?' Though this time when she spoke, she couldn't help the tears from falling. She shook her head. Since she'd gotten out of hospital, she felt more emotional than usual. But she didn't want to talk about what happened all those years ago, especially not with Jack. Some things were better left in the past. Taking a deep breath, she smiled. 'Just promise me you'll look after yourself. Sometimes, I think you're like a magnet to troubled souls, and to be blessed with such looks, Jack . . . Please be careful of Ollie. I think he'd be happy to kill any man that looked at Amy.'

'Time, everyone,' the prison officer sitting in the corner bellowed before looking straight back down at her magazine.

Jack stood up, then leaned over and kissed Maureen on the cheek. 'I have to go, Reenie. I'll see you next week.'

'Jack, be careful.'

He went to go, but turned back and stared at her before saying, 'What *you* need to remember is, I may have turned my back on Soho, but it doesn't mean I've forgotten how to look after myself. If Ollie comes after me, he needs to make sure he's able to kill me first – before I kill him.'

43

AMY

Twenty miles away, Amy stood in the bathroom, slowly getting dressed. She stared at herself in the mirror. Even after these few weeks, she hadn't quite got used to being able to go into the bathroom without queues of women clamouring for space and privacy. The other thing she hadn't quite got used to was the loneliness. It was stupid, because when she'd been there, all she'd wanted at times was peace. And now . . . well, now she'd got it, and it seemed pretty much overrated to her.

Before she'd gone into Ashcroft, she hadn't realized how isolated she'd become. How getting together with Ollie had taken her from being a social butterfly, loving going out with the girls, loving having fun and a bit of banter with the guys, to someone that couldn't go out most of the time without permission, someone who'd handed over their freedom, albeit unwillingly, to her husband.

Taking a deep breath, Amy touched up her make-up on her black eye: a reminder from Ollie yesterday that when he said a certain time to be home, he meant a certain time. Some things never changed.

Refusing to cry, she jumped as Ollie came into the bathroom.

'Hello, darlin'.' She tried to sound cheerful but her nerves were on edge as she noted the way he inspected the place, making sure everything was how he liked it. Everything about life was about how Ollie liked it.

Not saying a word, Ollie stared at the double towel rail. He pointed to it. 'What's that?'

Amy quickly looked in that direction and, seeing what he was staring at, ran across to straighten the fluffy white towels and make sure they were perfectly aligned with each other. 'Sorry . . . sorry, I . . . I didn't notice.' She heard herself and hated how she sounded, hated how she'd become, but it was either his way or no way.

'Five years inside, and this is what it's become. You're a slob. Look at your hair, you haven't even brushed it.'

'I did.'

He grabbed her face, squeezing it hard, then he kissed her hard on the lips. 'What have I told you, Amy? Don't talk back to me. Not unless you want to make me angry.' His voice was velvety smooth, but his eyes were full of hatred.

She stared into them. So beautiful, so handsome . . . so cruel. 'I ain't talking back, Ollie, I was just telling you that I *have* brushed it.'

He smirked. 'You see, not only are you a cheeky little bitch, Amy, but you're also a dumb one. I'd say that was talking back, wouldn't you? Go on, say it.'

Amy frowned. 'Say what? What are you talking about?'

Ollie glanced at himself in the mirror. Picking up the pearl-handled brush on the side of the marble washbasin, he brushed his hair, patting it down into the perfect position. He moved his gaze to look at her in the mirror. 'Say that you're a dumb bitch.'

She looked away, staring at the ground, her heart racing and her mouth becoming dry. 'Stop it, Ollie.'

'*Stop it, Ollie.*' He mimicked her, and as she looked up, she saw a sneer appear on his face. 'I want to hear you, say it. Say you're a dumb bitch. Don't look like that, all you're saying is what we both already know.'

She paused and stared at him.

He turned to her, spinning her around to face him. Then he looked at her, brought his hand back and slapped her hard across the cheek. 'SAY IT.'

Holding her face, Amy nodded, fighting back the tears. 'I'm a dumb bitch.'

'*Louder*, I can't hear you.' Ollie grinned, his hand beginning to move down her body.

She shivered inwardly in disgust, and trembling, she continued to cry. '*Ollie*, please.'

'*SAY IT!*' he bellowed, although he was right next to her.

'I'm a dumb bitch.'

'Again.'

'I'm a dumb bitch.'

'*Again!*'

'I'M A DUMB BITCH!' She screamed her words, her voice echoing off the expensive marble bathroom tiles, then she began to sob loudly. The time off she'd had from him in Ashcroft had made her forget; ironically, five years inside had made her softer. Made dealing with Ollie harder to cope with. After all, when she'd first met him, her life had been care homes, foster homes, working in clubs, stripping in clubs, selling herself to the highest bidder . . . that all took its toll and she'd built up defences that shielded her from what unfolded with Ollie. Even though she'd got in too deep with him and was too scared, too weak, too broke, too worn down to try to get away, back then it felt like she was tougher, it felt like his cruelty was something she could just about manage. But now? Now, even after only six weeks, it felt unbearable.

He pushed back her long hair, tucking it behind her ears. 'You see, that wasn't too hard now, was it? I'm so pleased you're home, Amy; I really did miss you.'

He moved in and she saw his erection straining against the joggers he was wearing.

'I . . . I need to go.'

Ollie looked puzzled. 'Go where?' he laughed.

'I, er, I'm not feeling so great . . . I've got a bit of a head-ache . . . I need to go and get a painkiller. I don't want it to turn into a migraine.'

'I'll tell you what, I've got the perfect solution for a head-ache . . . Turn around.'

'Ollie . . .' she trailed off, knowing in her heart whatever she might say would be pointless.

He kissed her again and then aggressively turned her around, pushing her up against the sink. He grabbed her hair with one hand, and with the other he pulled up her dress, dragging her knickers to one side.

She squeezed her eyes shut, not reacting – she knew that only made things worse: she'd learned the hard way. Trembling, she could feel his growing erection against her back.

'I bet you missed me, didn't you? Five years, I bet you dreamt of this, didn't you, babe?'

'Yeah.' Her voice was quiet, but she knew he expected that answer.

'That's what I thought.' Ollie's breathing began to change, and she heard it getting faster as his kisses on her neck became more urgent, then she felt his teeth biting down on her. She let out a yelp which made him groan louder as he grappled with his jog-gers. Then the next moment, Amy felt his penis enter her, roughly and painfully, thrusting deeper, harder.

'Am I expected to sit in the car and wait for you while you get your end away?' Martha stood in the doorway of the bathroom, staring at Ollie in disgust. 'For fuck's sake, you take the piss. You're like a fucking dog. And all that grunting and groaning is very triggering for me.' She smirked nastily and winked. 'I thought for a moment I was back in bed with you . . . Now get off her and come on.'

'Do you mind? I'm busy – and you know something, I think you're a bit sick in the head, coming in here, like it's nothing.'

'Believe me, I remember it well, and it is nothing . . . And by the looks of Amy's face, I'd say she feels the same.'

In the mirror, Amy could see Ollie's expression, screwed up in anger. '*Get out!*'

Martha shook her head, and Amy knew that she was loving this moment, not only to wind Ollie up, but to make sure that Amy would know who was in charge, that Martha could come in and out of here as she pleased. And Ollie would jump when she told him to, do whatever she said, while she stood terrified, being fucked against the sink, taken against her will and helpless to do anything about it. Oh yes, Martha Jones knew exactly what she was doing, how to humiliate and to make sure everyone knew their place. 'Didn't you get enough of that whore you picked up last night?'

Ollie spun his head around to look at her. 'Get the fuck out of here! *Get out!*' he yelled, but got only a cold laugh in return.

Martha stood her ground, her sharp features hard and pronounced. 'Oh sorry, wasn't I supposed to say, Ollie? Oh, come on, we're all adults here. I think Amy knows by now she ain't the only one.' She walked into the bathroom, staring contemptuously at Ollie as he stood behind Amy. 'Never has been, has she . . . Now hurry the fuck up, because we need to finish clearing up your mess, don't we?' She tapped him on his back. 'Oh, Ollie, what would you do without me? But one day, either your head' – she looked down contemptuously – 'or your dick is going to get you into serious trouble.'

With that she turned and left the bathroom, leaving Amy wondering what the hell Martha was talking about.

44

IRIS

'Are you sure that was him? Are you sure, Mina?' Opposite the prison, Iris sat in her car, excitement in her voice. 'Are you sure that was Matt?'

In the dark, Mina glanced out of the window, her knees pulled up to her chest as she sat on the passenger seat. 'I already told you, he ain't called Matt. He's called Phil. The fucking governor.'

'Think hard, Mina. Are you sure? Because don't forget you were out of it. Maybe you made a mistake?'

Mina shook her head. 'I can't remember a lot of what happened that night, but I can frigging well remember his face in mine. *Come to* fucking *daddy*. Sick bastard . . . Look, why are we still here? We've been here for hours. Dotty's charging extra for looking after Flo so late without notice. What's the point in sitting here when we could be back at mine or yours?'

'Don't worry about it – the money I got from Mum this month will cover us for a while. I think it's guilt money, she gave me double.'

Mina frowned. 'What do you mean?'

'Nothing.' Iris suddenly felt a pang of sadness. The wall she put up to protect herself sometimes came down, and when it did, she missed having her mum about, she missed having a life which wasn't spent in prison visiting rooms. And when the wall was fully down, it made her think about what those men did to her.

'Iris?' Mina touched her leg gently.

Putting on a fake smile, Iris pushed away the feeling and

returned to the matter in hand. 'Did he recognize you? Mina, did the governor know it was you?'

Mina shrugged. 'I have no idea. I was hardly going to sit there staring at him, was I? The minute I saw who it was, I tried to hide my face. Jesus, I hope he didn't recognize me . . . If my mum finds out, she'll kill me.'

Iris was agitated. 'That's not the point. Don't you get it?' She grabbed hold of Mina's hands. 'It's brilliant.'

'*Brilliant?*' Mina stared at her, taken aback. 'Now I really don't have any idea what you're talking about.'

Letting go of Mina's hands, Iris put the car into gear, driving speedily off in the Range Rover, but not before she glanced at Mina and said, laughing, 'Yeah, Mina, *brilliant*. Just trust me, you'll see.'

They drove for over three quarters of an hour, mostly in silence, with Iris occasionally switching radio stations but remaining entirely focused on the road ahead. From time to time headlights of oncoming vehicles lit up her face; seeing the look of intense concentration, Mina left her to her thoughts.

It began to rain and she put her windscreen wipers on, listening to the squeak of them as they dragged on the glass. She could feel her heart racing, the adrenaline kicking in. The idea that Matt was actually the governor was beyond brilliant, even if Mina couldn't see it, though that didn't matter because she could. Things were certainly looking up.

'What are you doing now?' Mina asked as Iris pulled into a cul-de-sac and parked under a tree.

Iris quickly shut off the headlights and swivelled around in the heated seat to look at Mina. 'Where do you want to go?'

Mina giggled. 'What do you mean, *where do I want to go?*'

Blowing a bubble from the gum she'd been chewing on for the

past hour, Iris bounced in her seat in excitement. 'If you had a choice, if you could go anywhere in the world, where would it be? Go on, it can be anywhere.'

Mina nodded and looked thoughtful. She frowned, mulling it over.

'Oh my God, it ain't a maths quiz, Meen,' Iris said with warm impatience.

Her blue eyes twinkling, Mina laughed. 'OK, OK . . . I think I'd go to Canada.'

'Canada . . . That's rubbish.' Iris grinned.

Mina shrugged, going along with the banter. 'You said where did *I* want to go – no one's asking you to come!' She laughed again. 'Canada's beautiful – well, it is in the pictures, and I saw this drama series that was set there. It's like, the air is well fresh and there's all these rivers – not like the Thames; proper massive ones, with grizzly bears and salmon, and you can go horseback riding alongside them.'

Iris stared at her. She sounded so young, so childlike, and once again she thought about how meeting Mina was the best thing that had happened in her life, and it was certainly worth going through all the shit with her mum being sent down just to meet her. 'Then Canada it is.' She leaned over and kissed Mina on her cheek, then turned her face towards her before gently kissing her on the lips. Then she glanced out of the car window, gazing into the darkness.

'OK . . . Now can we go home, please? Or at least tell me what we're doing.' Mina yawned noisily. 'Iris, come on, it's getting late. Can we go.'

Iris turned back and looked at her. 'I'm being serious. Canada it is.'

Mina's light mood looked like it was beginning to fade. 'And I'm serious too: I want to go.'

'You're not getting it, are you? We're going to go to Canada. You and me. You and me and Flo. That's what you want, isn't it? That's what you've just said.'

Mina slumped in her seat. 'Iris, please, enough now, yeah?'

'Enough . . . We haven't even started.' She smirked and pointed into the darkness. 'Right there is our ticket out of here. It's our ticket to Canada.'

Mina sat up and peered into the darkness. 'You're not making sense.'

'Didn't you see that all the way here I was following that black Audi? The four-by-four?'

Mina shook her head and began to look worried.

'Well, I was. And the person driving it was our very own meal ticket . . . Matt, aka the governor. By the time I'm finished, we'll be rich.'

'Iris, no, don't be stupid. Let's go. *Now.*'

Iris shook her head. 'No. Unless of course you want to keep scrimping and scraping for money. I don't want to work for Roz, not after what she did to you, but you know I will. I'll do anything for you. But this way . . . well, think about it: the governor of Ashcroft, fucking the daughter of one of his inmates. The governor of Ashcroft, taking coke and spiking his whore's drink.'

'*Whore?* Thanks very much! I wasn't the only one on my back that night, remember!' Mina sounded indignant.

'I'm not getting at you – just thinking what the headlines would say. He'd be ruined. Finished, and I don't think he'd want that, do you?'

'No, but why would anyone find out?'

Iris could hear the nervousness in Mina's voice, but this was perfect. It couldn't be better. 'They won't, unless . . .' she winked at Mina, '. . . unless he doesn't pay up, that is. If old Phil wants to keep this quiet, he'll need to do exactly as we tell him. That way he won't have a problem.'

'Iris, don't! You can't, you can't blackmail someone.' Mina began to panic.

'Just watch me.'

She reached round and pulled her bag from the back seat, opened it and began to rummage around in it as Mina continued to talk: 'This is crazy! You can't, Iris, listen to me.'

Iris retrieved a pen and a tiny notepad from the bottom of the large Chloé tote bag, then glanced up. 'I'm listening, but you're wasting your breath. What would be crazy is if we were to let this opportunity slide. It'll be easy, Mina. How much should we ask him for? Twenty grand?'

'Twenty grand!'

Iris nodded. 'Yeah, you're right, that's not enough. Let's double it.'

'No! No! No, I ain't saying that.' Mina's eyes were wide open. 'It's too much, any amount would be too much . . . Iris, take me home. Just take me home *now*.'

Finishing writing on the notepad, Iris grinned. 'There, I reckon that will do it . . . Stay here, I'm going to pop it through his door.'

'Oh God, Iris, what did you write . . . Iris, Iris, come back!'

45

THE GOVERNOR

. . . Hello Matt, I think we need to talk. I think it's in your best
interest, don't you? Here's my phone number, call me . . .

Phil Reed stared at the note, rereading it for the tenth time, then
he sat back in his black leather chair, poured himself a glass of
whisky and picked up the phone.

A gruff voice answered. '*Hello?*'

'It's the governor.'

There was silence for a moment.

'*What do you want?*'

'I've got a little problem, one you might be able to help me
with . . .'

46

STEPH

Sunday in Ashcroft started with the usual head count. The noise was loud and, unlike most days, there was no yard exercise due to the weekend staff being minimal. As always, Steph's head was filled with her daughter. Her head was filled with how she was going to get revenge on everyone who had hurt her little girl.

Sighing, Steph contemplated eating the crap on the plate in front of her: fried eggs, fried bread, beans – overcooked – and chipolatas, sitting in a pool of grease. There were times when she was distinctly ravenous, the lack of healthy food or even edible food sometimes got to her, and right now was one of those times. However, no matter how much she wanted to ease her hunger, she wasn't sure she could put herself through eating breakfast.

Annoyed, and channelling her pain, she pushed her plate away, watching Tess blatantly dealing on the wing. 'She's a fucking disgrace. Lynn ain't even back yet and she's still carrying on with her crap like nothing's wrong.' She stared at Tess as she spoke to Maureen, who sat sipping on a hot cup of coffee and nibbling a piece of burnt toast which looked more appetizing than the Sunday breakfast in front of her.

'So, are you ready to say that you were wrong about Amy?' Maureen glanced at her.

'I wasn't wrong. Just cos Tess is still dealing, that doesn't mean Amy wasn't part of it. And let's not start this again. I've got too much shit in my head.'

Maureen turned and looked at her. 'Steph, I don't know what's going on with you, but isn't it time you put that pig-headedness of yours away? In this place we need all the friends we can get. You haven't spoken to Ness since the fight in the laundry room.'

'That's right,' Steph snarled. 'And I'm not going to either. She's gonna get what's coming to her.'

Maureen slammed down her hand on the table, causing the other women to turn and look, but they soon turned away when they saw Steph glaring at them.

'Enough! Enough, Steph.' Maureen lowered her voice, but her tone was still powerful. 'I nearly died, and I don't know how long I have left—'

'What?' Steph looked at her, shocked. 'What do you mean?'

Maureen took a deep breath, rubbing her chest. 'I've got heart failure, there's nothing they can do. Only the good Lord knows how long I've got left, but my days are numbered . . . It's OK, Steph.'

Steph looked away. She couldn't believe it. Not Reenie. Life without Reenie in Ashcroft would be unthinkable. How much more terrible news could she take? She didn't know, but it felt like she was beginning to crack. The pressure of life in Ashcroft was becoming too much. The prison was winning, taking her down like it had taken down so many other women before her. 'I'm not ready to lose you yet.' She held back tears, but she could hear her voice breaking.

Maureen tapped her hand. 'Well, I'm not ready to go just yet – unless of course this piece of toast chokes me. Jesus wept, how long have I been in here? Years, and I can't think of one decent meal I've had.' She chuckled. 'Maybe that's all part of their grand plan. If losing our liberty won't break us, then maybe their dietary food plan will . . . Oh Steph, don't look so sad.'

'What the fuck do you expect me to do? I think even you'd be shocked if I started doing an Irish jig.' She hurriedly wiped away her tears. She couldn't be seen to be crying. She was going to challenge for top dog, and she couldn't show weakness yet. Some of the women had asked her why she hadn't just taken the crown already, but the truth was, she was exhausted. Emotionally drained. She hadn't the energy to go for it, and she didn't want to fuck up because she knew she only had one chance at this.

Maureen winked cheekily. 'I dunno, I'd be impressed if you could do an Irish jig. After all, I've seen you dance and, let's face it, you've no rhythm at all.'

They both laughed, though it trailed off as Steph sighed again. 'I can't get my head around it. Are you sure?'

Maureen gave her a sad smile. 'Am I sure that I've got heart failure, that I'm going to die sooner rather than later? Yes, Steph, I'm sure.'

Steph put her head in her hands, but within moments she felt Maureen move them away. 'Steph, come on now, it hasn't happened yet. I'm still here.'

'Does Ness know?'

Maureen shook her head. 'No, and I can't tell her. It would destroy her, she's ready to have the baby any day now and there's no place in the mother and baby unit, and she's got no family to take the bairn, which means social workers will snap him up within minutes of him being born. The last thing she needs is my news. This is the first time she's ever been clean, even with Tess waving temptation under her nose. And if she's got any hope of having a life after she gets out of here, to continue being a parent to Mina and to her son – if by some miracle they don't adopt him and she manages to get him back – then she needs your support. Because if she goes down the rabbit hole again and starts on the gear, there'll be no coming back for her . . . Steph, please, I need you to put all this hostility to the side. Remember how we all used to be?'

Steph as usual turned her hurt into anger. 'Yeah, back before Amy and Ness became fucking idiots. Before Ness thought she could go up against me in front of everyone.'

'Then why are you still talking to me?' Maureen's face flushed red. 'Why are you sitting here in conversation with me? Don't forget I was with them.'

Steph stared at Maureen. She'd heard rumours that Maureen had helped Amy get away, she'd made a deal with one of the bent screws in Ashcroft – Jenkins, most likely. And although she should be mad at Reenie because she'd gone against the rules of women, the rules of being inside, she knew that Reenie had done it because she cared. She had a good heart, and it wasn't about trying to bring anyone down, more about who she could protect and care for. Still, it rankled. Loyalty meant everything to Steph, and if she thought about it too hard, she could easily come to the conclusion that Reenie had betrayed her.

'I'd rather not talk about that.' She gave a tight smile. 'It is what it is. But Ness, she disrespected me in front of everyone.'

'No, she didn't. She saved you from yourself. Things went too far with Amy. You brought your own dirty laundry into it all. You know what I'm saying's true . . . Steph, *please*.' She stopped and stared into Steph's face. 'How can you refuse a dying woman's wish?' Then she burst out into laughter.

Steph shook her head, laughing along with her. 'Did anyone tell you you're a wicked woman?'

'I think the judge at my trial said something along those lines . . . So, is that a yes? Will you put everything to one side for me? Ness needs you, and when I'm not around she'll need you even more . . . And when Lynn comes back, you'll be no use to her if you're fighting amongst yourselves.'

Steph glanced across to Ness. She knew it was true what Maureen was saying: they were stronger together and there was no doubt it was easier getting through the days when they were friends rather than enemies. She'd already accepted that she'd be behind bars for the rest of her life, carried out of Ashcroft in a body bag. But it was the friendships, the laughs, the bond they had, that made it possible to get up each morning. Most days, it was the only thing preventing her and so many other women putting a noose around their necks.

After four weeks of not speaking to Ness, she missed the crack. She missed not being able to confide in her. She missed Ness.

'You wouldn't be losing face, Steph, if that's what's worrying you.' Maureen broke into her thoughts. 'The rest of the women on the wing will be behind you. Most of them don't know which corner to stand in. There's enough pain in here because of what happened to Lynn and Evie, without adding to it. It's divided us, which only makes Tess and her cronies stronger, and I believe that's exactly what she's wanted all along . . . Come on, Steph, what do you say?'

Steph stared into Maureen's eyes, then she nodded. 'OK, I'll think about it.'

Maureen smiled. 'That's good enough for me. You'll see it's the right thing to do.'

'Howay, look who's back!' Tess's voice was loud as she sat at the other end of the canteen, calling across to Officer Earle as he walked in.

Earle scowled but said nothing.

'Cat got your tongue?' Tess roared with laughter as Earle's face flushed red. The other women in the canteen joined in, banging their cutlery on the table.

'Or was it someone else that got your tongue?'

Earle, clearly unable to take the banter, exploded. He pointed at Tess, 'I didn't come back here to listen to your rubbish.'

Tess became even more animated. 'Have you heard him. He sounds like fucking Daffy Duck!'

'No, it's Sylvester the cat!' another woman bellowed across. *'Sufferin' succotash!'* She squealed with laughter as she did an impression of Sylvester's catchphrase.

'It's fucking Looney Tunes!' Tiny yelled, then started singing the cartoon theme tune, getting up and dancing with some of the other women who joined in raucously.

'Is that what happens when you have your tongue sliced, *Tone*!' Above the singing and noise, Tess shouted at him.

Earle, enraged, stepped towards Tess, screeches of laughter rising around him. 'Who told you that?' He slammed his fist on the table, losing his cool altogether. 'Who told you that I had my tongue cut?'

'Mind the spray, man, I need me brolly!' Tess waved Earle away as a light mist of spit landed on her. She smirked in delight. 'You need to watch that.'

'That's a lie . . . What you just said is a lie . . . If you must know, I . . . I . . . I . . .' He looked around at some of the other prisoners. 'I had abnormal cells, they found them in my mouth, and they were worried and . . . and needed to . . . to operate on the tip of it.'

Cackling with laughter, Tess clapped her hands in delight. 'Whatever you say, Daffy!'

Earle looked like he was going to implode, but at that moment Officer Bailey walked in, clicking her fingers. 'What's with the noise, ladies? Keep it down and get to your tasks. Everyone, go to your jobs *now*. This may be a Sunday, but the Devil never rests. So move it.'

There was an audible groan.

'Come on then!' she shouted, and Steph got up, taking Maureen's breakfast tray and her own across to the dirty dishes trolley.

What Maureen had said was rolling through her mind. How was she supposed to act now she knew? But like so many things, she decided that not thinking about it might be the easiest approach.

Suddenly, she felt her arm being grabbed and she was surprised to see it was Earle. His face twisted in fury. 'How long are you going to be?'

Steph pulled back slightly, experiencing the same thing Tess had: the light spray of spit leaving his mouth, no doubt a consequence of whatever had happened to the tip of his tongue.

'How long am I going to be what?'

'Stop with the attitude.' He glanced around, then his eyes returned to Steph and he whispered, 'Tess – when are you going to take her down?'

Steph glared at him. 'When I'm ready, but there's been other things going on. Like Lynn, like Evie, like . . .' But she stopped.

There was annoyance in Earle's tone: 'I thought you wanted to be top dog. Aren't you sick of her throwing her weight about?'

She looked at him coldly. 'Are you sure this is about me, not you?'

Earle sniffed, gesturing with his head for one of the women to move away. 'It's about both of us. You need to take her down, there's no place for her here anymore. She's trouble, for everyone . . . So you need to do it, sooner rather than later. Otherwise, she's going to bring us both down.'

Five minutes later, Steph walked into Ness's cell. She smiled at Maureen, who was sitting on the bed next to Ness. 'Do you mind if I come in?'

'Well, you're already in, ain't you,' Ness snapped.

'Nessie, stop,' Reenie gently commanded.

Ness lowered her eyes and folded her arms, though it looked difficult with the size of her stomach.

'Ness,' Steph's voice sounded strained, 'I'm sorry . . . Everything got out of hand. I ain't making an excuse, but when someone puts a knife to your head, you're hardly going to have a cup of tea with them after, are you? And in front of everyone too.'

'It wasn't like that,' Ness said defensively.

'Nessie, what did I just say? Let her speak.' Maureen's soothing tone had the desired effect. Once again, Ness complied.

'This place can get to you sometimes. I've had stuff on my mind which I haven't spoken about and it's messing with my head a bit, so I'm on edge. Then all the stuff with Evie and Lynn – like a lot of the women, I find it triggering,' Steph continued. 'But Reenie, well, she made me see that our friendship meant something, and I don't want to throw that away.'

The women fell into silence, which was broken a moment later by Ness.

'I'm sorry too. I know you're going for top dog, and it ain't good that I did that in front of the other girls. And I know that you could have easily put me in my place, but you didn't cos I'm pregnant . . . I appreciate that. Not all the women in here would be so considerate . . . So yeah, I'd like to be mates again . . . I missed not having you around.'

Steph, uncomfortable with the compliment, just nodded.

'Are you still going to take her down? I'll back you all the way if you are,' Ness spoke hurriedly, lowering her voice. 'The women want to have some sort of leadership again; they're hating all this division. On top of the stuff with Evie and Lynette, they find it unsettling.'

Steph, hearing Tess's voice from the corridor, nodded as she turned to watch her larking around with some of her cronies. 'Oh yeah, I'm going to take her down, and I have the perfect plan to do it.'

47
AMY

It was just past three o'clock, and it was still raining as Amy sat in Ollie's blacked-out Range Rover: one of the numerous cars he owned and kept in the twenty-four-hour private car park in Lexington Street. Not that she liked to borrow his cars, but her own cars were being serviced after not being driven for five years. They'd had to send off to Ferrari in Italy for parts, so it was taking forever, but in all honesty, she was in no rush to get them back. She liked to use her cars less than she liked to use Ollie's, mainly because Ollie had put trackers in hers, so whenever she drove them, it always made her feel nervous, because she was well aware if there was a diversion or she happened to take a different route to wherever she was going or coming from, then he'd question her, wanting to know where she'd been and why she'd gone a different way. His jealousy, his possessiveness of her, crept into every aspect of her life. Ironically, she felt more of a prisoner on the outside than she had during her five years in Ashcroft.

Parked up in Hyde Park Street, which was far enough away from Soho but near enough to get back quickly if she needed to, Amy was about to get out of the car when she heard her phone ring. And in that second, it felt like her heart had leapt into her mouth. Automatically she sat up straight, dusting down her clothes from the sandwich she was eating, something she knew she shouldn't do in Ollie's car, but she'd been feeling faint with hunger.

Chucking the crisp packet and sandwich wrapper on the seat

as if she'd been caught doing something wrong, Amy retrieved her phone from the Mulberry clutch bag beside her, not bothering to look at the screen. If his call wasn't answered within a couple of rings, he'd be furious. But in her rush to grab it, she dropped the phone, missing the call. Shit.

Spotting a couple of crumbs, she dusted herself down again, then checked the driver's seat for crumbs. She needed to get back to Soho. If Ollie was calling her, it probably meant he was looking for her. The only reason she came to this area was so she could relax. She could sit back and not worry about seeing anyone she knew. It was the only escape she had.

She leaned across to the passenger side and picked up the sandwich wrapper. Again she checked for crumbs, inspecting the cream leather seats and the footwell. She knew what Ollie was like.

Leaning over even further, she retrieved the crisp packet which had fallen into the footwell. As she did, something caught her eye and she frowned.

Hopping out of the driver's seat, she walked around to the passenger's side, opening the door to look under the seat.

A bracelet. She picked it up. A cheap, plastic bracelet with hearts and letters spaced between various multicoloured beads. Shaking her head, she threw it into the small row of rose bushes. Ollie made her sick; he was happy to pick up slags and screw around with them, but she couldn't even go from Soho to Marble Arch without him interrogating her. He was a total shit, and she didn't have to find another woman's bracelet in the car to know that.

48

MINA

A few miles away, Mina watched happily as Iris tickled Flo, reducing her to helpless giggles. The moment Iris paused to let her get her breath back, Flo got up and ran into the small bedroom they shared to get her teddy bear so he could join in the fun.

'Flo, why don't you show Iris your colouring book as well?' Mina called, then turned to Iris, who was lying stretched out on the couch. Although she'd always hated the tiny bedsit, having Iris here and not having to keep secrets anymore, made all the difference. The place had patches of mould on the walls, and the furniture was tatty and old. When they moved in, she and her mum had cleaned the place from top to bottom, throwing out the stained, flea-infested cushions and bedding. They'd bought bright material from the market and thrown it over the chairs to cheer them up, but nothing could dispel the air of gloom that filled the dump.

Until now. Iris had brought a cheerfulness that she wouldn't have thought possible. Now, the place seemed like a cute, messy, chic home rather than a rundown hole in Soho.

'You're so good with her, Iris,' Mina beamed. 'She's usually really shy, but she took to you straight away.'

'She's great . . . and she'd love it in Canada.'

'Don't say that. You know I can't go. I can't leave Flo.' A sadness washed over Mina.

'I ain't asking you to leave her, I'm saying bring her. We'd be a great little family.'

'I can't just go and wave goodbye to everything, I can't get up and move to the other side of the world.'

Iris winked at her. 'Technically, it ain't the other side of the world.'

Suddenly Mina froze, staring at the floorboards, seeing the dark stain where Steve's blood had discoloured them after she'd knifed him. She hadn't meant to hurt him, or at least she hadn't meant to kill him, but it had happened so quickly. One minute Flo was screaming for him to let her go, the next he had a kitchen knife sticking out of his chest.

Quickly she dragged the rug back over the stain, having rolled it up so Flo could play with the sparkly marbles that Iris had bought her.

Taking a deep breath, she tried to put the images of him lying there out of her mind, but sometimes, especially at night, his face would haunt her, and then she'd end up burying her head in the pillow so Flo wouldn't hear her crying.

'Mina, you OK?'

Iris's voice broke through her thoughts, and she looked up and smiled. Like so many other things, she didn't want to talk about it, so she nodded. 'Yeah, I just can't think about what it'll be like when you leave. Do you have to go?'

Iris slid down onto the floor next to her. She put her arm around Mina's shoulder, pulling her gently in towards her. 'I ain't leaving here without you. Somehow you and Flo are going to come with me, even if I have to kidnap you.'

'We couldn't even come to Canada if we wanted to. I ain't got a passport and neither has she. She ain't even got a birth certificate, I don't think. Mum had her under her sister's name in the hospital, then she scarpered, so fuck knows if she has or not. I doubt it though.'

Iris pushed her away gently and looked into her face. 'Then

let's not go to Canada. They say Scotland is lovely at this time of year.'

Mina laughed. 'Scotland?'

'OK, Wales, Ireland – who fucking cares, as long as we're together. That's all that matters: you, me and Flo. Away from here, getting our happy ever after. Please, Mina.'

Before Mina had time to answer, Iris's phone beeped. She rolled her eyes. 'Please don't tell me this is my mother texting to check up on me again. She's off her head. She's constantly worrying about me now. I don't know which is worse: her being a cold cow, or her being all kind and caring. Well, she can . . .' Iris brought the phone to her mouth and did an exaggerated shout: '*Fuck off!*' then she roared with laughter and started checking the text that had just come through.

'She called me this morning, you know. I forgot to tell you.'

Iris looked bemused. 'You're joking. What did she say?'

'I didn't speak to her; I was getting out of the shower, so I missed the call.'

Iris grinned. 'I am so sorry; it was the worst idea, your mum giving my mum your number. You'll get no peace now she knows it . . . Do you know where she keeps her phone?'

Mina shook her head, feeling happy. She liked feeling good, and right now she couldn't think of anywhere she'd rather be. 'No, where?'

'Up her foo-foo!'

Mina screamed with laughter. 'You're kidding!'

'I'm so not. Haven't you ever wondered why she walks like this . . .' Iris jumped up, walking around like a bow-legged cowboy, causing Mina to hold her stomach in fits of giggles.

After a couple of minutes, Iris sat down, kissing Mina quickly on the lips before she glanced back down at her phone, reading the text she'd been distracted from. 'Oh my God!'

'Everything OK?' Mina stared at Iris.

'Yeah, yeah it is, it's better than OK. It wasn't from Mum.' She looked at Mina. 'Start packing your bags – it's Matt, he wants to meet me.'

'You can't just go and meet him. Iris, *no*.' She watched her beginning to text. 'What are you typing?'

Iris punched the text out on her iPhone with a large smile on her face. 'He'll be so shocked, he'll wonder who it is, who else knows, he'll be bricking it.'

'What did you write?' Mina tried to look at the screen.

'I've just told him straight: I want money, and if he doesn't want his name all over the papers, he needs to cough up.' She squealed with delight. 'Scotland, here we come!' she said in a bad Scottish accent.

Mina was about to tell her to stop being crazy, not to even think about blackmailing someone. But then she looked around the room and thought back to the last visit with her mum, the last phone call. Her mum was always so angry, and always making her feel guilty, and she was tired of it. And she certainly didn't want to do it anymore. None of it. The only thing she wanted was to be with Iris. She didn't ever want this feeling to go. 'Good.'

'What?' Iris's eyes lit up, but she also looked surprised. 'Good?'

Trying not to cry, Mina smiled. 'Yeah, and I'm going to come with you. I don't care where it is, but I'm done with all this. I'm done with my mum. I want to start again. You, me and Flo. Fuck her . . . Fuck them all . . . And fuck the governor – let's make him pay. Because, you know what? They owe us. All of them owe us.'

49

AMY

The next day, Amy walked through the glass revolving doors of St Agatha's District General Hospital, which was no more than twenty minutes from Finchley. She was taking advantage of not only being able to drive around without a tracker on the car, but also of Ollie being away for the day. On business, with Martha . . . As usual. Not that she minded; she would be happy for him to go and never come back. That, however, was too much to hope for. In the meantime, she was determined to make the most of her few short hours of freedom. And what better way than going to visit Lynette in hospital?

Finding herself in the high-ceilinged, air-conditioned reception area, Amy scanned the information board for directions to Juliette Ward, where Lynette had been moved to now she was out of intensive care.

Hitting the button on the lift, Amy tried not to be overwhelmed by the stench of bleach and cleaning products, though in truth her thoughts were very much distracted. She was really looking forward to seeing Lynn, but she wasn't looking forward to telling her that so far, they'd had no leads on Evie. She knew through Jack that Lynn had spoken to Maureen, who'd given her the briefest of updates, reasoning that Lynette probably couldn't take the whole truth. She also knew that the police had as good as closed the case, no doubt assuming Evie was just another kid who'd packed up and gone; after all, she was legally an adult.

Walking down the fifth-floor corridor, Amy took a deep breath to steady herself before she walked into the ward.

Pushing the double doors open, she rolled her eyes, seeing Lynette dressed in a blue hospital robe in the end bed, hand-cuffed and chained to the metal cot while a prison officer she vaguely recognized from Ashcroft ate an éclair while playing a game on his iPad.

'Fuck me, I'm surprised you ain't got a sign on her as well. She's hardly criminal number one, is she? She drove a fucking car through a semi-detached while her old man was kipping in front of the telly – it's hardly a ram-raid down Hatton Garden, is it?' Amy scowled at the officer. She placed her bag to the side. 'Oh, don't worry, darlin', I ain't brought her a file, so there's no need to look like that. There'll be no re-enacting *The Great Escape* this afternoon, not in these heels . . . But I'll leave that there, so you don't have to panic.' She shook her head, watching him look back down at his game.

Then she turned to Lynette. 'Hello, sweetheart. Oh it's so fuck-ing good to see you. Really good.' She kissed Lynette's cheek and smiled, genuinely pleased.

'I didn't think you'd be able to come . . . God, it's lovely to see you. You're the first visitor I've had, actually.' She looked more closely at Amy. 'Jesus, Steph did do a number – that scar looks nasty. Reenie told me what happened. It sounded like a right free-for-all.' Lynette's face lit up, but Amy could see the dark circles under her eyes. She looked like she'd been crying.

Amy touched the scar. She tended to forget about it unless she saw it in the mirror or someone mentioned it. 'Yeah, she did a number on me. Thought she was going to scalp the fuck out of me, stupid cow.' She laughed.

'So, what's it feel like to be a free woman?'

Amy suddenly felt a sense of relief at the prospect of being able to talk to Lynn, to talk to someone who might understand. The familiarity of a woman from Ashcroft felt warm and welcoming, and right there, she began to open up. 'It's a struggle. I know it's only been five years, but I feel so different. It sounds stupid, but I feel like I don't fit in anymore. Even going to the shops – it's like I'm abroad on holiday, everything seems new and foreign to me.'

'What about Ollie?'

Amy massaged her temples. 'What about him? He's worse than I remember, or maybe it's just a question of me having forgotten what he's like. And I miss it. Can you believe, I miss Ashcroft?'

Lynn nodded.

'It'll be different for you, Lynn. You've got family, you've got Ev—' She stopped. 'I am so sorry, Lynn, put a sock in my mouth, I didn't mean that. Hark at me going on, and . . . We're doing all we can, I promise. We're doing all we can to find her, and we will.'

Lynette's eyes filled with tears. 'Reenie said. She told me that, since you got released, you've been working hard to track her down . . . Thank you, thank you.'

Amy jumped up out of the chair she was in. 'Don't thank me. I want to help – I wish I could do more.'

'Yeah, yeah . . . Even . . . even if she hates me and never wants to see me again, I'll be OK with that. I mean, I won't like it, but as long as she's safe, that's all I care about.'

Amy looked into her eyes, staring at her intently. 'I swear to you, Lynn, I won't stop.' She paused for a moment, then smiled again. 'Jack's great – you'd like him. He can be a bit arrogant at times, but he's a fella, what d'you expect?'

Lynette tilted her head. 'From that smile, Amy, I'd say you like him.'

Suddenly flustered, Amy shook her head. 'No, no, it's not like that, he's just . . . well, he's different. He's so passionate about finding Evie, and he's . . . well, he seems like a good guy.' Emotion welled up in her.

'You know, it's all right to like him. I ain't going to say anything.'

'I know, I know you won't . . . but . . . but he's with some-one . . . so am I . . .' She trailed off, not wanting to think about Jack. It was too confusing, especially as she barely knew him.

'Did you know Ness asked me to take her baby,' Amy said, changing the subject quickly.

'What?' Lynn's tone reflected the look of shock on her face. 'You're kidding!'

'No, I wish I was. She walked into my cell and just asked me . . . She's desperate. I mean, a baby, it's a big deal. It broke my heart to say no to her, but Ollie . . . he'd never let me.'

Lynette reached out and held Amy's hand, the chain of the handcuffs clanking on the metal bedside. 'But you'd like to?'

Once again, Amy felt overwhelmed with emotion. 'I'd like to help her. But I can't. I mean, I always wanted kids. But looking after Ness's baby, even though we've got a huge house in Soho, and the money's there, and I'd look after him as if he were mine, it's impossible. Ollie's crazy. Five minutes with him and the social would run a mile. Ness doesn't get that. But you know yourself, when you're inside, you end up not thinking straight. She must be going through hell right now, thinking what's going to happen to her son—' She broke off with a frown and slipped her hand out of Lynette's, then gently raised her arm. 'Lynn, where did you get this bracelet?'

Lynette smiled widely. 'Evie made it for me. When I first got sent down, she brought this when she came to visit. I managed to sneak it in – you know what Ashcroft are like, you can't wear your own jewellery, but I managed to hide it, and I've kept it on me ever since. When they brought me in here, they bagged it with my possessions, so that's why I've still got it.' Her eyes filled with tears again. 'It makes me feel close to her . . . She's got one as well, but see, I've got the letters E-V-I-E on mine, she's got the letters B-E-A-R on hers.'

'Bear?'

'Yeah, as in Mama Bear – that's what Evie always used to call me: Bear. She used to say I was like a mama bear.' Lynette started to cry, and Amy held her in her arms, though her mind was elsewhere.

'Lynn, I hate to leave you like this, but I need to go. Is that OK?' Amy spoke hurriedly.

Lynette nodded. 'Of course it is, doll. Thanks for coming.'

'I'll be back – I'll visit next week.' She grabbed her bag quickly, scowling at the prison officer.

'Oh, didn't I say,' Lynette called out after her, 'I won't be here. They think I'm well enough to discharge me . . . I'm going back to Ashcroft on Friday.'

Amy skidded to a stop on the wet tarmac and pulled into the same spot on Hyde Park Street where she'd parked yesterday. She jumped out of the Range Rover and ran to the row of rose bushes by the black iron railings. Ignoring the looks she was getting from passers-by, she got on her knees and scrabbled around in the dirt under the bushes.

Then her fingers touched something. She grabbed it, bringing it out. It was what she was looking for: the plastic bracelet she'd thrown away. The bracelet was identical to Lynette's. The bracelet that Evie had made with the lettered beads B-E-A-R.

And now she needed to find out what the hell it was doing in Ollie's car . . .

50

MINA

It had been two days since Mina had spoken to her mum. Ness had left several messages on her phone, but she hadn't answered, and she wasn't going to either. Mainly because she needed to keep an emotional distance from her; she knew if she did speak to her mum, her resolve would break, and she'd end up stuck where she was. Feeling guilty, feeling like everything was her fault. But this wasn't a life, not for her, not for Flo, and she was determined she was going to start again with Iris.

Taking a deep breath, she zipped up her bag and smiled at Flo. 'You OK, baby?'

Flo shook her head, her bottom lip beginning to pout. 'No, my tummy hurts.'

Mina crouched next to her sister. She wiped her mop of curly hair out of her face, staring into her big brown eyes. 'Hey missus, do you reckon it's all that ice-cream Iris gave you yesterday?'

Flo nodded and giggled, but then she held her stomach and pulled another face.

'Why don't you go to the bathroom, yeah? Hurry up, though . . . call me if you need me.'

Her sister skipped off and Mina threw herself down on the couch. She was supposed to meet Iris, but it looked like she was going to be late now, though she wasn't sure exactly what she was meeting her for. Iris had been full of excitement and secrets, as if she were a child. No matter how many times she asked, Iris refused to tell her what it was all about.

All she knew was that she was due to meet her in less than an hour and, by the look of the address she'd texted, she was going to be way late. Plus, Doreen was meant to have Flo, but at the last minute she'd had to cancel, due to having to take her mum or someone to an appointment she'd forgotten about.

So now Mina was going to have to drag her sister across London to meet Iris, because she really didn't want to cancel. She wanted to see Iris, needed to see her because, no matter how bad she was feeling, no matter how upset she was with her mum, Iris always made her feel better. She'd never felt like this before about anyone . . . In fact, Mina had a feeling she was falling in love.

'This is it.' Just over two hours later, the Uber driver stopped the large people carrier which felt hugely oversized just to take her and Flo across the bridge to South London.

'Are you sure?' Mina glanced around: it was an abandoned industrial site, and she could see a large derelict warehouse in front of her. The other thing she could see was what looked like an old shipyard, with the River Thames beyond.

'Yeah, otherwise why would I bring you here?' the driver, who wore a large black cap, snapped irritably.

'It just looks . . . I dunno, that it might be the wrong place.'

'Look, I brought you to the postcode you said. This is it – now either you want to get out or you want to go somewhere else. I don't care, as long as I get paid for it.'

Flo was starting to wake up so Mina gave her a cuddle. She'd tried to call Iris on the way, but her phone had decided it was going to update itself, so she hadn't been able to use it. But this was definitely the address that Iris had given her. When they spoke, Iris had been so excited and spoken so quickly, she'd made her text it over so she could be certain she had it right. 'OK, yeah, that's fine.' She opened her bag and pulled out the thirty-five pounds that had been quoted to her on the app.

She gently took Flo's hand and helped her out of the people carrier, watching as it sped away.

'How's your tummy?'

Flo's sweet eyes shone as she sucked on her thumb. 'Good,' she mumbled, and Mina began to walk with her over to the derelict warehouse.

Pulling out her phone, she glanced at it, relieved to see that it had finally finished updating. She scrolled to Iris's number and immediately pressed call. It rang but then switched to voicemail.

Sighing, she wandered along in the summer sun, wondering what the big secret was that Iris had been so excited about. On the phone earlier it had been all she could do to contain her excitement. Clearly, this place, this abandoned site, was something do with it.

She felt the warm breeze coming from off the Thames, and she thought how peaceful it was. Maybe this was what Scotland was going to be like. Though as long as it was away from here, she didn't care where it was.

Looking around, she couldn't see or hear anyone, which was a huge change from Soho. The only sound was her and Flo's feet, crunching on the stony gravel as they walked along the side of the warehouse, which was surrounded by rusting debris and broken glass.

Calling her again on the mobile, she hoped that Iris hadn't gone home without texting her, annoyed that she was late. Maybe she'd ruined Iris's surprise by not showing up on time. A sudden rush of disappointment washed over her, but then she stopped. What was that? She listened again.

'Can you hear something, Flo?' Her sister ignored her, too

busy kicking a rusting paint can to pay attention. Mina smiled to herself and carried on listening. It was the sound of a phone ringing.

She wandered in the direction of the ringing sound, turning the corner of the derelict building.

Then she stopped.

'Iris . . . Iris . . . Oh shit. Iris! Iris, are you OK?'

Lying in the long grass in front of her was Iris. She sprinted towards her, worried that she'd fallen somehow, fainted. 'Iris?'

About to kneel down by her side, Mina suddenly froze. 'Oh my God, no . . . Oh God, no . . . Iris . . . Iris.' She began to cry, shake and then to scream. 'Iris! Iris! Iris, please, no!'

Blood trickled out of Iris's mouth and the top of her skull, and she lay motionless.

Mina pulled out her phone to call the ambulance at the same time as picking up Iris's bag, which was lying a few feet away.

'Hello, what is your emergency?'

Crying hysterically, Mina blurted out the address. As she ended the call, she suddenly felt sick and vomited, then she heard Flo begin to cry, no doubt terrified because of her screaming.

Wiping her mouth, Mina ran towards her sister, 'Flo, Flo! Flo!' gesturing her to come, her words tumbling out. 'Let me give you a piggyback, come on, come on, we need to go, we need to get out of here, get on my back.'

As she began to run, carrying her sister, a cold dread passed over Mina. It felt like someone was watching her.

51

THE GOVERNOR

Phil Reed, dressed in a newly dry-cleaned suit, wandered down the corridor of HMP Ashcroft, humming to himself. It had been a busy day: an inspection, a meeting with journalists about a new scheme they were going to launch here at Ashcroft, and then he'd had a leisurely lunch with the board. Now it was time to catch up on the inevitable paperwork.

Making his way to D wing, he smiled to himself: life was busy, but good. He had no complaints.

The noise of the women laughing and chattering echoed around. He supposed it was something to do with this part of the old building which seemed to make the sound louder. 'Hello, sir, when's Lynn back?' A small thickset woman who, off the top of Reed's head, was serving a fifteen stretch for her part in a forced organ harvesting organization, called over to him.

'If all goes well, later today.'

She grinned widely. Her East European accent strong, she said, 'It'll be nice to have her back.'

Disinterested, Reed answered witheringly, 'If you say so.' And with that he continued to make his way through the wing, nodding at the various prison officers dotted around.

At cell number 32, he stopped, and once again smiled to himself. Yes, life was certainly good.

The door of the cell was open, and he walked inside, then he closed it behind him.

'Did I ask you to fucking close it? I may be inside, but I still have a right to privacy,' Ness growled. 'You can't just walk in here without asking.'

He winked at her. 'OK, well show me the rule book on that one.' He laughed and regarded her with disdain. Her hair was greasy, and an outbreak of spots had appeared on her face. Her large pregnant belly looked enormous, stretched under a faded grey tracksuit top.

'So, how's everything going, Vanessa? Any day now, another of your offspring is going to come into the world. Oh, how the human race has been waiting for that. It's just what we all need.'

'Get out!'

Reed walked up to Ness, crouching by her as she sat on the bed. 'Like mother, like daughter. Like whore, like hooker.' He grinned.

Ness tried to get up, but he pushed her back down on the small metal bed.

'What are you talking about?' She sounded and looked upset.

'Mina, isn't it? That's your daughter's name.'

Panic spread across Ness's face.

'Her skin's so soft.' He grinned.

'What . . . what . . . Get out, get out!' Tears and words rolled out. 'You sick fuck!'

'Now, that's not very nice.'

'I said, OUT! I don't want to hear anything you've got to say.'

Reed shrugged and Ness attempted again to leap up, but Reed pushed her down, lying almost on top of her on the bed as he pressed his hand over her mouth. 'She was little miss tight pussy, when she was sitting on daddy's dick.' He laughed as Ness, wide-eyed and crying, squirmed underneath him. 'She loved it though, I could tell . . . I wonder if you're as sweet as her, hey? Or have you been used too much?' He slid his hand between her legs. 'Shame . . . Anyway, now, I'm going to get up, and you're not going to scream, are you? In fact, you're not going to do anything. You know why?'

She shook her head.

'Because if you do, I will make sure that the report I'm going to write on you, and the suitability of you keeping your baby, or even having anything to do with him, will be so damaging by the time I've finished writing it, you will never, *ever* have the chance to lay your eyes on him.'

He took his hand off her mouth and stood up, brushing down his suit, which looked slightly creased now.

'Your daughter should have never played with fire,' he sneered. 'It was inevitable that she was going to get burnt.'

Right at that moment, Maureen walked in. Her eyes went straight to Ness, who was shaking and crying on the bed. 'Is everything all right?'

'Oh, everything's fine . . . Well, it is now.' Reed patted Maureen on her back as he walked out of the cell. 'You have no idea how fine it is now . . . Have a good afternoon, ladies.'

52

AMY

It had gone six and Amy wasn't 100 per cent sure when Ollie was going to be back, but she couldn't leave it any longer. She needed to go and speak to Jack. She'd called a few times, leaving messages, but she knew he probably wouldn't risk returning her call in case Ollie was about.

She'd even gone to St Patrick's and left a note behind the row of dusty prayer books, the ones which were never used, where they'd arranged to leave messages for one another. She'd asked him to meet her in a coffee shop just off Oxford Street, but he hadn't showed up, so she'd gone back to see if the note had been taken. It was still there.

So she'd come home, afraid it would set Ollie off if she was late. Only he wasn't back yet, and all she could think about was the bracelet – Evie's bracelet in Ollie's car. Ever since she'd made the connection, she'd been running over the possibilities in her head. She needed to get Jack's take on it urgently, because her head was a mess.

Pulling on a thin cream jumper, she walked out of the newly decorated bedroom and was about to head down the stairs when she heard the front door open. Ollie was back.

She scrambled quickly into the shadows, trying to hide – if Ollie saw her in her outdoor clothes, he'd go crazy. Then she heard a woman's voice and realized Martha was with him. Wanting to hear what was being said, she crouched on the landing, listening.

'. . . *he's a wanker. I'm telling you, Martha, if he didn't have that stuff, I'd wipe that smug smile right off his fucking face. Who the fuck does he think he is with his demands? What, am I supposed to be at frigging Reed's beck and call whenever he feels like it? Muggy cunt.'*

'For fuck's sake, Ollie, give it a rest, never mind about the governor, what we need to worry about is Fat Eddie – he was on the blower again. He's got himself in a right state – personally, I think he's snorting too much of that shit and it's making the fucker paranoid and now—'

The door of the lounge closed behind them, making it impossible for her to eavesdrop on the rest of their conversation.

Amy frowned to herself. The governor? Why would Ollie have anything to do with Reed? Maybe he had something to do with the drugs coming in to Ashcroft? But no, that didn't make sense, because when she'd overheard Tess speaking about the drugs to Earle, it sounded like they'd been working together for a long time, and the governor hadn't been around long. Or perhaps the governor had got involved after he'd arrived, but then that seemed unlikely. Had this something to do with Evie? Did Reed have something to do with her? No, the timeline wouldn't fit. So what the hell was going on?

Amy crept down the stairs. She knew the risk she was taking, but what else could she do? She comforted herself with the thought that, most nights, Ollie wouldn't come upstairs until the early hours. She needed to know what shit he was involved in. How was he connected to both Evie and the governor? More than ever, she needed to speak to Jack; maybe it would make more sense to him than it was making to her.

Taking care not to make a sound, she opened the front door and stepped out into the balmy Soho evening.

Walking into the club in Richmond Mews, Amy glanced around. The place was small, though the music was cranked up loud. It was dimly lit, and the heat and smell of bodies and alcohol hit her immediately.

She noticed how crowded it was, certainly for early evening, though she guessed sex sold anytime; it certainly did in Soho.

Weaving through the throng of men, Amy scanned their faces, looking for Jack. She couldn't see him and suddenly it occurred to her that coming to the club hadn't been such a great idea. As she turned to go, she felt a hand on her arm.

'Amy.'

It was Jack.

She smiled at him, but she could see his eyes were bloodshot. Drunk? High? She wasn't sure which, but maybe that was the reason why he hadn't been in touch. Maybe Soho, as it did to so many people, had started to pull him under.

'Hey, Jack . . . Is there somewhere we can go to talk?'

He looked around, a puzzled expression on his handsome face. 'Yeah, sure . . . I'm surprised to see you here.'

'I've been trying to get in touch with you.' Her tone was harsher than she'd imagined.

'I'm not saying it isn't good to see you, it is, but . . . Let's grab that table over there.' He gave her his lopsided grin, and she put her head down, not wanting to look at him, not wanting to feel the way he made her feel – not that she was sure exactly what that was, but she knew it was pointless. She also knew she was here to talk about Evie and Ollie, nothing else.

'Actually, do you mind if we go outside, Jack? There's too many eyes in here.' He nodded without saying anything and she followed him, weaving back through the club. She kept her head down, hoping that no one recognized her and put in a call to Ollie. Trying not to think what would happen in that event, she let Jack lead her up the stairs to the cobbled mews, where they stood in the shadows by the row of garages.

'Sorry I haven't been in contact.' Jack shrugged. 'It's Rebel – she hasn't been too good recently. She's back on the gear, hitting the hard stuff.' He shrugged again. 'It's tough to see, and it's hard not to care when you have history with someone.' He smiled and she thought he looked uneasy as he added, 'But if any of my leads had come up with anything, I would've been in touch. You know that. Finding Evie is still my number one priority.' He smiled at her again, a hazy glaze in his eyes which was probably from the alcohol she could smell.

'That's what I wanted to talk about. I think . . . I think Ollie might know something about Evie.'

'Why would you think that?' He frowned.

'I found Evie's bracelet in his car . . . I know it's hers, I saw Lynn – she told me Evie made them identical bracelets. The one in the car was definitely Evie's.'

Jack looked thoughtful. 'He could've just given her a lift. It could be innocent.'

'Yeah?' She raised her eyebrows. '*Nothing* Ollie does is innocent. Besides, why didn't he mention it? I've told him about Evie going missing. He knows how worried Lynn's been. When he came to visit me in Ashcroft, even then I talked to him about it, and he said nothing. And since I've been back, he's . . . well, he seems distracted, like he's got something on his mind . . . then this evening, I heard him and Martha talking. They were talking about the governor – Reed. Ollie was pissed off with him, something about being at his beck and call.'

Jack looked surprised.

'I know, it's weird, right? I've got a bad feeling about it all.'

'Was there anything else? Did he say anything else?'

Amy thought, and after a moment she nodded. 'Yeah, he mentioned someone else – or rather, Martha did . . . she said that Fat Eddie—'

'Fat Eddie?' Jack's face darkened. 'Are you sure?'

Amy nodded. 'Positive. Why, do you know him?'

'I do – we go back a long way. Someone else I've got history with.'

'What kind?' Amy asked gently.

Jack didn't say anything for a moment, just rubbed his temples.

'A long time ago, I did some business with him. Him and a guy called Raymond, who was supposed to be my best mate. The pair of them turned me over, Raymond in more ways than one.' He paused, then shrugged. 'Rebel, she was hard on it at the time, *again*, bang on the gear, I wasn't really giving her the attention she needed. Back then, I was more of a prick than I am now.' He laughed, but it was edged with sadness. 'She ended up with Raymond.'

'Some best friend.'

He shrugged, but Amy knew that he must have been hurt at the time, even if the wounds had since healed. 'Yeah, what can you do . . . Anyway, Eddie always had his fingers in a lot of pies. He still owes me money, but I don't care about that. He was always a slippery bastard though.'

'So, what are you going to do?'

'I think I'll pay old Eddie a visit. After all, it's about time . . . And if he knows anything about Evie, don't worry, I'll get it out of him.'

'Let me know what happens, won't you?' She glanced at her watch. 'I have to go; I want to get back before Ollie notices.'

He nodded. 'I'll walk you to the corner.'

'No, it's fine. It's best we're not seen together.'

'OK.'

They locked eyes for a moment before Amy turned and hurried away. She didn't want to start making things any more complicated in her head. It was just a stupid schoolgirl crush. So, Jack was handsome, so were lots of guys, but it was more than that. He made her feel . . . She frowned, scrambling around in her mind for the word . . . Safe. That was it. He made her feel safe.

'Oi. I want a word with you. Amy, I said I want a word with you.'

At the corner of Wardour Street, Amy turned around. Swaying in the road behind her was Rebel. 'I want you to stay away from Jack.'

'I beg your pardon.' Amy was taken aback.

'Don't play the innocent. I've seen the way you look at him, pushing yourself up on him like some little whore.' Even from three feet away, Amy could smell the alcohol on her breath. 'I was watching you two tonight, outside the club, getting all cosy.'

'You have totally got the wrong idea.' Amy stared at her. 'Whatever you thought you saw, you certainly didn't.'

Rebel scoffed. Her make-up was smudged across her face, her breath reeked of booze. 'Oh, come off it, you don't fool me, darlin'. You seriously trying to tell me you ain't thought about Jack in that way? You ain't thought about what it might feel like if he was to kiss you?'

'No . . . no, of course not.'

Rebel shook her head. 'Right there. I can see it in your eyes: you're lying to me.'

'I ain't got time for this.' Amy went to turn away, but Rebel grabbed her arm.

'I lost him for a lot of years, and I ain't goin' to lose him again to someone like you. Understand?'

Amy glanced down at her arm, pulling herself out of Rebel's grip. 'Oh, I understand, all right.'

'Good, I'm glad you do. So I don't want to see you sniffing around him again, otherwise, believe you me, you'll regret it.'

53

MINA

Sitting on the floor in the corner of her bedsit, Mina shook so hard that she was struggling to scroll through her phone. She'd been sick twice, once in the Uber cab and once in the street. The cab driver had kicked them out halfway through the journey, but she was so upset she didn't even put up a fight. But from there she had no idea how she'd actually made it back home.

Everything was a blur, a mess, and the image of Iris lying in the grass, blood coming from her head, whirled through her mind. She didn't even know if the ambulance came – she'd been too terrified to stay around to wait, she'd been so sure that someone had been watching them. And apart from being scared for herself, she'd been terrified for Flo.

With a trembling hand, Mina finally managed to see through her tears and steady herself enough to dial a number.

It rang a few times, then a voice answered.

'Hello?'

'Steph . . . Steph, it's me . . . Mina . . . I . . .' She trailed off. She couldn't, she couldn't speak, she felt like she was about to have a panic attack.

There was a pause. 'Mina, you all right? Mina?' Steph's voice sounded loud in the quiet of the room. Phoning Steph on her mobile was the only thing she could think of. There was no way she could get through to speak to anyone otherwise.

'Mina? You sure you're fine?'

'Yeah . . . yeah.' She pulled the phone away from her mouth and bit down on her arm to stop herself screaming.

'Mina? You there?'

She took a deep breath and spoke again, 'Yeah, I'm here.'

'You don't sound too clever, girl. What's happened? Mina?'

Mina squeezed her eyes shut, desperately trying not to break down.

Steph's voice sounded unsure. *'You want me to get your mum? I'll have to be quick, lockdown is soon, and those fuckers can't wait to put us to bed.'*

'No . . . No, no, not my mum, no, I don't want to speak to her . . . Reenie – is Reenie there? . . . Please, please don't let my mum know I'm on the phone.'

'Reenie?' Another pause, then Steph spoke, *'OK sweetheart, wait there, I'll try and find her.'*

Waiting, Mina held the phone in her hand, wrapping her arms around her knees as she rocked back and forth, terrified.

A couple of minutes later, Mina heard Maureen's voice on the phone.

'Mina? What is it?'

'Reenie . . . Reenie, help me . . . Help me!' She burst into tears, long gut-wrenching sobs.

'Oh Jesus, what's happened, sweetheart, tell me what's happened.'

Eventually, Mina managed to calm herself down enough to say some more: 'Reenie, it's Iris . . . I think Iris is dead, and I think I'm going to be next . . .'

54

JACK

'Hello, mate. How's it going?' It was late now, gone midnight, and as Jack walked into the small messy office his thoughts kept jumping between Amy and Evie, but right now he had to put those thoughts on hold, separate them from what he was about to do. Right now, his priority was dealing with something he probably should've dealt with a long time ago.

'Remember me, Eddie?' Jack grinned, cocking his head to one side. 'Course you do. You owe me money!' He laughed as Eddie, who'd been stuffing his face with a double cheeseburger, practically choked on it in surprise, his whole body visibly tensing at the sight of Jack.

His face white, Eddie growled, 'Who the fuck let you in?'

'Now that's not very nice, is it? After all this time, I would've thought you'd be pleased to see me. And a word of advice, you need to get better security, your goons on the door are hardly SAS in the making, are they?' He blew on his fists, feeling the sting of the broken skin on his knuckles; it had been a while since he'd had to batter anyone.

He wandered around the office, sweeping ashtrays, photo frames and other items onto the floor. 'Whoops . . . sorry about that, but then this place is a shithole anyway, I doubt it'll make any difference. Some things never change; it's like they say, a home reflects its owner . . . or should that be a dog reflects his owner?' He sneered.

'What do you want? Raymond said you were back, but he thought you were still bible-bashing?'

'And what would Raymond know? Are you really still listening to him?'

It was Eddie's turn to sneer. 'Well, clearly Rebel is, or so I've heard.' He winked.

Jack slammed his hand down on the table, making Eddie push back in his chair with a panicky glance at the door. 'Oh, come on, Ed, what are you looking over there for? You're a fat cunt, by the time you get there, it'll be sunrise.'

Eddie shook his head. 'I knew it wasn't for real, when Ray told me, when other people told me about you. I knew all this . . . this priesthood shit was crap. You need to brush up on your act, Jack. For a start, what priest talks like that?'

Jack shrugged and winked at Eddie. 'Well, that's the good thing about it, Ed. I can sin until the cows come home, then say a few Hail Marys, and all will be forgiven. Who'd've thought, hey?' He laughed louder than he needed to, but he could see that Eddie was well and truly worried.

'Look, tell me what you want, then get the hell out of here . . . You want money? You want girls, is that it? Drugs? Come on, Jack, there must be a reason you've come to see me. You ain't just here to visit, I ain't one of your parishioners.'

Jack walked around the desk which Eddie was sitting behind. 'Tell me about Ollie Jones . . . What's your connection with him? And let's not go through the whole thing of you denying knowing him. Let's make this quick, shall we?' He kicked Eddie's chair.

Eddie shook his head, his lips pursed.

'Ed, this can only end one way. Don't be an idiot, you don't want to see who I used to be, do you? You don't want the old me.'

Eddie licked his lips nervously. 'I ain't a grass.'

Jack nodded slowly. 'Maybe, but that's not the point. The

question is, are you stupid? If you don't tell me, then you know what's going to happen and I don't think you'd like that . . . Because if you aren't a grass, then you give me no other choice.' He winked. 'That's right, Eddie . . . Jack's back.'

He grabbed Eddie's hair, slamming his face down on the desk, smashing his nose. Blood spurted everywhere as Eddie cried out, but Jack continued brutally hammering his face against the hard wooden desk.

Eddie screamed in pain.

'Have you had enough?' Jack, panting, pulled Eddie's head back and stared into his bloodied face. 'Because I'm quite enjoying this. I'd forgotten how good it feels . . . You want more?' And with those words, Jack bashed his face against the desk again.

Almost immediately, Eddie waved his arms. 'OK . . . OK . . . OK . . . Stop . . .' Struggling to breathe through his broken nose, he was panting hard as he spluttered the words out. 'Ollie . . . me and Ollie . . . We deal in girls together . . . Filming – anything goes . . . punters, they can do what they want . . . That's it . . . No big deal.' He coughed, blood coming out of his mouth.

'And what about a girl called Evie? What do you know about her?'

'I don't . . . I've never heard of her. I swear, Jack . . . I'd tell you if I did.'

Jack could hear the panic in Eddie's voice. 'You know something: I think I believe you, but I always like to finish off a job, you should know that by now.'

Then, with one final slam of Eddie's head against the desk, he knocked him out cold.

He blinked and stared at the man lying motionless on the desk, then closed his eyes for a moment, trying to come to terms with what he'd just done. Trying to work out if he had enjoyed it, or if it was something that he had to do to help Evie.

Rubbing his temples, he opened his eyes, looked around, then he stared at the desk. Trying not to think too hard about it, he took a £50 note from the pile of cash on the desk, rolled it up and, pausing for only a moment, he leaned over the line of cocaine Eddie had laid out on his desk, and snorted it up.

The coke hit the back of his nose, his throat, rushing round his body, a euphoric high hitting his brain. Taking the edge off what he'd just done. Then he sank into a chair, his heart racing, holding his head in his hands. Feeling lost. Thinking of Amy. Thinking what a mess he'd made of everything.

His phone buzzed in his pocket. Wearily, the high washing over him, he pulled it out then audibly groaned. It was Maureen . . . Again.

Knowing he needed to answer this time, he tried to keep his voice even. 'Hi, Reenie. Sorry, I've been busy, I know you've called a few times.'

'*Jack, oh thank God, it's me . . . I need your help.*' Her voice was urgent but quiet, as if she was whispering. '*You need to go around to the address I'm going to text you . . . you need to make sure that Mina's all right. Once you get her, take her somewhere safe.*'

'What's this about?'

'*Just do it, now. Call me when you've got her – I'll explain when I see you. And Jack – be careful. Don't do anything stupid.*'

He glanced at Eddie lying unconscious in a pool of his own blood, and said, 'Of course I won't.'

55

NESS

Yawning, Ness walked back into the cell after her early-morning shower. It was one of the positive things about being pregnant in this place: they allowed pregnant women and the older prisoners to hit the shower room first. It wasn't much of a perk, but it was better than nothing.

'Morning, Reenie,' she said sleepily.

Reenie's face was drawn with worry. 'Who's Flo? Sweetheart, who's Flo?'

Ness stumbled back; she leaned her hand on the wall. Her mind began to race, her heart beating faster. 'What are you talking about? I don't know anyone called Flo.'

Maureen's voice was warm but firm. 'Ness, you need to tell me who Flo is . . . you know can trust me.'

Ness began to shake. 'What's happened? . . . Reenie, what's happened?'

'Please, Ness, tell me.'

Ness started to cry. She covered her face with her hands. 'She's my daughter . . . she's my daughter.'

Maureen went across to Ness, holding her as she cried. 'Ness, is there anyone who can look after her. Has she got anyone?'

Trembling, Ness nodded, dropping her hands. 'Mina . . . Mina looks after her.' She could hardly speak; her mouth was dry, nervous. Even though she wasn't sure what was happening, fear sat in the pit of her stomach.

'Apart from Mina, sweetheart. Think, is there anyone else?'

Confusion ran through her. 'What's happened? Please tell me that Mina hasn't gone out partying and left her sister. Please tell me that she ain't that irresponsible . . . Oh my God.'

Maureen shook her head. 'It's not that.'

Ness screamed. 'Then what? What? *What's happened?*'

'Sshhhh, Ness.' Tears were running down Maureen's face as well. 'Mina's not there. Jack needs somewhere he can take Flo. Somewhere to keep her safe . . . Something's happened to Mina, and we don't know what yet. When Jack arrived at the flat, she wasn't there.'

Ness couldn't believe what she was hearing. 'What? How . . . how did you know where we live? I . . . I don't understand.' Her words tumbled out. 'Reenie, please, just tell me.'

'Mina, she called me last night.'

Ness stood up, swiping away her tears, angry now. 'What the fuck do you mean, she called you? What's going on? Why's she calling *you*, why the hell didn't you tell me. What the fuck, Reenie?' She began to pace.

'That's what I'm trying to explain: Mina's got herself involved in some things that . . . well, things have got out of control, Ness.'

Shaking, her thoughts rushed to what Reed had bragged about, but she didn't say anything, just pointed at Reenie. 'You need to tell me what she's done.' Nausea washed over her, and suddenly a cold uneasy feeling rushed through her.

Maureen spoke gently. 'Before I do, tell me where Jack can take Flo, then I can call him back and let him know.'

Ness stared into her eyes. 'OK . . . OK, there's a babysitter called Lottie, she lives in the new flats on Berwick Street, it's on the ground floor, the first door you get to . . . But her number should be on the pinboard by the sink.'

'Thank you.' She squeezed Ness's hand. 'Why didn't you tell me about Flo?'

'I couldn't . . . I couldn't tell anyone . . . I'm sorry, but I couldn't let them take her.' Ness was still shaking, but she took a deep breath. 'Please, tell me what's happened.'

'When Jack went round, Mina wasn't there. But he found blood. There was a pool of blood.'

Ness shook her head. 'Maybe . . . maybe she fell and banged her head . . . Maybe she went to Casualty, and that's why she left Flo. That must be it.' Ness spoke quickly and desperately. 'Tell me that's what it is, *tell me.*'

'I wish I could, but she thought someone was after her. She and Iris—'

'Iris?' Ness cut in. 'What's Iris got to do with it? I mean, I know they're friends. I know . . .' She trailed off, shaking.

'She and Iris . . . well, lovey, they got themselves in a spot of bother.' Maureen paused. 'Look, I don't want you to be upset, you've got the bairn to think about.' She pointed to her bump.

Ness's face darkened. 'Just tell me what you're talking about.'

'OK, OK . . . Look, Iris thought it might be a good idea to sleep with men to get some money, Mina . . . well, Mina went along with her, then things got out of hand, and . . . and from what I can gather, Mina's drink got spiked and, well, that's when things happened.'

Ness shook her head as she glared at Maureen. Reed's words came back into her mind. Her eyes filled with tears. 'My girl ain't a hooker, she ain't a whore.'

'That's right, she's not, she's not any of those names, and neither is Iris, they're just two young girls who got caught up in something. Nessie. I'm so sorry, but please, you've got to try to calm down. Ness, please.'

The wail of agony which came from Ness filled the cell with a cold chill, she leaned against the wall, facing it. Then she felt Maureen's hand on her back, rubbing it gently.

'Oh my God, oh my God, oh my God.' Full of pain, Ness continued to wail and cry.

'Ness, try to take a deep breath, I know it's hard, but you need to think of the baby. And Ness, I want to say how proud and brave I think you are. I don't know all the ins and outs because Mina was obviously in a state, but she managed to tell me what you did. I know you took the blame for her. She told me that she was the one who killed Steve. I think she was relieved to tell someone. I know how much she loves you, Ness, that was clear, and how much you love her.'

Ness turned around. 'You won't breathe a word – not about Flo, not about Steve, promise me.'

Maureen nodded, her eyes full of warmth. 'I promise. On my life.'

Ness was only partly listening. Her voice wavered with emotion. 'You think it's . . . it's a . . .' She struggled to say the word, '*punter*, you think a punter has come around and knocked her about? That's happened to me before, I've had guys do that.'

'*Breakfast, ladies,*' an officer shouted as he walked along the corridor.

'No, Ness, I don't . . . Again, I don't know all the ins and outs, there wasn't time to go into it, but Iris and Mina got it into their heads to blackmail one of the clients from this brothel.'

'What? Who?' Ness was stunned.

'It was the governor, Ness . . . They were blackmailing him.'

Shocked, Ness didn't say anything at first. 'The governor? The governor took her?' She felt sick. 'Oh my God, he was saying . . . He was saying about Mina, and I thought he was just winding me up, tormenting me. That's what he must have meant when he said about Mina getting burned if she played with fire . . . That was him telling me what was going to happen . . . Jesus Christ.'

Then she stared ahead. 'And . . . and he talked about Mina, you know, he made out . . . I'm going to kill him.'

Ness rushed out into the corridor, trying to get some air, trying to get her head around what Maureen had just told her. 'I'm going to fucking kill him.'

Maureen ran after her as Steph, looking shaken, came to join them.

'Wait! Wait! Ness, don't do anything silly. Don't forget, Mina is still missing. We don't want to do anything that will jeopardize her safety – plus we don't have any proof.'

'I don't need proof. I know Reed did this.'

'But think about it: Reed was here yesterday, so he couldn't have done . . .' Steph stopped.

'Couldn't have done what?' Ness's agitation, anger and fear mixed together. 'Steph, for fuck's sake.'

Steph took a deep breath. 'Jack's just told me that Iris – she's in a coma, she's in a bad way.' And with those words, Steph collapsed to the floor.

56

STEPH

Later that afternoon, Steph, feeling shaken still, sat opposite Jack in the visiting room. Thankfully, Jenkins had been on duty, and as usual she'd been easy to bribe, so Steph had been allowed to join Maureen and meet with him. But now she was here, her thoughts were so full of Iris that it was all she could do to concentrate on what he was saying.

She felt like she was drowning. How could she just sit here when her daughter was miles away in a hospital bed, hanging on to life by a thread? Right now, she envied what Lynette had done. If only she could inject herself with smack, get rid of the pain, because the agony she felt in her heart was unbearable.

'I think it's for the best, don't you, Steph?' said Reenie.

'Sorry, what?' She looked up and saw the worry in their faces.

'It's for the best that we don't draw attention,' said Jack. 'We need to make out we don't know anything, that we're not on anyone's trail. Iris is safe in hospital, but Mina's missing, and if she is still alive, we don't want whoever has her to become spooked and do something to her in panic . . . Right now, the police have no idea who Iris is. Mina picked up her stuff, so the police just have her down as a Jane Doe, no clue as to who left her for dead on a patch of wasteland.'

Steph gasped, putting her head in her hands. She took a deep breath and tried to stop the wave of nausea.

She felt Maureen rub her back. 'That's it, you take a deep breath.'

After a moment, she dropped her hands and stared straight at Jack, but she didn't say anything. It was taking everything she had to stop herself screaming, but she continued to let him talk.

Jack nodded. 'I know it's tough, Steph. It means that you can't ask permission to go and see her, but I think this is the best way to handle it.'

'That sounds a sensible idea,' Maureen said.

'It's only a matter of time, though, before they discover who she is.' Jack's stare moved between them both. 'A few days maybe, if we're lucky. But we haven't got long. We need to find Mina before the heat gets too much for whoever it is that took her. We don't want it to get out there. That's the best hope we have of keeping her alive.'

Steph glanced around the visiting room; it was quieter today than on a weekend, but she saw Tess grinning at her, and dark rage ran through her veins. She had planned to take Tess out next week, but there was no way she was going to let her walk around a moment longer than she had to. She couldn't help Iris right now, nor could she help Mina, but what she could do was help the women in D wing by getting rid of her. And the pain, the fear and helplessness she felt in her stomach for her daughter, well, she was determined to channel it into giving Tess a goodbye she'd never forget.

Sighing and turning her attention back to Jack, Steph asked, 'And what about Evie?'

Jack paused. 'Before Amy found the bracelet in Ollie's car, I had an outside hope that maybe she ran away with some boyfriend that no one knew about.' He shook his head, pain in his eyes. 'Now, I'm so sorry but I think she's dead.'

57

AMY

Later that afternoon, in a café off Wardour Street, Amy met with Jack. 'I can't stay long – I don't know when Ollie's due back – but I needed to find out how Steph and Ness are.' As she spoke, she noticed how tired he looked.

'Steph was in a bad way. She looks broken, but she was trying to put a brave face on it.'

He gave her a sad, weary smile, and once again she had to resist the feelings that surfaced whenever she was with him.

'I did think about calling her but, I don't want it to seem as if I'm sticking my nose into her business. There's a lot of bad blood between us and maybe now's not the time to start phoning her up.' She took a sip of her tea, which was almost cold.

'Maybe now is the perfect time. It's times like this when we need our friends around.'

'Maybe.' She shrugged, doubting that, even at the worst of times, Steph would want to hear from her, even though she'd love to reach out, just to let her know that she was thinking of her. 'And Ness, what about her? How's she doing?'

'I didn't manage to see her. Reenie is looking after her though. She's in good hands.'

'It's all such a mess.' Amy took a deep breath, watching the summer rain pour down the window. 'Who's going to tell Lynette about Evie?'

'Maybe she doesn't need to know yet. I mean, it's only a hunch at the moment, we can't be sure. She might turn up alive. Miracles do happen.'

Amy laughed bitterly. 'Not here in Soho they don't.'

Jack sighed, and Amy thought how the past few weeks had taken a toll on him. 'And what about you?' he asked. 'How do you feel, knowing that Ollie might be a part of it.'

'*Is* a part of it,' Amy corrected him. She'd followed her usual strategy when it came to Ollie: pushing away how she felt. It was easier that way. The enormity of the situation was almost too much to handle. It was clear that Ollie was up to his neck in whatever had happened to the three girls. 'Guilt. That's the main thing I feel. If it wasn't for me, they'd be safe. I feel like I've walked them into a lion's den.'

Jack picked up a paper napkin and wiped away Amy's tears. 'Guilt . . . Guilt is a strange thing. It never seems to go away.' He spoke softly, his voice almost too quiet for Amy to hear. 'I know it's not the same, but that's what eats away at me. That's what had me coming back to Soho to see Rebel.'

'Why did you leave in the first place?' Amy asked.

Jack leaned back in his chair. 'I was dealing drugs – *big* time. Really big time. I wouldn't let anybody get in my way . . . If they did . . .' He stopped and shrugged, and Amy knew exactly what that meant.

'I made a lot of enemies, but I didn't care, and I didn't care who I hurt. That's when Rebel got involved with drugs. I took my eye off the ball – maybe I didn't give her enough attention. Before I knew it, she was bang on the gear. But I ignored her, I didn't have time for her or what she was going through, even though she was struggling. The way I saw it back then, it wasn't my problem.'

He paused again, and Amy could see it was difficult for him to talk about it.

'Then she started fucking my best friend, which I think was her trying to get some sort of reaction from me, or I dunno, revenge maybe, and she got so high one day that she drove off the road. Our daughter was in the back of the car – she was only a few months old.'

'Oh my God, I'm so sorry.' Amy looked at him, smelling the alcohol on his breath. 'I had no idea.'

'Maybe I should've stayed around to help her, maybe I should've stayed around to share that grief that eats away at you like a cancer, but I couldn't. And I ran, I ran, I ran so far because I couldn't stand to look at her. Because, if I'd stayed, if I'd stayed a moment longer, I might have killed her for what she did . . . But that doesn't stop me feeling that I let her down. Like you, even though I know I didn't force her to pick up the drugs, I feel like I led her to the den.'

'Is that why you let her treat you like that? You shouldn't. You shouldn't let anyone treat you like that.'

He gave her another sad smile, then reached over and touched her face gently. The bruise on her cheek from Ollie still stung. 'I think that goes for both of us, don't you?'

Tears welled up in Amy's eyes and he took her hand in his as the sound of the noisy café faded into the background. They held each other's stares, his dark green eyes gazing into hers, though it was Amy who eventually broke away. 'I have to go.'

'No, wait. Please.'

Amy glanced up at the clock, then nodded. 'Five more minutes, then I really do have to go.'

They sat in silence, still holding each other's hands, not needing to say anything, though Amy was aware that she was being reckless. Right now, she didn't care. Right now, she felt alive for the first time in as long as she could remember.

Then, reluctantly, it was time for her to go. Getting up from her chair, she nodded to him. But what neither of them saw was Rebel, standing watching from the other side of the street.

58

OLLIE

It was early evening the next day when Ollie locked his car, having parked it right outside the address he was going to. He could feel the sweat running down his back, wetting the black shirt he was wearing, and he could also feel the tension in his neck. He cricked it to one side, rolling his head round at the same time. The past twenty-four hours had been full on, though now there was a pressing matter he had to deal with, and he was certainly going to look forward to it.

He looked up and nodded at the person waiting by the stone stairs which led down to a basement.

'You'll find him inside. He's out of it. He's been drinking a lot. He came home a bit of a mess. The club's closed today. There's no one around and I've left the door open, OK? If you go up the stairs, through the back room, you'll find him. He's up on the first floor but he's crashed out at the moment, so it'll be easy.'

Ollie looked at the woman. He could smell the alcohol coming off her, he could also see when someone had been smoking a rock.

'Jesus, what did he do to deserve you, hey?'

'Piss off . . . Cos let's face it, it ain't my wife who's been fucking him, it's yours. You should be thanking me that I came and found you, told you what your slut of a wife has been up to. They deserve payback.'

He grabbed her around the throat. 'Don't ever call my wife a slut. And the day I thank a cracked-up whore for anything will be the day hell freezes over.' He let her go, throwing her to the floor and making his way into the club, calling over his shoulder, 'But you're right about one thing: Jack is certainly going to have payback . . .'

A couple of hours later, Ollie, with splatters of blood at the bottom of his trousers, walked into his house. He was greeted by Amy, who smiled at him.

'Hey, it's good to see you. You OK? You want me to get some dinner for you?'

He stared at her. 'Maybe we need to have the entrees first?' Then he clenched his fist and laid into her with the first punch.

59

STEPH

It was almost lockdown the same evening, and Steph was pacing, her face drawn in anger. Yes, she'd been crying on and off, going through a range of disbelief and full-on rage, but the main thing driving her was the desire for revenge. The anger she felt rushing through her was welcome, it was what was going to see her through the next few hours. It was what was going to make her strong, and right now, that's exactly what she needed to be. She needed to do this for Iris. For Mina. For the women. Right now, she needed to be one badass bitch.

She looked at Ness, who herself had gone through difficult emotions: terrified for Mina, worrying she was in labour, relief that she could talk about Flo, as well as having full-blown panic attacks throughout the day.

Maureen sat on Lynette's bed. She looked ill and she'd been struggling for breath, but she'd refused to go to medical. She rubbed her chest, speaking quietly, subdued. Her face strained and pale. 'Are you certain this is the best way? Jack thought it would be best to wait to see how it unfolds. Though he's not answering the phone now.' Her concern cut through the air.

Steph, whose eyes were puffy, shook her head. There was a hardened edge to her voice. 'Reenie, no disrespect, but it should be *my* decision, not his. It's Iris who's lying in the hospital because of that bastard. It's Mina who's missing. And I will never be able to rest while he's still walking around.' Her hatred oozed out of her, and she bit down on her lip, battling not to cry or scream.

'We don't know the full story though.' Maureen sounded worried.

'Does that matter? Does that fucking matter?' Steph raised her voice and smashed her hand against the wall, causing it to become red and swollen.

'She's only asking, Steph.' Lynette, who'd joined them after being discharged from the hospital, gently intervened. 'Reenie's only saying it because she cares about the girls. She's not digging you out.'

Steph nodded but said nothing. There was no room for softness, not now; that would only lead to weakness.

'And are you all right with this, Ness? You don't think it'll make things worse for Mina?' Maureen turned to Ness, who wasn't looking at all well.

'How could it be fucking worse? Whatever we do now can't make anything worse . . . That fucker needs to get what's coming to him. To think he screwed Mina. It makes me sick to my stomach, she's a kid, a fucking kid and he's . . .' She trailed off, taking noisy deep breaths. Then she began to cry. 'I can't, I can't think about what's happened to her, I can't think about where she is, and what he's done to her. The police won't do anything – they never did anything for Evie, did they?'

Lynette sucked the air hard, and the women saw she was battling the tears.

'This way we've got a chance, haven't we?' Ness continued. 'This way we can find out where Mina is, we can make him talk.'

Steph nodded, her hands shaking. 'Yeah, and by the time we've finished with him, he'll be begging to tell us . . . The governor won't know what's hit him.'

Maureen nodded and stared at Steph. 'You think we'll be able to pull it off?'

'I don't think, I know . . . It's all arranged.'

'*Get back in your own cells, ladies,*' an officer called loudly as he walked through the wing.

Steph turned to go, but Lynette waved her back. 'Wait!' She stood on the top bunk bed and stretched up to the fluorescent lighting, moving her hand around, then she grabbed something and jumped down. 'Here, you might need this.'

In her hand she held a home-made weapon.

'Tess dropped this in my cell a couple of months ago, when she was being hauled off to solitary. I thought you might want it.'

Steph took it. 'Thanks,' she said. Then she walked out, followed by Ness and Maureen.

As Steph walked along D wing she nodded to Earle, then sauntered into her cell, waiting for it to begin . . .

It was just past nine o'clock and Steph heard her cell door being opened. She knew who it would be, and she stood up, readying herself, trying to push everything out of her mind, which she was becoming so good at.

'Are we all set?' Speaking quickly, Earle stepped inside. His face was slick with sweat.

'Yeah, I'm ready . . . have you done what you need to?'

Earle nodded, his speech still not right. 'It was easy. There's only a couple of us on at night, so making sure the CCTV was off in the wing wasn't a problem. It's always playing up, so no one will be suspicious.' He paused and stared at her, a twinkle in his eye. 'I'm glad you agreed to do this. It's long overdue.'

'Yeah, you're right, it is. So let's go.'

She followed Earle out and into the corridor until they came to a cell further along the wing. They stood outside for a moment while Earle made sure they were alone, then he whispered, 'I'll come back in five minutes when it's done and get you back in your cell.'

Steph nodded. 'That's fine.'

'Tomorrow, I'll make sure the cells are all unlocked as normal, I'll be the one doing it, and then, after about an hour, just before breakfast, I'll raise the alarm. With the CCTV cameras down, no one will know when she was actually attacked. It will look like someone got in after the cell was unlocked in the morning.'

Steph gave him a thumbs up.

'Make sure you do a good job on her, won't you? I don't want Tess coming back on the wing, ever. I want her out of my life – understand.'

Steph pulled the home-made blade from the pocket of her trousers and smiled. Earle gave a wide grin in return.

'Ready?'

Steph winked. 'Oh yeah, so ready.'

Putting the master key – which was attached to his belt – in the lock, Earle turned it, nodding to Steph as he did so.

As the cell door swung open, Steph suddenly shoved Earle hard in the back, pushing him forward.

Tess, who'd been waiting behind the door, dragged him into the cell. There was a look of shock on his face as Tess tripped him up, flinging him to the ground.

'Surprise!' Tess laughed and winked at Steph, who followed him in and quickly closed the cell door behind her. Immediately both women set about kicking Earle, who was unable to respond to the battering blows to his skull and body as he lay on the floor, being booted around like a ragdoll.

Laughing, Tess sat astride Earle as he lay face down.

'Get his keys. Get the fucking keys!' Steph urged Tess. 'Hurry up, let's leave him, come on.'

'Where's the fun in that?' Grabbing the keys off his belt, Tess grinned, then she pulled Earle's limp head backwards and slid her forearm round his neck. She winked at Steph again and with one expert heave, she wrenched his head round as far as it would go. A loud crack sounded as she broke his neck.

'Howay, Steph, don't look like that. Daffy was getting on me nerves, and I never did like cartoons.'

'For fuck's sake, hurry up. Go and open all the cells and the wing gate, OK? But hurry.'

Tess nodded, but as she got up to leave Steph scowled at her, hatred in her voice. 'Us setting Earle up was purely because I want payback. I haven't forgotten what you did to Lynette – don't think for a minute, Tess, that you and me are mates.'

Stepping over Earle's body, Tess sneered and leaned in close to Steph. 'Don't kid yourself for a moment that I'd want that, pet. Me agreeing to help you was totally because I want a bit of fun . . . Now come on, who's next!'

Within half an hour the women on the wing were out of their cells, the doors having been unlocked by Tess. The air was filled with the deafening sound of emergency alarms, and shouts and screams from the women.

It was chaos, and on the bottom landing, Ness huddled in a corner, leaning forward in pain. 'I don't want to get involved, I can't.' She took a deep gulp of air. 'I just don't want to risk it, I ain't feeling too clever.' She bent further forward, holding her stomach. 'Oh fuck, oh fuck, that hurts.'

Steph looked at her, then at Maureen. 'Reenie, can you take her somewhere? Get her out of the way?'

'Yeah, of course.'

As quickly as she could, Steph helped Ness to her feet, watching the scene unfold as the women looted and fought between themselves. She saw Tiny punch one of the women from the top landing in the face, sending her sprawling across the floor. Clouds of smoke hung in the air, one of the women having set fire to the mattresses which had been thrown out into the corridor, an acrid smell wafting through the cells.

'Do you think you can make it to the chapel, Ness? That will be the safest place for you, the women are going crazy out there.'

With difficulty, Ness spoke. She winced. 'Yeah, I think so.'

'Reenie, take her up there and I'll try to find Samantha. I'll send her up to you. She used to be a nurse.'

'Yeah, before she killed her patients and ended up in here.' Ness attempted a smile.

Steph didn't smile though, her mind had moved elsewhere, she knew time wasn't on her side. She wasn't sure how long it would be before the screws took control again, so she needed the women to go crazy, it was in her best interest.

As she raced along the corridor, it occurred to Steph that she hadn't seen Lynn in a while. Ahead of her, a woman was standing on a chair, laughing and waving a rolled-up burning newspaper under the smoke detectors, setting off the sprinklers.

'Has anyone seen Lynette?' she yelled, but her voice couldn't compete with the alarms and the screaming of the women.

Charging onward, she turned a corner and spotted Tess at the far end of the first-floor landing, surrounded by her cronies. As she drew closer, the air of danger ratcheted up a notch or two and she noticed a woman who'd only come into Ashcroft the previous week, out cold at their feet, lying face down, blood coming from her ear as she shook violently, fitting and rasping, vomit in her mouth.

'Tess? Have you seen Lynette?' she panted.

Tess, who had blood smeared on her face, grinned nastily.

'Last time I saw her she was heading for the library. But I don't know if you'll be able to get there – apparently the screws have surrounded the place. Some of them managed to get in via the gym, which means I need to make the most of it while I can.' She laughed, nodding to the women standing with her. Obeying her unspoken command, they picked up the woman lying on the ground and threw her over the balcony.

Tess glared at her. 'You next? Fancy a bungee jump, love?'

'Fuck off.' Steph took off, her lungs burning with the effort. She could hear prison officers yelling commands, the sound of batons banging against cell doors. She'd seen a few officers dressed in riot gear over by the kitchen, but so far they'd been held back by the overwhelming number of women on the wing. It wouldn't be long before reinforcements arrived, which meant she needed to find the governor fast. She knew that this might be her only chance. But she also needed to know Lynette was all right.

Nearing the library, Steph skipped around a woman who was crying in agony. She didn't have time to stop.

Running through the double doors of the library, Steph, trying to catch her breath, looked around her. It was quieter in here, although the place had been destroyed: most of the books had been thrown on the floor, posters ripped off the walls and lipstick graffiti scrawled everywhere. Chairs and tables had been over-turned and Steph saw someone had tried to start a fire in the far corner.

Seeing no one, she was about to make her way out when a voice rang out.

'Looking for me?' The governor entered the library from the other door.

Steph's heart raced, and she charged towards him, but she stopped in her tracks as three women with a reputation for being grasses came through the door and stood behind the governor.

THE WOMEN

Steph looked at them in disgust. 'You're joking. When word gets out that you stupid bitches backed him, your lives won't be worth living.' She held the home-made blade which Lynette had given her in her hands.

'But for it to get out, you need to be able to walk out of here alive,' Reed laughed.

Steph glared, her hatred for the governor overwhelming her fear of the three women who stood next to him.

'You're going to pay.'

The governor laughed. 'No – but I think Iris did. She's certainly a chip off the old block. You'd be proud. Ollie told me she put up a good fight, or she tried to.' He laughed but it sounded like he didn't realize Iris was still alive. As tempting as it was to tell him, her instincts told her not to.

'You piece of fucking scum!' She clutched the blade in her hand harder.

He winked at her and pulled a face. The coldness in his eyes cut right through her.

'You're not going to get away with this.'

'I think I already did, don't you? You're the one who'll be leaving here in a body bag.' He nodded to the women, who immediately lunged at Steph.

She dodged them and charged through the door, the sound of their pounding feet following her as she ran along the corridor and clambered up the metal stairs. She felt her hair being grabbed and kicked out at her assailant, but one of the women snatched her ankle, trying to pull her down. Steph clung to the railings, kicking out as hard as she could until the hand released her from its grip, enabling her to spin around and slam her foot into the face of the woman, smashing her nose with the heel of her shoe.

'Fuck off, you stupid bitches!' she yelled as she charged on up the stairs.

'You're a dead woman, Steph!' one of the women shouted as she ran after her.

Panting, at the top of the stairs, Steph turned right, towards the bathroom, but she saw a pile of burning mattresses blocking her way, so instead she charged the other way, only to find two of her pursuers standing in front of her, grinning. She spun around to be confronted by the third woman, who was holding a broken broom handle.

Surrounded, Steph waved the blade at them. 'Come on then, you stupid cow, come on, if you want it . . . Let's see, shall we?' She gestured with one hand and stabbed the air with the blade still clutched in her other hand.

The woman, her face screwed up in anger, swung the broom in the air. Steph ducked but, hearing the other women coming up behind her, she turned. The next thing she knew, the broom connected with her wrist, knocking the blade out of her hand. She scrambled to get it and as she did, she heard Lynette yell.

'*Steph!* I'm coming! Steph, I'm coming!'

From the corner of her eye, she saw Lynette charge towards her.

'No, Lynn, stay there! Stay there, it's fine.'

But Lynn kept running towards her, only to be grabbed from behind by one of Tess's cronies.

'Let her go! Let her go!' Steph had managed to pick up the blade, but she couldn't do anything as she was surrounded herself.

Tess chuckled as she walked towards the group of women. 'And what fun would that be, hey?'

'Just let her fucking go. This has nothing to do with her. It's me you want. Do what you like with me but leave her alone.'

'How noble, but I think my way's better.' She nodded to the

women, who held onto Lynn, and immediately she let out a scream as they laid into her.

'Stop! Stop! *Stop!*' Tears ran down Steph's face as she watched in vain, blocked by a wall of Tess's cronies, as Lynette tried to fight back. Laughing, the women knocked her off her feet then kicked her down the metal stairs to the bottom landing.

'No! Lynn! No! *Lynn!*' Steph screamed as the women stepped out of the way, still laughing, and slipping on the wet from the sprinklers, skidding on the streaks of blood which smeared the floor, Steph ran down the stairs to where Lynette was lying.

'Lynn! Lynn? Oh my God, oh God, darling, no.'

Steph dropped to the floor and cradled Lynette's head in her arms. 'Look what you've done to her.' Her scream rose above the noise. 'Look what you've done. She was my friend. She was everyone's friend.' The tears and the hatred rushed out.

She looked up and saw Tess moving down the stairs towards her. 'Oops. That was unfortunate.' She let out a deep roar of laughter. 'Oh well, no point in crying over spilled milk.'

'You and me, bitch, you and me.' She leapt up, charging at Tess, dragging her down the stairs with a clatter. A look of surprise crossed Tess's face for a moment as Steph jumped, leaping on her back.

She dug her fingers into her eyes, and Tess, trying to get her off her back, spun round on the spot. Unable to shake Steph off, she ran into the wall, crashing them both onto the floor.

Steph flew forward, but managed to scramble to her feet and grab the broken broom handle. She raised it above her head and charged at Tess, who was slower getting up.

The other women stood back as Steph landed a blow to Tess's face, splitting her nose and spurting blood all over the floor. Then she charged again, driving Tess into the wall with the broom handle pressing against her throat, pushing with all her might.

She heard Tess gag as she struggled for air, her arms flailing, trying to push her away; then her body started going into spasms, but it only made Steph more determined to finish her off. She pressed with all her strength, watching as Tess's face turned purple, her eyes wide open, the whites of them bursting with red veins, until eventually she stopped moving altogether.

And as Tess dropped to the floor, Steph had only one thought in her mind . . . The governor.

60

AMY

Her mouth, her face, her whole body was sore. She wasn't sure how long she'd been lying there. All she knew was that Ollie somehow had found out about her and Jack, and now she was paying the price. She moved her wrists, the rope tying her to the bedpost cutting into them. Her feet were tied as well, her legs spread-eagled.

Terrified, she knew that when Ollie came back, he'd continue what he started, though she wasn't sure that he'd kill her. It would give him more pleasure to keep her alive so he could go on torturing her, making her suffer. Ollie had always preferred to play with his victims, prolonging the pain as long as possible rather than put them out of their misery.

She froze as she heard a hammering on the door. Knocking. Constant, incessant banging. Then she heard a voice. A voice that she recognized calling through the letterbox.

'Hello! Ollie! Ollie! Ollie, open the fucking door! Please, I was wrong, OK . . . I wasn't thinking straight . . . You hear me, I got it wrong. Ain't nothing happening. Ollie, please, if you're there, open the door. I don't want you to do anything, you hear me. I don't want you to do anything to him. Ollie! . . . *Open the fucking door!*'

'Rebel! Rebel! Rebel!' she screamed. 'Rebel, it's me, Amy! Rebel! I'm tied up. Ollie's tied me up . . . Can you hear me? Rebel? If you can hear me, I need you to help get me out of here!

Rebel, can you hear me! *Rebel!*' She cried, her mouth stinging from where Ollie had split her lips open. 'Rebel?'

But when she listened for Rebel's reply, there was nothing but silence: she'd gone.

Her heart sank, hope fading away. She swallowed down her tears and lay staring up at the ceiling in the dark, watching the dancing of lights pass across it from the cars outside. For her, the waiting game would continue; he'd leave her here, helpless, imagining what he was going to do to her, how he would hurt her, when he came back from wherever he'd gone.

A loud crash broke through her thoughts. The next thing she heard was footsteps running up the stairs, and then Rebel appeared at the door with three guys she'd never seen before.

'Thanks, John. I'll take it from here.' Rebel's voice was full of worry.

'You sure? What about the door? It's well and truly fucked, anyone can come in.'

Rebel shrugged. 'Not my problem – but thanks . . . I'll see you at the club tomorrow.'

She switched on the light and they turned to go, but not before Amy caught them looking at her, an expression of shock on their faces.

She watched as Rebel came over to her. 'I had to get them to break down the door . . . They won't say anything though, they're good guys.' She walked towards the bed. 'Fucking hell, Ollie's done a number on you. I take it this was Ollie's doing?'

Amy spoke quickly while Rebel untied her. 'Yeah, it was, thanks to you. Why did you do it? Why did you tell him?'

Rebel paused for a moment. She glared at her, and Amy had no doubt how much Rebel hated her.

Once the ropes had been loosened enough for Amy to free herself, she stood, but was immediately hit by a wave of dizziness.

She held on to the bed for a moment, struggling to see out of her swollen eye. 'And Jack, is he OK?'

Rebel looked away.

'Rebel, I said, how's Jack?'

'I don't know.'

Amy caught a glimpse of herself in the mirror but turned away. Her face was purple and blue, cuts across her mouth, and one eye was the size of a golf ball.

'That's why I'm here. It was stupid, what I did. I was jealous. I saw the way he looked at you. He don't look at me like that. He's never looked at me like that. It's either pity in his eyes or loathing.' She paused. 'It don't change the way I feel about you, but I'm sorry . . . and we need to find Jack.'

Amy pulled on clean clothes, her others were covered in blood. She slipped her trainers on.

Rebel was still talking: 'Ollie took him somewhere. He knocked him about and then bundled him into a car.'

'What— How? I mean, Jack can look after himself, can't he?'

'Yeah, he can, but Jack was drunk when Ollie got to him so he didn't stand a chance.'

Amy shook her head, fear for Jack rushing through her.

'I was hoping that it wasn't too late, that Ollie might be here still. That I could talk him out of doing something to Jack, but . . .' Her voice trailed off and she stood there looking ashamed.

Amy didn't know whether to laugh or cry. 'There's no way Ollie would ever be talked out of it. He will enjoy every minute of torturing him. You have no idea what you've done, Rebel.' Fear was in Amy's voice.

Rebel chewed on her lip, and Amy could see she was shaking. 'Then where, where might he take Jack? Where could he have taken him? Look, if there's a chance, even a small chance of finding him alive, we need to go and look for him.'

Amy thought for a moment, then she nodded. 'We've got a house in the country, there's a possibility that he took him there . . . I'll get the keys.'

'Will it take a long time to get there?' Rebel's voice was urgent.

'I hope not. For Jack's sake, I hope not.'

They jumped in the car and sped along Shaftesbury Avenue, driving towards the Thames embankment. Amy drove in silence, her head hurting, one eye swollen closed. She struggled to concentrate on the wet road as thoughts of Jack came into her head.

Turning left, they headed past the Tower of London and picked up the A13, with Amy driving at speed, her foot pressed hard on the accelerator. The tension between her and Rebel hung heavy in the air.

Amy weaved through cars and lorries, breaking the speed limit all the way, pushing the Range Rover to well over a hundred.

Eventually, an hour or so later, she turned onto a slip road and followed the winding country lanes as fast as she dared until she reached a lay-by just ahead of the entrance to a large house.

She pulled in and turned off the engine. From where she was, she had a good view. 'It looks like there's no one there. His car isn't on the drive, the whole place is in darkness. No lights, no cars.' She slumped down in her seat, defeated. 'He ain't here, Rebel.'

'Maybe not.' Rebel's voice was sharp. 'But we are, and we might as well have a look. Let's just check.'

'OK. But I'm telling you, it's a waste of time.' Amy touched the side of her face; her swollen eye was throbbing and she had a splitting headache. Her mouth hurt when she talked; her lips were split and it felt as though a couple of teeth were loose.

She started the engine and set off along the drive, coming to a stop directly outside the house.

Without speaking, they rushed out of the car. Amy, who hadn't visited the place in over six years, got out her keys, hoping Ollie hadn't changed the locks. She let out a sigh of relief when the front door swung open, then went inside and switched on the lights in the hallway, illuminating the domed ceiling and grand sweeping staircase.

'This way. Let's start from the kitchen and work our way around.'

Rebel nodded and they rushed from room to room, but found no tell-tale signs of Jack having being here. In fact, Amy found it strange that after so many years away, the house looked exactly the same as she remembered. It even smelled the same.

As they were making their way back to the hallway and staircase, Rebel stopped by a heavy wooden door and looked at Amy. 'What's in here?'

'Last time I was here, it was the basement.'

'We might as well see what's down there. Come on . . .'

Without waiting for a reply, Rebel opened the door and made her way down the stairs. Straight away Amy could see how much this part of the house had been altered. For a start, there was a narrow corridor with a series of doors that certainly hadn't been there before. Each door seemed to lead to a small room which had been fitted out with a bed.

Rebel stood at the door of one of the rooms and whistled. 'Someone's been watching *Fifty Shades*.'

Amy peered over her shoulder and saw an array of chains and handcuffs, whips and clamps and sex toys strewn around, as well as filming equipment.

'This shit's in every room. What the fuck is he into?' Rebel chewed noisily on a piece of gum as she looked around her. Amy, not wanting to talk about Ollie or anything else with the woman, ignored the question and walked in. The temperature was several degrees higher than in the corridor, but her blood froze when she looked at the floor.

'Oh my God . . .' She crouched and examined the dark stain on the wood. 'Someone's been here recently, look . . . Rebel, look, that's fresh blood.'

'Jack? You think it's Jack?' Rebel's voice was full of panic.

'No . . . No, I think it's more likely to be Evie, or Mina . . . Oh my God, what's he done to them?'

They looked at each other and neither of them said anything for a moment. Amy suspected the fear she saw in Rebel's eyes was the same fear Rebel saw in hers.

'I can't believe this is happening.' The anger she felt towards Ollie was overwhelming, but she breathed deeply, counting to ten, pushing her feelings aside. The only thing that mattered was finding Jack because, looking at the blood, she doubted that either Mina or Evie was still alive.

'What now?' Rebel asked.

Amy thought for a moment. 'There's one other place we could try. I know when Ollie was dealing in stolen goods and that sort of shit, he used some lock-ups. You want to take a look?'

Rebel looked at the blood on the floor, then nodded. 'We ain't got nothing to lose.'

'You think that, you don't know Ollie.'

'Look, there's his car . . . Over there, that's Ollie's car.' Amy turned off the headlights. She could feel her heart racing and she took a deep breath, wanting to run, wanting to go back. Terror rushed through her, but she needed to focus on Jack, on Evie and Mina. She had to try to find the strength for them.

'You ready, Rebel?'

Before she'd finished asking the question, Rebel jumped out of the car and headed off in the direction of Ollie's four-by-four.

Amy hurried after her, using the torch app on her phone and dimming it with her hand as she made her way down the gravelled track onto the industrial site.

'Which one is it? There are loads of them,' Rebel whispered as she looked along the rows of lock-ups, most of them disused.

Amy glanced to the left, then gestured silently to Rebel to follow her.

They tiptoed along the back of the row, past abandoned garages and the wreckage of burnt-out cars. Wooden pallets and old paint cans with grass growing through them were strewn around and the whole place smelled faintly of oil.

'I think it's this end one,' Amy whispered, switching off the torch. She pressed herself against the side of the wall and listened intently, then she took a few steps towards the side door. 'Sshhhh, I think someone's in there.'

Rebel frowned, concentrating. 'I can't hear anything.'

Amy continued to listen. Again, she edged forward as close as she dared to the ill-fitting door. Then she stopped and strained to hear, her heart pounding in her chest. 'I can hear groaning . . . There's definitely someone there. We need to go and take a look.'

'Fucking hell, Amy, are you sure? How do we know your husband ain't in there? I ain't looking for my boat race to end up like yours.' She could hear the fear in Rebel's voice. 'Ollie's a nutter, and he's obviously about, his car's here.'

Amy shrugged. Her heart was racing, but she steeled herself. 'If Ollie's here, this could well be where he's keeping Jack. Are we going to check it out or not?'

'This is crazy,' Rebel whispered.

Inwardly, Amy shared her unease, but she glared at her and snapped, 'Tell me about it . . . Come on, give me a hand with this – it ain't looking too clever, I reckon between us we can get it open.'

They began to pull at the old rusting door, heaving at it, until eventually the eroding frame gave up, allowing them to force it open. With only a slight hesitation, Amy switched on her torch and stepped inside.

She shone the light around the cold, wet lock-up. There were piles of bricks and scrap metal, crates and boxes piled up. But then she gasped; over in the corner, slumped on a chair, was Jack. He'd been badly beaten, his hands were tied behind his back, and a bloodied gag had been stuffed in his mouth. His clothes were ripped and torn, and Amy fought back tears when she saw the slashes across his chest – deep wounds, caused by a knife or a blade.

She ran over to him. 'Jack, Jack, Jack, can you hear me? Jack, are you OK? Jack?'

He groaned, then slowly lifted his head. His face was battered, almost worse than hers. Through half-closed eyes, he looked at her, his lips sticking together with blood. 'Amy . . .' He stared at her for a moment, as if he was trying to focus. His voice was weak, his breathing ragged, but she could sense the anger when he looked at her swollen eye and asked, 'Did Ollie do that to you? Did he fucking do that to you?'

'It's fine, I'm fine now, don't worry about that,' she whispered. 'Look, let's just get you out of here.'

His gaze moved to Rebel, then he spoke to Amy. 'Get *her* fucking out of here . . . Get her *out!*'

'Jack, leave it.' She tried to calm him, desperate to keep the noise down. 'Whatever she's done, she was the one who helped me get out . . . I wouldn't be here now if she hadn't.'

'None of us would be here if she hadn't opened her fucking mouth.'

Rebel stepped towards him. 'Jack, I'm so fucking sorry, I didn't know he'd do this to you, I . . .' But she trailed off as they heard another groan coming from the darkness.

Amy frowned. She stared towards the back of the lock-up. 'There's someone else there.'

'I'll . . . I'll go and see,' said Rebel. 'You sort Jack out.'

Amy nodded. 'Be careful.'

Rebel hurried away as Amy started to untie Jack: the knots were tight and she struggled to undo them, though partly that was because her hands were shaking so much and she was struggling to see properly through her damaged eye.

'Amy?'

Hearing her name being called, she glanced up. 'Mina? Oh my God, Mina!' She rushed over to her, throwing her arms around the trembling girl, holding her tightly.

She could feel Mina shaking and she spoke softly, 'It's so good to see you, baby, we've all been going out of our minds. Your mum will be so pleased to know you're OK.'

Mina, looking traumatized, nodded. 'I'm sorry, Amy.'

Amy's gaze roamed Mina's face. 'Don't say that . . . You ain't got nothing to be sorry about, darlin', you hear me?'

Mina was crying hard now. 'Flo – is Flo safe?'

'Yeah, she's fine. She's being looked after.' Amy stroked Mina's face.

'And Iris? Is she . . . is she . . .' Unable to finish the sentence, she covered her face with her hands.

'Is she still alive? Yes, yeah, she is. She's in hospital, she's hanging in there, darlin'.'

Amy gently took Mina's hands away from her face.

'I don't suppose you've seen Evie? We think Ollie took her too.'

Mina shook her head, and Amy nodded, not wanting to push it. Then, dreading the answer she might get, she forced herself to ask, 'Did he hurt you? Did Ollie hurt you, darlin'?'

Without saying anything, Mina nodded. It took everything Amy had to stop herself from screaming. She looked across to Rebel. 'You take Mina and get in the car. I'll help Jack, we'll be right behind you.'

As Rebel and Mina hurried out of the lock-up, Amy glanced quickly at him and attempted a smile, her injuries painful. 'I thought he'd killed you.'

'No, you don't get rid of me that easily.' He squeezed her hand weakly, emotions welling up in her.

They began to head out, but froze as the sound of a gunshot rang out.

Then there was silence, but a moment later, Martha appeared at the door, her face twisted and cold as she pushed Mina back inside the lock-up. At the sight of Amy she laughed coldly. 'What is it about my ex? Seems he can't be trusted to do anything properly. Always has to prolong things to get his kicks. It's a good job I'm here to finish off what he started, ain't it?'

She pointed the gun between Jack and Mina and smiled nastily at Amy. 'Go on then, your choice: who's it going to be? Loverboy here, or the cock tease? You can only save one.'

'You're a sick bitch, Martha.'

Martha smiled. 'You should know me by now, I take that as a compliment . . . So go on, Amy, choose.'

But before Amy could speak, she stepped inside the lock-up. 'Oh well, I'll choose then.'

She aimed the gun at Mina, but Jack sprang and pushed Mina out of the way as the gun went off.

He yelled in pain as the bullet tore into his shoulder, splintering the bone. He dropped to the floor, but before Martha could fire another shot, Amy grabbed a discarded piece of metal and leapt at her, slamming it down onto Martha's skull with all her strength.

There was a sickening crunch and Martha dropped to the

floor, blood and grey matter oozing out of her head. Amy stared at her for a moment; then, snapping herself out of it, she turned and grabbed Mina by the hand. 'Come on, we need to get out of here . . . Let's go, yeah. Sweetheart, it's going to be all right.' With Jack leaning on her, bleeding profusely, the three of them made their way as quickly and quietly as they could through the rows of lock-ups.

As they turned towards the car, Amy saw the lifeless body of Rebel, lying on the ground outside one of the burnt-out garages. Half her face had been blown away; presumably by the gunshot they'd heard earlier. Sadness passed through her, but she knew she had to focus. There'd be time to think about this later, provided they made it out alive.

They rushed along the gravelled track to the car and Amy opened the door for Jack and helped him in while Mina jumped in the back. She rushed round to the driver's seat and turned on the ignition, but before she could take the car out of park, Mina started screaming:

'Amy! Amy, drive! *Drive!*' Her voice was high and hysterical. '*Drive*, Amy!'

Amy looked up and saw Ollie charging towards them. Panicking, she tried to get into reverse, but Ollie grabbed the handle of the driver's door and started to pull it open.

'*You fucking stupid bitch!*' he bellowed, his eyes blazing with anger.

The car lurched backwards, followed by a loud bang as it slammed into a tree behind them which she hadn't noticed in the dark. '*Oh fuck.*'

'Amy, Amy, he's coming! Hurry!' Mina shouted again, while Amy continued to fumble in the dark, trying to select drive on the gear shift selector.

In front of them, Ollie smiled maniacally and began walking slowly towards the stalled car.

'Hurry, Amy, for God's sake,' Jack's voice was quiet but urgent, barely audible below Mina's screams.

Her heart racing, Amy turned the engine back on, revving it loudly. She looked through the windscreen and locked eyes with Ollie. For a moment they held each other's stares, then she put her foot on the accelerator and floored it, driving at speed into Ollie, throwing his body into the air . . .

61
STEPH

Steph limped slowly along the corridor. Every part of her was aching, but suddenly she began to run, seeing Maureen leaning against the wall.

'Reenie, Reenie, are you all right?'

Her eyes were half closed but as Steph came to kneel by her, she opened her eyes, a smile on her face. 'Steph . . . Steph, it's good to see you.' Her voice was faint. 'I got Ness to the chapel. She's safe.'

'That's brilliant, but we need to get some help for you, Reenie.'

Pale and ashen, she shook her head. 'No, no. It's pointless, lovey.'

Steph's eyes filled with tears. 'Don't say that. Don't say that. We need you. The women need you. I need you.'

'You'll be OK. The women are lucky to have you.' Tears ran down Maureen's face. 'Look after Ness for me, won't you?'

'You'll be able to look after her yourself, you hear me. Reenie, you hear me?'

She reached up, her hand shaking as she touched Steph's face. 'Tell Jack I love him.'

Then she closed her eyes, her breathing staggered, and her head fell forward.

'Reenie? Reenie? Reenie, no, no – don't you die on me, Reenie, don't you dare!' She grabbed her shoulders, shaking her gently. 'Reenie?' Then, lying her down on the floor, she tried to revive her, pumping her chest, crying with each compression. 'Reenie, please. *Please.*'

But it was no good. Reenie had gone.

Taking a deep breath, Steph wiped away her tears. She glanced around the wing; the place was in chaos, though she was certain any minute now, the prison officers would overwhelm the women and take back control of the wing. She was almost out of time.

Running up the stairs, which were stained with blood, she got to the top knowing exactly where she was going . . . where she needed to be. Passing the library at the end of the corridor, and the gym, which was strewn with rubbish, Steph turned the corner and darted up another flight of stairs, then she stopped and stared at the tall figure in front of her.

'I thought I'd find you here. Hiding away in your office.'

'Hello, Steph, we meet again.' He chuckled nastily and walked nearer to her. 'You know, this riot you and your friends started, destroying my prison like a bunch of animals . . .' He leaned down, whispering a threat into her ear. 'When I've finished with you, you're going to wish Tess had finished you off.'

He straightened up and glared at Steph, who stared back at him. His face was covered in a light film of sweat and dirt.

'All those women who've been hurt or have died in this riot,' he went on. 'They died because of you. You do realize you have blood on your hands, Steph.'

She smiled widely at him. 'Then one more won't make a difference, will it?' And with that she opened her hand and slashed the blade she was holding across the governor's throat.

Wide-eyed, he stared at her. His hands flew to his throat and he clasped the wound, but he couldn't stop the blood bubbling through his fingers, gushing from the deep laceration. She watched him gasp for air, struggling as his eyes began to roll to the back of his head, and he staggered forward, rasping, then fell, slamming onto the floor, his body thrashing for a moment before it went still.

Emotionless, Steph, her hand red with his blood, slipped the blade into her pocket, then turned and walked away.

PART THREE

THREE WEEKS LATER

62

STEPH

Confined to solitary, Steph sat on the bed reading the paper Jenkins had brought in for the hefty price of fifty quid. Nothing changed in this place, though they did have a new governor. A female governor this time. Steph hadn't met her yet, and who knew how long she'd last.

Fighting back tears, she finished reading the account of Evie's murder. Her body had been found in a shallow grave in Epping Forest. A dog walker had come across it. And although it broke her heart that Lynn wasn't still around, right now, Steph was grateful that she wasn't. It was some small comfort that she'd died still with a sliver of hope they'd find her daughter alive.

Sighing, she threw the paper to one side. She wasn't sure when she'd get back on the wing, but she needed to as soon as possible. She'd put feelers out already with some old contacts, trying to find out the names of the scum who'd abused her daughter. If it was the last thing she did, she'd track them down. Word had gotten back to her that her scumbag of a husband had slipped below the radar. But she'd find him too. She'd find them all. She wouldn't stop until she did. No one was going to get away with hurting her daughter.

But there was only so much she could do while she was stuck in solitary. It would be good to get back to the wing. The women were in no doubt that she was top dog, at least for now. They'd been jubilant about her finishing off the governor, though so far officials couldn't pin it on her. No doubt someone would eventually challenge her for the crown – after all, this was Ashcroft and the place was filled with long sentences but short memories.

The flap of the cell door suddenly opened. It was Jenkins. 'I've got news for you.'

'Yeah, it cost me fifty fucking quid, remember?'

Jenkins snorted. 'Actually, I'm going to give this news for free. Your daughter's woken up. Looks like Iris is going to be all right.'

63

MINA

Mina stood by the window of Iris's room and blew kisses to her, giggling as Iris blew them back. She wasn't allowed to go in and see her. The doctors weren't allowing anyone in. She'd woken up from her coma yesterday, and although she was now stable and they weren't worried about her, she was still having to stay in ICU, so for the time being, she had to put up with waving through the window.

Blowing a final kiss goodbye, Mina moved along the corridor and made her way down the stairs and into the maternity unit.

At the far end of the ward, she saw her mum holding her little brother. She smiled, ignoring the fact that her mum was chained to the bed. The reality of the situation they were in was never far away.

'Mina!' Ness's face lit up.

Mina glanced at the prison officer sitting half asleep in the chair.

'Come on in and see him, come and meet your baby brother.'

She rushed over to them; it was the happiest she'd seen her mum in a long time, and in fact it was the happiest she'd felt too.

'Isn't he beautiful?'

'Can I hold him?'

Ness nodded. 'Of course – he needs to know what an amazing sister he's got.'

Mina's eyes filled with tears as she took her brother in her arms. 'I'm sorry, Mum, I'm so sorry. This isn't right, he needs you, I can tell the police it was—'

Ness grabbed Mina's hand: 'You don't tell them anything, you understand me? I want you to live your life like you should. Happy and free. Nothing has changed. I love you, and I ain't angry. It's me who should be saying sorry to you. You deserve so much more than I've given you. And hopefully you and Iris can make a go of it.'

Mina smiled, feeling the love for not only her mum and new brother but also for Iris. For the first time in her life, she was excited by the future.

'And guess what. I got good news: the new governor has got me a space in the mother and baby unit. So, it means I'll be able to keep him until he's two. And because I'll only have a couple more years to serve after that, they won't put him up for adoption.' Tears dripped down Ness's cheeks.

'That's amazing.' Mina could hardly get her words out. 'And Flo seems happy with her foster carers. Social workers are letting me see her three times a week. And it's not too far from Iris's house, so it's easy to get to, and my support worker thinks I might have a chance of getting Flo back full-time. She says it might take a few months or so to sort it all out, but if it's done officially, they'll help me get a flat, and help with day care so I can stay in college.'

'I'm so proud of you, Mina.' Ness's voice trembled.

'Are you?'

'Of course I am. I should have told you that before, I should have said it every day, every chance I got. Fucking hell, I should have shouted it from the rooftops, because I'm lucky to have you as a daughter, Mina – you really are the most incredible young woman I have ever known.'

64

AMY

Amy smiled at Jack as the sun beat down on her back. This wasn't how she'd envisaged her life, but she couldn't think of anyone else she'd rather be on the run with. She laughed at the thought as she watched him carrying two glasses of wine back from the bar on the edge of the beach.

They'd thought about staying in England, but after what had happened it was too risky. She'd also thought about handing herself in, but Jack had persuaded her not to. She certainly didn't want to rot in prison for killing the likes of Ollie and Martha. So South America it was, thanks to Jack's contacts, and looking across to the crystal waters and the white sandy beach, she certainly wasn't complaining.

Jack kissed her on the top of her head as he sat down opposite her. He stared into her eyes, smiling, and raised his glass. 'To you.'

Amy shook her head. 'No, to Reenie.'

Jack nodded, a flicker of sadness coming into his eyes. They'd heard through a contact what had happened, and although Jack hadn't spoke about it, she knew he was devastated by Maureen's passing.

Amy smiled, picking up her glass, raising another toast. 'To the women.'

ACKNOWLEDGEMENTS

A huge shout out goes to my wonderful editor, Wayne Brookes, who has been so patient, kind and supportive during a tough year. Working with you is everything I've ever wanted – so much love. Thank you.

Also a huge thank you goes to everyone at Pan Mac, especially Rebecca Needes, the best desk editor around. And massive thanks to Anne O'Brien, who is the unsung hero of getting this book reading-ready – her copy-editing skills are simply phenomenal.

Thanks and love as always to my loyal and supportive agent, Darley Anderson, who is a force of nature. I'm truly blessed to have you in my corner. The whole of the Darley Anderson team are a reason to celebrate. A fantastic team who so hard for each and every book. A special thanks too to Rebeka Finch at Darley Anderson agency, who patiently replies to all my endless emails!

To the readers, a huge thank you, for your constant support.

And lastly to my family and my three wonderful children who have blossomed into three wonderful young adults who I couldn't be prouder of. My life is full because of you all.

ACKNOWLEDGMENTS

THE STREETS
JACQUI ROSE

She thought her secret was safe . . .

Ten years ago, Jo Martin was released from prison after serving twelve years of a life sentence. She is now out on license – and she isn't Jo anymore. Given a new identity by the courts, and with a different appearance, a ready-made history and even a change of age, Jo can pretend to be anyone . . .

Cookie Mackenzie is not only Ned Reid's lover – but she also works for him. She supplies the girls – and boys – for Ned's clients. There's always some runaway kid who needs shelter.

Natalie Ellis works at Barney's bar. A fierce and loyal friend, she's a shoulder to cry on, a listening ear – but should everyone really trust her to keep their secrets?

Lorni Duncan needs to keep running, always looking over her shoulder, especially with a young child in tow. But how will she survive? The refuges are full, and the last thing Lorni needs is the authorities getting involved. Who is she trying to escape from?

Everyone has something to hide and a lot to lose, but which of them did Jo become?

The streets of London's Soho hide a multitude of secrets in this hard-hitting gangland thriller from bestselling author Jacqui Rose.